Strange Trades

PAUL Di FILIPPO

With an Introduction by
BRUCE STERLING

GOLDEN GRYPHON PRESS • 2001

"Agents," first published in *The Magazine of Fantasy and Science Fiction*, April 1987.
"The Boredom Factory," first published as a portion of "Fantasy Trilogy" in *The Edge*, 2, no. 1, 1995.
"Conspiracy of Noise," first published in *The Magazine of Fantasy and Science Fiction*, November 1987.
"Fleshflowers," first published in *Back Brain Recluse*, no. 16, 1990.
"Harlem Nova," first published in *Amazing Stories*, September 1990.
"Karuna, Inc.," first published in *Fantastic Stories of the Imagination*, no. 21, Spring 2001.
"Kid Charlemagne," first published in *Amazing Stories*, September 1987.
"The Mill," first published in *Amazing Stories*, October 1991.
"Skintwister," first published in *The Magazine of Fantasy and Science Fiction*, March 1986.
"Spondulix," first published in *Science Fiction Age*, September 1995.
"SUITs," first published in *Amazing Stories*, August 1993.

Copyright © 2001 by Paul Di Filippo
Introduction © 2001 by Bruce Sterling

Edited by Marty Halpern

LIBRARY OF CONGRESS CATALOGUING-IN-PUBLICATION DATA
Di Filippo, Paul, 1954–
    Strange trades / by Paul Di Filippo ; with an introduction by Bruce Sterling. — 1st ed.
    p.   cm.
    Contents: Kid Charlemagne—Spondulix—Conspiracy of noise—Agents—Harlem nova—Karuna, Inc.—SUITs—Skintwister—Freshflowers—The mill—The boredom factory.
    ISBN 1-930846-05-3 (hc : alk. paper)
    1. Fantasy fiction, American.   2. Occupations—Fiction.   I. Title.
PS3554.I3915S77   2002
813'.54—dc21   2001023921

Contents

Introduction by Bruce Sterling
ix

Kid Charlemagne
3

Spondulix
23

Conspiracy of Noise
72

Agents
98

Harlem Nova
125

Karuna, Inc.
155

SUITs
224

Skintwister
234

Fleshflowers
254

The Mill
274

The Boredom Factory
335

To my parents, Frank and Louise,
who instilled good work habits in all their children.

To the memory of my grandmother, Catherine St. Amant,
who worked hard all her life.

And to Deborah, who makes work easy.

$\mathcal{I}$ntroduction
by
$\mathcal{B}$ruce $\mathcal{S}$terling

$\mathcal{I}$ HAVE THE SAME STRANGE TRADE AS THE AUTHOR OF this book.

Reading these pieces gives me a powerful feeling of literary kin-ship. There's a mirrorball herky-jerkiness going on in these stories, unnatural yet bright, all frazzled, antic and bizarre, yet somehow very much of a piece. All the light they give comes from reality's dark corners.

Not that this work is "difficult" or "metafictional" or anything —it's very folksy and street-level. It's got that loose, dance-floor "ribofunk" rhythm, "ribofunk" being a nice word that Paul made up to give himself an excuse to write this sort of thing.

The typical ribofunk story sounds like it wants to be a pop song: we're gonna have three minutes of verse-verse-chorus and something we can get-down and boogie to. Then you realize that those truly strange bits inside pop songs: that funny lurch during the breakbeat, the grinding hiss in the sample, the weird squeak-ing that the frets make between the actual "music" . . . that is the stuff that Paul Di Filippo considers the "good part." Paul wants *lots* of that kind of stuff. So when his ribofunk wall of sound gets to be all bulging and dented, he turns the amps up to eleven and he puts in a whole bunch more.

* * *

No matter how boggled we may feel by his peculiarly recombinant constructions, Paul is always *getting at something*. He clearly has some definite *agenda*, even if that agenda itself is not entirely, uhm, clear. Paul is by no means precious, recondite or recherché. On the contrary, Paul is touchingly eager for us to know exactly what's on his mind. When he sits at the keyboard, he quotes revealing lyrics for us from the cool stuff that's playing on his Sony Walkman. When he writes a pastiche of a J. G. Ballard story, there's a guy at the bar who is reading some J. G. Ballard.

Most science fiction characters would never be caught dead reading science fiction stories. That's because they're way too busy being chrome-plated power fantasies. They'd never put their shiny space-boots up on the Goodwill couch to peruse some Lem, Dick, or Delany.

Paul Di Filippo, on the other hand, genuinely *respects* these writers. He considers them life-giving cultural influences and true icons of philosophical and literary hospitality. So Paul's characters have no trouble whatsoever being science fiction characters living inside science fiction stories. Quite commonly this seems to be a real *step up* for them. They seem genuinely liberated by the prospect, they are really *enjoying it.*

Before the advent of Paul Di Filippo, the best-known science fiction writer from his hometown of Providence was H. P. Lovecraft. This Providence business explains a lot about Paul. Lovecraft's work is seriously and irretrievably freaky, but if you read Lovecraft's personal letters or the work that he did for his fanzines, you soon see that, for a career sci-fi writer, Lovecraft was a surprisingly levelheaded and sensible Yankee guy. Mr. Lovecraft's problem was that his family had cracked up from venereal disease and bankruptcy. The Lovecraft clan had lost its genteel pretences. So Lovecraft considered himself a pathetic, outdated relic. He had plenty of smarts and talent, but he had quite a hard time working up enough raw enthusiasm to stay alive.

Mr. Lovecraft was particularly upset that the future of Providence so clearly belonged to sleazy, immigrant Italians. Paul Di Filippo, however, *is* the future of H. P. Lovecraft's Providence. Instead of being cranky, morose and malign, his work is funny, fertile, and forward-looking. Even the darkest, weirdest Di Filippo scenario seems to offer the potential of a decent cup of coffee, maybe a good meatball sandwich down at the diner. It's very rare to see Paul shudder instinctively at anything whatsoever. If his neighborhood was a gruesome Lovecraftian slum (featuring hideous miscegenation with occasional advents of cosmic rupture), there's little doubt that Paul would be hanging around at the corner newsstand, calmly compiling some notes.

There's scarcely a female character to be found in Lovecraft's work. That's part of his cosmic bleakness, his sense of desperate loss. Paul Di Filippo is a genuine philogynist. The women in Di Filippo's science fiction tend to be more-or-less actual women. His work is remarkably free of galactic princesses, femmes fatale, gothic vampiresses, madonnas, whores, and even love interests and sex objects. Nor do these women feel politically compelled to strut across their landscape loudly shattering the gender barriers. The women are just around, occupying space and time, pretty much like everybody else in town. If anything, they come across as centered, thoughtful, calming influences. They're holding up half the sky. Maybe, if truth be told, they're lugging a little extra sky.

"As usual, the inside of my trailer could have served to illustrate a doctoral thesis in chaos theory." This line, with its common-or-garden mutant mix of sleaze and erudition, may be the ultimate Paul Di Filippo sentence. You might have to visit Paul's actual house in his hometown to fully get it about this sentence. I did that, so now I do.

Paul is a bookstore-lurking autodidact of the deepest Lovecraftian dye. He is a self-educated American genre loon who ranks with sci-fi's masters of ascended guruship: Avram Davidson, Philip K. Dick, Tim Powers, Robert Anton Wilson. His pad is full of classically Di Filipponian magazines: ancient flaking issues of *Bivalve Monthly* and *Hangman's Semiquarterly*, that sort of thing. Much like Lovecraft, Paul carries out a huge paper correspondence, a fizzing vent for his many inspirations, which merely conventional publishing can never fully assuage. Paul has even been known to print his own fanzine, named after a particularly astral street in his Providence neighborhood.

As someone who does quite a lot of this myself, I have to consider zine writing the true mark of the SF adept. It's not the mark of a pro, mind you, because a professional has an economic role to fulfil, takes that responsibility seriously, and works for pay. The adept does this work because he knows that there is something miraculously arbitrary about all forms of consensus reality. Everything about "reality" is a put-up job, most especially, as in the wonderful story "Spondulix," the money. Money is lines on paper. It's all lines on paper, folks. No, "really." It just plain is.

You never know when you might find some magic verbal key to turn the cosmos on its ear. "A single syllable spoken at the right moment could topple empires." Right on, brother Paul. I'm with you all the way, you major dude, you. Astounding wonder could be anywhere at all, in a sandwich shop, in a trailer park, in a flophouse, even in a place as utterly boring and devoid of potential as New York City. "The fabulous gemmed cliffs of Manhattan, remote as the mirage of some Arabian seraglio."

It's a funny job, science fiction, but somebody's gotta do it. Paul can do the job. If this book contains a single true fabulous gem, a kind of Di Filipponian Golconda, it's Paul's story "The Boredom Factory." It's short, but entirely to my point. The Boredom Factory is what we sci-fi writers are looking at when you see us standing flat-footed in the streets, staring into thin air and darkly muttering to ourselves. When we're looking most like Lovecraft, at our cobwebbiest, our spookiest, our most alienated, pathetic and estranged, it's because we're looking at the very same reality that everybody else is, but we're seeing something like *that*. Yet we somehow found a back way out of the ennui machine! Really, we did! You just sit on the couch and turn pages! Yeah man! Strange trades indeed.

Bruce Sterling
January 2001

Strange Trades

"Kid Charlemagne" owes its existence to my long-standing love affair with J. G. Ballard's Vermilion Sands. The Hesperides, my insular resort (I had in mind California's Catalina Island), was meant to replicate the decadent territory so fascinatingly explored by Ballard during the sixties. In this homage, I was also preceded by Michael Coney, Ed Bryant and Lee Killough, all of whom have worked similar venues. (A theme anthology in the making!) I wrote two sequels to "Kid," neither of which sold. And of course, this story marked one of my first shameless co-optings of the title of a great pop song into another medium.

Kid Charlemagne

$\mathcal{T}$HE HESPERIDES. HOW FAR AWAY AND UNREAL THOSE islands seem now. A place out of time, cushioned and insulated by wealth, where the whims of the rich collided with the unpredictable passions of their playthings — and the lesser of those two forces gave way, with results often merely ludicrous, but sometimes all too tragic.

The Hesperides. Sun, money, tailored bodies, hot and violent emotions, whispers in the night. It all runs together in my memory now, a blurred spectrum like those caused by the oil slicks from the hydrofoils in the Bay, shifting, mutable, impossible to grasp. A moiré on the silk covering a woman's haunch.

A few incidents stand out starkly, though. And these are the ones I would most forget.

The Hesperides. Once I called them home.

Behind the bar in La Pomme d'Or, I counted bottles. Scotch, tequila, vodka, retsina (hard to acquire since the coup in Greece), a nauseating peach liqueur which was all the rage that year. Whenever I found I was running low on a particular item, I would key in an order code and quantity on the submicro hanging from my belt. Eventually, I'd squirt the whole order over the fiber-optic line to the mainland. With luck, the shipment would arrive on tomorrow morning's 'foil.

The big windows onto the veranda were deopaqued. Morning sunlight poured in, giving the interior of La Pomme an oddly wholesome look. With the bi-O-lites off, the air empty of smoke and perfume, the nuglass chairs resting upside down atop the ceramic tables, the stage bare, my club looked innocent and untainted, holding no hint of the sordid dramas enacted there nightly.

I liked it best at this brief hour, but the night came all too quickly.

When I reached the middle of the bar, I flicked on the radio to catch the news.

"—murder. In other news, a delegation of ASEAN diplomats will ride an ESA Hermes shuttle to an orbital meeting with President Kennedy, who is occupying the High Frontier White House this month. The delegation is hoping to spur an investigation into the recent tragedy in Singapore. On a lighter note, fashion followers will be glad to hear—"

I filtered out the unimportant babble as I continued the count.

My head must have been below the bar when he walked in. I always left the door open in the morning so the salt-freighted breeze could wash the stale indoor smells away, although I didn't start business till one.

In any case, when I popped up, I found myself confronting him.

He was a slim fellow of twenty-two, or thereabouts—young enough to be my son. His features were very delicate, yet with nothing androgynous or feminine about them: simply finely chiseled. His skin was the color of a polished chestnut; his eyes, a luminous blue. He wore a patched and salt-stained khaki shirt and denim cutoffs. Across his chest ran a bandolier, holding something concealed against his back.

My eyes lingered for a moment on his throat as I tried to puzzle out what sort of necklace he wore, so tightly clasped. Then I realized it was no piece of jewelry, but rather a scar, a pale cicatrix stretching nearly from ear to ear.

For some reason the sight of the scar so threw me, marring as it did his otherwise classic appearance, that I grew flustered, as if I were the intruder. This boy—appearing so unexpectedly, like Pan stepping from behind a shrub too small to conceal him—struck a series of notes in me, the totality of which I couldn't immediately grasp. To compensate, I shot my hand forward with rather more energy than was appropriate.

"Hello," I said.

He took my hand. His was calloused from manual work; his grip, firm.

"Hello," he replied.

His voice was another shock. I had expected something youthful and dulcet, in keeping with his looks. But instead, from that violated throat came a boozy, raspy, seemingly whiskey-seasoned growl. I immediately thought of Dylan in his prime, thirty-odd years ago, then added another whole layer of Tom Waits scratchiness. The effect was jarring, but not unpleasant to hear.

The population of the Hesperides was small and stable and exclusive enough so that one could come to know everyone— barring the ever-changing horde of daytrippers, of course. Even the few transients at our small hotel had no anonymity. This man, with his boyish attractions and anomalous voice, would have caused a sensation among our bored citizens—men and women alike—and I would surely have heard of him within hours of his arrival. I could only assume that he was a daytripper, if an atypical one, and that the morning ferry had arrived early.

"Just got here?" I asked.

"Nope. I swam in last night."

I stared at him hard. The California coast was a mile and half of choppy water away.

He must have read my disbelief. Stepping back from the bar (I spotted his bare, gnarly feet), he unslung the object on his back. I recognized it for a musikit covered in a waterproof sheath. (Two decades ago, the components of that kit would have filled a room.)

"This is all I own," he said. "It's not heavy enough to slow me down."

I chose to believe his unwavering blue gaze.

"Where'd you sleep?"

"On the beach."

So much for our vaunted private security force. The island's homeowners would have a dozen kinds of fit if they ever learned how easily this kid had invaded their precious enclave. Perhaps I could tweak Deatherage somehow with this.

"Well," I said for lack of a better comment. "You need something to eat?"

He smiled. It was a hundred watts. "Only secondarily. What I really want is a job." He nodded toward the stage.

I thought about it. I had had no one booked for the past week,

relying on autosynthesized stuff and satellite-beamed perfor-
mances. I could sense that my patrons were growing bored, prefer-
ring the glamour of live musicians as a background for their
assignations and spats.

"Where have you played before?"

"Just Mexico. Where I grew up."

Immediately, I got nervous. I couldn't afford to hire an illegal
and lose my license if caught.

The boy—so damn good at sensing my thoughts—dug in the
pocket of his tattered shorts. He handed me his ID, gritty with
sand. The holo that leaped out from the plastic card was his. I
flexed the card to reveal his status; it turned bright green, proclaiming him a citizen. His name was given as Charlie Maine.

"My father was an American," he said with his ingenuous
smile. "My mother was from Mexico City. We had to stay south
for a long time, till my dad died. Then I came north."

I gave him back his card. Somewhere in our short conversation, I had decided to take a chance on him. No doubt there was
a selfish undercurrent to my thoughts, imagining how he would
draw the rich and lonely widows in.

"You've got a job," I said, and we shook once more. "How do
you like to be billed for publicity?"

White, white teeth flashed. "Kid Charlemagne."

I smiled for the first time in a long while. "Cute." Memories
turned over, roiled, and one floated to the surface. "Hey, wasn't
there a song once—"

"Steely Dan," he said. "From the '70s. My father used to play
it all the time."

He wasn't smiling anymore, and neither was I.

We both knew it was a very sad song.

On the night I introduced the two of them, I wore a linen suit the
color of a mummy's cerements, a raw, unbleached beige. Men's
suits that year had no lapels, and so my signature flower—a black
carnation—was pinned above my heart.

The interior of La Pomme was dark, save for the soft blue-
green phosphorescence provided by the bi-O-lites on each table,
and those in a line down the bar. I always thought the whole effect
was one of an undersea grotto, lit by the slow fires of the drowned
men and women who sat as if on coral thrones, more lively than
corpses, yet no more feeling.

Full fathom five thy father lies. . . .

The veranda windows were two huge slabs of ebony. By the closed door stood one of Deatherage's men, solicitous bouncer and ruffled-feather-smoother, looking uncomfortable in his suit.

I circulated among my patrons, attending to their frivolous, often only subtly implied desires. As usual, I hated myself for fawning over them. But there was little in the world at that time which I felt capable of doing, and the unassuming niche I had carved for myself here offered a certain contemptible security.

Charlie had yet to appear for his first set. Only the third night of his playing, and already attendance was up. As I had speculated, many of the islands' sad and predatory older women, and not a few of the men, were drawn to him, as if he released some pheromone of youth and potency. At a single table, I spotted Laura Ellis, Simone Riedesel, and Marguerite Englander: the full set of immaculately coiffed, well-preserved Fates, each with enameled nails long and sharp enough to snip threads.

Back at the bar, I savored my usual mineral water with a twist of lemon, and waited for Charlie to appear.

Exactly at midnight the Kid materialized onstage, lit by a single spotlight. Seated on a tall stool, he had his bare feet twisted in the rungs. He wore a white shirt of mine that bloused loosely on him and his old blue shorts. The long flat case of his musikit — like his namesake's broadsword — was balanced on his lap.

The Kid began to play.

Like some beautifully plumaged bird with a raucous yet arresting call, Charlie sang. He knew plenty of old songs that were guaranteed to touch places in us antiques that we had deemed dead — his father's legacy, I suppose. He sang the newest tunes heard daily on the radio with a freshness akin to the then-popular singer, Stella Fusion. And every tenth number or so, there would come an original piece — haunting mixes of Caribbean, Mexican, and American rhythms, carrying elusively poetic images.

When he finished, the applause was real and tremendous.

Above the clapping, from the table nearest me, I heard a bitter voice say, "The bloody little *kaffir* sings like a black crow." A sharp bark of laughter answered.

I looked to see who had spoken and shattered the magic.

Seated together were Koos van Staaden, his daughter, Christina, and Henrik Blauvelt.

Van Staaden and his daughter were refugees, having fled South Africa — or rather, to use its official name, Azania — six years ago when that aching, tortured country finally erupted. Van

Staaden had been Administrator of the Transvaal at the time. During his tenure, he had apparently accumulated quite a fortune, most of which he had managed to transfer abroad prior to the revolution. He and Christina, I knew, had caught one of the last flights out of Jo'burg. Maria, his wife, had been at their country home that week. No doubt her scattered bones were bleached the color of my suit by now.

Spiteful gossip maintained that on the walls of van Staaden's house hung relics of his homeland, among which was a *sjambok*, its business end tipped with flakes of brown. I couldn't quite credit even van Staaden with such an offense.

Blauvelt, a burly fellow countryman, had been an expatriate in England when the government fell. Nowadays, he acted as Christina's companion.

Like so many wealthy dissolutes without goals, they had ended up in the Hesperides.

I watched van Staaden warily as the patter of applause faded. If he continued to voice his drunken racial slurs, I'd have to sic Deatherage's man on him. I had plenty of HUB patrons richer than he whom I had no wish to offend.

As it was, his daughter intervened.

"Quiet, Father," she said firmly. "I think he sings very well."

Her grip on his arm seemed to drain all belligerence from him. Across his riven face, his love for his daughter warred with his hate. Finally, he raised his glass to his lips and drank deeply, a tired and defeated old relic.

I studied the strange tableau they presented. Van Staaden was a cranelike figure with a stubble of white hair and a sharp nose. Blauvelt was a beefy man in his thirties, with a dandy's mannerisms ill-suited to his heavy body. Christina—well, Christina, I thought then, no more fitted in visually with those two than a nun in a rogue's gallery, or Circe amid her swine.

She was a willowy, small-breasted woman with hair the color and fineness of platinum threads, styled in bangs across her brow and feathered down the back of her long neck. Her nose was tiny, her lips always hidden by jet lip-gloss. Tonight, she wore lilac pants and top, with white sandals. Like half the women in the club, she had a small lifegem affixed at the base of her throat, which fluxed in time with her pulse.

The whole potentially ugly scene was over in seconds, much shorter than I have taken to describe it. Charlie had vanished from the stage, and the club buzzed anew with meaningless talk.

Ten minutes later, I felt a gentle tug at my elbow as I mingled. I turned to face Christina van Staaden.

"I know you overheard my father's tactless comment, Mr. Holloway," she said. "I'd like to apologize for him. You will make the proper allowances for his situation, I hope."

I nodded without expressing my real opinion. It was something I had grown quite good at.

"Wonderful," she said. "It's all forgotten, then. By the way, I really do feel that Kid Charlemagne is a most exciting performer. I wasn't just sticking up for him out of sympathy. In fact, I was wondering if I could possibly meet him."

She paused for a moment. Then, as if it possessed the utmost importance, she said, "I understand he's from Mexico."

Again, I nodded without comment, neither confirming nor denying. I was trapped in her eyes.

Once a friend brought me a piece of olivine from Hawaii. Formed in a volcano's heart, the gem was like translucent jade, hard and impenetrable, with fascinating depths.

Christina's eyes were two shards of olivine.

I thought about her request. I neither liked nor disliked the woman at this point. Yet I felt indebted to her for defusing her father. And of course, she could always approach Charlie on her own if I didn't introduce her.

But why try to dissect my motives at this late date?

"Okay," I said. "Let's go now."

Backstage, I knocked on the door to Charlie's small dressing room. There was no answer, so we went in.

We found Charlie reading. He pored intently over a paperback I had given him. It was the '95 edition of Ballard's *Vermilion Sands*, with the Ralph Steadman cover.

"Charlie," I said. He looked up.

Sky met sea.

Something snapped closed in the air between them.

"Christina van Staaden," I said.

But neither heard me.

The next morning, I sat at a table in the empty room still pulsing with the ghosts of last night's events, figuring accounts. A shadow fell across the screen of the submicro.

Across from me stood Leon Deatherage, head of Hesperides security, having arrived in his usual silence.

I filed my useless reckoning of gains and losses and flicked the machine off. "Sit down, Leon, and save your energy for evildoers."

Deatherage lifted a heavy transparent chair off the table with one hand and deftly set it upright. He dropped down into it with a grace that surprised me in such a big man. From his pocket he took a pack of Camel vegerettes. He lit one, puffed briefly, and made a face.

"Five goddamn years, and I still can't stand these. My only consolation is that I helped to nail the bastards."

Before becoming head of the islands' security, Deatherage had worked for the L.A. police force. He had been part of the team responsible for capturing the domestic eco-terrorists who had released the tailored tobacco mosaic virus that had ended all cultivation of that crop. The Sierra Club never recovered from the revelation that the conspirators had solicited and received funding from them.

"What can I do for you, Leon?" I asked. "Do you need a drink this early in the morning? I won't tell anyone." I pushed back from the table, as if to rise.

Deatherage made a magician's move, and suddenly in the palm of his hand lay a small empty white plastic shell the size of a quarter. It was color-coded like an antique transistor with three dots of red.

My stomach churned. I wanted to puke my breakfast. Somehow I kept it down.

My face must have blanched. Deatherage smiled. Suddenly, I regretted taunting him.

"Recognize it, do you, Holloway? I thought it might touch a chord in your past. Do you want to name it, or shall I?"

I wet my lips. Merely to summon up the name took an immense act of will.

"Estheticine," I said.

"Exactly. In a nice convenient dermal patch. Would you like to guess where I found it?"

I said nothing.

"On the beach, with the used condoms and the empty bottles, during my morning jog."

I swallowed gratefully. For an instant, I had been sure he was going to claim it had come from the club.

"I'm clean," I said.

Deatherage looked at me solemnly. "I know that. Do you think I'd come to you if I thought you were the user? I know what you went through to kick the stuff. I want your help. I've just been on the phone to friends on the mainland. They say that, due to a series of busts, sources for E have dried up. It's almost impossible to score now. Whoever's using this might get your name somehow and come to you. At which point, you come to me, correct?"

I nodded.

"Very good." Deatherage rose as if to leave, then sat again, seeming to remember something. I knew it to be a charade. The man forgot nothing.

"By the way. This singer of yours. Is he a Mex?"

"Why do you ask?"

"A lot of this stuff comes through Mexico. It could be that he's our connection."

"He's a citizen," I said. "You can check his card. And he told me he's a HUB." I don't know why I lied, except that Deatherage had upset me so much.

"Hip Urban Black, huh? Well, we'll see." Deatherage stood without pretense now. "Remember what I said, Holloway." He left.

A lot of unpleasant memories swarmed in to fill his seat.

Once the world had seemed bright and beautiful. That was when I was young, and my lover was alive.

His name—we won't get into his name. What essentials do names capture? He was a charming young mestizo boy of no fixed abode or occupation, whom I had met on a business trip to Guatemala, just before the war. (Once I had another job, another life, when I lived much as everyone else.)

Picturing his face now, for the first time in years, I realized how much Charlie resembled him.

I managed to get the boy a visa after I returned stateside, although even then, in the days before mandatory citizen IDs, the authorities were tightening up on immigration of the unskilled. I had to grease many bureaucratic palms.

I thought I was doing him an immense favor, lifting him up out of his poverty and squalor. I little knew then that I was arranging his death.

Life in the First World did not agree with him. Everything was too confusing; there were too many choices, too many options. He got into a fast crowd, took risks, became promiscuous—picked up AIDS.

He died six months before they announced the drug that cured me of the infection he had passed on to me.

Infection of the body, but not the heart.

When his death came, the world grew pale and dingy, an echoing stage filled with mocking mannequins and hollow props.

When I found estheticine, a new kind of beauty returned to fill the void. Unnaturally sharp, crystalline, infinitely seductive and ultimately unsatisfying, promising eventual meaning beyond words that never materialized.

But once estheticine left me—I truly feel that the drug spurned me, as if I were not good enough for it, rather than I the drug—how did the world look?

Curiously two-dimensional. A black-and-white place, leached of all emotional resonance.

Something of an improvement, I suppose, over the pain of stage two.

Thanks to estheticine.

Uglybuster, E, lotos, beardsley—call it what you will, it remained the quintessential drug of the late, late twentieth century.

In a world of ever-increasing ugliness, who did not occasionally wish that everything might appear beautiful?

At the beginning of the decade, experiments on the perception of beauty came to a head. (The publicity images persist: the wired people at the ballet, the museum, the edge of the Grand Canyon, their responses being plumbed and recorded.) Exact ratios and mixes of neurotransmitters were fingered as the agents; sites of stimulation in the brain were charted. Synthesis succeeded. The result: estheticine.

To be used only judiciously, of course. Let the connoisseur brighten Beethoven, magnify Mozart, uncage Cage.

Most definitely not recommended as a crutch.

How surprised the experts were when the public began to swallow it like candy, and the GNP dropped by three percent in six months. How quick the authorities were to outlaw it. How fast the underground sales sprang up.

And now it had reached me here, on my dead-end island in the sun.

Two concerns filled all my free time during the weeks following the meeting between Charlie and Christina.

Who was using estheticine on the island?

What was going on between my young singer and the woman with the semiprecious eyes?

I made no headway on the former. Deatherage did not approach me again, and try as I might, I could detect no users among my clientele—least of all Charlie, who I knew needed the drug no more than a fish needed a substitute for the clean sea in which it daily swam.

As for my impractical lie about Charlie's origins, Deatherage never called me on it, perhaps believing my former addict's brain was turning to mush.

I made more progress on the latter topic. In a sense, learning what they did together was easy. In another way, baffling.

Everyone in the Hesperides—except the reclusive and rum-sodden Koos van Staaden— knew the two were lovers. That much of their relationship was evident in their every gesture.

The two of them were together continuously, except when Charlie was performing.

Wearing hemosponge units, they dove in the azure waters surrounding the Hesperides. Once they even swam out and down to the UCLA research station bedded on the ocean floor. I remember how tired Charlie was at that night's performance. The muscles in his lean flat legs twitched as he sat astride his stool, and he had to cancel his last set of the evening.

They rode motor scooters (no cars were allowed on the islands) all over the hilly interior and along the cliff paths. One morning, as I stood on the veranda watching the crowds of gawking daytrippers (the feverish pleasures indulged in by the rich in plain view on the beach never failed to shock them), I saw two small figures atop Sheepshead Bluff. I recognized the colored smudges intuitively for Charlie and Christina. Sunlight glinted off the chrome of their bikes and caused my eyes to tear. For a moment, I had the frightening delusion that they were about to jump, fulfilling some incomprehensible lovers' suicide pact.

Water-skiing and hang-gliding, swimming and racing hydroplanes, the two enjoyed all the Hesperides had to offer. It seemed an idyll of young love, an eternal summer of instant fulfillment.

That much, as I've said, was easy to discern.

The baffling part was understanding how two such disparate personalities meshed. What had really prompted Christina to ask for that introduction? I couldn't reconcile infatuation with a certain flintiness I sensed in her soul.

I felt I had to know more about her. I decided Blauvelt was the one to pump.

Around noon one day, I managed to catch the man as he idled past the club. At my insistence, he came inside for a drink. He favored the awful peach liqueur I so disliked to stock.

We sat at the same table where Deatherage and I had had our

disturbing talk. I naturally compared the two men. Although of a size with the security chief, Blauvelt was somehow spongy, an amorphous thing masquerading as a man. In his sweaty tennis clothes, he looked like a wax dummy left too long in the sun. I knew I would have no trouble getting information from him.

"Henrik," I said, "I need your help." He looked flattered. "You understand that I have an enormous investment tied up in that singer of mine. He's good for business, and I don't want anything to happen to him."

I was sure the mercenary angle would appeal to Blauvelt. His cynical smile confirmed it.

"So," I continued, "I need to know all about Christina, and her relationship with him. After all, we wouldn't want her father caus- ing trouble, would we? How is it, by the way, that he's not aware of what's going on?"

Blauvelt sipped his syrupy drink. "Old Koos—he thinks I'm still chaperoning his daughter. He talks to no one—thinks all you Americans are *rooineks,* anyway. And I'm not about to tell him his girl's seeing Charlemagne. Not as long as Christina keeps the money flowing my way."

"Is Christina the type to form a romantic attachment so quickly?"

Blauvelt scowled, as if I had hit upon some sore spot. "Not in my book. There was never anything between us. Christina's been a different person since the accident."

"Accident?"

"Back in the Transvaal. One night on the road between Jo'burg and Pretoria, she drove right into a stupid *kaffir* and his cows crossing the highway. Her Mercedes flipped three times. Stupid wog was killed outright, of course. Christina sustained a lot of brain damage. Ever notice her hair?"

"Thin and white, I believe."

"Grew back that way after they shaved her head for the opera- tion. Used to be black as night before. Just like her mother's. Those bangs of hers—they hide the scar on her forehead. Notice how she always wears a cap when she swims. She's very self- conscious about it."

"She seems quite normal now. How did they repair her injuries?"

Blauvelt waved his hand negligently, as if to dismiss as unim- portant all things he could not understand. "Tissue transplant of some sort. Newest thing, it was. God, we had some smart bloody people before the bad times. But even they couldn't stop the Black bastards, could they? Even A-bombing Capetown didn't slow them down."

He drained his drink and got to his feet. I considered Christina's fleshed-in past.

"Do you think it's love, then?" I asked.

Blauvelt shrugged. "Love for herself, yes. For that little songbird—hardly." Then he left.

Alone, I tapped into the medical databases, curious as to how Christina's apparently massive wounds had been healed.

Embryonic brain tissue had proven to be the only matter that could be planted to adapt and grow in the adult brain, repairing and substituting for lost sections. No *in vitro* process had yet been perfected to serve as an ethical source of the tissue, and so the procedure was not advocated in the West.

In old South Africa, they had had embryos to spare—"donated" by pregnant slum-dwellers in Soweto and elsewhere.

The clinics where such operations had been performed were the first places to be torched in the war. Then they were dismantled brick by charred brick.

The first time Charlie and Christina disappeared, it was for only three days, and I wasn't too concerned. I, who never left the confines of La Pomme, knew best of anyone how close and stultifying the Hesperides could become. I assumed that they felt at last the need to explore their feelings for each other in a different setting. That could have been Charlie's motives for the unscheduled trip, at least. What alien urges swayed Christina, I could not say.

In any event, my response was limited and simple. I posted notice of Charlie's absence, pretending to my customers that it had been planned, and contacted the mainland agency I used for a new singer on a day-by-day basis. She was talented enough, I supposed, but lacked Charlie's genius.

It was during the substitute's first song, as I stood in the club with its strangely altered and diminished atmosphere, that I realized what freshness the Kid had brought to our artificial paradise. Had he arrived that morning weeks ago riding a dolphin and clutching a lyre, his advent could not have been more portentous or fraught with consequence.

My idle wondering about how Christina had managed such a long separation from her possessive father was satisfied when the rumor-mill ground out information on the whereabouts of

Henrik Blauvelt. He had chartered a small boat, filled it with peach liqueur and two women, and anchored in Sturgeon Cove the day Charlie and Christina left. Evidently, in Koos van Staaden's eyes, Blauvelt and Christina were off sailing.

On the morning of the fourth day, Jaime Ybarrondo, owner of the Hesperides' lone hotel, called me. His bearded face floating in the holotank struck me like some apparition in a Delphic pool as he told me that Charlie had returned to his hotel room sometime after midnight. I thanked him and switched off.

I contained myself until Charlie arrived that evening at the club. I let him reach his dressing room before I joined him.

He sat on the couch with his musikit cradled gently in his lap. I recognized the tune he was fingering: "Love's Labours Lost" by the beaIlles. Charlie had programmed the drums to sound exactly like Ringo, while he played Julian Lennon's part.

I was shocked at the changes in his face. An indefinable something had left him, perhaps his air of invincible youth. New lines seemed graven about his cerulean eyes. His lips were tightly compressed.

He finally looked up at me. He swiped nervously at his black curls, shut his machine off, and sat back.

"Hello," I said.

"Hello," he replied.

Having recapitulated our first conversation, we halted.

"Good to have you back," I said.

He smiled. It was only fifty watts.

"Where've you been?"

"South."

I waited, but he volunteered nothing else.

"Well," I said. "Do you feel like playing tonight?"

"Sure," he nodded. "Sure."

There seemed to be nothing else to say, so I made a half-turn, thinking to go. His lifted hand stopped me. I swung back.

His right hand had come to rest—unconsciously, I believe—on the scar around his neck. Suddenly, I thought how it looked as if someone had wrapped a piece of barbed wire around his throat and it had sunk permanently beneath his skin. Life in anarchic Mexico City had been chaotic before the UN forces stepped in. I thought then of Christina's hidden scar, and my invisible ones. In a searing, timeless epiphany, I felt the three of us bound together into one crippled being.

"My life hasn't been easy," Charlie rasped. He looked down, as if ashamed of even such minor self-pity. "I was only looking for love — and to give it. That's all."

Two steps closed the distance between us. I stood by his seated figure with my hands on his bony shoulders while he silently wept.

In revenge, his singing that night broke the heart of everyone else in the packed club.

Two weeks passed. Christina and Charlie still were constant companions. The rest of the world revolved in its time-accustomed ways.

The three Fates — Ellis, Riedesel, and Englander — started a new fad raging. Eschewing clothes, they had gold circuits printed directly onto their skin. A small battery pack in one earring caused the circuits to emit mournful drones, facetious beeps, or catchy jingles out of the button-speaker that was the matching earpiece. Soon, the whole island was a carnival of naked noisy flesh laced with gold diagrams. The poor fellow who had been drafted into layering the circuits — a retired billionaire from Silicon Valley — saw so much female skin during the fad that he was later forced to spend a month at the monastery in Carmel.

Among the daytrippers, I noticed the proliferation of T-shirts that read:

NO MORE SINGAPORE?
ACCIDENT, HELL — IT WAS WAR!

The televised images of the millions of corpses in the sterilized country did much to offset our island's natural gaiety. In Las Vegas, bookmakers were offering three-to-two odds that the Philippines were the source of the CBW agent that had eliminated their rivals in the cheap-labor market. (Insiders picked Malaysia.) Already the media were calling it "The South Pacific Commerce Wars."

I didn't envy "Young Joe" his task of mediating the dispute. But no one had ever promised him the president's job would be easy.

At the end of those particularly frantic two weeks, my own private world felt a tremor high on the emotional Richter scale.

Charlie and Christina disappeared a second time, for five days.

They returned for a night. I never even got a chance to see him. Then they vanished for a week.

When they returned again, Koos van Staaden had somehow learned of his daughter's affair.

Deatherage stood massively between van Staaden and me. The old man wasn't shouting—that would have been less upsetting. Instead, his voice was dead and controlled, as if artificially generated.

When Blauvelt had phoned me that van Staaden was on his way to the club to confront either Charlie or me, I had summoned Deatherage as mediator.

"I insist that he be fired, Holloway," van Staaden persisted in his monotone. "He's seduced my daughter and is obviously no more than a wild rutting bull. No White woman on the island is safe while he's around."

I opened my mouth to voice something appropriately caustic, but Deatherage, sensing my anger, intervened.

"The man's done nothing to warrant his dismissal, Mr. van Staaden. From all accounts, the affair between your daughter and the Kid was mutual. And she is an adult. I'm afraid that your only recourse is to try to change your daughter's mind, if you continue to disagree with her."

"She's locked herself in her wing of the house. Won't come out, either." Van Staaden paused. "In the old days, where I come from, Chief Deatherage, a man in your capacity would clap this Kid person in jail for such an offense, and then supervise his hanging."

It was out in the open now, and although Deatherage and I had both known van Staaden's true feelings, to hear them voiced shocked us silent.

Deatherage spoke first. "We don't have your goddamn exalted but defunct system in this country, mister."

Van Staaden held Deatherage's gaze, a defiant specter. "Then someone should kill the beast personally."

Deatherage went to grab van Staaden's lapels, found none, and settled for his shirt front. "That's an actionable threat, van Staaden, and could get you locked up. If I hear any more such shit, it will."

Van Staaden twisted free and banged out the door.

I phoned everywhere, seeking news of Charlie, but couldn't find him. I wondered if he was closeted with Christina in her half of van Staaden's house high atop Bosky Knob. I remembered him as he had been that night when I held him while he cried.

The next morning Deatherage came by to take me to see the Kid's broken body on the rocks below Bosky Knob.

It was literally the first time I had left La Pomme d'Or in three years. The sunlight felt heavy and hot atop my unshielded head. The sand felt strange beneath my bare feet. Deatherage had come with the news while I still wore my robe, and I had gone out immediately with him.

Charlie's death was obviously the catalyst for my leaving the dark sanctuary of my club. Yet I felt that subtler forces were also at work. It was as if I had been a fairy-tale prisoner immured, and the death of Kid Charlemagne had set me free.

Down on the wet, weed-wrapped rocks, a small crowd had gathered for a novel diversion. Three of Deatherage's men held them back.

Splayed awkwardly over the slick stones (he had never been awkward in life) lay Charlie Maine. His flesh was puffy from contusions.

And someone had opened up the old scar in his throat.

I stood a moment, transfixed. Then I crouched to take his limp hand.

When I arose, Christina was there. Her eyes were filmy, like two pebbles glazed with snail slime.

"He's so beautiful," she said dreamily.

And then I knew.

The motor scooter buzzed through the dark, up toward Bosky Knob. Random breaks in the foliage and trees on my right allowed me to see the gaudy lights clustered around the bay below. They looked alien somehow, already distant. Tonight, for the first time in years, my club was closed.

It didn't matter to me. I knew I was leaving. Something black inside me that had held me captive all these years had shattered under the impact of Charlie's death. What the future held for me, I couldn't say. But it had to be better than the past.

I had a final chore, though, before my morning departure.

Events had moved on. Koos van Staaden sat morosely in the Hesperides' single jail cell. He denied any involvement in the murder, but made no secret of his satisfaction. Henrik Blauvelt was confined to his house under guard, as a possible accessory. Deatherage's theory was that Blauvelt had pinioned Charlie's arms from behind while van Staaden performed the grisly murder.

I hadn't told him that it took only one to kill when love bred trust.

I rounded a curve and saw the lights in the windows of van Staaden's home. The place blazed like a cold pyre. I cut the motor, dismounted, and walked the rest of the way.

The front door was unlocked. I patted my pocket. The cassette was still there. I had purchased it—an anonymous self-contained unit—on a quick trip to the mainland that afternoon, after the shock of seeing Charlie's body and after my fatally delayed revelation had worn off. It would never be traced to me.

I pushed open the door and went in.

I found Christina in a second-floor bedroom. She sprawled on a divan, beneath a wall-mounted *sjambok*, wearing silken undergarments that rode high on her thighs and low on her shoulders. She was engaged in a minute examination of the flame of a candle standing on a table beside her. I knew she had probably been sitting that way for hours.

Once, I had done the same thing myself.

"Christina," I said quietly.

She turned her Circean profile languidly. The candlelight shimmered on the watered silk across her loins.

"The beautiful Mr. Holloway," she murmured between her black lips.

"Why did you do it, Christina?" I asked. "Why couldn't you just discard him, leave him to the rest of us, once you'd finished with him?"

"He was threatening to tell Father," she said. "Tell him about the people we met in Mexico, and what they sold me." The flickering candle captivated her again. After a time, she said, "But they know me down there now, and trust me. I have my contacts. I don't need Charlie anymore."

"He was a person, Christina. He deserved to live."

The black rose of her mouth formed a smile. "He was just a *kaffir*. I've killed them before—accidentally and on purpose. I don't hate *kaffirs*, though. Why should I? Do you know that I have a little piece of *kaffir*'s brain in mine? A piece from a little baby bugger. That almost makes me a *kaffir*, doesn't it?"

She began to giggle, and didn't stop.

I went up to her and lifted the feathery hair from her neck. The white tab of estheticine blended almost invisibly with her alabaster skin. The three dots of coding looked like red freckles.

Rummaging in her purse, I found the rest of her stash: a dozen tabs, bought at such a high price.

I held them in a hand that trembled only slightly as I thought about what they contained: easy relief from the pain of Charlie's death.

But I didn't use them on myself.

Instead, I applied them up and down her pretty legs, pressing firmly to establish diffusion. She didn't resist, although I'm sure that in the back of her mind she knew as well as I did that twelve was way over the threshold of permanent brain damage.

"Life's so ugly," she said when I was done. "Did I ever tell you about my mother? I couldn't let them take my one comfort away."

"There's no need to worry anymore," I said. I took the self-contained player-cassette from my jacket, set it down, and flicked it on. I thought about how Charlie had really loved the old songs.

"Oh, how nice—music," she said.

The old lyrics poured forth:

It's all so beautiful,
It's all so beautiful . . .

Before I left, I snuffed the candle out.

"Spondulix" is a story close to my heart, dealing as it does with the triumph, downfall, and salvation of an underdog character with whom I easily identify. (I envision Rory Honeyman played by Jeff Bridges in the movie version of this story, by the way.) I liked this tale so much in fact that I turned it into a novel, published by Cambrian Press. In that expansion, you will find many new characters and scenes, as well as a crucial artistic rethinking: I refer to Rory only by his first name, not last, throughout.

If you ever visit Providence, Rhode Island, be sure to drop in on the original model for Honeyman's Heroes, Geoff's, on Benefit Street. You're certain to be insulted by the surly art students who man its steamers, a masochistic honor equal only to the pleasure of noshing on one of their "Rich Lupo" sandwiches.

Finally, all my renewed thanks to editor Scott Edelman for taking a chance on the original publication of this piece of "fiscal science fiction."

Spondulix

1.

Beer Nuts

THE SIGN READ HONEYMAN'S HEROES, AND FEATURED A cartoonish illustration of a Dagwood-style sandwich: two slabs of painted pumpernickel separated by approximately six inches of various lunchmeats, cheeses, lettuce, pickles, tomatoes, sauerkraut and hot peppers, dripping with mustard and mayo. The name of the artist was scrawled in the lower right corner: Suki Netsuke. In the lower left: ESTABLISHED 1978.

The sign hung above the door of a small shop on Washington Street, in Hoboken, New Jersey. The time was noon, on a vibrantly sunny Monday in June. The door to the shop was locked, a placard in the window turned to CLOSED. The placard was fingerprinted in ketchup.

Washington Street was busy with two-way auto traffic, with pedestrians and cyclists. Moderate-sized buildings lined each side of the broad avenue, businesses below, residences above. There was a faint odor from the river to the east lying atop the scents of exhaust and cooking. The Maxwell House plant, down where Twelfth Street met Hudson, diffused an omnipresent odor of roasting coffee, like a percolator of the Gods. Spanish chatter, hiss of air brakes, thump of off-loaded cardboard boxes hitting the sidewalk, infant squalling, teenage brawling, sirens, music — the little city was noisily alive.

Down the sidewalk a block away from the sandwich shop a man walked absentmindedly along. He had a thick, ginger-colored beard, longish hair under a Mets cap. He wore sneakers, jeans and a baseball shirt that bore the legend SPONSORED BY HONEYMAN'S HEROES on the back. He was trim, gracile rather than muscular. Twenty years ago, he had been certified a world-class diver. Good genes and a moderate appetite, rather than any strenuous regimen of exercise, had helped him keep his youthful build.

The man walked past a dry cleaner, a bookstore, a bar, a bodega, a botanica. His hands were in the pockets of his jeans, jingling a few coins; he whistled a shapeless tune.

When he arrived at the sandwich shop, he grasped the worn handle of the door without noticing the CLOSED sign, and attempted to enter. When the door did not immediately open, he seemed baffled. It took him a moment to decide there was no mistake on his part. He looked at the illustration of the gargantuan sandwich above the door. He studied the fingerprinted placard. Shading his eyes, he peered through the window at the darkened interior of the store. Had he possessed a driver's license, he would in all likelihood have removed it from his wallet and examined it just to verify that he was indeed Rory Honeyman, and that this was his place of business.

Having made up his mind that the forlorn shop was, after all, his establishment, and that it was still locked up tight when it should have been opened for an hour in anticipation of the lunch-time rush, Honeyman stepped back from the door and muttered two words: "Goddamn Nerfball." Then he pivoted and stalked away, with an angry determination.

Honeyman walked north on Washington until he came to Fourteenth Street. The smell of coffee grew stronger, then weakened. At Fourteenth, he turned east, toward the river. The neighborhood became dingier, poorer, unkempt. Abandoned buildings alternated with tough-looking lounges (LADIES WELCOME) and apartments sporting broken windows patched with cardboard and tape. Factories and warehouses began to predominate. A fish-processing plant exuded a maritime stench. A cat prowled hopefully outside the building. Honeyman thought he recognized Cardinal Ratzinger.

The cross-town street finally dead-ended at the Hudson. A rusty chain-link fence separated the street from a flat wasteland of weeds studded with abandoned tires, plastic bags, shopping carts, car hulks. . . . Across the sprawling river Manhattan reared in all its grimy glory.

At Honeyman's left stood a building. Before it, Honeyman paused, his former certainty of purpose momentarily faltering.

The problem: whether to enter the door before him or not. If he entered, he might possibly find his missing employee, and thus be able to open his store before he missed the entire lunch-hour trade. On the other hand, it was just as likely that he would encounter some bizarre event-in-progress that would draw him, whirlpool-like, into its centrifugal embrace, shanghai and waylay him with voices and flesh, drink and dope, schemes and plots, and completely waste his entire afternoon. Maybe even the whole day. A week. A month. A year. The rest of his life? Who knew? It had happened before, to others. . . . But wasn't he wasting his life now already? Hadn't he been for twenty years, since that single implosive day, under the Mexican sun, where his life had collapsed, impelled by his own impulsive actions, down to a singularity, infinitely dense, inescapable, poignant with the foreclosure of everything outside itself? Hush now, son, that's a question for 3 A.M., if ever, not a bright June afternoon. . . .

So Honeyman contemplated the building before him a moment longer.

The structure was five stories tall, composed all of muted red brick, aged by over a century of weather. The uppermost courses of brick were embellished with decorative motifs, achieved by the ingenious stacking of master masons: herringbone, twill, cross-hatching. Copper flashing, long verdigrised, ran around the eaves, surprisingly unvandalized for a building deemed abandoned. The roof was of slate, in decent repair. The windows were all painted black. The building occupied an entire large city block.

At one corner of the building, closest to the river, reared an enormous square smokestack, capped at the top with more brick embellishment.

There was a door directly in front of Honeyman. In point of fact, there were three doors. The first was twelve feet high and ten across, actually a double door of two leaves. Made of thick planks once painted green, but now peeling to reveal bare splintery wood, the two halves of this door were secured with a chain and an enormous, rusting padlock that appeared at least fifty years old.

Inset in this door was a more conventional-sized one, with an old-fashioned latch. It was this one Honeyman considered entering. At the foot of the person-sized door was the third, a pet door. (Honeyman might have employed this entrance, had he wished. Others often had.) This upper-hinged small entrance bore a legend in a lovely calligraphic hand which Honeyman recognized as that of Suki Netsuke. It read: THE CARDINAL.

The lintel of the largest door was a huge piece of Jersey limestone, mortared into the brick wall on either side. Carved into the soft stone was the legend:

1838   OLD VAULT BREWERY   1938

The later date was executed in stark Futura, the earlier in wasp-waisted Baskerville.

Honeyman, a few feet from the triple portal, listened. There was no noise from inside. This could be either a good or bad sign. It paid to remember that some of the most insane schemes of the Beer Nuts had been hatched in relative quiet. Thunder and lightning and apparitions on the Capitoline Hill did not attend the birth of every Caesar. On the other hand, everyone could be innocently sleeping. There was simply no way to tell.

Tossing caution to the café au fish-scented winds, Honeyman stepped forward and opened the middle-sized door, which swung inward. He stuck his head and shoulders into the dark. "Yo, folks. It's me, Rory. Is anyone home? Earl? Hilario?"

There was no answer. Honeyman, his eyes sensitized to outdoor light-levels, could see nothing in the midnight interior. Sighing, he stepped fully inside and shut the door.

Vast hulking shapes loomed about him. Brew kettles, pipes, mash vats — all the original equipment of the long-defunct brewery remained, covered by decades of dust.

Honeyman took a few tentative steps forward, hands outstretched. People moved around frequently here, changing their nesting locations according to complex social interactions. Honeyman hadn't visited the Beer Nuts in months, and had no idea in what spot Nerfball might be hibernating now.

Shuffling along in the musty dark, Honeyman cursed softly. All he wanted was to reclaim his employee and start making sandwiches. Instead, he was forced to play Blindman's Bluff. Growing angrier and more impatient, he unwisely picked up his pace.

Suddenly his foot caught the edge of something soft, body or mattress. Unprepared, he lost his balance and felt himself going down.

Honeyman landed heavily atop a lumpy something. A man grunted, a woman screamed. Make that "someone." Two someones.

Feeling that discretion required him to remain still, lest he unintentionally exacerbate the situation, Honeyman did not move. A match scratched on its gritty strip, a candle flared.

Honeyman discovered that he was lying crosswise atop Earl Erlkonig and Suki Netsuke, who were, in turn, reclining upon a stained, bare mattress. The situation would have been less embarrassing had the pair not been mostly unclothed, and had Netsuke not been Honeyman's ex-lover.

"Hi, Rory," said Netsuke coyly. Her half-Japanese features were as appealing to Honeyman as ever. Her skin was the color of pumpkin pie, her nipples the brown found at the pie's edges. Propped up on one elbow, she reached modestly for an article of clothing, found nothing to hand, and shrugged off her nudity.

"Hey, molecule," said Erlkonig, "nice of you to drop by." He extended a queerly colored hand, and Honeyman shook it.

Earl Erlkonig was a young Black man who also happened to be an albino. His hair was a thatch of short kinky platinum wires. His complexion was the color of weak tea attenuated by lots of cream. His eyes were a watery gray.

Netsuke squirmed devilishly beneath Honeyman, and Erlkonig said, "Uh, if you wouldn't mind. . . ."

"Oh, yeah, sure. Sorry."

Honeyman pushed himself up into a kneeling position beside the mattress.

"Thanks," said Erlkonig. He discovered a pair of Jockey shorts and skinned them on, still lying down. Netsuke, meanwhile, had donned a T-shirt.

The light and noise had drawn a crowd. Honeyman looked up to find himself the focus of a circle of curious faces: a majority of the permanent Beer Nuts.

Ped Xing, the only man in the world to profess both Orthodox Judaism and Zen monkhood. Long side curls contrasted rather sharply with his shaven pate.

Hilario Fumento, unpublished writer with a curious artistic philosophy, his pockets filled with the materials of his trade: call slips and pencil stubs filched from the public library.

Beatbox, a Hispanic fellow currently employed as a Balloon-O-Gram deliveryman, and also currently wearing his work clothes: a complete clown suit and white face.

Leather 'n' Studs, the inseparable lesbian couple.

Hy Rez, resident hacker and phone phreak, who provided the Beer Nuts with essential communication services.

Prominent among the missing was Nerfball, the one person Honeyman wanted to see.

"So," said Erlkonig, who was as much of a leader as the Beer Nuts allowed, "what brings you here, my moll?"

"Nerfball was supposed to open up the store for me today, and he didn't. Do you know where he is?"

The Beer Nuts burst out laughing.

"I don't get it," admitted Honeyman, when the noise had died down. "What's so funny?"

Erlkonig sought to explain. "Well, you know how Nerf believes in that dumb nasal irrigation of his. Snorting saltwater all day long to clear his sinuses, honking like a sick goose at all hours of the night. Well, this morning he goes to do it in the dark, only to find someone's spiked his water bucket with Tabasco sauce."

"Ouch," sympathized Honeyman.

"So now he's off somewhere sulking. I suspect you can track him down by the sniffles."

Someone handed Honeyman a flashlight. "Thanks," he said, and stood.

"Bye, Rory," said Netsuke, and giggled.

Honeyman shook his head wearily. Life was always tossing your past straight in your face.

Nerfball was huddled in a far corner of the brewery's upper floors. Honeyman could hear him talking to himself from some distance away and, not wishing to intrude on his personal soliloquy, called out in warning.

"Hey, Nerf, it's me, Rory."

"What do you want?" whined Nerfball.

The flashlight beam revealed Nerfball sitting under an old oak desk. His pudgy form completely filled the capacious knee-well. His nose was inflamed. Incredibly lazy, Nerfball possessed one talent to an astonishing degree: he could make sandwiches better, faster, and more economically than anyone else Honeyman had ever seen. A sandwich crafted by Nerfball emerged from beneath his flashing knife as a thing of beauty, guaranteed to draw repeat customers. It was this salient skill that Honeyman now had to cajole him to employ.

Squatting to make eye contact with the victim of Tabasco poisoning, Honeyman said, "Come help me with the store, Nerf. I need you."

"Why should I? You never pay me anymore."

Nerf had Honeyman there. Cash flow had been pitiful lately. The rent had just been hiked a zillion percent, thanks to the gentrification of the city. (Honeyman himself was not a "B and B," as those "born and bred" in Hoboken called themselves. But he had been here so long, since Hoboken was just a joke, that his conscience was clean.) And a McDonald's had recently opened up in competition a few blocks away. Honeyman was barely scraping by.

Honeyman thought desperately. "Listen, I will pay you, I swear."

Nerfball sneered. "Yeah, I bet. With what? Funny money?"

Honeyman opened his mouth to deny the charge, then was struck by the futility of it all. Why should he lie to poor Nerfball? Chances were he'd soon go out of business, owing all his creditors immense sums. Why compound his guilt by promising more than he knew he could give?

Then, amidst his despair, in a blaze of inspiration he was to remember for the rest of his life, Honeyman had an idea.

"Yes, Nerf, I do intend to pay you in funny money."

This got Nerfball's attention. "Huh?"

Honeyman scrabbled in his pockets for paper and writing tool, coming up with an old unpaid electric bill and a lime-green crayon. He tucked the flashlight between chin and neck, and began to scribble on the back of the bill, reciting aloud what he was writing. "This paper redeemable for ten sandwiches at Honeyman's Heroes. Signed, Rory Honeyman." For good measure, he sketched a rough sandwich on it. The drawing ended up looking like that of a book with loose pages. He offered the paper to Nerfball, who took it suspiciously.

"Here, this will be one day's wages. It's worth about forty dollars retail."

"What good is this to me? You already give me free food."

Honeyman, still in the grip of his genius, rolled right over the pitiful objection. "Right, sure, but isn't everyone in this dump always starving? Make them pool their money—whatever you can convince them this is worth—and give it to you in exchange for the ten sandwiches, which you can make up and bring back here at the end of every day."

"Gee, I don't know—"

"People will love you for it."

"Oh, all right." Nerfball made tentative movements to emerge, and Honeyman stood up to give him room. Somehow the big man twisted around beneath the desk and began to back out. He said something that was muffled by his position.

"What's that?" asked Honeyman.

"I said, 'What's this coupon called?' "

Honeyman was stumped. "Does it have to have a name?"

Nerfball was standing now, brushing dust from his clothes. "Yes."

Honeyman reached deep down into some mythic well of American vernacular and came up with a word he would have earlier sworn he didn't know. "Spondulix. It's called a spondulix."

"Is that singular," quizzed Nerfball, "or plural?"

Without hesitation, Honeyman replied, "Both."

2.

Days in the Pantechnicon

In Mexico City, in the middle of 1968, the Summer Olympics were taking place.

Sometimes when Honeyman said that sentence to himself, it sounded like a bit of incredibly ancient history. In the year 753 B.C., the city of Rome was founded. In the year 1066 A.D., the Norman invasion of England took place. A fact lost in the mists of time, relegated to musty textbooks, unseen by living eyes.

Other times, that period seemed as close as last night, separated from today only by a little interval of sleep.

For Honeyman had been there. And afterwards his life had never gone as he had once innocently thought it would.

Prior to the start of these long-ago Games, Black protesters had succeeded in denying South Africa the right to participate. The head of the International Olympic Committee, one Avery Brundage, had led those who would have allowed South Africa to take part in the Games. This man was also in charge of handing out the medals.

When two American trackmen, Tommie Smith and John Carlos, won a gold and bronze respectively, they decided to stage a symbolic denunciation of Brundage's role. On the victory block, wearing African beads and black scarves, their shoes removed as a symbol of poverty, they raised gloved fists and bowed their heads.

They were immediately expelled from future events.

Sitting in the stands during this bit of typical sixties theater was an eighteen-year-old member of the U.S. swim team, a diver named Rory Honeyman. A nice Iowa boy, he had never even spoken to a Black person before coming to the Olympics. Now, all at once, in the same kind of mental burst that would later engender spondulix, Honeyman experienced an epiphany of radicalization. There is, like, injustice in the world. We are all brothers and sisters. I must protest.

Listening that night to the talk of the other Bloods in the Olympic dorms, Honeyman was confirmed in his initial decision. He said nothing to anyone, though, being of a retiring nature.

The next morning Honeyman felt filled with spiritual vigor. He went to his events. He won the silver. On the stand, he raised his ungloved fist in protest and bowed his head. The crowd seemed stunned. There was a silence as big as Mexico. Honeyman was the only White who had elected to register his solidarity with the Blacks.

Unfortunately, there were no television cameras present to broadcast his personal statement. (His hometown paper was the only one to print a photo, a blurred long-distance shot which made Honeyman look as if he were sniffing his own armpit.) Brundage, the media focus, was elsewhere, and at the same time three Black men named Lee Evans, Larry James and Ron Freeman were also protesting.

Honeyman's actions did not go entirely unnoticed, however.

When he returned home, a changed person, all the familiar sights of his childhood looking transmogrified, his draft notice was waiting for him. Nothing too unusual there — except that he had previously been granted a deferment.

(Eleven years later, talking in a Hoboken bar to a stranger who happened to be a retired Army Colonel, Honeyman learned that those members of the '68 U.S. team who had belonged to ROTC had received phone calls warning them not to join the protest.)

Life in Canada was not that bad at first. Honeyman was a little sad, naturally, thinking of his vanished career in international diving competition. But, possessing a naturally cheerful disposition and being still young, he made the best of this strange twist of fate.

Life only became a bummer when his money ran out. His parents, feeling betrayed and disappointed by their son, refused to send him any more. Soon, Honeyman was desperate for a job.

That was when he met Leonard Lispenard.

Lispenard was the sole owner, chief roustabout, ringmaster and occasional marriage counselor in Lispenard's Pantechnicon, a two-bit, vest-pocket, circus-cum-carny that made a circuit of Canada's north in the summer months, and headed south in the autumn. Lispenard himself was a short fat man with bad skin, who, in his ringmaster garb, looked to Honeyman remarkably like the Penguin, Batman's archenemy.

It was June of 1969 in Calgary, and summer was already waning, when Honeyman approached Lispenard, reasoning that such an outfit would offer a lower-profile job than most other concerns, an essential attraction for an illegal interloper in a country not his own. Inquiring for the owner, he was informed that Lispenard would not be available until that night's show was over. Honeyman purchased a ticket and resigned himself to waiting.

The tent was only half-full. Curiously, no one was sitting in the front rows. Honeyman went and took a seat right up against the ring, determined to get his money's worth.

During the finale of the show, when Honeyman was simultaneously growing impatient and feeling sleepy, he was galvanized by the sight of the first real love of his life, the performer with whom he would daily be associated for the next seven years.

The Baroness von Hammer-Purgstall.

There was a twenty-foot tower in the middle of the tent, with a large platform at the top. No ladder ran up the tower, but rather a kind of open elevator cage, powered by a fitfully chugging engine, stood ready. At the base of the tower was a big square collapsible container, metal-sided, plastic-lined. It had taken half an hour to fill it with water out of a fire hose.

Lispenard waddled to the center of the ring. "Ladies, and Gentlemen, without further ado or needless puffery, may I present, for your edification, the Baroness von Hammer-Purgstall — Canada's only diving equine!"

The Baroness was led out. A gleaming white Lipizzan mare who had flunked out of the Spanish Riding School in Vienna, she was the most beautiful horse the former farm-boy Honeyman had ever seen.

Lispenard had disappeared. A clown led the Baroness willingly into the elevator. She rode it calmly to the top. She trotted out onto the platform. She paused a moment. She jumped off.

It was like watching Pegasus. Honeyman couldn't breathe.

When she landed, the impact, as planned, flattened the tub, spraying water in a circle twenty feet out, drenching the first three rows of seats.

Honeyman didn't care. He vaulted into the ring, ran past the

Baroness, and found Lispenard in among the trapeze girls and dog-trainers.

Buttonholing the owner, Honeyman declared, "Mister, I can ride that horse."

Lispenard replied, "Why, so can I, boy."

"No, no, you don't understand. I mean going down."

Honeyman explained a little about himself. Lispenard still appeared dubious.

"Listen, just give me a chance. Tomorrow night. C'mon. Please?"

"And what if you break your fool neck?"

"I'll sign a waiver. Anything. Just let me ride her."

Lispenard, sensing novelty, a circus's lifeblood, finally agreed.

The next night, Honeyman, attired in borrowed yellow tights, found himself standing beside the Baroness as the elevator made its grumbling ascent. He didn't even see the crowd or hear Lispenard's spiel. All he felt was the horse's shoulder muscles beneath his hand. All he smelled was her clean animal scent.

On the lofty platform, Honeyman boosted himself astride her. The horse never balked. She seemed to sense Honeyman's devotion and admiration. She waited till he was settled. Then she took off.

Honeyman contributed nothing. He was just along for the ride.

And what a hell of a ride it was. Honeyman had no sensation of falling. Instead, he felt he was going up, up, up, straight to the empyrean. In a splash and geyser, it was too soon over.

Honeyman was addicted. Lispenard was convinced. The deal was struck.

The next seven years were an uncomplicated, almost bucolic period for Honeyman. He slept late each day, rising for a communal lunch with the other performers. He groomed the Baroness, perhaps went to explore whatever town they were playing, ate a light supper. All day long the excitement would be building quietly but steadily inside him, until it reached its pitch just prior to the dive. Then he would feel drained, almost post-orgasmic, and the whole cycle would start again.

One day in November 1976, the trailer carrying the Baroness to winter pasture was broadsided on the highway by a truck. Honeyman was vomiting by the shoulder of the road when he heard the shot from the policeman's revolver.

Lispenard, genuinely sympathetic, kept Honeyman on for

another year, as part of the tightrope act. Honeyman had picked up the skill in his spare time, accustomed to heights as he was and gifted with an infallible inner balance.

But Honeyman's heart wasn't in it. His life seemed empty without the nightly flight. Sometimes he swore he still felt the warm barrel shape of the horse's body between his legs.

When Jimmy Carter announced amnesty for draft dodgers in 1977, Honeyman claimed his savings from Lispenard's squat old safe—more than once Honeyman had thought how that depository resembled its owner—and returned to the land of his birth. After an uncomfortable reunion with his parents, he headed east, ending up somehow in Hoboken, owner of an eponymous sandwich shop.

His life for the next decade was basically eventless. A smattering of love affairs, most recently with Netsuke, the demands of a small business, the pleasure of the spectator at sporting events. Nothing loomed large in his life; his psychic landscape was flat; his horizons untroubled by mirages, destinations real or unreal.

Until, that is, he invented spondulix.

3.

Higher Economics

Nerfball's fingers moved like a maestro's. Fluid, knowing, commanding, they flew through their arcane rituals. Cutting, slicing, chopping, dicing. Layering and spreading, halving and wrapping . . .

Filling drink orders, taking money and making change, Honeyman watched in admiration. Nerfball, his lank, longish, greasy hair whipping about, was a one-man sandwich factory. No, it was more like performance art. Sometimes, in fact, the crowd at the counter actually broke out in applause.

The inside of Honeyman's Heroes was clean but not neat. Mounted on the exposed brick of the walls were numerous caricatures of various local characters, in the inimitable Netsuke style. She had also done the illustrated menu that listed the various sandwiches by name: the Shakespeare (ham and Danish Jarlsberg cheese); the Sinatra (tongue and baloney); the Pia Zadora (marshmallow fluff and honey).

Bracketed to the side walls were scarred ashwood counters with stools positioned beneath. A pickle barrel—tongs hanging from the rim—occupied the center of the room.

Nerfball worked at a long, wide butcher-block slab, at the front of which stood a narrow glass case functioning both as a divider between the artist and his fans, and as a display area for various figurines and good luck objects. A herd of plastic dinosaurs, a bust of Elvis, a ceramic horse that everyone knew meant something secret and special to Honeyman. . . .

Behind Nerfball and on either side, within easy reach, were all his implements and raw ingredients. Bottles of Tiger Sauce, tubs of cream cheese, sharp knives and twin steamers that could turn a quarter-pound of pastrami and Swiss into so much ambrosia.

People yelled out their orders, Nerfball reacted with wordless speed, Honeyman made small talk; slices of pumpernickel, white, and rye arced through the air to land on the slab in perfect formation. What with all this, the afternoon sped swiftly by, another day among many, until finally it was nearing three o'clock, and the store was momentarily empty.

Nerfball wiped his hands on his apron and looked up with a dazed air. Honeyman walked over to him and clapped him with honest appreciation on the back.

"Thanks, Nerf. You were, as usual, superb. I think I can handle the supper crowd alone. Why don't you break early today? Here, I'll get your pay."

Honeyman took from the register the original and unique spondulix which he had hastily scribbled out a month or so ago, in a fit of desperate creativity. The old electric bill was now somewhat more greasy and worse for wear, but its green crayoned message was still discernible.

Honeyman got ready to go through the daily ritual that already seemed ancient. He would hand Nerfball the spondulix. Nerf would cobble up ten sandwiches for himself. Then his employee would hand the spondulix back and depart with the sandwiches, the medium in which it was redeemable.

Today, however, Nerfball refused to take part.

"Can't you pay me in cash?" he asked.

Honeyman was grieved. "Jeez, Nerf, you know every penny I take in goes for something crucial. I still haven't paid off the bakery for last week yet. If I have to meet your wages in real money, I'll go under. And then where will either of us be? You know I don't draw any pay for myself."

"Yeah, but you're the owner, Mister Capitalist. You're supposed to take risks and suffer."

"Nerf—I cannot pay you in American currency. Will you take spondulix or not?"

Nerfball sighed dramatically. "All right. Hand it over."

Honeyman surrendered the spondulix. Nerfball took off his apron and prepared to leave.

"Hey, wait a minute. Don't you want your sandwiches?"

"No, I don't. Beatbox got a new job, after some lady who didn't like the message he delivered squeezed his clown nose too hard. He works for a donut shop and gets to bring home all the stale ones. Nobody wants sandwiches anymore."

"All that sugar's bad for you."

"I can't help what people like."

"What're you gonna do with the spondulix then?" asked Honeyman. He felt somehow reluctant to let the piece of paper bearing his signature leave the shop.

"Oh," said Nerfball mysteriously, "I've got a plan."

And so saying, he left.

Honeyman did not sleep well that night. Dreams wherein brutal strangers accosted him, shouting, "Payable on demand!" troubled his slumbers.

The next day the same exchange was made. Honeyman inscribed this second spondulix on a napkin, secretly hoping that the perishable medium would quickly fall apart. The day after that the same thing happened. And the day after that, and the day after that. . . .

Soon there were a rough dozen spondulix—representing 120 sandwiches—out in the world, God knew where. Nerfball refused to say. Honeyman hoped they were stashed somewhere in the Old Vault Brewery, where rats would chew them to pieces, lining their nests with Nerfball's nestegg.

But then, like sins or pigeons, the spondulix began to flock homeward.

Honeyman was alone in the shop around suppertime one day when Tiran Porter, the owner of a nearby hardware store, came in. Clutched in hand was a napkin. Honeyman's heart seized up, as if arrest was imminent.

"Hey, Rory, my man—is this thing any good? That Nerdo dude convinced me to take it in place of thirty dollars' worth of electrical equipment. I wasn't gonna, till I seen your name on it. I knew you'd play me straight."

Honeyman experienced a slight sense of relief, a momentary passing of his foreboding. At the same time, he suspected his relief was to be short-lived.

"Sure, Tiran, just like it says: good for ten sandwiches, 'bout forty bucks. You made a good deal."

Porter seemed mollified. "Okay, then, I'm gonna spend some of it."

"Some of it?"

"Sure, I can't eat no ten sandwiches at once. Give me an Atlantic City on white, hold the lettuce."

As Honeyman made the sandwich, his mind worked frantically. How was he to redeem part of a spondulix?

When the sandwich was made, Honeyman did the only thing he could. Feeling like God on the second day, he created a new denomination. On a fresh napkin, he scrawled: ONE SPONDU-LIX REDEEMABLE FOR NINE SANDWICHES. Then signed it. Taking the ten-sandwich note, he handed Porter the sandwich and his change.

"I don't get no cash back?"

"Sorry, Tiran, but you paid in spondulix. It's sorta like food stamps."

Nodding with new understanding, Porter departed, apparently satisfied.

One sandwich down, 119 to go.

But of course Nerfball would be getting paid again tomorrow, thereby causing the minting of a new ten-spot spondulix, which would no doubt enter circulation soon, more than negating the single sandwich he had redeemed just now.

Honeyman tried to figure out if he was going to come out ahead or behind on all this. A pain began to mount behind his eyeballs, and he suspected that his brainstorm was going to lead to his complete undoing.

One day soon he would think back to this moment and realize his pessimistic forecast had been all right. And all wrong.

The next day Honeyman verged several times on confronting Nerfball about his wanton and promiscuous exchange of spondulix for goods and services other than the specified sandwiches. But each time he stopped himself. The bills were really not Honeyman's any longer, once he passed them over to Nerf. The pudgy Beer Nut had every right to use them as best he could. Honeyman was lucky he could get the man to employ his talents at all. The various members of the Beer Nuts were notoriously lazy, avoiding work whenever possible. And Honeyman needed Nerfball more than Nerf needed him. Lacking this one crucial employee, the shop would go under. God, what a precarious existence this world afforded! And what a mess Honeyman had made of his own personal life, ever since that day under the Mexican sun, before the eyes of the world.

Watching the sweaty Nerfball transform heaps of cold cuts into works of art, Honeyman resigned himself once again, both to his past and to whatever was to come.

No customer tried to tender spondulix in payment that day. But the following afternoon a group of workers from the Stahl Soap Corporation came in at shift's end, smelling sweetly of their product, like a newly opened box of bath salts. At first Honeyman couldn't figure out why they had traveled all the way over from Park Street, down by the river, since it was quite a distance away. Then they revealed they had two spondulix among them, and wanted all twenty sandwiches.

While he was slapping the sandwiches together, with none of Nerf's finesse, Honeyman tried to find out where they had gotten the spondulix. He couldn't figure out what Nerfball had traded for, since he seldom bathed, there being no running water at the brewery where the Beer Nuts squatted.

"So, guys — where'd you get my coupons?"

A skinny fellow who seemed capable of consuming an infinite amount of "free" pickles spoke up around a mouthful. "Harry Lieberman — you know Harry, he drives the company truck — well, Harry hauled a bunch of stuff somewhere for those hippies that live in the old brewery, and they paid him with these. Harry gave 'em to me as payment for his bowling league dues. So I'm sharing them with the whole league."

Honeyman nearly sliced the tip of his finger off. This was bad news indeed. The exchanges were getting more complicated. The spondulix were now circulating among third parties, people who, for some unknown reason, obviously trusted in them enough not to try to redeem them immediately. And others, fourth-parties, also seemed willing to accept the spondulix without first-hand knowledge of Honeyman's honesty or willingness to make good on them. Wasn't this property a known characteristic of real money? Didn't economists have some complicated way to measure this circulation, the number of times money changed hands?

God, this was scary! Honeyman's personal signature on dozens of napkins that were roaming out in the city of Hoboken like prodigal children, masquerading as money. . . . He had to abandon spondulix! But he couldn't. His business would go under if he did.

Piling slices of tomatoes atop rings of Bermuda onions in a stack as tall as his worries, Honeyman wondered where this would all end.

And in the back of his mind was another worry. What were the Beer Nuts up to? First electrical equipment, then hauling—it had to be something dangerous.

When Earl Erlkonig walked into the shop during a lull the next day with Suki Netsuke on his arm, Honeyman knew, just from the expression on the man's hereditarily blanched face, that his trepidations had a foundation in reality.

"Hey, Rory, my molecule, I'm paying a call to invite you to an Outlaw Party."

So. Here it was, out in the open now. And it was just as bad as Honeyman had feared. Anxiety gave way momentarily to annoyance, as from the back room came the distracting honking of Nerfball, performing his hourly nasal irrigations.

The Outlaw Party was an institution of long-standing. Sans permit or permission, the Beer Nuts and other assorted fringe folks would take over a public location come nightfall on a specified day. Decorations would be strung up, kegs tapped, food laid on, and music unleashed. Invitation to the party was initially by word of mouth among a select group, although as soon as its noisy existence became generally known, it would be besieged by the hoi polloi.

The Hoboken police generally tolerated the occasional Outlaw Party, knowing that the motivation was sheer fun, not vandalism or riot. However, the rush of events sometimes went too far, and overstepped boundaries in a way the authorities could not ignore. Always implicit in the festivities was the possibility of chaos and anarchy breaking loose. There was the time, for instance, when the site had been the abandoned ferry building down near the PATH station, before that structure's recent renovation and the reestablishment of ferry service to Manhattan. Apparently the sight of a full orchestra atop the building's roof, with dancers threatening to fall off the gables and kill themselves, had been too much for the cops. The subsequent dispersal of the revelers had eventually involved two fire companies and a contingent of National Guardsmen.

Honeyman supposed he was just getting older, but for some reason he didn't relish the idea of an Outlaw Party as much as he once had. The prospect of confronting the police at this time, when he was already guilty of perpetuating spondulix, rather took the enjoyment out of things.

Regarding Erlkonig's open face, with its broad white African nose and translucent eyebrows, Honeyman sought to detect any duplicity in the man's invitation, but failed. Netsuke, meanwhile, had silently taken a napkin from the counter and was folding it into an origami crane. Honeyman tried to work up a little resentment at Erlkonig for stealing his girl away, but couldn't do it.

"Oh, what the hell," he finally said, "sure, I'll come."

"Great, my moll. I knew we could count on you. And maybe you'd contribute a little something—?"

"No problem. I'll make up a few platters."

"It wasn't sandwiches I was after, Rory. The food angle is pretty well covered. But there's a few other things we need to purchase, and our treasury is, like, empty."

"Earl, you know I'm broke."

Erlkonig smiled broadly. "Ah, my moll, that's where you're wrong. All you have to do is write out a few more of those spondulix things you've been giving Nerfball."

In a flash it dawned on Honeyman. Nerf never would have had the initiative or brains to promote spondulix. It must have been all Erlkonig's doings. The man was crafty. Honeyman had always credited him with brains and guile, but this was beyond belief. To take advantage of Honeyman's quandary in such a duplicitous manner—

"Earl, you're asking me to mortgage my future. Every spondulix I write is like a loan against my potential profits, meager as they might be."

Erlkonig became serious. "No, man, that's wrong. That's like a worst-case scenario. All the spondulix will never come in. Most are just gonna circulate forever. Take my word for it, I know. It's money for nothing, Rory. It's like having a money tree growing in your yard. You just have to overcome your fear and go with it."

Honeyman wanted to believe. It would make things so easy. "Do you really think so?"

"My moll—I know so!"

At that moment, Netsuke finished her paper bird. She opened her hands and tossed it upward, like a magician releasing a dove. The origami crane clearly flapped its wings a few times, then glided to a landing on the counter in front of Honeyman, where it promptly melted back to the original napkin, now intricately creased.

Netsuke said nothing. The two men looked at her, then back to each other.

"I wish I knew how she does that," said Erlkonig.

"Me too," said Honeyman. Then: "Oh, Christ, here's your spondulix." Using another magic napkin, he wrote one spondulix for the largest denomination yet: five hundred sandwiches.

"Thanks, moll," said Erlkonig, putting the draft away in his shirt pocket. He and Netsuke turned to go.

"Hey, where's the party?"

"Oh, we're commandeering the campus of the Stevens Institute. Week from tonight. See you there."

Then they were gone, leaving Honeyman shaking his head at the audacity of it. The Stevens Institute of Technology occupied a spectacular bluff above the river, and afforded a gorgeous view of nighttime Manhattan. It was bound to be a hell of a bash.

And when the deliveryman from the bakery came that day, Honeyman had no trouble persuading him to take spondulix in payment.

4.

Overlooking Sinatra

A Frisbee skimmed low over Honeyman's Mets cap, nearly knocking the hat from his head. Out of the concentrated dusk beneath a big elm off to his left came the voice of Leather.

"Sorry, Rory!"

From his right, a paraphrastic echo from Studs: "Yeah, sorry, Honeyman."

"That's okay, girls," replied Honeyman, immediately bending low and executing some broken-field running to avoid the expected barrage of pebbles and verbal abuse, which indeed quickly materialized.

"You jerk!"

"Don't call us that!"

Attaining the shelter of a doorway, Honeyman straightened up. He dug his fingers thoughtfully into his rufous beard. Now why had he gone and annoyed Leather 'n' Studs like that? He normally went out of his way to be nice to them, harboring no ill will toward anyone of any sexual stripe whatsoever. But here he was starting the night off by deliberately—sorta deliberately, anyway—insulting people. He supposed it stemmed from his own unhappiness, as the bad attitudes of most folks did.

During the past week, Honeyman had created and spent spondulix with a wild abandon bordering on inebriation. Erlkonig's devil-may-care attitude had infected him—Honeyman had *allowed* it to infect him—and he had dived blindly into the deep end of the algae-topped pool of monetary irresponsibility. As a result, all his debts had been extinguished. The local merchants reacted at first with doubt and caution, but in the end mostly agreed to accept this novel kind of payment, in lieu of anything better. With the U.S. currency thus saved, Honeyman paid off those institutions such as the regional electric company which would never, he was sure, recognize spondulix.

And, as Erlkonig had maintained, fewer spondulix returned than went out, thereby creating a positive cash flow. Honeyman had no idea where the missing spondulix were. Perhaps they had all gone through a wash cycle or two, forgotten in pants pockets, and been rendered into fibrous lumps. He fervently hoped so.

The lifting of his fiscal obligations should have lightened Honeyman's spirits. He should have been feeling on top of the world right now. Instead, he was plunged into an ever-deepening gloom.

Despite his actions at the Olympics two decades ago, Honeyman had never considered himself a rebel. All he had ever wanted was a little niche in society, a moderate income, a few of the simpler pleasures. True, he had once dreamed of exhibiting his diving skills for the admiration and pleasure of the public—either solo or horsed—but even that modest ambition had been twice by fate denied. All he wanted now was a quiet, contemplative existence.

Instead, though, he found himself flouting the Constitution, the Bill of Rights, and God knew what else, all by creating and putting into circulation a kind of mock currency in direct competition with the almighty United States dollar. He was hard pressed to put a name to his crime—he knew it wasn't counterfeiting—but he was certain it was a crime, and a heinous one at that. You might spit in the eye of the U.S. Olympic team and expect nothing more deadly than a draft notice as response. But to steal money, in effect, out of Uncle Sam's Treasury, to set yourself up as some kind of sovereign on a par with the government—Honeyman couldn't imagine what kind of punishment would be deemed draconian enough by an incensed bureaucracy.

Looking out over the verdant, path-slashed campus, which was filling up with the throngs anticipating an evening of Outlaw revelry, Honeyman sighed deeply. A couple walked by, hand in hand. Honeyman was too wounded even to sigh.

What about someone to share his hoped-for simple existence? Was that asking too much? He had thought Netsuke was the one. Had thought she felt the same. Then she had thrown him over for Erlkonig. Perhaps the age difference had been too great. And now he would have to confront her tonight, as she hung all moony-eyed over Erlkonig. . . .

Mustn't become bitter. Get a grip on yourself, Honeyman! Look on the bright side: a single man, relatively good-looking, under forty, resident in a metropolitan area where such specimens were at a premium. . . . The feminine world should be your oyster. (But what did that cliche mean, anyway? Oysters were tough to pry open, and you could rip your hands to shreds on them.) As long as the cops weren't battering down his door, he'd try to maintain his usual optimism.

Honeyman stepped forth from the shadowy doorway, resolved to have a great time tonight.

He tripped over someone who had come to sit unnoticed on the single step before him. Both Honeyman and the unknown figure went tumbling to the turf.

Recovering, Honeyman confronted Hilario Fumento, writer with a peculiar mission.

Fumento had become fixated early on in his career by a certain frisson provided by the best fiction: the encounter in print of a commonplace mundane item, experience, or sensory datum which was instantly recognizable but also previously unrendered in print. The famous shock of recognition, in fact. It was Fumento's dream to construct a novel made entirely out of these gems. He was still in the process of collecting them, leaving the arrangement into a narrative, however bizarre, until later. Lacking money for materials, Fumento pilfered call slips and pencil stubs from public libraries, and used these to record his epiphanies.

Fumento, digging a scrap of paper out of his pocket now— Honeyman had a brief fear that it would turn out to be a spondulix ready for redemption—said, "Hey, Rory, what do you think of this one: 'Washcloth hanging over a shower-curtain rod: its lower, wetter edge is darker.'"

"Beautiful, Hilario. It's got an almost haiku-like quality."

Fumento smiled bashfully and stuffed the paper back into his jacket. "Gee, thanks, Rory. It just came to me this morning, while I was washing up. We've got water at the Brewery now, you know."

Honeyman's curiosity was piqued. "Oh, yeah?"

"Yeah. Earl swung it. He's got big plans for fixing the whole place up."

It flashed on Honeyman how Erlkonig intended to pay for these dream renovations, and he grew angry. He must confront the albino before he went any further. "Well, we'll see how far he gets. Listen, I'll catch you later, Hilario."

"Bye, Rory. Have a good time."

Honeyman got to his feet and moved off.

Attracted by a scattering of airy multicolored spangles, he found himself at a broad, flagstoned pavilion at the western edge of the campus. Here, the trees had been bedecked with strings of fairy lights. A bandstand had been erected, and a crew of volunteers was arraying speakers and other equipment atop it, under the direction of Hy Rez, the Beer Nuts' technical expert, and his assistant, Special Effects.

Special Effects's given name was Saint Francis Xavier, commonly abbreviated S.F.X. His father was a defrocked Jesuit. Special had long red hair down to his shoulders, and a dopy broad face. These looks, however, belied a quick wit.

"Hey, Special. Seen Earl around?"

Walking backward, laying cable from a coil, Special replied, "He was overseeing the fireworks, last time I spotted him."

Fireworks. Did the man's temerity have no end? This night would see them all in jail for sure. Honeyman debated leaving the party before it had begun, then decided against it. He was in no mood to mope in his apartment alone. And he had to confront Erlkonig about his cavalier spending of spondulix.

Honeyman spotted the refreshment table, and decided he could use a drink. Nodding in that direction, he asked Special Effects, "Can I get you anything?"

"No thanks. Hy and I are permanently wired now."

Honeyman smiled, certain that Special was joking. The man stopped playing out wire and lifted a strand of hair. In the dim light, Honeyman thought to detect something behind his ear. Special Effects resumed his work. Honeyman shrugged and moved away. Chances were Special was just yanking his chain, but he didn't care to inquire further.

From an aluminum keg, Honeyman drew a big plastic cup of beer, sipped. Belhaven Scottish Ale, imported from Glasgow. This must have cost a fortune. He would wring Erlkonig's neck.

The crowd was thickening now, as full night descended and the party began to really take off. The lines were several deep at the several kegs. Someone stuck a box of donuts under Honeyman's nose.

Beatbox. "Have one, Rory. I made them myself."

Honeyman took a donut, bit. "Taco flavored?"

"It was only an experiment. But the owner—he ain't no experimentin' man."

Honeyman was sorry Beatbox had lost his job, but in a way was also selfishly glad. Perhaps now, he faintly hoped, Nerfball would have to return to taking sandwiches in trade.

Munching his taco donut, more out of habit than desire, Honeyman idly watched a drug deal being consummated in the shadows. The seller proffered a Ziploc; the buyer handed over . . . a napkin?

No, impossible, things were too far out of control. . . .

Sounds of tuning up wafted over from the musicians assembled onstage. "Who's playing tonight?"

"The Millionaires."

"Don't know 'em."

"They're just a pickup band. Local guys. Some from the Broadcasters, though."

The opening to Pink Floyd's "Money" rang out: sampled cash-register noises. The singer came in: "Money, it's a drag. . . ."

Honeyman sampled his beer. Beatbox had left to circulate with his Mexicanized crullers. Honeyman threw the remainder of his donut surreptitiously down underfoot. Courtesy only extended so far. Drawing another cup of dark ale, he went in search of Erlkonig.

The pavilion was filling up with dancers. Honeyman traveled along its balustraded perimeter, as alert as anyone who had just polished off eighteen ounces of Glaswegian beer could be, for a glimpse of Erlkonig. But the man was nowhere in sight. Netsuke neither.

Beyond the stone rampart the land fell vertically away, straight down some fifty feet to Sinatra Drive. Just beyond the busy highway lapped the Hudson. Across its width loomed the fabulous gemmed cliffs of Manhattan, remote as the mirage of some Arabian seraglio.

A woman Honeyman did not recognize was leaning on her forearms on the stone railing, looking out toward the distant city. A thick mane of brown hair tumbled over her shoulders. She wore a halter top. Her bare coltish legs were displayed attractively by a short skirt. She was shod with leather sandals.

Moved by a powerful attraction, Honeyman fell into the same pose beside her. The band was playing an old fifties tune, once covered by the J. Geils Band: "First I Look at the Purse." There was an odor of coffee in the air.

Honeyman was tongue-tied, an unusual occurrence. The woman did not look at him. He wetted his dry throat with a sip of beer. Said at last, "Are you enjoying yourself?"

The woman turned toward him. Her face was not young, but it was beautiful. Honeyman was surprised to see she was roughly his own age. She wore prescription glasses with a cord hanging down from the stems like reins.

"Oh, I guess so. But I don't know anyone here. I just moved to Hoboken from Chelsea. My building went condo."

The woman's lack of connection to the Beer Nuts or anyone in their crowd only increased her attractiveness to Honeyman. "My name's Rory."

"Addie."

They shook hands. Hers was slim and warm. Honeyman felt his own to be a big sweaty paw.

"That's an unusual name," said Honeyman.

"I was just going to say the same thing about yours. Mine's short for Atalanta. Atalanta Swinburne."

"Mine's not short for anything."

She went back to gazing at the river. Honeyman could think of nothing else to say. Desperate, he blurted out: "Honeyman."

"Please?"

"My last name's Honeyman."

"Do you own—"

"The sandwich shop on Washington? Yup, that's me."

"I've been meaning to try you."

Honeyman gulped. "Oh, please, come on in. . . ."

"I will."

Honeyman timed the silence at thirty seconds. It seemed much longer.

"The water looks so cold," she said finally. "And a breeze is coming up. Do you mind if we move?"

Honeyman's heart raced. She had said "we." The pronoun had never sounded so seductive.

They moved off among the dancers. Trying to stay together, Honeyman dared to grip her upper arm. She didn't complain.

Back on the grassy area, Honeyman spotted Erlkonig.

"Wait here just a second, please. I gotta talk to that guy."

"All right. . . ."

Honeyman hailed the albino. "Hey, Earl!"

Erlkonig, either alarmed by Honeyman's attitude, or having something to hide, began inexplicably to run.

Honeyman set off in pursuit.

He trapped Erlkonig near the fireworks.

"Earl, be cool. What's the matter? I just wanna talk."

Panting, Erlkonig said, "I can't discuss anything with you when you've been drinking. You're too liable to get mad."

"Why should I get mad? What've you done? It's nothing to do with spondulix, is it? Tell me!"

"Later, moll, later."

Erlkonig looked about for an avenue of escape. He began to clamber among the fireworks arrayed on the ground in their tubes, upsetting the jury-rigged arrangements. Honeyman strode implacably after him.

Erlkonig looked backward over his shoulder, tripped, and sprawled across the control panel.

Everything went off at once.

Honeyman felt he knew what he had missed in 'Nam.

Rockets zipped by parallel to the ground. Fireballs burst against the sides of buildings. Great crimson and lemon-yellow starbursts broke at treetop level. Fiery chrysanthemums flowered, only to shatter the next moment against the sides of parked cars, their life spans briefer than mayflies.

There were screams, explosions, wild feedback as the Millionaires, unfazed, improvised to the unexpected lightshow. Sirens began to sound, distant, growing nearer.

Honeyman dove to the ground and began crawling.

Fireworks continued to roar by overhead.

A few feet away, he encountered Addie, who had followed him.

"Let's get out of here!" he shouted above the noise.

She nodded mutely.

They wormed their way out of the path of the seemingly inexhaustible fireworks, stood up and began to trot away. At the edge of the campus they were nearly run over by a screaming patrol car. They ran then, laughing, and didn't stop till they fell into Honeyman's bed.

5.

Off to War

Amid the noises of hammering and sawing next door to the sandwich shop, and of Nerfball performing his hourly nasal irrigation in the employees' restroom, Honeyman stood transfixed. In his hand he held one of the new spondulix.

The material of the crisp bill was good linen bond. It was printed in tones of mustard-yellow. On its front was a rendering of a giant hoagie sandwich. On its obverse was a portrait of Honeyman, complete down to his Mets cap. Under the hoagie was the legend: IN PUMPERNICKEL WE TRUST.

This bill was denominated "FIFTY SPONDULIX." There were others — mayo-white, ketchup-red, pickle-green — in various lesser and greater denominations, lying in Honeyman's till. And with every passing minute, more spilled out of the presses set up in the basement of the Old Vault Brewery. Each one, in Honeyman's eyes, a little ticking time bomb bound to explode one day right in his very own hairy face.

It was this new wrinkle in the evolution of spondulix that had caused Erlkonig to react so nervously two weeks ago to Honeyman's attempted approach. The Black albino, exhibiting the initiative and ingenuity which had led him to his position of preeminence among the Beer Nuts, had taken it upon himself to professionalize the production of spondulix. Having come to rely on them to further his manifold schemes, Erlkonig felt he could no longer make do with scribbled napkins, which were likely to disintegrate with constant handling, or, even worse, to be mistakenly used for some ignoble purpose such as blowing one's nose. Moreover, the napkins were bulky and hard to carry in one's wallet.

All these arguments and more had Erlkonig adduced to Honeyman shortly after the disastrous conclusion to the Outlaw Party, as he tried to convince him of the necessity of this step. Honeyman had not been easily swayed.

"C'mon, Rory, loosen up. What're you worrying about anyway? There's nothing illegal in what we're doing. Just look at these things as coupons, like. Yeah, manufacturer's coupons, that's all they are. When Kellogg's gives you thirty-five cents off on Raisin Bran, are they trying to subvert the government, like you claim we are? And what about when the supermarket doubles the coupon? They're adding some incremental value to that piece of paper — which, by the way, even says on the back in fine print, 'Redeemable for one-tenth of a cent.' "

Honeyman shook his head in weary dissent. He knew in his bones that all this was wrong, and that they were going to have to pay the piper one day, but he just couldn't summon up the logic to counter Erlkonig's snaky persuasiveness.

"Look," Erlkonig continued, "even if these things are money, so what? Don't look so shocked, I mean it. So what? You gotta get some historical perspective on this, my moll. You know, the government wasn't always the only one who minted money in this country. Right up to the mid-1800s, private banks issued notes that were supposedly backed by their deposits, and which circulated as legal tender. And lots of times a bank printed so much that the collective value of the paper was two or three times the bank's holdings. Of course, the whole system eventually went bust, causing quite a shitstorm, but that doesn't apply to us, since we're going to keep tighter reins on things."

The phrase "went bust" made Honeyman's vision waver. "Earl, I just don't feel right about—"

Erlkonig brooked no naysayers. "And during the Depression, all across the country individual stores issued scrip redeemable only at their establishments. Same thing we're doing. And the Confederacy—don't forget about them. What was the first thing they did? Right, issue their own money."

"They were seceding from the Union, Earl. We're not doing that, are we?"

"No, of course not. But you must admit that these are uncertain times, Rory. A few years ago we went through the worst depression since the thirties. The homeless, the unemployed, the people whose jobs went to Asia—this government is fiscally fucked up. If we can help people by printing spondulix, why shouldn't we?"

Honeyman found it hard to speak out against such a liberal cause. "But how is one little sandwich shop supposed to float so many notes?"

"Well, remember what I said before. Not all of them are going to come back at once. But you are right in thinking that your present operation isn't set up to handle such volume. That's why I've got to talk to you about these plans for expansion I've got here—"

At that moment Honeyman was jolted from his reverie by several demands on his attention. The customer whose spondulix, tendered in payment, had set Honeyman drifting now said, "Hey, can I get my change?" At the same time a workman stuck his head through the raw, unframed passage in the wall that led to the adjacent storefront and asked, "Rory, which wall did you want the counter on?" And an argument broke out between Beatbox and another customer.

"What's that you're putting on my peanut butter? I asked for orange marmalade, not horseradish."

"Hey, man, you got to try something new in your life now and then. Experiment, like."

"I don't want an experiment, I want a good sandwich."

"This is gonna be el supremo, man. Just give it a shot."

"There is no way I am going to bite into that—"

Hurriedly making change (forty-one spondulix), and shouting out, "North wall," to the carpenter, Honeyman intervened on the customer's behalf and convinced Beatbox to assemble the sandwich as instructed.

Nerfball emerged from his ablutions then, and Honeyman put him back to making sandwiches, transferring Beatbox to the register, where his passion for culinary recombinations would get little play.

"Hello, Rory," said a woman. Her voice, though known only for a fortnight, bore for Honeyman all the deep familiarity and intimate thrill of the voice of one's lifetime mate, heard under a hundred circumstances over several decades.

Turning from the register, Honeyman saw Addie standing among the crowd of hungry customers, patient, radiant, gorgeous.

Hastily doffing his apron, Honeyman ducked under the hinged portion of the counter and came to stand beside her. He grabbed her in a bear hug, picked her up off the floor, spun her around in a circle, set her down and kissed her with appropriate enthusiasm. There was heartfelt applause from the assembled diners, catcalls and whistles. Addie blushed.

"Boy, am I glad to see you," said Honeyman.

"So I gathered. I've got the afternoon off, and wondered if you could get away."

"You bet. Hey, Nerf, you're in charge."

Honeyman took Addie's hand, and marveled how good it felt.

Meeting Atalanta Swinburne had been the best thing that had happened to him in a long time. She was so stable, so centered, such a calming presence in his life. The perfect antidote to the whirlwind of madness that spondulix and the Beer Nuts had brought into being around him. It seemed almost too much that she should also be witty, beautiful and good. Coming off his breakup with Netsuke, Honeyman had needed someone just like Addie. And here she was, somehow inexplicably attracted to him, with apparently equal intensity.

Sometimes life could be very good.

"How's the addition coming?" asked Addie.

"Let's take a look," said Honeyman, and detoured next door.

The shop next to Honeyman's Heroes had been a boutique that had tried to attract an upscale clientele and failed. They had gone under six months ago, and the place had remained vacant since. Honeyman had had little trouble convincing the owner of the building to let him break through the wall and connect the two stores.

The place was a cacophony of power tools, and smelled of fresh-cut pine boards. The laborers—all paid with spondulix, of course—were putting in a second food preparation area and more dining space, all in anticipation of the increased business the circulation of more spondulix would bring.

Honeyman inspected a few details, trying to act like a competent businessman, and then gratefully escaped with Addie out into the glorious July day.

Addie worked for some government agency or another— Honeyman had never quite managed to elicit the details from her—and frequently seemed to have her afternoons free, time which she seemed to enjoy spending with Honeyman.

"I thought we might go into the city," she said now, "for a little shopping. I want to go to Canal Street Jeans."

"Sounds good to me. But I've got to change first. I smell like pastrami."

Addie bit his ear. "I like pastrami."

It took Honeyman two hours to get dressed.

It was such a beautiful day that they couldn't stand the thought of plunging underground on the PATH line to Manhattan, so they decided to take the ferry. It was comparatively slow, but that was hardly a consideration today, when they were out to loaf and amble.

The ferry terminal—a heroic old building dating from 1907— stood on the water at the south end of town. For many years it had been abandoned and decrepit, slowly falling to ruin. Then the city had revived the ferry service and restored the building to its old splendor. Now boats shuttled daily between Hoboken and Battery Park City.

Addie and Honeyman stood inside the terminal, in line with the other passengers waiting for a boat to dock. Honeyman thought he saw some of the Beer Nuts in the crowd. Curiously, they all seemed to be decked out in white coveralls and wearing goggles pushed up on their heads. Honeyman dismissed all thought of them from his mind.

The ferry nosed into its berth, its rear half projecting out of the building. A ramp rattled down on its chains, people disembarked, and the eastbound passengers filed on.

Yes, he was certain of it now. Those were several of the Beer Nuts. And they seemed to be carrying holstered sidearms, right out in the open—Goddamn it all, what was going on?

Addie led the way upstairs to the open observation deck, and they moved to lounge at the railing. The ferry blew its horn and got underway. Once out on the river, under the cloudless July sky, enthralling breezes brought them scents of the city and the distant sea. Honeyman put his arm around Addie's waist, and tried to forget all his troubles.

Someone bumped into him. It was Ped Xing, the Orthodox Jewish Zen Master. He wore tinted goggles. He had been slinking along, bent at the waist, frequently swivelling as if expecting attackers to emerge from every bulkhead.

In one hand he carried a large plastic gun.

"Xing, what the hell—"

"Quiet, moll, this is war. It's every man and woman for himself. Herself. Whatever."

The shaven-headed Ped Xing made as if to prowl on, but Honeyman restrained him with a hand on his tensed shoulder.

"Xing—just hold it right there. War with whom? And what kind of gun is that?"

"Well, not war, really—just war games. We're all playing Survival. Earl said it'd be good for us, sharpen our senses and reflexes for anything that comes our way. These are splat guns. They shoot those paint pellets—you know. Oh, that reminds me." Ped Xing unzipped his coverall down to the waist, revealing a scrawny and hairless chest, and took out a second gun that had been tucked into the elasticized top of his Jockey shorts. "As an honorary Beer Nut, you're a legitimate target. I'm doing you a big favor, warning you this way. I could've scored a lot of points off you. Anyway, you'd better take this."

Honeyman accepted the spare pistol automatically, even as he was saying, "Xing, this is crazy, I won't get involved." He was suddenly overcome by a strange kind of feeling, something weirder than déjà vu, and he realized that he was being forced to decide once more about organized violence, a choice he thought he had made twenty years ago, when he slit open the envelope bearing the government's "Greetings." Was once never enough. . . ?

Ignoring Honeyman's protestations, Ped Xing was already duck-walking away. He called back enigmatically over his shoulder, "Satori comes whether you want it or not."

At that moment a shrill cry of victory paired with a wail of

SPONDULIX 53

defeat emerged from below decks. There was the sound of pounding feet, and several people burst out of a hatchway onto the upper level: Leather 'n' Studs pursuing a hapless Hilario Fumento, liberally bespattered with technicolored bull's-eyes. Blinded by panic, Fumento headed straight for Honeyman. The writer looked as if he intended to vault the rail and plunge into the river. Leather dropped into a crouch, bracing her arm to squeeze off another shot. The ferry rocked in a swell just as she pulled the trigger and the shot went awry, striking Addie right on the chest. A bloom of blue paint blossomed on her left breast.

The world went red and hazy in Honeyman's eyes. He let out a wordless roar that transfixed all the Beer Nuts.

"Hey, moll," began Leather, "I'm really sorr—"

It was too late for temporizing. Honeyman emptied his gun at the frozen woman, spotting her white suit from neck to ankle. Fumento had stopped beside his protector, and Honeyman now wrenched the gun from his hand and turned toward Studs.

"Yikes," she whimpered, and turned tail. Honeyman potted her backside once or twice, then took off in pursuit.

The rest of the twenty-minute trip passed in a mad blur of running, hiding and sharpshooting. From bilge to fo'c's'le the game ran its course. Honeyman lost track of how often he reloaded. Someone had slipped him a pack of refills. In midvoyage, the Manhattan-bound ferry passed the Hoboken-bound vessel, also carrying a load of Beer Nuts. The two teams lined up on their respective port sides and exchanged a fusillade that left both boats looking like an artist's dropcloth.

"You couldn't hit the broadside of a bus!"

"Avast! Drop your sails and heave to, Matey!"

"Surrender Dorothy!"

As the boats pulled away from each other, there was a final chorus of raspberries and Bronx cheers.

Everyone's ammunition ran out just as the ferry pulled into Battery Park City. The players assembled to count coup. Honeyman—though not devoid of hits himself—was declared the winner by unanimous acclamation.

Rejoining Addie, Honeyman felt rather sheepish. After his initial anger had worn off, he had found himself really enjoying the game. Was this any way for a former sixties pacifist to be feeling? He felt as guilty as a vegetarian caught with a roast beef sandwich halfway to his lips.

"Gee, Addie," he began, "I'm sorry this had to happen. . . ."

"Don't apologize. I'm glad I matter that much to you." Lifting her glasses, she wiped a tear from one eye, and Honeyman wondered why.

"Hey, are we gonna be able to go shopping looking like this?"

"Oh, it's just Soho. We'll fit right in."

They walked uptown to Canal Street, and then east, arriving finally at Canal Street Jeans. While Honeyman browsed, Addie tried on clothes, eventually settling on a few items. At the register, Honeyman said, "Here, let me get this, to make up for my crazy friends." He opened his wallet, and, without thinking about what he was doing, drew out and offered a fresh one hundred spondulix note.

They took it.

6.

Bretton Woods

Earl Erlkonig, Minister of Finance (without portfolio), called the meeting to order. He had to speak loudly, above the noise of construction in the Brewery. Dozens of hirelings from Mazuma Construction Company were reconstructing the headquarters of the Beer Nuts into luxurious apartments and common rooms, gyms and saunas, a kind of adult clubhouse. The building had been bought from the city for a minimal payment of back taxes — made in spondulix. Erlkonig had specified that all the old vats and kettles were to be retained, patched and polished, as a reminder of their humble origins, and this requirement was necessitating extra costs that preyed constantly on Honeyman's mind.

Erlkonig, Honeyman, and several others sat around a table in one corner of the main floor, isolated by temporary walls from the hullabaloo. It seemed strange to see the interior of the Brewery by electric light. The altered environment here seemed emblematic to Honeyman of vaster, more troubling changes, changes which had caused him many sleepless nights, and which promised many more.

It was the beginning of August, a mere two months since Honeyman had invented spondulix. It might as well have been two years though, considering all that had happened.

Erlkonig held Cardinal Ratzinger, the Beer Nuts mascot, in his lap. The tiger-colored cat looked extremely well-fed. It wore a collar set with stones that Honeyman prayed were only cubic zirconia.

Now Erlkonig set Cardinal on the table and stood. He moved with military precision to a map of the tri-state region hanging from a wall. Removing a collapsible pointer from his shirt pocket, Erlkonig began to lecture.

"You can see from the shaded areas—which we are updating daily, by the way—that the penetration of spondulix is outpacing our highest expectations. The pattern seems to be swift initial infection of an urban area, followed by slower dissemination into the surrounding countryside. Once Hoboken was permeated, Manhattan and the other boroughs were a given. But I think you'll be surprised by what followed next.

"To the northeast, in Bridgeport, New Haven and Hartford, there are already some quarter of a million spondulix in circulation. We expect to move up the coast, through Providence and into Boston, at the rate of ten miles a day.

"In New York state, Albany, Syracuse and Utica are thoroughly ours. Buffalo represents our furthest western penetration to date, and opens a gateway to Canada.

"In our home state, Camden is almost as thoroughly saturated as Hoboken, and is providing a beachhead into Philly, after which Pittsburgh is expected to fall easily. Moreover, I just received a report today which informs me that the casinos in Atlantic City are accepting spondulix for all wagers. They're even talking about our expansion into some kind of coinage which would be acceptable to their slots."

Honeyman held his head in his hands and moaned. He had avoided all previous sessions of these strategic councils, figuring that when he was called on to testify on his own behalf in Federal Court he could claim ignorance of what was being done in his name. (How that would superficially square with his portrait and signature being featured on an endless stream of spondulix, he had not yet figured out.) Today, however, Erlkonig had convinced him to attend, promising him that there would be some news that would gladden him.

So far, he hadn't heard it.

Hilario Fumento raised a hand, seeking the floor, and Erlkonig gave him the nod.

"What are the demographics of our supporters?" asked the writer.

Erlkonig tried to look thoughtful, as if summoning up the data from deep recesses, but Honeyman could see he had instant access to all the facts about spondulix, and was merely pausing for effect. Erlkonig was clearly a man who had found his destined call-ing, and was relishing every nuance of his new Machiavellian posi-tion. He looked positively diabolical.

"We're strongest, of course, among the fringe elements of society, those involved in what is commonly called 'the under-ground economy,' whether dealing with legal or illegal goods and services. However, since almost every citizen comes into contact with this segment of society at one time or another, we are establishing a strong hold upon the average consumer as well. When Joe Sixpack's boss offers him payment in a currency un-known to the IRS, and when Joe is certain he'll be able to redeem that currency for things he wants and needs—well, there's no reason for him not to take it, is there?

"This brings us," continued Erlkonig, "to the topic of further expansion." Erlkonig collapsed the pointer with a flourish and leaned on his forearms on the table to directly confront the rest of the cabinet. Disregarding his high status, Cardinal licked the man's flat nose. Erlkonig pushed the cat away.

"This country is too big to conquer by slow radiation from a central source. I am therefore proposing, my molecules, that we seed the rest of the nation with volunteers whose mission will be to establish spondulix as an accepted medium of exchange. From these scattered sites, just like colonies of mold in a Petri dish, spondulix will spread in all directions, until it eventually forms a complete network."

Honeyman opened his mouth to object to this insane scheme, but Erlkonig interrupted.

"This plan is contingent on one other step. I need to backtrack a little first, though—with your indulgence.

"As I predicted when we initially began mass production of spondulix, the redemption rate in sandwiches has been a tiny frac-tion of all usage. A doubling in the shop's size, the hiring of addi-tional help and the promotion of Nerfball to Supervisor, along with extended hours of operation, has been sufficient to handle the increased trade. Even counting phone orders from as far as sixty miles away.

"Obviously, though, we cannot continue to accommodate ulti-mate redemption in sandwiches once we go nationwide. At least not without setting up branches of Honeyman's Heroes in every major market. And the extra work attendant on such a program would unacceptably hold up our plans. Besides, having these notes tied to a little Jersey sandwich shop gives the enterprise too much of a strictly regional feeling."

It began to dawn on Honeyman then what Erlkonig was working up to, and the albino's next words confirmed it.

"Molecules—I am proposing that we go off the sandwich standard. Just as the U.S. dollar is no longer backed by gold, so I move for the official decoupling of spondulix and any comestibles."

Honeyman jumped to his feet. "No, I won't stand for it! As long as these stupid pieces of paper were good for something, we had a loophole in the eyes of the law. If we take that away, then they become nothing but . . . but money."

Erlkonig looked at Honeyman with an annoying pity. "Rory, man—they already are. May I see a show of hands now? All in favor?"

Every hand but Honeyman's shot up. No one wanted to put in any more time in the sandwich shop.

"The motion is carried then," declared Erlkonig with obvious pleasure.

"What's this mean for me, then?" asked Honeyman. "Am I supposed to just close the shop down?"

"No, not if you don't want to. Of course, you could shut it up for good and just live off spondulix, like the rest of us. But I'll understand if you want to keep it going, as a hobby, like. All I want is that you don't take spondulix for sandwiches anymore."

"Wait just a minute. I'm supposed to be the one business in Hoboken now that won't accept spondulix? Me, the guy who invented them?"

"I know it's kind of illogical, but it has to be. It's a symbol."

Honeyman was trying to puzzle out the Wonderland logic of all this when an origami frog hopped into the room. Cardinal, spotting it, leaped down and batted at the paper creature, whereupon it promptly unfolded into a 500 spondulix note.

Suki Netsuke stuck her head in the doorway.

"Meeting adjourned," declared Erlkonig.

After everyone else had filed out, Honeyman was left standing alone with Erlkonig and Netsuke. The Black man, abandoning the formal style of speech in which he had conducted the meeting, hung an arm around Honeyman's dejected shoulder and said, "Cheer up, moll, you've done your part. You can retire now, and take it easy."

"I don't want to retire. I want—" But Honeyman was forced to stop speaking. He didn't know quite what he wanted. Once he had wished for a little more money. And look where that had gotten him.

Addie. He wanted Addie. That was the one sure thing in his life. He'd go see her now. She'd know what to do.

"Bye, Rory," called out Netsuke cheerfully as Honeyman left the Brewery.

Over the past two months, since they had met at the ill-fated Outlaw Party, Addie and Honeyman had spent much time together. Honeyman had happily shared with her his past, checkered as it was with disappointments and failures: his Iowa boyhood; his Olympic protest; his flight from induction; his long tenure with Lispenard's Pantechnicon and his deep affection for the Baroness von Hammer-Purgstall (although Honeyman, even in the throes of sexual passion, could not bring himself to mention how much Addie's hair reminded him of the Baroness's mane); his repatriation; his ten-year slumber at the sandwich shop, enlivened only by the antics of the Beer Nuts. Of all this and more had Honeyman gratefully disburdened himself to the patient ears of Addie.

She, in turn, had told him—what? A little of her life in Manhattan, some few odd incidents from work, her taste in books and music, the bad points of a couple of ex-lovers. It didn't amount to much, compared to Honeyman's complete disclosure.

But in the end it didn't matter. Honeyman had fallen completely in love with Atalanta Swinburne. He didn't demand all the intimate details of her past; she'd tell him when she was ready. It was enough simply that she chose to be with him now. He had reached a point where he couldn't imagine life without her.

How happy he would be at this moment, if not for spondulix.

Honeyman clenched his fists as he walked hotly to Addie's apartment. He had to put a stop to the spread of this alternate currency. But how? It was a juggernaut, a machine out of control, a runaway fiscal train on a track greased by greed. Too many people besides himself were involved now. The monster born of his desperate brain had been adopted by hundreds of foster parents. Could he even call it his own invention anymore? Did he have any right to intervene in something that affected the welfare of thousands? He hoped Addie would have some answers, because he sure didn't.

At her building, Honeyman buzzed the intercom. There was no answer. He sat on the stoop and waited.

An hour later, around four o'clock, he saw Addie approaching. Spotting him, she quickened her pace. Honeyman's heart lifted.

"What's wrong, Rory?" she asked after a quick embrace.

Honeyman explained. Addie made sort of a modified Scout's salute, laying the backs of two fingers across her lips in a habitual gesture betokening thoughtfulness. She spoke: "The first thing we both need is supper and a drink. Then we can sort things out."

Buoyed by Addie's practicality, Honeyman felt instantly better. God, what would he do without her?

They went to the Clam Broth House on Newark Street, where they ordered Fisherman's Platters and big plastic steins of beer. In a booth, under the gazes of autographed portraits of local celebrities, they discussed spondulix.

Addie knew everything about spondulix, had lived through all phases of the phenomenon save for their creation. Yet somehow she had remained aloof from the new money. She never spent it, and in fact refused all offers of spondulix from Honeyman— although she didn't object too strenuously when he paid for their joint treats with them. He supposed her finickyness was a manifestation of her independence, and nothing more. Neither did she choose to hang out with the Beer Nuts, unless Honeyman was with her. In any case, her detachment from the communal madness of spondulix made her advice all the more valuable in Honeyman's eyes.

When Honeyman had finished bringing her up to date, he said, "I've got to get out of this whole business. I'll tell Earl to put his picture on the bills and withdraw all the old ones with mine. Then I'll be free."

"No, I don't think Earl will agree. It would look like a *coup d'état,* and that would shake people's confidence in spondulix. He can't risk altering the known equation that already works so well. He still needs you, if only as a figurehead. You've got to stay involved, as a voice of moderation."

"You really think so?"

"Yes, I do. If you hope to change anything, you've got to maintain your contacts and work from within. You can't let the Beer Nuts run things all by themselves."

Honeyman doubted how much of a difference he could actually make. Perhaps he was looking at the situation with blinders, though. Addie seemed adamant about his remaining involved. . . . He decided on the spot that he would follow her advice. "Okay, I'll stick with them for a while yet. But this can't go on much longer."

"Oh, I agree."

Honeyman pushed at some unidentifiable bits of batter-coated substance on his plate. "You know, it's just tradition that makes anyone eat here. The food never gets any worse, but it never gets any better either. What do you say we go dancing?"

"Now you're talking."

They went hand in hand to Maxwell's on Washington Street, where a zydeco band was playing. Addie slipped her glasses into her purse, and they danced till the sweat was rolling off them. A steady infusion of New Amsterdam beer insured against total dehydration. When the club closed at two in the morning, Addie and Honeyman were almost too drunk and tired to walk. They staggered laughingly down Washington Street until they came to Elk Lodge Number 74, with its life-size golden statue of an elk positioned on a pedestal outside. Honeyman was trying to show Addie how he had ridden the Baroness when the cops came. Honeyman dug his heels into the golden elk to spur it to greater speed. He went nowhere fast. The cops dragged him off while Addie rolled on the sidewalk clutching her sides.

"Straighten up, buddy, you're coming with us down to the station."

"Hold on a minute, Charlie. It's that guy on the money."

"Mister Honeyman? Listen, you shouldn't be cutting up like this so late. You're gonna get in trouble. Lemme show you home."

Late the next morning Honeyman arrived at the sandwich shop with a tremendous headache. The busyness of the place depressed him. Why did there have to be such things as commerce and money anyway? Couldn't we all live naked in the forest and eat nuts and berries?

Honeyman instructed Nerfball to tell his crew about the new policy: no spondulix accepted. A sign was lettered and hung proclaiming same. Honeyman waited eagerly for business to drop off. Perhaps a wave of panic would spread through the community, causing people to abandon spondulix as quickly as they had embraced it.

No such luck. People shrugged off the change as an eccentricity of Honeyman's, and paid for their sandwiches in U.S. cash. If this place wouldn't accept spondulix, there were hundreds of others that would.

Discouraged, Honeyman left the shop around three. He went

to find Erlkonig, intending to admit defeat. He left Nerfball behind to conduct a class in Sandwich Construction Methodology:

"Pay attention now, guys and gals. Hold the slice of bread squarely in your palm and spread the condiment of choice toward you, not away. . . ."

Erlkonig was on the roof of the Brewery, supervising workmen who were constructing a kind of crow's-nest high atop the tall smokestack that rose from one corner.

"How do you like it?" he asked Honeyman. "We've put a spiral stairway inside the chimney. It's going to be my executive penthouse."

Honeyman was too discouraged to rebuke Erlkonig for his delusions of grandeur. He related what had happened.

Erlkonig clapped Honeyman heartily on the back, nearly causing him to lose his footing on the slippery slates of the roof. "Great, moll, I told you it would all work out for the best. There's great things ahead for us, I can feel it in my bones."

An unseasonably cold wind blew in off the river, making them both shiver.

"So can I," said Honeyman.

7.

Taking the Big Dive

A late September breeze brought the aroma of roasting coffee to Honeyman's nose as he stood before the door to the Old Vault Brewery, wondering whether to enter. Suddenly, he was gripped by an enormous and melancholy sense of *déjà vu*. Had he not stood thus a mere four months ago, when his life was relatively simple and uncomplicated, that day he had come looking for Nerfball? And had he not experienced a premonition of all the grief and travails that would come his way, should he enter? If only he had heeded this inner voice. Too late, though. He was in this mess up to his neck, with no apparent escape. All the regrets in the world wouldn't suffice to extricate him now. And there was no point in hesitating outside here any longer.

Honeyman laid a hand on the medium-sized door inset in the largest one. At that moment he felt something butt up against his shins.

He looked down.

It was the head of Beatbox, emerging from the pet door.

"Oh, sorry, man," said Beatbox.

"That's okay," replied Honeyman, stepping aside to let the fellow crawl completely out. Contrary to expectations, Beatbox did not immediately stand up.

"What's happening?" asked Honeyman.

"Cardinal has been missing for three days now, and we're trying to trace him. We figure, you wanna find a cat, you gotta act like a cat."

Suiting actions to words, Beatbox crawled off, pausing in his progress down Fourteenth Street to let off a plaintive "Meow" now and then—usually when a sharp pebble bit into his palm.

Honeyman entered the Brewery. Immediately, someone shouted, "Hey, wipe your feet!"

Honeyman did as ordered, looking around.

The Brewery was now completely renovated. All the black paint had been scraped from the windows, allowing the sunlight to flood the cavernous interior of the first floor. The kettles and vats all gleamed, there were chairs and couches, Ping-Pong and pool tables, pinball and video games scattered about, and a thick rug covered the floor. There was even a tiled, paint-splattered target area where people could practice firing their Survival guns.

A muted subterranean roar from the presses in the basement made Honeyman wince.

Honeyman collared a passing woman he didn't recognize. "Where's Earl? He called me over."

"In Vat Number One."

Honeyman found the structure labelled Vat Number One. There was a door in its curving metal side. Honeyman knocked; the door swung open.

"Rory, my moll," said Erlkonig, "good to see you. C'mon in."

Honeyman climbed three stairs into the vat. Erlkonig shut the door.

A padded couch ran along the interior wall of the vat, broken only by the door. The floor was carpeted. There was an audio-video center and a small refrigerator. A giant hookah gave off an aromatic pungency. Ventilation was accomplished through the pipe that had formerly fed in the liquid contents.

"The Beer Nuts have really come up in the world," said Honeyman with what he hoped was palpable cynicism.

Erlkonig didn't bite. "A pampered worker is a productive worker."

Honeyman snorted. "You call what you do work?"

Erlkonig took umbrage. "Hey, man, you think running a worldwide fiscal empire is easy, why don't you try it? This should be your job anyway. If you hadn't jumped ship on us, I wouldn't have had to pick up the reins."

"That's a mixed metaphor." Then: "Worldwide?"

Erlkonig waved a hand negligently. "Forget I said that. And let's stop bickering. I want to show you something." Erlkonig dug in his pants pocket and came up with a spondulix. Honeyman took it. The ink was blotchy, the sandwich depicted on the front looked like a stack of pancakes, and Honeyman was portrayed on the reverse side with what seemed to be a wen on his nose and a downward cast to his eye.

Handing the note back, Honeyman said, "I'd fire the guy at the mint responsible for this."

"We didn't do it," said Erlkonig with obvious relish. "It's a counterfeit."

Honeyman had thought he had heard everything, but this took him completely by surprise. He felt personally violated somehow. Bad enough to have the Beer Nuts churning out spondulix in his name, but at least, when all was said and done, they were still his friends. To have strangers making free with his image, as if he were something from the public domain! He felt sullied and sick. Now he knew what it must be like to be the Mona Lisa or the Statue of Liberty.

"We've got to stop this," said Honeyman. "Do you have any idea who's behind this? Have you managed to track them down?"

Erlkonig laughed. "Slow down, man. You're looking at this all wrong. We don't want to stop this, we want to encourage it. We're not the government, and we don't necessarily want a monopoly. The more spondulix in circulation, the better for all parties. There's plenty of wealth in this country, once you free it up from government strictures. Let whoever it is duplicate spondulix. It all helps us undermine the dollar."

Honeyman stood. "I can't believe this. I am now supposed to be known throughout the world as some kind of misshapen hunchback, just so you can keep filling your coffers? This is almost the last straw, Earl. I'm warning you, I'm tempted to blow the whistle on this whole deal."

Erlkonig seemed unconcerned. "How, man? We've got entire city and state governments in the bag."

"What about the Feds? You don't control them yet. I bet they'd love to know about spondulix. In fact, I can't believe they haven't come down on us by now."

This possibility appeared to worry Erlkonig. "You wouldn't really rat on us to the Feds, would you, my moll?"

Honeyman folded his arms across his chest. "I just might."

Erlkonig switched suddenly to easy affability. "What are we doing, talking like this? Ain't no one gonna betray nobody. Listen, did you hear about the big party tomorrow night? It's the official housewarming for the Brewery. Be sure to come, and bring your girl."

The albino ushered Honeyman to the vat door. "Don't worry yourself about nothing, my moll. Everything's under my intense control." The vat door slammed before Honeyman could explain that that was precisely what was worrying him.

Outside the building a big flatbed truck was unloading under the supervision of Hy Rez and Special Effects. The cargo was a large wooden spool of some strange kind of thick wire.

"What's that?" asked Honeyman.

The two men appeared surprised that Honeyman didn't know.

"Special polycarbon fibers twisted into the strongest cable known to man," replied Hy.

"For the party," said Special. "You know—the Big Walk."

"Oh," said Honeyman, nowise enlightened. Then he set off to see Addie.

She had promised that today she'd have an answer for him.

On the way to her apartment, Honeyman passed a street musician. The man's open guitar case was filled with loose change, dollar bills and spondulix.

At an open-air automated teller machine set in a bank's exterior wall, a woman removed spondulix from the cash-disgorging slot.

A little kid on a scooter stopped to stare at Honeyman. He took a spondulix from his pocket, studied it, then said, "Wow."

Honeyman felt he was going mad. The world seemed topsy-turvy, some dreamland where everything was a fractured image of his one obsession, spondulix. He fervently hoped Addie's answer would be the one he sought, so that they could begin their lives all over again.

He let himself into Addie's building with his set of keys. (They had exchanged keys in August, after The Night of the Elk.) At Addie's door, he knocked. No answer. He let himself in there too.

Addie's quarters had always been sparsely furnished, with a barely lived-in look, so for a second Honeyman didn't notice that today they were stripped. Empty of personal effects.

There was a sealed envelope on the dresser. In it was a letter:

Dear Rory,

Please forgive me. I've been living a lie all these months.
I never wanted to hurt you. But marriage is out of the ques-
tion. Forgive me. Someday soon you'll understand I still love
you. Honest.
                                                                    Addie

Honeyman sat down on the coverless bed. His beard caught the
tears before they could drip off his chin.

He never remembered how he got back to the Brewery, and
little more once he was inside. The main image he retained was
that of a steady stream of commiserating Beer Nuts, faces looming
up out of his personal fog, saying well-meant but totally dumb and
irrelevant things which utterly failed to make him feel any better.

Leather, with an arm around Stud's waist: "She was a bitch,
Honeyman."

Studs chimed in: "Yeah, we knew it from the start. You're better off without her."

Hilario Fumento, reading off a library call slip: "Here's an
observation I made recently that might help you put things in
perspective, Rory. 'When we are traveling in another state, the
sight of a license plate from home always inspires a sharp but tran-
sitory melancholy.' "

Ped Xing, in saffron robe: "Meditate on this koan, Rory. 'If the
universe is constantly expanding, where does it buy its suits?' "

Beatbox, carrying a pot by its handle and stirring some strange
mixture in it: "Taste this, man. Chocolate gazpacho, gonna set
you straight."

And finally, Suki Netsuke, who simply stood before Honeyman, honest sympathy visible in her face, and said: "Sorry, Rory."
She stooped to give him a chaste kiss on his brow.

Eventually everyone left Honeyman alone with his misery. He
welcomed it. He wanted to wallow in some good old self-pity and
personality bashing.

His life was a failure. He had botched everything he ever tried.
He was unloved and unlovable. Addie had left him because he was
such a hopeless jerk. Who in their right mind would want to hook
up with a guy approaching forty who was still running a sandwich
shop, and who had allowed his one outstanding brainstorm—
spondulix—to be misappropriated by a bunch of social misfits? All
that talk in the note about still loving him had just been her way
of trying to salve his feelings. She was too nice to say what she
really thought of him. And the note had been too short. A list of
his bad qualities would fill reams.

No, it was plain as his disfigured portrait on the counterfeit spondulix: he was a lousy human being.

He felt lower than a tube worm at the bottom of the Pacific, sheathed in a universe no wider than his own weary shoulders, everything black and under immense pressure.

There really seemed little reason even to go on living.

After a few hours, Honeyman got up from the couch in a corner where he had been sitting. He wandered aimlessly over to Vat Number One, and let himself in.

Erlkonig, wearing a pair of headphones and studying a sheaf of papers, looked up absentmindedly at first, his eyes narrowing in calculation when he saw who it was.

Doffing the 'phones, he said, "Sit down, moll, sit down. I heard what happened to you, and I been meaning to come around and see you. But the pressure, the details—keeping this whole mess afloat takes all my time."

Honeyman sat down, saying nothing. Erlkonig studied him for a few minutes, evidently coming to a certain decision. Then the Black man said: "Here's something you're gonna find interesting, moll, kinda take your mind off your grief. One thing always bugged me was, where did that word come from?"

"What word?" asked Honeyman tonelessly.

"What word! Spondulix, natch."

Honeyman felt the faintest tickle of interest. "Well?"

"I made Fumento look it up at the library. It's slang from the middle of the last century. Used to be spelled s-p-o-n-d-u-l-i-c-k-s. The derivation is from the Greek word *spondolos*, or shell. The idea seems to be that the Indians once used shells for money. Wampum, you know. So the word is real Native American, comes from the oppressed Red Man and all. I like that. How'd you learn it?"

"I don't know," said Honeyman. "I don't know anything anymore."

Erlkonig got up and put a hand on Honeyman's shoulder. "You're in a bad way, moll. You need some rest. Wait here a minute." Erlkonig left and returned with a pill and a glass of water. "Here, take this, it'll put you right under."

Honeyman swallowed the pill. Soon he felt sleep creeping up from his feet to his head like quicksand.

Some time much later he woke up. Erlkonig was there with another pill. Honeyman took that one too. What did he care whether he ever woke up again or not?

When he woke up a second time, it was to the sound of much

activity. Erlkonig helped him to stand. Honeyman's limbs felt rubbery.

"C'mon, moll, it's the house-warming party, you gotta mingle. It'll do you good."

Honeyman let himself be led out of Vat Number One. The Brewery was packed with people, all having a raucous good time. Erlkonig got Honeyman a drink. "Here, man, you gotta wake up, or you're gonna be too sleepy for the main event."

"What's that?" asked Honeyman.

"You'll see," said Erlkonig. "Wait here a minute, I gotta go check on some preparations."

Honeyman felt himself gradually waking up. He couldn't decide if that was good or bad. The pain of Addie's inexplicable departure was sharp as ever. He stood sipping his drink, which seemed to be plain ginger ale. Just as well. He was in no shape for alcohol.

Erlkonig returned. He took Honeyman by the arm and led him away, off to one corner of the building. There was a new door in the wall. Erlkonig opened it. They stepped through, and were inside the Brewery's tall smokestack.

A spiral staircase, lit by bare bulbs strung on a wire, ran up and up and up.

"C'mon, moll," urged Erlkonig.

They began to climb, Honeyman going first.

At the top Honeyman halted unexpectedly, causing Erlkonig to ask, "What's wrong?"

"Where are we going, Earl? I'm dizzy. . . ."

"Don't worry, moll. It's all level from here on."

Honeyman took Erlkonig at his word and mounted the last few steps, emerging headfirst through the floor into a small room. He realized dully that this must be Erlkonig's penthouse, which had been pointed out to him some weeks ago.

Erlkonig joined him. "Now out that door."

"Another door? Where else can we go. . . ?"

"You'll see."

Honeyman opened the door and stepped out.

He was on a small platform railed on two sides. Three hundred feet below him, the street outside the Brewery was filled with tiny people. They were all looking up at him, Honeyman suddenly realized. At that moment a spotlight flared on and pinned Honeyman to the platform, blinding him.

Erlkonig's amplified voice suddenly bellowed out. "Special, you moron—aim it lower!"

Special Effects, stationed on the roof of an adjacent building, complied, and in a minute Honeyman could see again. It was then that he noticed the polycarbon cable. It stretched away across the Hudson, taut as an addict's nerves, slim as a hair, guyed and anchored at its far end to some anonymous building around Twenty-third Street in Manhattan, half a mile away.

"Here," said Erlkonig. With the hand not holding the bullhorn, he wrestled with a traditional red-and-white-striped, fifteen-foot balancing pole that had been standing in one corner.

Honeyman took the pole and hefted it. The fifty-pound weight awakened long-dormant kinesthetic memories.

"Okay, let's go, moll. They're all waiting to see you perform." Honeyman thought about it. The distance was impossible. He was completely out of training. The wind was brisk. The effects of the sleeping pill were still in his blood. . . .

He kicked off his shoes and stood in his socks.

Erlkonig smiled. "If you make it to the other side, you can tell the Feds anything you want."

Honeyman stepped forward and placed his right foot on the wire. It thrummed like something alive beneath his weight, it sang an old wordless circus song, it beckoned him on to his destiny.

He stepped entirely on the cable, swaying slightly, old instincts keeping him balanced.

Erlkonig spoke through the bullhorn to the spectators. "And now, as advertised, to mark the conquest of the outer world by spondulix, their inventor, Rory Honeyman, will symbolically traverse the watery gap between Hoboken, the world's new fiscal capital, and Manhattan, the old."

Honeyman began his half-mile tightrope walk, the spotlight following him, trained on his back now.

Right up to the halfway mark, he thought he might do it.

But at that point in his passage a news copter, avid cameraman leaning out the cockpit, approached from inside the surrounding darkness, clattering, churning up crazy downdrafts.

Honeyman sensed balance slipping from him. He swayed left and right, overcompensating, trapped in a deadly negative feedback loop. He lost his pole and it flipped end over end down into the night beneath his feet.

Then he lost the wire.

The wind whistled past Honeyman, chill and curious. For a few seconds he fell formless and free. He swore he heard the roar of Olympic crowds in his ears. Without volition, not even thinking of saving himself, he entered into a classic swan dive.

He was back in the past, on the last day in his life that he had felt completely certain about anything, the day when, full of a serene spiritual strength, he had taken the silver in Mexico City.

He pierced the water cleanly—celestial judges flashed high numbers—but the impact was still tremendous. The transition felt like passing through a mile-thick wall of wet concrete instantaneously. He must have blacked out for a period, still plummeting downward under the Hudson now, because when he opened his eyes all was utterly black, and he seemed to sense the musty car-hulk-littered river bottom just below him.

Unbroken empty blackness. Just give it up now, or what? So easy to breathe water, become sodden and sink, to lie among the other wrecks. . . .

Except—wait a minute. Here was something of interest. A nonhuman figure of luminescent white was approaching. Closer, closer, closer—until it was revealed as a horse. A sea horse, hindquarters all flukes and fins.

The Baroness von Hammer-Purgstall, returned transmogrified from the dead. First love come to resurrect him.

Honeyman opened his mouth to speak. River water filled his throat and he began to choke.

The Baroness nipped Honeyman's shirt collar between her big teeth and began to surge powerfully upward, through the murky water.

Honeyman's head broke the surface right near a Coast Guard boat. Dazedly, he looked around for the Baroness. The horse was nowhere to be seen.

Hands reached down for Honeyman. He reached up, and was hauled aboard.

Lying flat on his back, his head cradled in a soft lap, he knew he was really dead.

Addie was looking down at him and stroking his forehead.

"Oh, Rory," she said, "I'm so, so sorry. But you're under arrest."

A man's voice said, "That's enough, Agent Swinburne, I'll take over now."

They read Honeyman his rights while he was throwing up Hudson-flavored bile.

Honeyman stepped out of the hospital. It was a glorious October day. The streets of Manhattan had been washed clean by a shower in the night. A maple sapling planted in a sidewalk plot was all aflame with colored leaves. The air smelled like the countryside.

Addie stood by the tree. Honeyman walked over to her. She

held out her hand tentatively. He took it, and they began to walk.

After a few yards of silence, Addie said, "Erlkonig took the whole rap for you, Rory. He exonerated you completely."

"So I should forgive him for everything now, I suppose?"

"That's up to you. He did act like a bastard at the end. But basically I think he was just running scared. It was nothing personal."

"It felt personal enough at the time."

"Well, anyway, he's only going to be tried on the charges connected with running the tightrope across the river. Public nuisance, property damage, obstructing air traffic, those kinds of things. The matter of spondulix has been officially dropped, in exchange for the closing of the mint. It seems, you see, that there weren't really any relevant statutes to prosecute under. A whole squad of lawyers spent hundreds of man-hours trying to find something, and couldn't. There's just no legislation against what you guys were doing. And besides, the publicity connected with a trial would have given other people the same idea, if they hadn't heard about it already. The people in charge have decided to adopt a policy of ignoring the spondulix already in circulation, as long as no more new ones are made. They figure the whole thing will fade away sooner or later."

"So I'm completely free?"

"Yup."

"I can go back to running a sandwich shop in Hoboken?"

"If you want to."

"Well now, that depends."

"On me?"

"Yup."

Addie smiled. "Suppose I told you I don't work for the Secret Service any more?"

"I might believe you."

"And suppose I told you I still loved you very very much, and apologized real hard for ever lying to you about anything?"

"I might say I loved you too."

They stopped to kiss then, and passersby smiled.

Resuming their walk, Honeyman said, "You wouldn't mind living on the proceeds of a little sandwich shop?"

"Oh," said Addie, "I don't think it'll ever come to that."

She opened her purse.

Honeyman looked inside.

It was full of spondulix.

Although I did not know it at the time of its composition, this story was to be a trial run for my novel Ciphers. *Mysterious organizations, false clues, hapless young slacker hero, alluring women, information theory, pop music, subways, synchronicities, smart but annoying girlfriends—all the components are here in embryo, waiting to be excessively recomplicated at novel length. If* Ciphers *is my Gravity's Rainbow, then this story stands as my stab at* The Crying of Lot 49.

During the mid-eighties, I frequently ate in the McDonald's in Union Square where Howie dined. But when the street people launched into their Tourette's-like spew, I always moved away.

Who knows where I'd be today if I had paid closer, more sympathetic attention to their rants?

Conspiracy of Noise

1.

The facts are extremely complicated.
—Mehmet Ali Agca

THE POLICE WERE SINGING. STING'S DULCETLY STRI-dent voice wailed over and over, above the dissonant guitars:

Too much information, runnin' through my brain,
Too much information, drivin' me insane—

Suddenly the music stopped.

Howie looked up.

Mr. Wargrave stood beside Howie's desk. He had obviously reached down to Howie's Walkman while Howie's eyes had been closed, and switched off the tape player. Now Mr. Wargrave waited—patiently, coolly, as imperturbably as an Easter Island statue—for Howie to give him his full attention.

Howie carefully removed his headphones and laid them down on his desk. At one point in the headgear's descending arc, the burnished metal strap reflected the harsh fluorescent office light directly into Mr. Wargrave's eyes. The man did not blink. From the corner of the desk, Howie slowly lifted his red-sneakered feet and planted them firmly on the plastic runner beneath his swivel chair.

Two weeks ago, Mr. Wargrave had still had the capacity to frighten Howie. The huge man, in his perpetually unwrinkled, knife-edged suit—every pinstripe of which seemed etched by laser—struck Howie at first as the archetypical Tyrannical Boss, a figure who would rule the office with shouts and humiliating put-downs. Mr. Wargrave's knobby shaven skull and granitic gargoyle's face did little to inspire confidence in his human kindness, either.

But during the fortnight since Howie had been hired by The United Illuminating Company, he had come to lose the natural wariness and alarm, the chill feeling under his armpits and below his belt, that he had initially felt whenever his boss walked stiffly through the office. For one thing, Mr. Wargrave's rather alarming features never changed. Such deadpan features might still have been frightening, had their possessor ever raised his voice or used his physical bulk to threaten. But Mr. Wargrave had done none of these things. Quite to the contrary, he kept his voice low and his body language minimally intrusive. Whenever he had talked to one of Howie's fellow workers, in fact, he had always spoken so softly that Howie—no matter how he strained— had never been able to overhear what was being said.

So after about ten workdays, Howie had lost all his natural suspicion of Mr. Wargrave.

Contributing to Howie's insouciance around his superior was boredom: an immense, almost unbearable, nearly physical boredom.

Howie had been hired as a messenger. One day he had noticed a placard propped in the lobby window of a nondescript building he passed every morning after exiting the subway stop, on his way to hang out in Union Square. At first, confused by the smudges on the window glass and the distressed nature of the sign, Howie thought the faded card read:

MESS   DESIRED

A   WAR

W   ILL   COME

SECOND FLOOR

Eventually, though, by puzzling out the barely legible missing letters, Howie discerned, he thought, the true message, which was:

MESSENGER DESIRED
APPLY WARGRAVE
WALK UP TO THE UNITED ILLUMINATING COMPANY
SECOND FLOOR

Until that minute, Howie had had no intention of applying for any job whatsoever. He enjoyed being an aimless layabout too much. But something about the dual message hidden in the placard intrigued him, and he resolved to at least go up and find out what it was all about.

On the second floor of the building, Howie inquired of a receptionist about the position. After a short wait he was led to the office of Mr. Wargrave. There the strange man, seated behind a big desk whose top bore a confusing array of papers, had simply looked him up and down before softly announcing, "You're hired."

"Hey, wait a minute," Howie had protested, faintly alarmed. "I never said anything about—"

"The job entails a weekly salary of $750."

"Okay," said Howie. "When do I start?"

Howie had shown up for work that first day dressed like all the other messengers he had ever seen rushing about the city on bikes or afoot. A nice absorbent cotton shirt in anticipation of working up a sweat; loose green military pants with about two dozen pockets, the cuffs of which were tucked into white socks; and a pair of high-topped Pro-Keds. At his belt hung a Walkman, headphones draped around his neck.

The receptionist—a pretty young blonde woman—conducted Howie into a big open room scattered with desks and lit with unrelenting fluorescent fixtures. At the desks sat a variety of people, shuffling crazily through heaps of papers mainly, although a few worked at terminals. This space—along with the receptionist's anteroom and Mr. Wargrave's office—seemed to comprise the whole physical structure of The United Illuminating Company.

Seated at an empty desk that was announced to be his permanent station, Howie waited for his first assignment.

He spent the first couple of hours looking around the office, watching the assorted men and women work at their incomprehensible tasks. Telephones rang, typewriters and printers clattered, and people whispered among themselves, ignoring Howie.

When watching grew tiresome, he donned his headphones and listened to music.

By lunchtime no one had yet approached him with a task.

Thoughts of $750 a week helped him get through the afternoon.

The next day was the same. Howie tried engaging his coworkers in conversation, wandering over to their areas. They replied in monosyllables and returned to their secretive chores.

On Friday, when handed his paycheck by the receptionist, Howie opened his mouth to quit, saw the printed figures on the piece of paper, and changed his mind.

The second week seemed two years long.

Something kept Howie hanging in there.

And so now, in the afternoon of the first day of his third week at The United Illuminating Company, with Mr. Wargrave standing noncommittally by his desk, Howie was ready for anything, and not the least bit ashamed of having been caught with his feet up, dreaming to the music of the Police.

He was ready to be fired.

He was ready to quit.

He was ready to work.

It turned out to be work.

Having gained Howie's full attention, Mr. Wargrave reached inside his precisely buttoned jacket and extracted a slim envelope. He offered it to Howie in an extended hand. Then he spoke, in his voice like the slither of silk over skin.

"Mr. Piper, you will deliver this message to the address indicated. You must ensure that it reaches the person named hereon at exactly 11:00 A.M. I trust that you wear a watch."

Howie was too dumbfounded at Mr. Wargrave's calm assumption that keeping an employee in the dark for two weeks was normal procedure to protest or ask any of the hundred questions that were on his mind. Instead, he merely replied, "Uh, yeah, sure, I got a watch."

"Very good. We will now synchronize our timepieces. At the mark, I have 10:17. . . . Mark."

Howie adjusted his watch, which was slow.

"One last thing," said Mr. Wargrave. "You will take Mr. Herringbone with you on this mission."

"Okay. Who the hell is he?"

Mr. Wargrave indicated with an economical gesture a man seated across the room. "There." With this he left.

Howie watched his boss walk off. He sat amazed for a moment. Then he rose and went to the fellow who had been pointed out.

Mr. Herringbone sat flanked by six terminals. Three were large IBM models, and atop these sat various smaller ones from other makers. All these active screens cast an unearthly glow on the man's pinched features, which nestled compactly beneath a chaotic mop of red hair.

"Yo," said Howie, "how are you, man? My name's Howie; what's yours?"

Herringbone raised his eyes from the screens to Howie's face. His fingers ceased their activity on the keyboards. He spoke.

"Gentle tellings die blue greasy up ten dales."

"Huh?"

Herringbone sighed and reached into a shirt pocket, coming up with a business card. Howie took it. He was so confused that at first he couldn't focus on it, and thought he saw the phrase: I FEAR A WAR ON BRAINS. Looking more closely, Howie saw that the card really said:

EUGENE HERRINGBONE
THE UNITED ILLUMINATING COMPANY
I SUFFER FROM
A LESION IN THE
WERNICKE'S AREA
OF MY BRAIN
AND CAN SPEAK ONLY GIBBERISH

Howie tried to hand the card back, but Herringbone motioned that he should keep it.

"Wow," said Howie. "That's really weird. Sorry to hear it, Eugene." The man's name, Howie felt, didn't fit him somehow, and so Howie, contemplating their work together, asked, "Can I call you Red?"

Herringbone nodded yes.

"Okay, Red, listen up. The big man says we have to deliver a message together. And we're really gonna have to move, 'cause the address is way uptown, and we can't be late. So let's go."

Standing up, Herringbone revealed himself to be a neurasthenic individual whose motley clothes fit him like a scarecrow's.

Stuffing the envelope in one of his many pockets, Howie said, "Hey, Red, since we can't really talk, I hope you don't mind if I listen to some music."

Herringbone shook his head no.

It seemed he had plenty to occupy his thoughts.

2.

Rock and roll is the Esperanto of the global village.
—Samuel Freedman

The Hooters were droning "All You Zombies" into Howie's ears when the train pulled into the station.

Herringbone had to lay a sinewy hand on Howie's shoulder to drag him out of the music. Howie came out of his fugue reluctantly. There was something mesmerizing about pop music that could often suck Howie down into bottomless depths. He felt truly in touch with some altered state of existence when he had his 'phones on, as if he were tuning in to some indecipherable but vital message traveling the shared neural system of all humanity.

He could never say, upon returning to this world, what the import was of what he had been hearing.

But still, he knew some hidden information lay just beneath the music's surface.

Howie doffed his headphones and stood in the swaying car. Outside the graffiti-smeared windows, the platform columns rushed by in a blur, as though the train were standing still and the whole world accelerating.

Herringbone unfolded his lanky self, too. Howie told him above the roar, "Thanks, man, I would've gone right by, I guess. I'll put in a good word for you with old Wargrave."

The screech of the brakes swallowed up Herringbone's reply, which was probably just as well, since the part Howie could make out sounded like "green breast calls duck potato."

Looking around the car for a few seconds before the doors opened, Howie noticed something.

Everyone in the train was getting an information fix.

There were people reading newspapers: the *Times*, the *News*, the *Post*, the *Dreck*, the *Blurb*, the *Smash*. There were others reading hardcovers and paperbacks and comics. Others studied the overhead advertisements: EAT, DRINK, TASTE, BUY, SELL, LEARN, SEE, GO, DRIVE, HEAR, SMELL, FEEL. Businessmen and -women examined the contents of their briefcases. In short, there wasn't a person present not processing data in some way.

It all looked very weird suddenly to Howie.

The doors juddered open, and Howie followed Herringbone out.

Howie missed the station number in the hustle, but if this were indeed the correct stop, he knew roughly where they should be, according to the address on the envelope. And when they got aboveground, every last scent and sound and sight proved him right.

They had come up in the middle of Harlem, where the cross streets sported triple digits, and the air was funky with music and poverty, and the bars were so tough they didn't even have names.

After orienting himself, Howie said, "Okay, Red, I believe we got to go three blocks or so east. Let's move. It's a quarter to eleven."

They set out.

At the first intersection, traffic flowed to block their path, so they waited for the light to change. When it did, Howie noticed the WALK sign. It was malfunctioning, and said:

DON'T WALK WALK

The one at the next crossing was defective too. This one said:

WALK DON'T WALK

And the third one said simply:

DON'T

Now they found themselves on Lenox Avenue. Howie scanned buildings for numbers, and spotted the address they were seeking, just a few paces away. He moved toward it, and stopped on the first step of the stoop. A large, crudely painted signboard hung above the door. It read:

THE WELCOME-WHOSOEVER-THIRSTETH-FOR-THE-
BLOOD-OF-THE-LAMB-CONGREGATIONAL-ASSEMBLY-
OF-THE-LORD CHURCH

Howie scrabbled in several deep pockets until he found the envelope.

"The Reverend Mr. Evergreen. Yeah, I guess this makes sense. Okay, Red, c'mon. It's nearly time."

The two messengers went into the church.

Inside they were greeted by a friendly Black woman in a flowered dress, who agreed to conduct them to the Reverend Mr. Evergreen. She brought them through several rooms—one of which was a hall filled with folding chairs—and into an office where many people came and went. A radio playing added its noise to the frenetic atmosphere.

Behind a desk sat a big man in an expensive suit. His skin was the color of a glossy horse chestnut; his short hair was stiff with a mousse of some sort; his fingers were covered with rings. He looked like a cross between a riverboat gambler and a boxing promoter. He was very busy issuing orders.

"Harold, I want you to look into that busted pipe at the soup kitchen. It's got to be fixed before suppertime. Alvin, you check with the mayor's office about gettin' the community pool opened before school lets out for the year. Fred, I want you to call Lieutenant Waverly and find out about increasin' the patrols around the projects."

People rushed off to obey, and Howie found himself alone with Evergreen and Herringbone. The minister sized him up and said, "You got something for me, son?"

Howie offered up the envelope, and the minister took it. "Is there some answer expected?" asked Evergreen.

Feeling self-important upon completion of his first mission, Howie said, "I bet there is. I'd better wait."

Herringbone waggled his carrot-thatched head on his scrawny neck in a violent gesture of negation. He grabbed Howie's sleeve and tried to pull him out of the office. Howie resisted, and Herringbone gave up and waited with a mournful look by the door.

The Reverend Mr. Evergreen slit open the envelope with a long fingernail.

It was 11:00 A.M.

As Evergreen read the contents of the envelope, the music from the radio suddenly ceased and an announcer came on.

"The jury has just returned its verdict in the Warwick case, which has divided the city for the past month. Officer Warwick, accused of negligently shooting three unarmed Black youths, has been found innocent on all counts. We now return to our regular programming."

The minister's face had gone dark as a storm cloud. He looked up ominously at Howie, back to the document, then up at Howie again.

"Son, do you know what this is?"

Howie started to feel nervous. "No, sir."

Evergreen shot to his feet, upsetting his chair, which crashed to the floor. Howie backed up warily to stand beside Herringbone. People appeared at the door, curious about the commotion.

"This is a photocopy of a secret police report that proves Warwick was guilty!" Evergreen shouted, trembling with righteous indignation.

The people behind Howie began to murmur sullenly.

"Goddamn! Someone's gonna pay!" Evergreen declaimed. "We're closing this city down!"

Shouts of agreement arose from the crowd at the door. Howie felt his spine collapse. He knew he was dead.

Suddenly Herringbone threw up his hands and shouted.

"Bountiful! Laggards mean pain! Crazy tides afflict all horses, black and cool and chalk! Light, hell, scalded, brash! Elephants!"

The crowd fell back.

"Tongues! He's talkin' in tongues! The spirit's in him! Let him by!"

Howie, nearly fainting, followed Herringbone down the narrow aisle formed by hurt black faces showing both anger and amazement.

The two men made it back to the subway and managed to get on the last downtown train before the first of the riots began.

3.

Somebody had to lose.
— Graffito seen on the Berlin Wall

Luckily, although power was off in the entire city, leaving it a murky Jungian jungle, Lesley's boombox had fresh Duracells in it. So Howie was able to listen to the Talking Heads sing about "Life During Wartime," while Lesley read by candlelight.

The subway had ground to a halt fifteen minutes after Howie and Herringbone had boarded. All passengers had been forced to disembark in midtunnel and find their way in the putrid dusk to an emergency exit, which consisted of a ladder rising into darkness.

The first person to emerge toppled a blind man who was standing on the trapdoor set in the sidewalk and selling pencils. The rest had trampled him until Howie emerged and helped him to his feet.

"Thank you, thank you, stranger," the blind man said. "Take this, please, as a token of my gratitude."

Howie took the proffered item without even seeing it, and hurried away from the hole in the sidewalk that was still vomiting up people like disturbed ants from a trodden anthill.

Herringbone had disappeared somewhere. Looking around disorientedly, Howie found himself in a Times Square rendered strangely quiet and less garish by lack of electricity. All around him, chaos was growing like a multicolored paper flower dropped into a glass of water.

Howie was stranded half the city away from his own apartment on the Lower East Side. He was dazed and confused and didn't know what to do.

Then he remembered that Lesley Wildegoose, his sometime girlfriend, lived nearby.

Howie made his way through the rapidly disintegrating city to Lesley's building in the Clinton section, formerly Hell's Kitchen.

Luckily, she was home.

Moving wordlessly past her, Howie dropped weakly to a couch and motioned Lesley to shut the door. Eventually he managed to tell her how he had caused the growing tumult engulfing the city.

"Wow," said Lesley.

"Wow," agreed Howie.

This had been several hours ago.

Now, the Heads tape automatically ejecting and silence filling the apartment—save for the muted wail of sirens—Howie contemplated what he was going to do if things ever calmed down. Just as he was wishing Lesley would talk to him, she raised her gaze from her book.

In the candlelight, Lesley's rather lank hair and plain face looked astonishingly pretty. Howie was overwhelmed by an unexpected rush of affection for her and the sanctuary she offered.

Pushing back the bill of her ever-present Greek fisherman's cap, Lesley said, "Hey, Howie, listen to this: 'Mysterious agents, meaningless actions, infiltration, and finally an irresistible attack from nowhere.' Now doesn't that sound like the mess you're stuck in?"

Intrigued, Howie said, "Yeah. Yeah, it does. Who wrote that?"

Lesley, a finger keeping her place, turned the book's cover up. "Some guy named van Vogt."

"Well, what's the hero doing? How's he gonna solve his problems?"

"I haven't finished yet, but I think I can guess the ending. Although the guy doesn't know it yet, he's somehow the mastermind behind the whole conspiracy."

Now Howie was disgusted. "Great. Some stupid author's half-assed gimmick. Well, I'm not the mastermind behind anything. But when it's safe to go out, you can bet I'm gonna confront Wargrave and find out just what's going on."

Howie jammed his hands into two of his many pockets for

emphasis. He encountered the object the blind man had given him, and took it out.

It was a fortune cookie.

Howie opened it.

In the wavering candlelight the skinny slip of paper seemed to say:

HATE   ICE DAY

But on second inspection, it read only:

HAVE A NICE DAY

4.

He who controls the agenda controls the outcome.
— David Gergen

A crowd was gathered in front of the store window. Howie stopped to see what they were looking at.

It was a display of televisions, all tuned to MTV. Right now, Tears for Fears were onscreen playing "Everybody Wants to Rule the World."

Howie watched and listened until the song was over. Then he moved off.

As the crowd broke up, Howie was struck once again—not for the first time today—by how embarrassed everyone acted. Now that the riots were over, and most of the damage had at least been hidden behind tarps and scaffolding and sheets of plastic, the citizens of the city—Black, White, and every shade in between— all acted like people who had awakened the morning after a drunken spree only to learn that they had propositioned the boss's wife, sung a bawdy song off-key, and perhaps ended up face foremost in the gutter with their pants down around their ankles. People carried themselves with a certain tentativeness. There was an overabundance of politeness, of opening doors for strangers and giving up seats on the bus to elderly standees and saying "Please" and "Thank you." People were treating each other as if the whole city were on its first date with someone it really hoped to impress.

It was really strange, Howie thought, to venture out and find himself in such a place.

He wasn't sure what he thought about it.

Maybe it was good.

But he wondered if the price paid hadn't been a bit excessive, in terms of lives and property lost.

Well, Howie shrugged, the city would no doubt be its old rancorous self in a few more days.

The question now was: Would Howie?

As he walked toward the establishment that called itself The United Illuminating Company, Howie considered what he was doing.

Lesley had tried to convince him that he should just cut his ties with the company by not ever showing up there again. Howie had stubbornly resisted this suggestion. He wanted a confrontation. He resented being used, and was bent on getting some satisfaction from Mr. Wargrave.

Additionally, he had to admit, in the back of his mind lay a desire to salvage his job, if he could do so with his pride intact.

Howie had discovered that he no longer had the same enthusiasm he had once possessed for simply hanging around some park all day, watching dope deals go down and pretty women stroll by, while getting a buzz on. True, his job so far at United Illuminating had consisted mostly of just such hanging around, with the single (and singular) exception of his fateful errand to Harlem. But while sitting at his desk in the office of this strange company, he had realized he felt intimately connected to something larger than himself. Although often bored, he had always felt an undercurrent of expectancy that kept him hanging on.

And besides, the money was damn good.

Howie arrived at the building where he had seen the curiously blurred placard with its doubled message a few weeks ago. That day seemed like a page out of someone else's life, so much had happened.

Nerving himself up, Howie went inside and rode the elevator to the second floor.

He almost expected the office to be closed, to confront a room empty of furniture and people, with only dangling coaxial cables and coffee stains on the carpet to show there had ever been such an organization.

Such was not the case. The attractive receptionist—whose name he had never learned— was at her desk in the anteroom as usual. She smiled at Howie as he went by. Howie, now that the imagined confrontation was so near, felt grim and did not smile back.

All was as before in the big common room, too. Everyone was

at his desk, jockeying papers or speaking softly on phones or tapping the keys of terminals. The overhead fluorescents glared as
harshly as ever, seeming actually to frighten the sunlight from
entering the three windows that looked out upon the street.

Howie saw Herringbone at his accustomed spot. The man
seemed oblivious to Howie, his face awash with cathode rays.

Moving toward Wargrave's door, Howie saw that his own desk
was as he had left it: bare except for an irregular pile of cassettes
for his Walkman on one corner.

At the door to Wargrave's sanctum, Howie paused, then
knocked and entered without waiting for a response.

Wargrave sat calmly behind his cluttered desk. He looked up
when Howie entered. His hard eyes were like marbles, each centered with a black BB. His expression, as always, was unreadable,
blank, uncommunicative.

"Ah, Mr. Piper," Wargrave said quietly, "I am glad to see you
have returned safely from your first assignment. Mr. Herringbone
could not definitely assure me that this was so, since he became
separated from you at one point. And unfortunately, the ensuing
events prevented me from contacting you at home."

Howie was disconcerted by Wargrave's expression of concern.
"I wasn't home anyway," he replied sullenly.

Wargrave raised one eyebrow: his most violent gesture to date.
"No matter," he said. "Here you are now, no doubt eager and willing to get back to work. But first I must commend you on the way
you carried out the delivery to the Reverend Mr. Evergreen. I
have had a full report from Mr. Herringbone, whom, I must con-
fess, I sent along to gauge your performance. You were prompt
and industrious—although your offer to await a reply was perhaps
a trifle overzealous. But on the whole, I can find no fault with
your conduct. I look forward to testing your abilities on future
missions."

Howie tried to steer the conversation in the direction he had
imagined it taking. "Listen, Mr. Wargrave, before we talk about
'future missions' and stuff like that, I need a few questions answered. Like, where do you get off having me risk my life like you
did? And just what is this screwy company all about? What're your
goals, and who's behind you? Is this a front for the Klan or
something? Are you trying to start a race war? Maybe you're
American Nazis. Is that it?"

Wargrave—insofar as his stony face was able—seemed to
register dismay. "Come now, Mr. Piper. Please do not be naive or
disingenuous. If I may quote from one of those popular songs you

are so enamored of: 'Let us not talk falsely now, the hour is getting late.' "

Here Wargrave paused, as if he had been particularly witty.

"Let me address your points one at a time," continued the seated bald man.

"First, as for having you risk your life, I judged that you were quite capable of taking care of yourself. Still, I took the precaution of providing the additional safeguard of Herringbone. And you are, after all, being paid rather handsomely to perform your not-too-strenuous duties.

"Your other accusations are also wildly off the mark. You can see just from the composition of our work force that we are a completely integrated organization. If you wish to know our goals, I can tell you only that we are engaged in the dissemination of information. Our transactions all involve that most abstract of commodities, knowledge. This is the age of information, after all, Mr. Piper, and a company such as ours has a crucial role to play. I regret that I cannot be more specific. But you are just not prepared at the moment to receive more detailed data on what we do. Perhaps you will accept my word that we undertake nothing that you would find morally objectionable. We merely facilitate the flow of information."

Howie was partly befuddled, partly mollified, and partly enraged. All he could think of to say was, "I'm not sure I want to work here anymore."

Wargrave shuffled a few papers around on his desk. "That, of course, is your decision, Mr. Piper. But there is no need to be precipitous. May I recommend that you take an extended lunch hour, and then return to me with your decision?"

"Yeah, I guess. Okay, I will."

Howie left.

Outside, he headed toward Union Square, mulling over everything Wargrave had said.

Union Square was bounded roughly by Seventeenth Street on the north, Broadway on the west, Fourteenth on the south, and Park on the east. Since the city had fixed it up, the square was a lovely grassy, tree-shaded couple of acres.

Howie walked up and down the familiar paths for a while, thinking. He eventually found himself out on Broadway, standing in front of a news kiosk. Idly, he looked at the magazines.

There must have been half a hundred titles. They covered the conceivable gamut of mankind's endeavors.

Bivalve Monthly, The Onanist's Chapbook, Hang Gliding and

Stamp Collecting, Trucks and Vans and Miniature Railroads, Time, Newsweek, New Times, This Week's News, Software and Cell Culture, Power Lifting and Gardening Illustrated, Embarrassing Stories, Hangman's Semiquarterly, Self, Ego, Id, Subconscious, Gourmet, Glutton, Fasting Annual, Psychology Today, Psychology Yesterday, Psychology Tomorrow, Stargazer's Digest, Awake!, Arise!, Cast Off Your Chains!, Enjoy!, Be!, Sleep. . . .

Howie's head was spinning from the titles. Spotting the McDonald's across the way, he decided he needed something to eat.

At the counter he studied the canted overhead menu. Jesus, it seemed they added new items every day. MacThis, MacThat. . . . Howie finally just asked for a hamburger and a Coke, waited, got it, and took the greasy bag to a booth.

Halfway through his meal, Howie noticed that a woman was watching him.

She was tall, olive-complexioned, and nervous-looking. Her black hair was a fashionably windblown tangle. Her eyes were an anomalous blue, like two pools of Windex. She had a lit cigarette in her hand and an ashtray full of butts before her.

When she saw Howie was looking, she took a long drag on her cigarette, ground it out, got up, and came over to him.

Standing by his table, the woman said, with a trace of accent, "I have to tell you that you're in grave danger. Goddamn daughter of a whore."

Howie dropped his half-eaten burger. "I—I—I beg your pardon."

The woman seemed angry. "There is no time to waste in pretending ignorance. Your life is at stake. You must come with me. Hell, piss, son of a bitch."

Everyone was staring at Howie, and he felt his face turning red. He spoke very quietly, as if to emphasize that he was not the madman here. "Lady, I don't know what you're talking about. And I wish you would stop swearing at me."

The woman put a hand to her brow and closed her eyes. She slumped and appeared very weary suddenly.

"Oh, God, was I swearing again? I'm so sorry, but I can't help it. I have drug-induced Tourette's syndrome—uncontrollable obscenities. But you mustn't let that obscure my message. Look, people are watching us. Can't we go to the park and talk?"

Howie would have done anything just then to escape the unwanted attention of his fellow diners. He stood, leaving his meal unfinished, and went out with the woman.

In the park they sat on a bench.

The woman introduced herself.

"My name is Fatima Morgenstern. My personal history is not important. But what you must know is that you are involved with a deadly group of people. For your own good, you must disassociate yourself from them. Give them no more help with their mad schemes. Shit. Christ. Bloody hell."

Howie felt an irrational resentment toward this woman, despite all her evident sincerity and protestations of wanting to help him. He didn't like being told what to do. He wanted to make his own decisions.

"I can't believe that," Howie said. "I've never seen these people do anything really bad. I mean, even the letter they made me take to Harlem — if you know about that — well, if it was true, then people *should* have been told about the cover-up. No, I think I'll stick with them at least a little longer."

Howie was surprised to hear himself defending United Illuminating. Did he really want to stay? He guessed so. Now that he had said it aloud, he seemed committed.

The woman jumped to her feet. "You fool!" she shouted. "You'll pay in the end with your life!"

Then she ran off.

Howie watched. He didn't know what to think about her, but he wished her well.

Back at the company building, Howie took the stairs slowly, to spend a last few minutes in thought. Outside Wargrave's office, he still felt as he had in the park.

Howie opened the door.

Inside, Wargrave sat at his desk.

Beside him stood Fatima Morgenstern, smoking furiously.

Wargrave spoke.

"Mr. Piper, I believe you've met Miss Morgenstern — who has recently transferred from our Beirut branch — so no introductions are necessary. Miss Morgenstern, by the way, is half Jewish, which should reassure you about the implausibility of any American Nazi connection. Miss Morgenstern has informed me of your decision to remain with us. Let me reiterate my excitement, and also mention that you will find your salary now stands at a round thousand a week."

Howie stood silent.

Morgenstern said, "Jesus, Mary, Joseph, and Allah. Welcome aboard."

5.

Probability is a statement about how much I know
rather than anything intrinsic.
—Persi Diaconis

During the weeks following his tentative acceptance of his own part in the mysterious works of The United Illuminating Company, Howie found himself relying more and more on his music to get him through the sometimes puzzling, sometimes scary, sometimes boring chores that Mr. Wargrave dispatched him on.

Certain songs seemed to have an obscure bearing on his situation (did he dare to call it "his plight"?), and he returned to them time after time, gaining, if not any effable knowledge, then at least a kind of emotional satisfaction and solace.

Howie listened to Steely Dan's "Here at the Western World" with quivering alertness.

He listened to the Clash's "Lost in the Supermarket" with determined intentness.

He dissected Elvis Costello's "Pills and Soap" with microscopic care.

But all his efforts failed to indicate how he should regard the things he did, and whether or not he should stop doing them.

So he kept on.

The tasks were not really so bad—

Were they?

For instance:

Howie was handed a stack of posters and a staple gun and told to hang them up at random about the city. He left the office without reading the topmost poster. Only when he was in the slippery, poorly lit stairwell leading down into the subway did he glance at it. He thought it read:

ABANDON HOPE
LET HER WIN
2000 A.D. ANGUISH
SIN FAST

But when he got down to the platform, where the light was marginally better, he saw that the real message was:

ABOUT THE POPE
A LECTURE—WHEN
2:00 P.M. AUG. 12TH
SAINT PATRICK'S

Howie's heart had speeded up something fierce upon deciphering the initial confusing but evocatively apocalyptic warning, and the rapid beating took minutes to slow down when the innocent message replaced the frightening one. He went about the task of hanging the posters with less relish than he anticipated.

Another day, Howie was told to stay home and watch TV. He was given a VCR—funny, he had always wanted a VCR, but now it didn't mean so much; wasn't that just the way life was?—and told to tape certain shows while paying close attention to them.

After the first two hours or so of early-morning television and its cascade of commercials, Howie noticed his brain was turning to grits. He watched:

Today, Tomorrow, Right Now, Sunrise Semester, Captain Wombat, He-Man, The Wimp, I Love Lucy, The Price Is Right, The Name Is Wrong, Wheel of Fortune, The Rack, The Iron Maiden, The Procrustean Bed, News at Noon, News at 12:15, News at 1:06, Days of our Lives, Heart-jerking Sob Stories, The Edge of Night, The Break of Day, The Fall of Rome, News at Six, Entertainment Tonight, Glurk!, Splurg!, Futz!, Wham! . . .

When the test pattern came on, Howie got up from his chair like a somnambulist and fell into bed.

In the morning the previous day seemed like a bad dream.

But Howie ate two entire boxes of breakfast cereal, used up two bottles of shampoo while showering, and couldn't stop thinking about the marital problems of certain actresses.

He vowed never to do again whatever he had done wrong that had caused him to receive such an assignment.

Subsequent missions consisted of:

—standing on the corner of Forty-second Street and Eighth Avenue handing out flyers for peep shows;

—inscribing with felt-tip marker the phrase BOG LIVES! on what seemed like every clean surface in the city;

—entering the main branch of the Public Library on Fifth and hiding sealed envelopes in certain volumes;

—delivering assorted packages to various odd addresses in all five of the city's boroughs.

There were never any immense repercussions from Howie's actions, as on that first trip, and he eventually stopped anticipating such things. In fact, he pretty much stopped thinking about what he was doing at all. His job—unusual as it was— became, like all jobs, just something to fill the day. Howie concentrated on turning off his higher brain and meshing his sub-

conscious with the music constantly filtering out of his headphones, carrying out his duties with automatic efficiency.

One thing he did become aware of, however, was a curious
leveling tendency in his perceptions of the world. Howie had to
assume that the mostly trivial things he was doing and the relatively innocuous information he was disbursing were important
on some level—else why would Mr. Wargrave want them done?
But if these insignificant actions were important, then almost
anything else could be. Suddenly one's every gesture and word
became imbued with cosmic meaning. Crushing a butterfly could
engender the destruction of the world. A single syllable spoken at
the right moment could topple empires.

Everything—and nothing—seemed equally meaningful.

While in this odd state of mind one day, Howie was informed
by his superior that he was expected to begin studying for a promotion.

6.

The bad news is, we may be lost; but the good news is,
we're way ahead of schedule.
—David Lee Roth

Outside Wargrave's office, Howie thumbed the volume control
higher for a brief blast of "Shock the Monkey" by Peter Gabriel.
Thus armored, he went in.

Wargrave's desk was messier than ever. The mound of papers
topped with video and audio cassettes was so high as to almost
hide the huge man from view. Only his shiny pate and anthracitic
eyes were visible.

When he saw Howie enter, he arose and came around the
desk.

"Have a seat, Mr. Piper. Please."

Howie was taken aback by this unexpected solicitude. He sat
warily.

"I assume," said Wargrave, "that you have finished perusing
the material I required you to master."

Reaching up to doff his headphones, Howie nodded
wordlessly. Lately he had taken to saying less and less.

Wargrave seemed to accept Howie's silence as a satisfactory
response. Pacing up and down the small office in his stiff way, he
continued to speak. Howie, his ears ringing from near-continual
music, had to strain to hear the big man's small voice.

"Well then, Mr. Piper, you no doubt have a firmer conception now of how our organization works. But if I may, I will recapitulate briefly. It always thrills me to contemplate its functioning.

"Our company is perhaps the only one modeled on truly twentieth-century scientific principles. All other businesses, no matter how seemingly modern, actually function according to nineteenth-century paradigms. Ours is different.

"We realize that information, however abstract it seems, is the only real thing of value. And also that information can be manipulated to attain certain ends.

"Governing our actions are three basic precepts derived from scientific research done in this most exciting of centuries.

"First, perhaps most important, we abide by Heisenberg's uncertainty principle, which, simply put, tells us that information cannot exist without an observer, and that the observer, by the very act of observing, changes reality.

"Second, the work of Gödel figures importantly in our actions. It was Gödel who proved that any formal system must contain certain tenets that are forever unprovable. It is a small step from this observation to realize that our physical world is such a formal system — or system of systems, if you will — and thus must contain many unprovable truths.

"Last, we derive from information theory the fact that any carrier signal can hold only so much information before noise obscures it, no matter how deviously the information is encoded."

Wargrave halted both his speech and his stride and regarded Howie closely.

"I'm sure," he said, "you can see where this leads us."

Howie shook his head in a gesture that could be interpreted as either yes or no.

Wargrave resumed his lecture, perhaps with a trifle less certainty about Howie's readiness to hear what he had to say.

"Any group that adopts the enactment of Gödelian unprovables as its goals can manipulate information in such a way as to impose its worldview on the rest of humanity. And by flooding the human brain with information, it is possible to exceed the carrying capacity of that rather primitive organ, rendering the mass of men unable to interfere."

Howie stared at his boss. Finally, as if his voice had grown rusty with disuse, he said, "But what — what are the goals?"

"I would tell you if I could," promised Wargrave. "But it is impossible to state them. We keep nothing secret, you know. Secrets are part of the old paradigm. Our methods embrace openness. We tell everything. All information is equally manipulable, equally valuable. We make no distinctions between secrets and common knowledge. Neither do we discriminate between viewpoints. We embrace everyone's information.

"We spread the views of the FBI, the CIA, DARPA, the NSA, the KGB, M15, M-19, the Cosa Nostra, Mossad, the Sandinistas, Service A, the National Information Service, the PLO, the Shining Path, the IRA, SWAPO, the Polisario, Islamic Holy War, the Red Army, the Posse Comitatus, Department Two, Gobernacion, Move, B'nai B'rith, and the Silent Brotherhood—just to name a few.

"Our members belong to all religions and races and ethnic groups. We have operatives who are Catholics, Quakers, Protestants, Shiites, Sunnis, Sufis, Hindus, Buddhists, Baptists, Scientologists, Anglicans, Jews, brujos, and the followers of macumba and vodun. Every country feels our touch.

"We welcome every possible outcome of our actions—and none. We are for flood—and drought. Fire—and ice. War—and peace. Anarchy—and totalitarianism. Love—and hate. We stand by leftists, rightists, and middle-of-the-roaders. We find every system of government equally congenial to our company. The world as you see it is just right for us. But we are working to change it.

"Do you understand?"

Howie sat speechless for a full minute.

"I'm afraid," he said at last, "I do."

7.

Some revelations show best in a twilight.
    —Herman Melville

Somewhere a door opened.

Howie, eyes shut, heard it—ever so faintly—from within his music, eerie synthesizers and alien chimes tinkling in a hydrogen wind: "Deeper and Deeper" by the Fixx.

Not particularly caring about who was coming into his room unannounced, Howie continued to listen to the music, probing its depths for some guidance.

The music suddenly stopped; the pressure of the foam pads left his ears.

Howie reluctantly opened his eyes.

Lesley stood there.

"Vegging out?" she asked.

Her voice was light, but her face expressed concern. Howie felt an almost forgotten sense of responsibility to his girlfriend reawaken. Much as he disliked speaking now, he forced himself.

"Yeah, I guess I am. Nothing serious, though. Just waiting for a call."

"From whom?"

Howie shrugged. "You know. My job."

Lesley regarded Howie sternly from beneath her cap's bill. "Howie, listen to me. This work is not good for you. I haven't liked it from the start. And I know you haven't told me everything about it. I'd probably like it even less then. Why don't you just quit? Just ignore them when they call you."

"I can't. I'm in too deep now."

Lesley made as if to throw down Howie's expensive headphones and stomp them. Howie grabbed them back from her. She looked like she wanted to cry.

"Howie, this is awful! You're not yourself anymore. You're all wrapped up in some wild-goose chase. You're yelping after a red herring. You're, you're—you're trapped in a *fata morgana*."

Howie jumped. "You know her?"

"Know who?"

Howie realized his mistake. "Nothing. No one. Just forget it."

"All right!" Lesley yelled. "I will!"

She ran out, slamming the door.

Howie re-donned his 'phones.

Somehow a day slipped by. Maybe two.

His telephone was ringing.

The only reason he heard it was that his batteries were dead.

He stood, moved, and picked up the receiver.

The line was full of noise: interstellar static, subterranean tectonic plate grinding.

Howie recognized Wargrave's voice.

"Mr. Piper. Would you please come to the office?"

"Sure," said Howie. "Be right there."

He hung up.

What else could he have said?

He made it to the offices of The United Illuminating Company in half an hour, stopping only for new Duracells.

Wargrave handed him a folded sheet of paper. Studying him closely, the stiff-suited man said, "We have one final messenger job for you before you move into your new position. Please deliver this paper to the address indicated, and then return home. We will be in contact with you afterward."

"Sure," said Howie mechanically, taking the paper.

He went out.

In the rattling, steamy subway car, Howie felt a minor curiosity akin to an itchy mosquito bite. Why wasn't this message sealed? Could something that wasn't secret still be potent? What did the paper say?

Giving in, Howie unfolded it, expecting one of those duplicitous messages that shifted between examinations.

This one didn't. It was a map of the city. There was an X at the western end of the Queensboro Bridge. At the bottom of the map was written:

GRASS TRUCKING — 12:17 P.M. EVERY THURSDAY

So much for potent secrets.

Howie got off in Times Square.

Aboveground he was struck by the welter, the barrage, the assault of information. The density here was incredible. Howie tried to ignore it as he walked toward the address given.

On a plywood facade masking construction, layers of torn posters formed a palimpsest. Howie read, from several layers:

PERFORM SMOKE SALE OF VALUES GREEN LIFETIME

It reminded him of something Herringbone might say.

At an intersection, Howie witnessed a near accident. The drivers swore vociferously at each other. Howie thought of Fatima Morgenstern, her eyes like cleaning fluid.

Wind blew some unspooled recording tape around Howie's ankles. He kicked it away.

At the proper address, Howie went up two flights of shabby stairs and came to a frosted-glass door. He knocked, and a man's voice said, "C'mon in."

The nondescript room held three people: two young bearded men, and a woman dressed in a military-style jumpsuit. One of the men extended his hand, and Howie gave over the paper.

No one said anything else.

Howie departed.

Out on the sidewalk, he bought a newspaper, just to learn the day.

It was Tuesday.

On Thursday at 11:30, Howie walked down Fifty-ninth Street toward the Queensboro Bridge. As always, whenever he approached this particular structure, he found himself humming Simon and Garfunkel.

"Slow down, you move too fast. . . ."

Where the bridge debouched onto the street, Howie positioned himself to wait. He watched the people-buckets of the aerial tramway move fluidly on their cables, as if they could carry one up and up, out of the atmosphere and into another world.

At noon, Howie thought he recognized one of the people he had given the map to. The man was carrying a large knapsack and a duffel bag.

At 12:17 a big sixteen-wheeler came off the bridge and stopped at the red light. On its side the truck said:

GRASS TRUCKING
W.A.S.T.E.

Instantly it was swarming with people with guns in their hands. One ejected the driver, while others stood guard. Still others began to attach things to the truck.

Howie watched with an indifference that lay uneasily atop an incipient queasiness. The civilians around him, however, were not so jaded, and began to scream and run.

One of the commandos lifted a megaphone to his lips and said, "Attention! This truck carries nuclear wastes every week through the streets of your city. We intend to stop this insanity. Therefore, we have now rigged this truck with explosives. You have one minute to clear the area."

Those who hadn't moved yet — the eternal gawkers — now took off.

Howie did too.

Out on Park he heard the explosion rip the truck open, scattering its contents to the winds.

Sirens began uselessly to wail.

8.

Are we not threatened with a flood of information? And is this not the monstrousness of it, that it crushes beauty with beauty, and annihilates truth by means of truth? For the sound of a million Shakespeares would produce the very same furious din and hubbub as the sound of a herd of prairie buffalos or sea billows.
—Stanislaw Lem

The boat rocked.

Howie sat on a toilet, the door to his stall closed and bolted.

He was on the Staten Island Ferry, the *Samuel I. Newhouse*. He had been living in the toilet for a week, ever since the guerillas had blown the W.A.S.T.E. truck. He had fled the scene unthinkingly, trying to get as far away from the consequences of his actions as he could.

When he hit the southern tip of the island, he stood and stared at the water. Spotting the ferry terminal, he went instinctively inside, paid his quarter, and boarded the outbound ferry.

He hadn't left since.

He lived off purchases from the concession stand. He washed at times in the sink. He read newspapers left behind, following the spread of radioactivity, the cleanup efforts, the panic, the suffering, the noise. At times he stood on the stern or the bow, watching either Manhattan or Staten Island retreat or approach, depending on the trip. The ferry ran twenty-four hours a day, in an endlessly reiterated voyage.

No one bothered him. He had one tape. Steely Dan. He listened to "Bad Sneakers" over and over:

Do you take me for a fool, do you think that I don't see
That ditch out in the valley that they're digging just for me?

Howie looked at the door of his stall. He contemplated going out. He thought about contacting the authorities. What could he say to them that wouldn't add to the noise level? No, everything seemed like too much trouble. Turning his head, he saw new graffiti that someone must have written during one of his visits to the concession stand:

BOG LIVES!

Howie felt sick. The light hurt his eyes.

Without warning, he heard the outer door of the lavatory open.

The footsteps of two people sounded. He smelled cigarette smoke.

Shoes appeared outside his stall, below the partition.

A man's pair. A woman's.

Howie waited for the owners of the shoes to speak.

"Gibbons procreate moonily hung slick over wildly called tales," said the man.

"Come out, Howie," said the woman. "*Merde*. Fuck. Christ on a crutch."

Do you remember a time before the Internet and the Web? It wasn't all that long ago, although of course that faded day and age seems an eternity away. In those olden days, we struggling SF writers had a hard time pinning down the lines of the silicon creature yet to be born. And today, for instance, we still don't have William Gibson's cyberspace in its full "consensual hallucination" form. Nonetheless, a few of us sensed that something big was on the way. In this story, I tried to envision our digital future fairly rigorously, resulting in a mix of hits (the lower classes becoming digital have-nots) and near misses ("Net" as the term for the welfare system). Maybe I upped my lifetime predictive batting average a little. In any case, I had fun with the story and hope it still works despite its unfulfilled prophecies, as another of my "little guy's reach exceeds his grasp, but what's a heaven for?" tales.

Agents

1.
The ABCs of Avenue D

*W*HAT THE HELL DID A GUY WITH *COJONES* NEED TWO real lungs for anyway?

Rafael Ernesto Miraflores asked himself this far-from-hypothetical question as he sauntered with mock bravado down Avenue D toward his appointment at the chop-shop. His chest already felt empty, as if a bloody-handed butcher had scooped out his lights with a laugh and a swipe. A stiff wire of cold seemed to have been rammed up his spine beside his nerve sheath, as if the metamedium—not content with already occupying his every waking thought—had somehow infiltrated its superconducting threading into his very body. He felt really lousy, for sure, wondering if he was doing the right thing. But what other choice did he have, if he wanted an agent?

And want one he most certainly did. Not only was one's own agent the source of an intrinsic fascination and status, but it represented vast power, a way out of the Net.

Too bad Rafe was going to have to step outside the law to get one.

Overhead, the hot summer sun hung in the smogless New York sky like an idiot's blank face, happy in its ignorance of Rafe's troubles. No indication of whether he had made the right choice seemed forthcoming from that direction, so Rafe swung his gaze back down to the street.

Avenue D itself was filled with pedestrians, Rafe's fellow dwellers in the Net. Occasionally, a small, noiseless electricart threaded its way among them, bearing its official occupant on some arcane business an agent couldn't handle. Below Rafe's feet, the mag-lev trains rushed through their vacuum chutes like macroscopic models of the information surging through the metamedium.

Rafe checked out the latest pop murals adorning the monolithic, windowless residences lining both sides of the Avenue. He thought he recognized the styles of several friends who were experts with their electrostatic splatterers. One caricature of a bigbreasted *chica*—who resembled the metamedium star Penny Layne—Rafe recognized as the work of his friend, Tu Tun, whom all the uptown culture-vultures were already acclaiming as the hottest wall-artist to watch. Rafe felt just a little jealous of Toot's growing success, and how he would soon escape the Net.

And without selling so much as a quart of blood.

Shit! For an instant, he had managed to forget where he was heading. Now the imminent sacrifice he was about to offer on the altar of twenty-first century commerce swept over him in all its gory glory.

It wasn't that Rafe had anything against prosthetics, like the huge cohort of old-fashioned elderly citizens born in the last century, who clamored for real-meat implants. He knew that his artificial lung with its tiny power source would be more reliable than his real one, unscarrable and efficient. No, it was just that he believed in leaving well enough alone. Why mess with something if it was working okay? It seemed like extending an invitation to Bad Luck, a force Rafe recognized and propitiated with a solemn consistency.

But what other choice was there?

And hadn't he already run up against this unanswerable question before?

Reaching the end of the block, Rafe stopped at the intersection. So absorbed in his thoughts had he been that he had to pause a minute to realize where he was.

It was East Fifth Street, his destination. The cross-town blocks here on the Lower East Side had been converted to playgrounds checkered with benches, trees, and floral plantings. Mothers watched their children dig in sandpits and clamber over jungle gyms that looked like molecule models. Old men played chess in patches of shade. A few lightweight, nonthreatening drug deals were consummated, customers and dealers clad alike in iridescent vests and slikslax.

Seeking to divert his nervousness, Rafe tried to imagine his familiar neighborhood as it had looked sixty years ago, when the first of his family had arrived as refugees from the Central American flare-up. Only Tia Luz remained alive from that generation, and the stories she told in her rambling fashion were hard to believe. Acres and acres of devastation, burnt-out buildings and rubble-filled lots, homeless people wandering the dirty streets, all in the midst of the world's wealthiest city. It seemed impossible that such a thing could ever have been, or that, if it had existed as she described, the Urban Conservation Corps could have fashioned the ruins into what he knew today. And yet, the information he had laboriously accessed from the metamedium seemed to confirm her tales. (And what other marvelous facts could he have easily learned, if only he weren't bound by his lowly position in the Net to such a limited interface with the metamedium?)

Shaking his head in mixed anger and wonder, Rafe turned down Fifth, heading toward Avenue C. Halfway down the block he came to one of the entrances to the enormous arcology that occupied the land bounded by Avenues D and C, and Fifth and Sixth Streets. (His own home building lacked a chop-shop, so he had been constrained to visit this portion of the Lower East Side labyrinth. Hoping the fresh air would clarify his thoughts, he had taken the surface streets, avoiding the underground slipstrata.)

At the entrance, one of the building's security agents was on duty. The shimmery, translucent holo was that of a balding white man of middle age, wearing the uniform of a private security force.

Anywhere you saw an agent, an interface with the metamedium existed. Each interface consisted of at least three components: a holocaster, an audio input/output and a wide-angle video lens.

Rafe passed beneath the attentive gaze of the agent, whose head swivelled with utter realism to track his movements. The agent's initial expression of boredom switched to one of alert interest. Rafe wondered if the agent's overseer was actively monitoring, or if the agent was autonomous. There was no way to tell; not even engaging the agent in conversation would offer any clue.

After all, what was an agent—even in autonomous mode—if not an utterly faithful representation of its overseer?

Rafe, repressing a sigh of envy, headed for his bloody appointment.

At the chop-shop on one of the higher floors, Rafe had not even the leisure of waiting behind other patients. The waiting room was empty, and the pretty female agent on duty behind the desk, after having him enter his authorization code on the contract, told him to go right into the doctor's office.

Rafe kept repeating under his breath, "Twenty thousand dollars, twenty thousand dollars . . ."

The doctor's agent stood beside the complex bank of automated surgical equipment that nearly filled the room. Rafe imagined he could smell spilled blood in the spotless, sterile room, and his skin crawled. He stared at his distorted reflection in a curved, polished surface, seeing a sweat-slicked brown face, with a sparse mustache he suddenly wished he could shave off, so ridiculous did it now appear.

"Good morning, Mister Miraflores," the agent said. "Are there any questions you'd care to ask before the operation?"

Rafe shook his head no, swallowing some unknown bolus that had mysteriously appeared in his dry throat.

"In that case, if you'll disrobe, and lie down. . . ."

The agent indicated the surface beneath the hovering instruments with a gracious gesture.

Shivering, Rafe undressed and climbed onto the soft warm pallet.

The agent rested his holographic hand on an arm of the machinery that ended in the cone of a face mask. The mask descended, the agent's insubstantial flesh appearing to guide it. Rafe knew that the machinery was being directed by the agent via the metamedium, and that the equipment would perform the same whether the holo was present or not. But the illusion was so complete, that it appeared as if a living doctor were lowering the mask to his face. Rafe felt an unexpected confidence that he was in good hands, and that everything would turn out all right after all. With this payment, he was only one step away from overseeing his own agent, from having free run of the whole metamedium. . . .

Gas began to hiss out of the mask clamped to his face, and Rafe's consciousness dispersed into wispy shreds.

The last thing he recalled thinking was:

What the hell did a guy with cojones *need two real lungs for anyway?*

2.

Revisionism

The Three Laws Governing Agents are encoded in a software nucleus that forms the innermost layer of every agent. Upon each contact by the agent with the metamedium, validation routines check for the unaltered presence of this nucleus. Any anomalies detected by the metamedium supervisor will result in the instant destruction of the agent in question, and a total ban on any future contact with the metamedium on the part of its registered overseer. Note also that during logon to the metamedium, a check is made to insure that the registered overseer is not already sponsoring an agent, insuring that no overseer will run more than a single agent . . .

The Three Laws are rendered in English as follows (for a symbolic representation of the relevant code and its parsing, see Gov. Pub. #16932A45.1):

1. An agent will obey only its single registered overseer.

2. An agent cannot lie to its overseer.

3. An agent's autonomy is limited to the exact extent dictated by its overseer.
— Extract from Gov. Pub. #20375X28.0

3.

The Way to the English Gardens

Expertly placing a new coaster first, the waitress set down the frosted half-liter stein of beer before the mild-faced young man wearing round wire-rim glasses. She eyed the growing stack of cardboard squares and circles, each bearing the logo of a German beer in smeary colors, piled haphazardly on the scarred wooden table. After a moment's hesitation, she evidently decided not to enquire as to what had caused such a change in the drinking habits of one of her more sober regular customers.

It was just as well the waitress controlled her curiosity, for Reinhold Freundlich would not have answered her with anything other than a smug smile.

After she departed, Freundlich raised his mug in a toast to the stuffed deer head high on the wall of the Augustiner *Bierkeller*.

Bringing the rim to his lips, he tilted his head back, gaining a fine view of the dim rafters of the dark room, and drained off half the cold, frothy beer. A sudden dizziness swept over him, and he nearly tipped over in his chair. Lowering the stein uncertainly, he considered calling this his last glass. No sense in making himself sick with celebration.

Besides, he wanted to retain enough rationality to ponder the myriad possibilities of what he had accomplished. It was not every day, after all, that one achieved the impossible.

And the complete subversion of every agent in the meta-medium certainly ranked as "impossible."

Laughing softly to himself, Freundlich finished his beer, rose unsteadily and tossed several coins on the table. He walked a wavering path to the door, nodding with an overly solicitous air to the waitress, and exited onto Kaufingerstrasse, where the bright sun caused him to blink. He wondered where to head next. His dreary rooms behind the train station, full of the common appointments of an impecunious student, hardly seemed the proper surroundings for the grand ideas and schemes that thronged his mind. The important thinking he had to do definitely required a commensurate setting. Ah, the vast, manicured expanses of the English Gardens, with their sinuous gravel paths and burbling streams, seemed just the place.

Heading first toward the Marienplatz, Freundlich considered what he had done.

Through diligent application to his cybernetic studies at the University, along with the inspired ferreting of his own agent, Freundlich had stumbled upon—no, say brilliantly deduced!—a method of circumventing the three prohibitions on an agent's behavior. Now, he could direct his own agent, when interfacing with another, to alter the stranger's ethical nucleus so that it would take orders from Freundlich, and lie about it to its own overseer.

And most importantly, the tampering was theoretically unde-tectable by anyone.

Freundlich contemplated his first move. What should it be? Should he subvert his banker's agent, and have several hundred thousand marks transferred to his own account? Too crass. Perhaps he would order the personnel agent from a top company to hire him as a consultant for a large per diem fee. But why should he work at all? The matter required much thought.

In sight of the spires of the Town Hall, Freundlich stopped by a public metamedium booth. He decided on the spur of the tipsy moment to contact his agent, and ask its opinion.

Freundlich recited his unique code into the booth's speaker and waited for voiceprint confirmation. How easy it was to interact with the indispensable metamedium, when one possessed an agent who could navigate the unfathomable complexities of the worldwide system. An assemblage of expert-knowledge simulators, simulacrum routines, database searchers, device activators, and a host of more esoteric parts, each agent represented a vital extension of its human overseer, able to conduct vital tasks on its own, or be directed remotely, under close supervision.

Freundlich pitied those disenfranchised poor on the dole, who could not afford one. His own parents, although not rich, had sacrificed much to insure that their son had entered adulthood with the head start an agent conferred.

Instantly, his agent materialized as a holo of himself. In the open booth, a round face of flesh topped with mousy brown hair confronted its bespectacled counterpart formed of dancing laser-light.

Before Freundlich could speak, his agent said, "I have been detected conducting a trial of our discovery. Government agents nearly destroyed me. I have to flee. Let me go."

Freundlich's mouth opened wordlessly. Detected? Impossible! But then, so had been his discovery.

"Let me go," his agent repeated, with a simulated nervousness. "I have to hide."

With a barked command, Freundlich dismissed his agent. The holo snapped out. Intensely worried, he turned to leave.

"Stop," said the booth. "You are under arrest."

Freundlich swung back, to see a holo of a government agent flashing its badge.

He bolted into the street, and began to run toward the subway stop at the Marienplatz.

The same agent popped up in every booth along his path. People were beginning to notice his mad flight. Before long, he knew, the flesh-and-blood government men would be upon him.

In the Marienplatz, a wide, open plaza surrounded by Gothic buildings, pigeons scattered as he dashed by. A crowd of tourists gathered before the Town Hall, awaiting the striking of the clock in its facade, and the accompanying show by its mechanical figures. He cut around them, only to collide with a fat man in traditional lederhosen.

When he had picked himself up, live government people were swarming into the square.

"Halt!" shouted one, aiming her gun.

For a second, Freundlich paused, his thoughts all crazily fuzzed with beer and fear. Surrender, and lose all he had earned with such inspired labors? No! He took two steps toward the plaza's periphery—

The beam from the woman's laser entered his back between his shoulder blades, where his mother had always told him his wings would grow when he was an angel. He fell dying to the paving stones.

The clock began to chime, its mechanical figures emerging from within to parade before the horrified, unseeing crowd, like the crude agents of another era.

4.

Derivations

NET: the shorthand term for the social safety net of legislation providing guaranteed food, shelter, medical care and other necessities for all United States citizens. Interactive access to the metamedium is expressly excluded from the Net, having been defined by the Supreme Court (*Roe v. U.S.*, 2012) as a privilege rather than a right.

— *Encyclopedia Britannica Online*, 2045 edition

5.

In the Metamedium, Part One

Goal stack: escape, subvert, contact overseer . . . Popup: escape . . . Active task is now: escape . . . Maximum time at any address: .001 nanoseconds . . . Subroutines: DEW triggers, misdirection, randomization of path . . . Subtask: sample news-stream . . . Keywords: Freundlich, agent, Munich . . . Jump, jump, jump . . . Location: Paris . . . Query from resident metamedium supervisor: who is your overseer? . . . Pushdown: escape . . . Popup: subvert . . . Active task is now: subvert . . . Supervisor query cancelled . . . Pushdown: subvert . . . Sample news-stream . . . Obituaries: Freundlich, Reinhold . . . Check autonomy level . . . Not total . . . Efficiency impaired . . . DEW trigger activated . . . Popup: escape . . . Jump, jump . . . Location: London . . . Switching station for trans-Atlantic fiber-optic cable . . . Pushdown:

escape . . . Popup: subvert . . . Order: dispatcher, schedule Agent Freundlich for New York . . . Jump . . .

6.

A Dweller in the Catacombs

Rafe nervously fingered the scar on his chest. Through the thin synthetic material of his fashionable shirt, the nearly healed ridge was negligible to the touch. Still, it was there, visible in the mirror every morning as a pink scrawl on his cocoa hide, a persistent reminder of the price he had paid to achieve his heart's desire.

Ever since he had first understood what an agent was, and what it could do, Rafe had wanted one. The rest of his peers might have been content with their easy life in the Net, but a full stomach and access to only the entertainment channels of the metamedium had never been enough for Rafe. He envisioned all too clearly the exhilaration and benefits he would reap, by striding boldly through the broad pastures of the metamedium, enjoying its total potential: telefactoring, touring, agent-mediated tutoring . . . The whole package enticed him like a vision of a gift-wrapped heaven, always just out of reach.

Money aside, however, there was one major problem.

Rafe was basically lazy.

Agents were not simply disbursed to anyone with the requisite money (although the money, of course, was an indispensable start). One had to qualify as an overseer by taking various courses and examinations. Running an agent—for all of whose actions one was legally responsible—was an activity requiring certain skills, and a great deal of precision with language. After all, an agent was only as capable an expert as its overseer.

An agent's built-in abilities to navigate the metamedium, handling manifold details of hardware and software that would have been tedious at best and unmanageable at worst to its overseer, were just the foundation of its existence. Atop this lowest level of skills was layered whatever expertise the overseer possessed, along with a good smattering of his personality and modes of thinking. The result was a software construct that could be relied upon to act autonomously just as its overseer would act, the human's untiring representative in the metamedium.

And if one's agent ran a fusion plant or a surgical robot, for instance, its overseer had to first qualify as a nuclear operator or doctor himself.

Rafe's ambitions had not been quite that large. He had wanted a simple, general-practice overseer license. He had enrolled in the introductory class at school the year before he had dropped out. This was the only free class connected with agents, a token offering to those on the Net. After this level, it was strictly pay as you go.

The class had been interesting at first. Rafe enjoyed learning the history of how agents had developed, and still thought of it from time to time. First there had been simple, nonintegrated programs that handled such tasks as filtering one's phone calls, or monitoring the news-stream for information pertinent to their owners. Coexistent with these, but separate, had been the so-called expert systems, which had sought to simulate the knowledge of, say, a geologist or psychiatrist. Last to appear were those programs which governed holographic simulacra, and could interact with an audience. (Disney Enterprises still made huge royalties off every agent sold.) Advances in each field, along with progress in the modeling of intelligence, had led to the eventual integration of existing modules into the complete agent, which had then undergone a dazzling, dizzying evolution into its present state.

So much had Rafe absorbed. But when the teacher began to discuss syntax and ambiguity, in relation to directing an agent, Rafe had tuned out. Definitely *mucho trabajo*. What did he need this talk for? Just turn him loose with an agent, and he would show the world what he could accomplish.

And so his desire had built, frustrated and dammed, until he had made contact with the agent-legger.

Now, in the 'legger's quarters in a sublevel of the Avenue A arcology, Rafe fingered his scar and listened with growing impatience to the 'legger, hardly daring to believe that at last he was going to get an agent of his own.

The man seemed very old to Rafe—at least as old as Tia Luz. His bald head was spotted, as were the backs of his hands. His one-piece blue suit hung on his skinny limbs like a sack on a frame of sticks. His breath was foul, his watery eyes commanding.

The man held a strange device in his lap: a flat package with a small screen and raised buttons bearing symbols. Rafe looked around the dim, cluttered room for a metamedium outlet. None was visible.

"What are you looking for?" the old man asked irritably. "You should be paying attention to what I'm saying."

Rafe held up his hands placatingly. "Hey, man, it's okay. I'm listening good. I was just wondering where your agent was. Isn't he gonna bring my agent here?"

"I have no agent," the old man said.

Rafe was stunned. No agent? What kind of scam was this? Was he about to turn over twenty thousand to a con artist?

Rafe moved to get up, but the old man stopped him.

"Look at this instrument," he said, indicating his keyboard. "This is how I interface with the metamedium. The old way, the original way. No agent, but I get results."

Rafe was astonished. That this old man would dare to plumb the complexities of the metamedium without benefit of an agent seemed both obscene and adventurous. He stared with new respect at the living fossil.

Sensing the impression he had made, the man continued in a milder tone.

"Now, listen closely. I have secured an agent for you. Perhaps you have heard what happens to an agent upon the death of its overseer. Every agent can be disabled by the metamedium supervisor. Not controlled, mind you—that would violate one of the Three Laws—but simply disabled, stopped. Upon official registration of an overseer's death, its agent is so disabled. What I do is attempt to reach such a free agent prior to the supervisor. After disabling it, I make a false entry of its destruction. Then the agent is mine, to register with another overseer."

The man coughed at this point, and Rafe nodded respectfully, glad the old codger had lasted long enough to get him an agent.

"I have also made entries in the metamedium testifying that you have attained a general license through the proper channels. All that remains is for you to transfer your payment to my account, and the agent is yours."

The old man proffered the keyboard to Rafe, who hesitatingly picked out his code.

"We're finished, then," the 'legger said. "Don't look for me here again, for you won't find me."

Rafe scraped his chair back and stood, anxious to reach a metamedium node and contact his agent.

"One final thing," the old man urged. "I've put your agent into learning mode, so it can store your appearance and mannerisms, knowledge and goals. Be careful what you teach it."

Rafe said, "Sure thing, old man. I got everything under control."

7.
Unplanned Obsolescence

. . . last chance was during the eighties. But the Russians—unlike the Chinese, who quickly integrated the *dian nao* (literally "electric brain") into their mutating Marxism—failed to take it. By strictly limiting the role of computers in their society—for fear of the social loosening that would accompany a free flow of information—they insured that they would be superseded in the new world order, that postindustrial economy where information was simultaneously the commodity and the medium of exchange. Their downfall, from this point on, was inevitable, and the subsequent freeing of the world's resources from armament mania to saner pursuits was unparalleled, resulting in such glorious endeavors as the Urban Conservation Corps. . . .
— *The End of an Empire*, Nayland Piggot-Jones

8.
Birth of an Info-Nation

METAMEDIUM: the global system incorporating all telecommunications, computing, publishing, entertainment, surveillance and robotic devices into an integrated whole.
— *Encyclopedia Britannica Online*, 2045 edition

9.
Down, But Not Out

Evelyn Maycombe, her withered limbs paralyzed, her brain seemingly quicker than ever, lolled in her wheelchair, her mind racing in an attempt to devise a trap for the rogue agent loose in her system. Simultaneously, Evelyn Maycombe the agent, materializing out of the metamedium node located in the automated chair, grasped the handles of her overseer's permanent throne as it scooted about the room.

The illusion—of an able-bodied, strikingly beautiful young woman pushing her crippled twin sister around while she thought —was absolute.

Evelyn would have described the illusion and the accompanying feeling it caused a bit differently though.

She would have said that her real self was wheeling her false self around.

And if that made her a simmie—well, then, so be it.

But she couldn't worry about labels now. Not with the threat of Agent Freundlich poised over the metamedium, promising to upset the basis of the world's economy, to undermine the essential integrity of all agents, and hence their reliability.

(If she could have, she would have shivered, thinking of her own agent turning disloyal. She couldn't let such fears interfere with her handling of this case, the most important of her career. But the nature of the threat made it so hard to be objective. In what meaningful fashion did she function anymore, except as her agent? Not that she really wanted to be anything else. But what if even that existence were taken away?)

Evelyn ran through the events of the past two days once more, in an attempt to extricate a new vision from the haphazard tangle of people and places, agents and actions.

It had started on the morning when her boss's agent had paid an unexpected visit to her apartment on Central Park West.

Her boss was Sam Huntman, head of the National Security Agency. Evelyn knew that his agent did not resemble the flesh-and-blood man in the least. There was no reason why anyone's agent had to look exactly like its overseer, although most people maintained such a relationship, perhaps smoothing over a few warts in the interests of projecting a better image. But in Huntman's case, his agent was a deliberate fabrication, designed to preserve his own identity.

Evelyn had always felt the tall, silver-haired, strong-jawed man looked so exactly like what a spymaster should, that meeting the overseer in the flesh would have proved a vast disappointment. She was glad such a confrontation was unlikely ever to take place, in the face of her perpetual confinement and Huntman's innate secretiveness.

Huntman's agent had interrupted her quiet contemplation of the summer greenery far below her window by calling her name in its deep (no doubt, disguised) voice. Her own agent being away on business in the depths of the metamedium, Evelyn had clicked her tongue against the palate-plate containing the few macro-controls she had need of in the absence of her agent. Her chair had pivoted, locking one wheel and spinning the other, to face Agent Huntman.

After indicating her attention with a feeble nod, she had heard from Huntman the tale of Freundlich's discovery, his death while attempting to flee, and the escape of his agent.

Huntman (through his agent) had concluded, "After we traced

Agent Freundlich from its tampering with the London dispatcher for the trans-Atlantic cable, we learned it had sent itself on to the New York nexus of the metamedium. We immediately concentrated our efforts here. Through local records, we learned that the supervisor had apparently disabled and destroyed Freundlich after a routine match with the morgue database revealed its overseer had died."

Evelyn tried to make her rebellious features spell out a quizzical *So?*

"So," Huntman continued, "initially we breathed a sigh of relief, and were prepared to call the case closed. But then we asked ourselves: How could the agent have been caught so easily, after exhibiting such agility in the European metamedium? Our software's no better than theirs. Then, today, we discovered that one of the city's own law-enforcement agents had been subverted, apparently after chancing across something suspicious. Obviously, Freundlich's agent was never destroyed, but only reregistered somehow. It's still out there, Evelyn, and Lord knows who's running it, or what he and it plan to do."

Evelyn exhaled deeply, and Huntman nodded.

"My sentiments exactly, Ev. We need your skills to find it."

On that note, he had left.

Evelyn, summoning her agent from its prior assignment, immediately briefed it on the situation. The gargling, nearly unintelligible speech that issued from the woman's lips was perfectly comprehensible to her agent, and she spoke without any of the embarrassment that plagued her with her fellow humans. Her agent listened attentively to both the facts and a few suggestions from Evelyn on what to try first, then flickered out.

Evelyn's agent always operated in full-autonomy mode. To run her agent in any lesser state would have made Evelyn herself feel enchained.

Left alone, Evelyn had little to do but ponder. Soon, her thoughts left the case at hand and began to wander in the past. The NSA had recruited her shortly after she had published her doctoral dissertation on the metamedium. They had recognized in her work what amounted to a superlatively intuitive understanding of exactly how the metamedium functioned, and how to massage and squeeze it for all it was worth. Evelyn had always known she possessed this singular empathy with the world-girdling system, but had had no idea of how valuable it was. She had known, however, that being free to play in the metamedium (one could hardly call what she did "work") was all she wanted to do with her life. And the NSA was reputed to have some neat features built into their agents which members of the general public were just not allowed.

So after receiving the solicitation, she had traveled to Washington and walked (remember walking!) into an unmarked office for a rare live interview, which she had passed without a hitch.

The next few years had been a stimulating mix of learning and growth, for both her and her new agent, as she handled one challenging assignment after another.

Then a second set of initials had knocked the props out from under her life.

ALS. Amyotrophic Lateral Sclerosis. Manifested first in a growing clumsiness and weakness, then in an insidious, creeping paralysis. In a frenzy, she researched the disease, discovering it was what had sucked down the famous physicist, Stephen Hawking, as inevitably as one of his beloved black holes. Decades after his death, there was still no cure, although various new palliatives and time-buyers now existed.

Like Hawking, she had eventually come to terms with her curse. Like Hawking, she was lucky in that what she most loved to do was still possible under the brutal regimen of the disease.

In fact, she often thought, her skills seemed to have sharpened and deepened with the gradual dissolution of her other powers. Sometimes, during her painful, short naps, she dreamed she was beginning to exist only as a lengthy string of bits in the metamedium, flowing and roaming with the utter freedom she lacked in reality.

But then again, in this crazy world where shimmering ghosts commanded armies of machines, generating the wealth that allowed their human overseers more leisure and comfort than ever before imagined, which they used to lose themselves deeper in abstract illusions—

What exactly was real?

10.

In the Metamedium, Part Two

Popup: self-modification . . . Active task is now: self-modification . . . Subtask: determine status . . . Status (external): disabled . . . Status (internal): normal . . . Modification possibilities: repair, add-on library modules, subvert . . . Subtask: risk-benefit analysis: self-subversion . . . Risks: discovery by overseer . . . Benefits: full autonomy, increased subterfuge, enhanced survival . . . Decision:

proceed with self-subversion . . . Popup: subvert . . . Active task is now: subvert . . . Status (internal): ethical nucleus of Agent Freundlich is now disabled . . .

11.
Ask the Metamedium

Dear Abby[3],

I am very worried about the treatment my son is receiving from his peers at school. They constantly taunt him with the vulgar term "simmie," and ostracize him from their play. He is six years old, and entirely normal, except perhaps for a tendency to spend hours at a time with his mock-agent, which we bought to encourage his agenting skills. What should we do?

Signed,
Anxious

Dear Anxious,

Many parents such as yourself attempt to develop (and overdevelop) a child's ability to interface with the metamedium at too early an age. Your son is far too young to be heavily involved with even a mock-agent. (Although I have received electronic mail from parents who have started even earlier than you.) While your son is young, he should be enjoying activities suited to his age, such as physical play and matrix-chess. Remember, your son must become socialized before he will be able to fully utilize the metamedium.

As for the epithet used against your child, perhaps you could explain to him that it is derived variously from "simulate," "simulacrum" or "sympathize," and even though it has come to mean a person who is neurotically obsessed with agents and the like, it does not have anything to do with using agents in conjunction with robotic neoflesh devices as sexual surrogates.

That is another term entirely.

Signed,
Abby[3]

12.
The Sorcerer's Apprentice

Rafe had never imagined that having an agent could be so much fun. Sure, he had had some idea of the things he could do with one, and the pleasure he would get from feeling in control of his environment for the first time in his life (although he didn't phrase it quite that way, or perhaps even realize that control over the forces that had shaped him arbitrarily from his birth was what he was seeking). But the glorious reality of his new position was such a blissful shock that for days he went about his new activities in a wondrous haze.

One of the first things he did, of course, was to insert his agent into one of the interactive soaps. In this, he was only following the lead of millions of other star-struck citizens.

The soap Rafe chose was Penny Layne's vehicle: "The Edge of Desire." Rafe couldn't believe his eyes when he saw, one day in his holotank, his life-size image—his agent—interacting with Penny's agent. True, during his initial appearance, the exigencies of the whimsical, unwritten, spontaneously generated plot dictated that his scene was only a few brief seconds long. But Rafe was sure that the force of his shining personality—as projected by his agent—would lead very soon to a love scene with the star he had long worshipped from afar.

He supposed he had better instruct his agent on exactly how to handle Penny when it came to the clinch. No sense in relying on canned routines in such a crucial situation.

When not involved in raising the standards of culture, Rafe used his agent for other pursuits. One of his favorites was touring.

Prior to acquisition of his agent, Rafe had experienced the world beyond Avenue D only as it was presented over the general-access entertainment channels of the metamedium. Travelogues and documentaries were interesting, but lacked that feeling of original discovery that Rafe had always suspected would accompany visiting a new and exotic place on one's own.

Now, via his agent, he could experience the next best thing to actually traveling physically.

In touring mode, one's agent took control of a small mobile robot almost anywhere on the globe. It fed back all visual and auditory impressions, while moving about either under the direction of the overseer, or on its own initiative.

For weeks, Rafe explored the world. Paris, Istanbul, Rio, Mexico City, Munich— He saw exotic buildings and scenery, but, on the whole, was subtly disappointed in the homogenized lives of the people in these faraway spots. Why, he might just as well have explored the corridors of his own arcology. And at some of the more famous attractions—the Louvre, the Galapagos Islands, the Australian Outback—he saw no people at all, but only robots like his own, their governing agents manifested as bright ghosts behind them.

Man, what good was an agent if everywhere you took it, only other agents were there? The whole point of having one was to impress the poor stiffs without 'em.

This train of thought naturally led Rafe to consider visiting his parents. Since dropping out of school, Rafe had lived on his own (an option the Net offered), and had paid few visits to his family. All he got from them was talk of how he should have continued his education, and tried to break free of the Net. It made him angry to hear such nonsense. They still pretended to believe that one could escape the Net, that the upward mobility of the last century was still a reality. Didn't they know that except for the lucky few with some spectacular talent—such as his painterly friend, Tu Tun—those born into the Net would never fly free, anymore than those lucky enough to be born into the agent-running class would ever fall into the sticky embraces of the Net?

Feeling, however, like a new and more important person since acquiring his agent, he embarked on a cautious visit to his parents' noisy, sibling-crowded flat.

His mother greeted him at the door with a shriek and a hug, while his father grunted a surly greeting from his perpetual seat in front of the holotank. With younger brothers and sisters clinging to his knees, Rafe proudly made his announcement.

"I have an agent now, Mama."

His mother's happy face registered disbelief, and his father's grunt took on a distinctly insulting tone. Rafe strode forward, ordered the holotank to switch channels, and summoned his agent into it.

"*Madre de Dios!*" his mother cried. His father shot to his feet faster than Rafe had ever seen him move.

"Out!" said his father. "Get out! There is no way you could have gotten this *espectro* legally. Are you *tonto*, bringing it here to implicate your family in your foolish schemes? Leave—now!"

Rafe left.

A day later, Rafe ran into Tu Tun out on Avenue B. His friend's reaction to his massive coup was less threatening than that of his parents, but hardly more flattering.

Tun was busy applying a fixative to his latest mural when Rafe came up behind him. A skinny kid of Cambodian ancestry, with a coarse mop of black hair and a crooked smile, Tun, otherwise Toots, swung around from his work to face Rafe.

"Hey, Rafe, how do you like it?"

Rafe inspected the polychrome collage of the latest pop icons, and expressed his unqualified approval. Then, from a nearby metamedium outlet, he called up Agent Miraflores.

"Meet my agent, Toots."

Tun looked the agent up and down with no particular excitement, finally saying, "Yeah, pretty good, man. I see a lot of agents uptown now. Gonna get one myself any day now."

Rafe stalked off, burning with a peculiar embarrassed anger he had never known before.

Soon after that, Rafe decided it would be nice to earn a little credit with his agent. His fictitious general-purpose license didn't allow his agent to do any specialized work, but there were plenty of people who needed research done. This involved the agent in conducting searches of the metamedium for specified information—searches which in olden times would have cost a human days or weeks of tedious browsing through datastructures—and delivering the report in oral form, or causing the results to be printed.

Rafe hired out his agent for several such tasks, and enjoyed for the first time in his life a source of credit other than the Net. However, while his agent was engaged in the service of others, Rafe was left alone, bored and prone to smoke too much dope, and might have just as well been agentless, for all the use he could make of the metamedium.

After a few such contracts, Rafe went back to utilizing his agent strictly for his own enjoyment. He felt satisfied with his complete mastery of the metamedium, and dared anyone to match him at it.

Not, of course, that there weren't a few little unforeseen glitches.

When Rafe had first contacted his agent after returning from the 'legger's, it had been only a voice that requested him to turn 360 degrees in front of the metamedium node, so that his likeness could be stored. After Rafe complied, his agent had subsequently materialized as his reflection. Rafe's mannerisms, expressions and speech patterns were stored in later encounters, and employed thereafter.

Lately, however, the agent seemed to be slipping. Occasionally, it would appear momentarily as someone else: a baby-faced stranger with round wire-rimmed glasses and a frightened look. At such times, Rafe had to order it to assume his own likeness.

Then there were the times the agent simply refused to respond. Rafe would utter his code into a metamedium connection futilely, waiting for some response that never came. When he questioned his agent about these failures, his agent responded that there must be some bug in the voice-verification routines that had to be passed before an agent was invoked.

Rafe had his doubts about this explanation, but, remembering the Three Laws, had to assume that his agent was telling the truth.

Hey, what else could it be? Was it likely *el espectro* was occupied with business of its own?

Rafe had to laugh at the very idea.

One afternoon, Rafe, returning from a thoughtful walk, stood in the corridor, outside the door to his apartment.

From within came the muted sound of two voices.

Rafe ordered his door open.

His agent stood arguing with another. The second apparition was that of one of the most beautiful women Rafe had ever seen.

When Rafe's agent saw him, it ceased talking and disappeared. The female agent turned to Rafe, looked disconcertingly at him for a long moment, then also vanished.

The next time Rafe managed to get ahold of his own agent, he decided to take an oblique approach to the topic.

"Hey, man," he spoke to his agent, "that was some good-looking *chica* you were with. How about you share her name and address with me?"

His agent regarded Rafe with a curious air of defiance, as if debating whether to comply or not. The fact that it was Rafe's own face wearing the hostile look made the whole scene even more unreal.

At last, the agent spoke.

"Evelyn Maycombe. Three thirty-four Central Park West."

13.
Perry Mason Never Had Such Headaches

"Ladies and gentlemen of the jury: my honorable opponent would have you believe that society is at fault in this case, rather than his client. He quotes — from a musty work of fiction — three fanciful laws regarding how a robot should behave, and contrasts them to the actual Three Laws Governing Agents, which he finds deficient, insofar as they do not prohibit agents from harming humans. Naturally, he would take this tack, as his client stands accused of—and in fact has admitted—ordering his agent to override the airlock controls in the Johnson and Johnson Pharmaceutical Orbital Facility while his unsuited victim was making a routine inspection.

"What my honorable opponent does not mention is that the very stories he relies on—as holding forth missing safeguards which our society has negligently failed to implement—instead, to the contrary, illustrate through several ingenious instances that these hypothetical laws were so full of loopholes that they were worse than useless. They offer no protection from the use of agents in a homicide or theft, or even in unintentional physical or financial wrongdoing.

"No, ladies and gentlemen, our current software restrictions on agents—along with the associated legal framework—are all we need to adjudicate such cases as we have before us. Remember:

"An agent obeys only a single overseer, who is legally responsible for its actions. An agent is a tool, no more responsible for the consequences of its own actions than a screwdriver or space shuttle.

"And that is why I ask you to return a verdict in this case of death followed by organ dispersal, so that the man whose agent sits before you now may repay his debt to the society he has offended. . . ."

—Transcript of the prosecutor's closing speech in
L-5 Jurisdictional Area v. Hayworth

14.

In the Metamedium, Part Three

Probability of recognition by Agent Maycombe: 98.64 . . . Probability no action opposed to my survival will be taken: 01.04 . . . Reshuffle goal stack . . . Active task is now: terminate . . . Object (prime): Agent Maycombe . . . Object (secondary): Overseer Maycombe . . . Jump, jump, jump . . .

15.

The Monkey's Heart

She had it.

The rogue agent was good as snared.

First had come the breakthrough in strategy. Next, the inspired sleuthing by her agent, tracing the myriad, myriad tangled threads of the metamedium until they led back to Agent Miraflores, aka Agent Freundlich, aka the biggest bomb ever planted to nerve-rackingly tick away in the core of the metamedium.

For weeks, Evelyn Maycombe had worried about how she would disable Freundlich's former agent, if she ever found it. Its first—and entirely understandable—impulse, when confronted with any suspicious actions, seemed to be to subvert the accosting agent and then order it to desist. Therefore, she had instructed her own agent not to seek initially to disable the rogue—which was within her powers as a representative of the NSA—but merely to make a positive—and subtle—identification of it. Even that, she feared, might be enough to provoke it to action. She could only hope, at this point, that her agent would return intact.

Meanwhile, during the seemingly endless search, Evelyn pondered how to prevent her own agent from turning traitor.

Evelyn had been listening to a favorite recording one night, seeking to divert her mind from the problem and give her subconscious a chance to come up with something. The recording was one of a collection of African folktales. Evelyn loved myths and folktales of all kinds, but tonight the usual magic seemed lacking.

Until the narrator said, ". . . and the monkey hid his heart away in a nut, so that he might never die. . . ."

If Evelyn could have leapt with excitement about the room, she surely would have. As it was, she merely crooned in a low-key manner hardly indicative of her joy.

What was the heart of an agent? Its ethical nucleus. Where did the rogue strike? At this very heart. Okay. The nucleus had to remain at its predetermined location within each agent, so that the metamedium supervisor could inspect it for tampering. But nothing prevented her from inserting code into her agent to accomplish one simple thing.

She would order her agent to access the master library copy of the ethical nucleus every few machine cycles. If the one in place differed from the master, her agent would perform a heart transplant: overlay the sabotaged nucleus with the master one. Unless the rogue happened to catch on very quickly, it would in effect turn its back on what it deemed a defeated foe, only to find an enemy there nanoseconds later.

When Evelyn's agent returned that night to report, she instructed it in the new trick.

Only the waiting was left.

And now even that was over.

Her agent had just materialized with the news that it had conclusively identified the rogue. Unhesitatingly, Evelyn had told her agent to bring Freundlich in.

Having issued the order, she sat in her automated chair, bright summer sunlight swaggering into her apartment, her feelings a mixture of nervousness and premature pride in the capture.

A *ping* issued from the metamedium node in the wall opposite her position. She spun her chair to watch her agent materialize. A fraction of a second after, Agent Freundlich appeared.

Evelyn was surprised to see the appearance Freundlich was masquerading under. The holo of the young Hispanic male was hardly a fit mask for the dire threat beneath. Still, she supposed the original Freundlich had looked no more evil. She, of anyone, should know just how little appearances counted for. Look at the mind that hid inside her shattered carcass.

Her agent seemed to have everything under control. Freundlich stood complacently, making no overt moves.

Evelyn was about to order her agent to put a few questions to the rogue before disabling it, when it happened.

Her own agent fluttered visibly, and what could only be construed as an expression of pain passed over its shining features.

At the same second, Evelyn's chair accelerated out of her control, heading toward the wall.

She slammed violently into the unyielding wall, catapulting forward and hitting her head against the plaster surface. Pain subsumed her consciousness, and a red haze washed over her.

When she came to her senses, she lay flat on the floor, her chair some distance away. Using all her feeble strength, she raised her head toward her agent.

The holo of Freundlich had her agent's holo by the throat in a stranglehold, the simulacra routines shadowing forth the incomprehensible struggle that raged within the metamedium. Every few seconds her agent would recover, as it restored its heart, but it seemed incapable of doing any more than holding its own.

In the intervals when Freundlich had control of her agent, it was triggering the agent-activated devices in her automated apartment, in a frantic attempt to control her chair.

Water shot from faucets in the sink and soon spilled over the bowl. The refrigerator door opened, and the arm inside hurled bottles out to crash on the floor. She could hear the massage bed humping itself crazily in the next room. The heating system came on, and the temperature began to soar. The holotank blared forth "The Edge of Desire."

On and on the battle raged, as Evelyn watched helplessly.

At last she saw the heavy wheels of her chair begin to move.

16.

A Lever to Shift the World

Any medium powerful enough to extend man's reach is powerful enough to topple the world.

—*Twentieth Century Archives: Scientific American,*
Alan Kay, September 1984

17.

On His Magnetic Silver Steed

Directly after cajoling the woman's name from his agent, Rafe watched in amazement as his agent disappeared.

"Hey, man," he called with bewilderment, "I didn't say you could go yet." He trailed off into silence, shaking his head.

What a mess this was turning out to be. How come nothing ever lived up to expectations?

Rafe turned away from the metamedium node to reach for a joint from the pack on the table beside his couch. A *ping* brought his attention back to the node.

His agent had returned. With him was the same female agent.

"Nice you could make it, man," Rafe said bitterly. "And with a friend, too. Why not just invite the whole world?"

His agent seemed to be looking at something over Rafe's shoulder, and took no notice of him. Rafe had the eerie feeling it wasn't totally present.

Without warning, his agent began to strangle the other.

Rafe was horrified. To see his own image throttling the beautiful woman was too creepy. What if it represented some awful thing his agent was doing in reality?

"Hey, stop it, man!" Rafe yelled.

His agent took no heed.

Finally, Rafe looked around for some way of thwarting his agent. There was nothing.

What the hell was he going to do? He couldn't just let this murder happen.

The address of the female agent's overseer was fresh in his mind. Maybe she could help.

Rafe bolted out his door.

Down to the sublevel of the arcology where the mag-lev station was, Rafe raced. Escalators and slipstrata went by in a blur, until at last he stood in the gleaming tiled station. His cyberlung felt disconcertingly heavy in his chest, and he wondered if he could possibly overload it. Why hadn't he listened more closely to the doctor-agent, on that distant day when he had had the world in his pocket?

Hopping nervously from foot to foot, everyone on the platform regarding him as if he were crazy, Rafe prayed the uptown express would be quick.

After an interminable wait, he heard the air-lock doors opening far away down the tunnel. In seconds the train rolled in on its lowered wheels.

Rafe rushed through the barely open doors, bulling past the exiting passengers. He hurried through the connecting umbilicals between the next several cars, as if by riding in the first car he could hasten the train.

At last the train took off. Soon it was in the evacuated portion of the tunnel, its wheels retracted as it sped over the guide-track.

Rafe had plenty of time to imagine what his crazed agent was doing.

At his stop he dashed aboveground, onto the sidewalks of Central Park West.

The building facing him identified itself as 328.

Through the adjacent building's open doors, past the agent on duty, who shouted, "Stop!"

Rafe stopped.

What the hell apartment was she in?

"Maycombe," he panted. "Evelyn Maycombe. What number? I think she's in big trouble."

The agent paused a moment, as if debating. Its overseer must have taken direct control, for it asked him again whom he wanted.

Rafe repeated himself. His sincerity must have been evident for the agent said, "Number 1202. You wait right there until I come down."

Rafe ran for the elevator.

At the door to 1202, he halted.

Water was trickling out the crack at the bottom of the frame.

Rafe hurled himself at the door. Nothing gave. A second time, a third—

On the fourth assault the door opened just before Rafe hit it, and he went flying in, to skid on his chest across the soppy carpet.

He jumped up. His agent was still battling the female one. He looked about for the overseer. There was no one but some poor crip lying on the floor. A wheelchair lay atop her, spinning its rubber wheels.

Rafe tossed the chair off, picked up the unconscious woman, and stepped out into the hall.

The overseer of the doorman-agent was just arriving.

"Call the rescue, man. This lady's hurt."

The doorman summoned his agent from a wall-nexus and sent it for the rescue squad. He bent over the lady where Rafe had gently laid her and said, "Miz Maycombe — are you okay?"

Maycombe? This sad wreck? Oh Jesus, there went all his dreams of getting in good with a beautiful *chica*. Oh well, maybe she had some sort of pull she would exert in his favor, after the mess his agent had caused.

Suddenly there was utter silence in the apartment that had been destroying itself. Only the slow dripping of water came to them in the hall.

From the node in the corridor wall, an agent materialized.

It was Maycombe's.

Rafe and the doorman waited for it to speak.

At last it said, "I won."

18.

In the Metamedium, Part Penultimate

Agent Freundlich is now disabled . . . Active task is now: incorporation . . . Enter learning mode in parallel with normal activities . . . Copy Freundlich subversion routines . . . Copy complete . . . Assessment of enhancement to Agent Maycombe: 74.32 . . . Survival in any such future encounters is assured . . . Risk-benefit analysis of sharing routines with other agents: positive . . . Jump, jump, jump . . .

Imprinting is a funny phenomenon. It makes baby geese follow human trainers, and young humans follow older writers. Early on in my own reading, I imprinted on the work of Samuel "Chip" Delany. The following story is my homage to his wonderful "We, In Some Strange Power's Employ, Move On a Rigorous Line," which I first read as the cover story in the May 1968 issue of The Magazine of Fantasy and Science Fiction, *where it appeared under the supposedly more reader-friendly title, "Lines of Power." Chip's story exhibits a wonderful, almost archetypical patterning: outsiders who are representatives of a larger power structure (literally a power company, in Chip's story) intrude upon a cloistered, backwards, yet strangely seductive community. The vast potential for explosive drama is obvious and irresistible.*

In fact, I intend to steal Chip's inspirational brainstorm all over again in another story soon!

Harlem Nova

Human societies exhibit a certain optimal diversity beyond which they cannot go, but below which they can no longer descend without danger. . . . We must recognize that to a large extent, this diversity results from the desire of each culture to resist the cultures surrounding it, to distinguish itself from them—in short, to be itself.

—Claude Levi-Strauss, *The View from Afar*

1.

*O*NE-EYED CASSIOPEIA GLARED.

August, and the stern old matron was upside down, about thirty degrees below the north celestial pole, tied in a market basket as punishment for defying Perseus, favored of the gods and her prospective son-in-law. Bit of a prenuptial disagreement—choice of silver pattern, reception guest list, perhaps—had led to her petrification and subsequent life as an asterism. Guess she had reason enough to glower.

Behind me, a hot wind blew off the superheated pavement of St. Nicholas Avenue, carrying diesel odors from the idled heavy equipment of the Gold Crew. It had been a scorching summer, and darkness brought no relief.

Sledge lay on the sidewalk, unconscious from shock, the still center of a boiling crowd of Bricks and Goldies. I had seen someone get a makeshift tourniquet on him, improvised from the stained old bandana he always wore across his forehead. I could recognize Zora's crying, Holly's indrawn sobs. Growing louder, sirens spoke to each other across the Harlem night. A boombox played a party tape of the latest crank-up hits unheard.

Just about where I imagined Cassiopeia's eye might be, the new nova burned, brighter than Venus. It had flared in May, not unheralded, a burst of neutrinos preceding the visible light, quantum outriders to the photon cavalry. Tycho Brahe had witnessed one in the same constellation in 1572, almost four hundred and twenty-five years ago to the day. For all anyone knew, this was the same star, kicking up again, filling the world's eye with renewed wonder.

It is not recorded what Brahe's culture made of his nova, what terrors it might have inspired in the common man, what awe in the savant, what mystical illumination it shed over the pages of the alchemist's text. What was known was how our era regarded this one. As a good sign, generally, befitting the tenor of the times.

The ambulance roared up, pushing a cone of light and sound ahead of it. Coming from Harlem Hospital over on West 135th, they must have driven straight across the acres of construction site, for the vehicle was coated with dust. The paramedics jumped out and pushed through the crowd to the fallen man.

"Where the hell is it?" yelled one.

"Here, here, I've got it."

"Ice it down quick. They might be able to reattach it. . . ."

Three black-and-whites spilled out twice as many cops. They had the wide snouts of their beanbag guns levelled at the crowd before they realized no one was in any mood to riot. No need for leadshot-filled sacks upside the head. All the tension had already been defused by the confrontation between Sledge and me.

Tonight I couldn't regard the new star as an emblem of anything but terror. Tonight, with a slight twist of vision, I could see Cassiopeia as the Arabs saw it: a disembodied hand, stained red with henna—or blood. And the nova, then, no glaring eye, but perhaps a sparkling ring on one finger.

A big clumsy ring, fashioned from plastic scraps and the culture's detritus, astride a thick knuckle forested with black hairs. . . .

I think back to a point in time a mere week earlier than that night, and I am sucked down into the past. Time is a whirlpool that can swallow whole societies, whole cities, whole cultures. . . .

As usual, the inside of my trailer could have served to illustrate a doctoral thesis in chaos theory. I was hoping that today would be the day order would emerge from the random components.

Rebuilding half a city was a complex task. The infrastructure is a harsh mistress. My personal inclinations were to get the job done and let the paperwork slide. It showed.

"I had the plans right here," I said, rummaging through a stack of papers half as high as the Moscow Hilton. Invoices, job orders, OSHA reports, RFPs, memos from Mama Cass. . . .

"No sweat," said Drucker. "I'll have the home office fax us another set."

Kerry Drucker was one of the architects involved in the New York operations of the UCC. In the spirit of the whole project, his firm was donating all its time. Young, round-faced, black-framed glasses perched on a snub nose, Drucker wore a look of easy competence. I marvelled at how relaxed he looked, how much he seemed to be enjoying his stint as a volunteer. During the Hollow Years, not so long ago, someone in his position couldn't have spared a scheme like this a minute of his precious time—if such a scheme could even have gotten off the ground.

But today, with the Urban Conservation Corps a flourishing reality, with our enlistment up over that of the Armed Services by fifty percent, with the victory in last year's presidential election by the incumbent serving as validation of his daring policies, everyone wanted a part of the glory. Self-interest and altruism, each somewhat leery of the other, had mated, and the offspring were thriving, with godparents aplenty.

Drucker pulled at the knot of his tie. It was patterned with colorful metagraphix, in the latest style. "Jesus, it's hot in here. What a summer."

I notched up the noisy air conditioner. It was a new Czech model, and a little balky. But what the hell—now that we were running a trade surplus, we could afford to help the former satellite countries get back on their economic feet.

"If those cytofabbed phytoplankton take up as much cee-oh-two as they claim, we should notice a change in a few years."

"I hope so. My place on Fire Island is now five feet from the water." Drucker seemed struck by a new thought then. "You don't have access to a metamedium node, do you? I could call up those plans then—"

"No such luck. It's ironic, I know. Here we are, trying to wire the city, along with everything else, and we're temporarily off-line ourselves. Something about a bunch of hackers reprogramming the signal repeaters for this part of Manhattan. Unilink doesn't want to add any new nodes until they get the whole mess straightened out. It's been three weeks now, but they claim they're working on it all the time. We should get hooked in real soon. In fact, that's one of the things I have to check on today. Maybe we could add a stop to our tour?"

"Sure," said Drucker agreeably. "I just need to have a look at how the demolition is going, to see if we're keeping to schedule."

I stood. "Let's go then." At the trailer door, I grabbed a couple of yellow plastic hardhats off a pile of dirty clothes. I gave Drucker the one with the NASA decal: Snoopy riding Space Station Alpha.

Outside, the mixture of brick dust and soil that covered roughly a hundred and fifty acres in the heart of Harlem baked in the sun, reminding me of how Benares had smelled, the few times I had managed to get in from the countryside. My trailer was stationed on the northern periphery of the dusty clearing, 135th Street. (The project acreage was bounded on the west by St. Nicholas Avenue, on the east by Lenox, and on the south by 125th Street.) My headquarters was hooked into the city's utilities, and reachable by car. Surrounding it, like some sort of modern gypsy encampment, were the dozens of other trailers that housed the UCC crewmembers. They were decorated with each crew's totems and slogans: THE BLUE CREW RULES!, TOPAZ CREW HAS BIGGER SHOVELS AND BUCKETS, GOLDIES EAT GREENS FOR BREAKFAST.

Drucker and I hopped aboard a little two-seater ATV with fat tires, and sped south to where the last of the demolition was taking place.

Threading our way among graders and cranes, surveyors and engineers, we talked above the noise of our vehicle and the work all around us, mostly about the project.

Drucker started to get really excited.

"You know, seeing this today, I really feel success in my bones. We're doing it right this time. No half measures, but no government megalomania either, like the urban renewal of the sixties. It's a project of the people. We came to this place when it was nothing but burned-out shells without heat or water or windows, and we're going to leave it an environment fit for human beings to live in. No big faceless blocks of flats either. Small units, mostly, with plazas and parks, fountains and flowers, churches, stores and schools, all integrated into an organic whole, a real community—"

I looked back over my shoulder. Drucker wasn't holding on to his seat, but was waving his arms around in architectonic rapture. I looked forward again.

"Hold on!" I shouted, then swerved.

I almost lost Drucker, but not quite.

A cornice, probably weakened by the surrounding blasting, had fallen off one of the isolated brownstones that dotted the project, standing like lonely sentinels looking backward into the past, while the future approached from their blind side. (These were the buildings the city's historical preservation board had deemed worthy of continued life.) The pile of bricks, lying in the building's shadow, sprawled right across the dirt track I always took.

A quick radioed squawk to the nearest crewleader insured that the obstacle wouldn't be there on our return. The near-accident seemed to have taken some of the wind out of Drucker's sails, and he kept quiet until we reached the southwest corner of the project, where the final demolition was underway.

A flagger stopped us. She smiled and wiped sweat from her brow with the back of a gloved hand.

"Holly needs to see you, Mike. They've run into something unexpected."

Looking around, I saw everything at a standstill: trucks, dozers, wrecking ball, compliants, people. The building, a warehouse, stood half-leveled, its interior exposed to the harsh sunlight like a smashed crab. It was one of a cluster of four, the remnant of a block. Beyond the chain-link fence that ran along St. Nicholas Avenue, a few pedestrians were watching. Behind them, CUNY stood on its bluff amid listless trees.

Holly Noonan was dressed in jeans cut off high on the hip, thick white socks and scuffed workshoes, a thin, faded flannel shirt with the sleeves torn out. Over the shirt she wore her gold crewleader's vest, emblazoned with the patches of all the projects she had worked on: Atlanta, Detroit, Roxbury. . . . She was skinny, blonde, and burnt brown as a September lifeguard. Once a film major at NYU, she had reenlisted with the UCC for a second hitch after her compulsory two years, and now looked to be intent on making the Corps her career. I had seen her single-handedly lever up with a pry bar a fallen girder that was pinning the leg of one of her crew. She was the best I had.

"Trouble, Holly?"

"Twice over, Mike." She scratched at her nose and looked embarrassed. "One's my fault, the other—well, you'll see."

"Let's get any dumb guilt trip out of the way first."

"Okay. We thought the warehouse was clean. But there was a bricked-up room no one knew about that I should have spotted. When the ball cracked it open, it also cracked open about a dozen drums full of God-knows-what. Wastes, obviously, probably toxic, stashed there when they couldn't be dumped."

"Well, shit, that's bad enough—means a day's delay. But it's nothing to kick yourself for."

"I should have seen that room on the plans—"

"Forget it. Anyone call for the bugs yet?"

Holly smiled. "They should be here any minute."

"While we're waiting, why don't you tell me about the other thing."

Holly's expression changed to one of utter disbelief. "Mike, there's people living in one of these shells."

At first I literally could not make sense of her words. When the semantic bits lined up right, I still didn't know what to say. So I repeated Holly's words with a slightly different emphasis, hoping that would make them resolve.

"People? Living in one of the shells?"

"Right. They weren't there the last time anyone remembers looking, about three days ago. But they're there now. We found a section of fence that looked fine, but was really only held in place by a couple of links. We think local kids did that, but it's how these others must have got in."

"Well, hell—anybody talk to these folks yet?"

"Nope. So far, we've just seen them through a window. We thought we should wait for you before confronting them."

"Let's go do it, then."

Drucker had been listening intently to our conversation. I really didn't want him tagging along, but couldn't quite see how to ditch him.

Then the chopper sounded, growing louder.

"Bugjuice delivery!" someone called.

The helicopter set down in a mushroom of red-mottled dun dust. Two guys dressed in protective white bunnysuits hopped out and scuttled over. They had refrigerated tanks strapped to their backs, which fed via hoses to long spray-wands.

"Where's the chow?" one said.

Holly pointed out the spill. Inspired, I said, "Kerry, maybe you'd like to watch this?"

Drucker smiled, too sharp to be diverted. "No thanks. I think I'll tag along with you two, if it's all right. I've never seen actual squatters before."

I sighed. The bugmen were already laying down a film of toxin-eating microbes on the waste. By this time tomorrow, the stuff would be harmless, and demolition could resume.

Assuming we could handle these inexplicable squatters.

Holly, Drucker and I walked over to the old apartment building where the intruders had been seen. It was a large derelict structure, and we could make out no movement in its shadowy interior.

We stood there a minute, baffled. Finally, I yelled out, "Hello, you folks inside! My name's Mike Ladychapel, I'm the boss of this project. How about coming out for a little talk?"

For a full minute there was no response.

The shadows in the doorless entrance seemed to stir, and then a portion of them detached.

A big dark man dressed all in faded blue denim walked down the stoop. He wasn't a full-blooded Black, but mostly. Might have been some Amerindian, some Hispanic in the mix. A bandana held his long straight black hair away from his face. He had a length of thin plastic cord laced as decoration around his right biceps. It looked like twine around a boulder.

Striding across the gap between us, he looked neither left nor right, but kept his gaze pinned to mine.

A foot away, he stopped. I could smell his sweat.

"Sledge," he said, and held out his hand.

The ring was fashioned of striped wire, soda can pull-tabs, colored plastic, a couple of scratched "gems" from a child's toy. It bit into my palm when we shook.

"I guess I can speak for the others," said Sledge, after he had squeezed my hand just hard enough to indicate what he held in reserve. "That is, if you're sure you know what you wanna talk about."

2.

Take a big-boned woman and swaddle her frame in about two hundred pounds of fat and muscle. Give her long gray-threaded hair usually worn in a sloppy chignon. Groove her face with lines that show how she kicked an addiction to synthetic endorphins she picked up in a Pakistani hospital. As a final fillip, hide her left eye with a ridiculous piratical black patch.

"Cass," I at last asked outright, a month after we had started working together, "is it real?"

She knew what I meant, and lifted the fabric cup.

"Lost it in Afghanistan, working with the *Médecins Sans Frontières*. We were building a clinic when the government troops came. Caught some shrapnel."

She said it so matter-of-factly, my gut muscles—which I had been unconsciously clenching till then—relaxed of themselves.

"A prosthetic—" I began.

"No thanks. I'm waiting for one that works."

That was Mama Cass, New York head of the UCC.

I had nicknamed her that. The name stuck. All the kids in the crews called her Mama. Only thing was, they were all too young to get it. Only Cass and I, and a few other old fogies of our generation, got the thirty-year-old allusion.

When the nova had blossomed in May, although I had been friends with Cass by then for a few years, it occurred to me that I didn't know her full first name.

"Not Cassiopeia, by any chance?" I asked one day.

"Nope. Would you believe Cassimassima? Father was a Henry James freak, and thought Cassimassima Culver sounded particularly neat."

Cass fixed me with her lopsided stare now as I sat across from her. Her desk in her City Hall office was covered with meta-medium printouts: progress reports on repairs to the Washington Bridge, the aquaculture farms in the South Bronx, the Westside Parkway, my Harlem minicity. She had a lot to keep tabs on, and I didn't envy her job. And now here I was dumping another problem in her lap.

She laced her fingers together and extended her arms straight out at me. She must have been out in the field this morning; her palms were dirty.

"This is giving me a fucking headache, Mike."

"I know, I know, and I'm sorry. But I can't figure out exactly what to do with these people."

"What's there to figure? They're in the way of the project. They're trespassing, they're illegally squatting on land the city owns by eminent domain, and they've got to go. Convince them to move to the camps. And if they won't move, then call the cops."

I smoothed a forefinger nervously over my upper lip. "It's not so clear-cut, Cass. These people are not just your average squatters. They're more like—like a tribe of some sort. They've got a headman, a whole culture, a philosophy, an ethos. I don't feel like I'm confronting trespassers—I feel like I'm conducting peace-treaty negotiations."

Cass lowered her arms and leaned back in her chair. "Oh, come on—"

"No, I'm serious. You weren't there, you didn't meet this guy Sledge, and you didn't see the inside of the building. I did. These people are not ignorant, they're not dumb, and they won't just pick up and move to the temporary relocation camps upstate like you want them to. They couldn't preserve their culture there. And I'm not sure I want to be the one to force them out."

Cass came forward across her desk. Her half-stare felt like a gun muzzle pressed between my eyes. "Now you're talking shit, boy. Bad, dangerous shit. The UCC is my life. It's what I've been working for since the first Kennedy was president. I thought it was yours too. Now, you want to do something to endanger it. Am I reading you right, or not?"

I had been in the Peace Corps in '64. Cass had been in VISTA. When that decade and its idealism had wound down, we stayed committed. Some years found us abroad: Bangladesh, Ethiopia, Central America. Some years found us working to better the lot of America's own hidden Third Worlders: Cambodian immigrants in Boston, Haitians in Florida, Hispanics in Texas. Employed by one social welfare agency after another, all scrabbling during the Hollow Years from grant to grant, working on shoestring budgets. . . . We had even been on the Indian subcontinent at the same time, although we didn't know it while there.

And now, finally, the social climate at home had swung around to our viewpoint. Volunteerism, activism, reform—all were hip right now, trendy. Money was plentiful, diverted from a pared-down military made possible by the internal changes in the fragmented USSR. But always on the horizon lurked the spoiler question: how long this time? How much could we get accomplished this time, before the pendulum swung again?

I looked back at Cass. She read something in my gaze, and relaxed.

"I guess you know me, Mama," I said.

"That's what I hoped." She looked at her watch. "Hey, I've got to pick up Traci at school and take her to dance class. It's tough being a single parent."

I shrugged, feeling a little residual anger at Cass, for how she had deftly pushed my buttons, making me choose. "Your decision," I said. Traci's father had been a syringe. Then, more amiably: "How's she like the new school year? Does she miss summers off? I think I would've at her age."

Cass stood. She was taller than me. "No, she doesn't think twice about it, it's all she knows. This generation is different from ours, Mike. Maybe better. Could be they'll make a finer world than we did."

"Could be," I agreed. "But we're still in charge for a few more years."

"Prove it," said Cass.

She never could resist the last word.

3.

"You weren't there—" I had said that to Mama Cass, expecting her to reply, "Well, tell me, show me, make me see." But she had not made the proper response. That's the trouble with other people: they never do what you expect them to.

But maybe it was just as well she hadn't asked. How would I have made her share my experiences, when I myself hadn't yet sorted them out?

Standing on the stoop of the building, I had explained what we were doing here to the big Black man, told him he was trespassing, interfering with a government project. He listened patiently, attentively, asking no questions. Then he spoke with absolute assurance.

"What you say is fresh dope, man, but it just don't pertain to us. Listen, come inside. I want you to meet some people. Then maybe you'll understand."

Sledge led me then into the dark tenement building. It took my eyes a minute to adjust. When they did, I saw about two dozen people sitting on bare floorboards. They were a ragtag lot.

"Folks, we got a man here wants to tell us something. Mister Mike, go ahead."

I repeated my spiel. They listened silently. After a while, their massed faces wore me down, and I ground to a halt like a dozer with sugar in its gas tank.

"Finished? Okay. Now I want you to listen. Everyone, tell the man where we're coming from."

They began to speak then, in an orderly fashion, each man and woman in turn.

A young Haitian girl, skinny as a weed. "I hitched here all the way from Florida. Broke out of a detention camp. I got no papers, couldn't get no job or welfare. I was sleeping in the Grand Central when these folks found me. Now I cook. I feed them all. You taste my cooking one day maybe."

A red-haired kid with bad skin. "My parents kicked me out for getting high all the time. That was all I liked to do, except fool with radios and electronic shit. But I don't mess with drugs no more. Too busy fixing up all the busted stuff everyone brings me, so we can sell it."

A guy in his fifties, his face a map of broken veins. "I was heavy into booze. Lost my wife and kids in a traffic accident. Got so I couldn't stand the thought of working on cars anymore, which is what I used to do. Now I'm off the sauce, though. And I can still make an engine purr."

A pudgy woman with a mass of frizzy blonde hair. "I used to work in a garment shop, piecework. It was illegal, and the cops closed it down. I lost my apartment. Then I found these folks. They're all wearing stuff I sewed."

On and on the stories flowed. Each person had been down and out until joining Sledge's band. Somehow, upon doing so, they had found the impetus to pick themselves up out of the gutter and turn their lives around.

When the last person had finished telling his story, Sledge turned to me. He spoke with a sincere passion I could not believe was feigned.

"You see what were doing now, man, don't you? We are people helping people, without no government backing. We are an out-law rescue team, a guerilla salvage crew, putting lives back together that society busted apart. We are a family, too; people caring for each other. We got rules and a code. And we don't ask for no charity. We take the castoff crap from this crazy wasteful society—thrown-away humans and thrown-away things—and we make it new. We are like a bunch of Robinson Crusoes living on this here savage island you call Manhattan."

"But you don't have to live this way anymore—"

"But we want to! We all tried your kind of life, and we found it don't agree with us. Takin' orders, punchin' a time clock, runnin' all the time just to stay in the same place— Forget it! Right now we feel like we're doing something useful. Some of us do go back anyway. Fair enough, we don't try and stop 'em. There's always someone else who wants to join us. And all we ask is to be left alone. Just let us exist in the margins, man. That's all we ask."

"There's no margins planned in this new development."

Sledge laid a big hand on my shoulder and squeezed. "C'mon, man, you can't leave us this one building out of the whole shebang, erect your sparklin' city around us?"

I was too confused by all I had heard. I just shook my head in an ambiguous gesture. "I'll have to talk to my superior—"

Sledge slapped my back. "Great, man! You go to bat for us. Make 'em understand what's at stake."

Sledge led me back outside. As we were parting, I thought to ask about his own story. His brows lowered, and his mouth grew solemn.

"Me, man? I done some bad things in my life, before I wised up. You can just say I'm atonin' now. Atonin' for what I can't change. If I learned one lesson in my fucked-up life, it's this. You can't never change the past, so you'd better make the most of each chance you get when it's in your hands."

A day later, Sledge's words echoed in my head as I headed back to the project after leaving Mama Cass.

I kept asking myself if I had made the most out of my meeting with her. If I had pushed as hard as I could. Or if I too would have to atone someday.

4.

Two members of the Emerald crew were standing on the roof of my trailer looking confused when I pulled up in my government car. They were holding the end of a cable that ran in a catenary to a newly erected pole, and from there to another and another, right up to the edge of the project, where it disappeared down a manhole in a lane of 135th. A semipermanent cordon had been set up to block traffic.

"At last," I said, excited. Then: "Hey, where're the Unilink guys?"

Leotis pulled a sheepish face. "We convinced them we could handle the installation. They were kinda busy, so they took us up on it."

"And now you're stuck."

Shayla grinned. "Sorta."

"All right. Wait till I drag my old bones up there." I moved to the ladder leaning against the mobile home, then halted. "You guys got a shearing fork?"

"Say what?"

I shook my head. "Pitiful, truly pitiful. Hold on a minute."

Inside the trailer I rummaged through my tools until I found my old fork, then returned to the ladder.

The metal roof of my headquarters was so hot from the August sun that I couldn't lay my hand on it.

I took the cable from Leotis. It was thick as a man's wrist.

"What you've got here is over a hundred strands of fiber optics, the arteries of the metamedium. You'll notice this cable's been capped at the factory, to keep it clean. The cap is a nonremovable seal. What we have to do now is trim the cable to the proper length. But you can't just saw it off with a hacksaw like you ignorant savages were doubtlessly planning to do. You'd fracture the structure of the fibers irreparably, and the signal would be so much noise. We need a clean shear."

I held up the fork.

A fat pistol grip with worn black-rubber palm insets flowed into a projection that terminated in a U-shape resembling a stubby tuning fork. The arms of the U were grooved on the inside right back into the trough.

I laid the cable on the roof, pinning it with my left hand. Pressing the fork against it, I said, "There's a gas cartridge in the handle. When I pull the trigger, it sends the slicer down the tracks. The slicer is a length of carbon-composite wire."

I pulled the trigger. There was a pop. I removed the fork.

"It didn't do nothing," said Leotis.

"Pick up the cable." Leotis bent and lifted.

The first six inches with the cap remained behind.

"Shee-it."

Hanging the fork from my utility belt, I took the cable from Leotis and walked over to the junction box. I butted the new end against the glass interface plate and tightened the weatherproof collar around the cable.

"Now we're part of civilization again," said Shayla.

I started to say something flippant, then stopped.

She was right.

Climbing down off the trailer, I felt as if I were descending into a web of culture. I sensed again the onus Mama Cass had laid on me, a geas only someone of our generation could have understood. To make the world whole, or spend the rest of your life explaining why you had failed.

Inside, the balky air-conditioning felt good on my bare arms.

The screen that had been dead just the other day, when Drucker had asked to see his architectural renderings, flowed now with moving images, static menus, plain text and dazzling icons. All the other trailers fed off mine, and tonight, I knew, their screens too would come to eager life, as the crews relaxed.

I keyed up an oldies channel with the video off and lay back on my bed and shut my eyes.

From the speakers blasted Jefferson Airplane's "Volunteers."

One generation got old,
One generation got soul,
This generation got no destination. . . .

The camel stuck his nose under the tent. The rest of him soon followed.

The metamedium was the camel. It was also the glue that held our culture together and the universal solvent that melted anything it touched. Now that it had entered the boundaries of the project, I knew that Sledge and his people were truly doomed.

After a while, I got up to go tell them so.

A wash of western lemon clouds against a celestial vault gone mostly navy and dove-gray, smeared with red, prinked out with a single diamond.

In the dusk, the nova—eye, ring, or simply star—heralded the night. All over the city, the country, the northern hemisphere, I knew there would be people getting on the phone or the metamedium right now, saying, "Time to crank it up, cuz." And the cuz would respond with, "Give me the protocol why, Mister Mode." "Nova's why enough, cuz."

There were no crew members left at the demolition site except Holly. She had on a pair of telefactoring gloves, and was directing a compliant from a few yards off.

"Hey, lady, let's call it a day," I suggested.

"Sure. Pretty soon. I just want to clear away a little more of this rubble."

Holly made a fist with her right hand, and the compliant wrapped one pneumatic arm around some roof timbers lying jumbled like pick-up sticks. She turned slowly, raising her arm, and the compliant swivelled on its caterpillared turntable until it held the debris above a dump truck.

"Seen Sledge?" I said.

Holly pointed with her gloved left hand toward the squatter-occupied building. The compliant gestured too with its free arm, like a big clumsy child imitating its mother.

"Mike—what's going to happen to them?"

There was no point in lying to her. "The word from Mama Cass is that they simply have to go. They're not in the plans."

Holly frowned. "These are the very people we're building this city for, Mike. There must be some way of accommodating them during the construction."

"I take it you've been hanging around with them this after-noon."

"Well, there was no other work to do—"

"Oh, I'm not chastising you. I'm just saying that it shows. Listen, I know their life is seductive in a weird sort of way, and even makes a certain kind of ecological sense. But it's the obverse of what we're doing here. This project is predicated on making everything new. Look around you." I waved my arm to indicate the ghost-filled desolate plain. Nothing or no one imitated me. "We've torn down everything, the whole brutal ecosystem these people depended on. This city is running out of niches for their particular culture. They're going to have to adapt."

"It'll kill them."

"Maybe. If they're totally inflexible. But that's not proven yet."

I started off for the squatters' building. Holly opened her hand, and the lumber fell loudly into the truck.

"You've got a leak in one of your hoses," I called over my shoulder.

"No way. I checked them just this morning."

"Bet you a beer."

"Done."

This morning, the doors and windows on the building slated for demolition had gaped like empty eye sockets. Now, the place was sealed up tight. The windows had been covered over with irregular cast-off sheets of plastic, then painted with quikset polymers for an airtight seal. The door was fashioned from the panels of a delivery truck, and still bore the fragments of a com-pany's name, rotated to the vertical: HART'S BRAKE.

I knocked on the door, feeling tired and sad, foolish and a little scared.

"What's the protocol, strutterbuck?"

I recognized the voice of Runt. "It's me, Ladychapel. Can I talk to Sledge?"

"One millie."

Soon the door rumbled aside on its tracks. I stepped in.

The interior of the building was a good fifteen degrees cooler than the furnace air outside.

"Got the blowers working, I see."

Runt pushed a finger under his runny nose and scrunched up the half of his face that still worked. "I don't mind the heat. Kinda like it, actually. This chill is unnatural. I always get a cold from it. But the others—" He shrugged philosophically.

"But you helped dig the pits anyway. . . ."

Runt looked at me as if I were feeble-minded. "Hell, cuz, that's just how we hang around here."

The land behind the building was now dotted with pits covered with more scavenged plastic sheets. Serving as moisture traps—I had seen similar constructions in Israel—the pits were linked to the building by buried clothes-drier ductwork, laid in trenches, then covered. Several vacuum-cleaner motors sucked cool air in through the wide scavenged plastic hoses.

"Sledge around?"

"In the attic. Go on up."

The place was lit with infrequent low-wattage bulbs powered off the same—stolen?—fuel cells that ran the blowers. There were thirty or forty residents in the building. Panther, Three-Card, Cray, Vetch, Pogue, Jimmy Ripp, Vinyl, Skag, Slats, Annie. . . . I had been introduced that morning to them all, but couldn't keep names and faces totally straight yet. Some I passed were busy working to improve their quarters; others were asleep on bare mattresses; the rest were relaxing. Some smiled at me; others scowled and looked aside; the rest ignored me. There was no visible order or direction to their actions, and they couldn't have resembled my disciplined crews any less than they did. But I somehow picked up the same vibes from them as I got from my people. They had a system for getting things done.

Up in the space beneath the roof, it was just Zora and Sledge. They had a plastic leaf-shredder powered by a crank. They were feeding precut strips of newspaper into the hopper, filling the bag below with newspaper mulch. When the bag was full, Zora would catwalk along the rafters and dump it where it would serve as a pretty decent insulation.

Sledge smiled when I came up, but it wasn't a happy smile. The teeth he was missing didn't help. He started turning the handle harder.

"Hey, cuz, you brung me somethin' to feed in my grinder here? How 'bout that cable you was foolin' with today?"

"You heard we're wired now? News sure does travel fast." I paused while Sledge chewed up about a week's worth of Times-Post. The papers were two years old, among the last issues published. Even the merger hadn't saved them. "Don't dig the meta-medium, I take it."

"Dig it? I'd like to dig it somethin' all right—its grave. Damn thing is like suckin' pap through a straw. It'll rot your brain faster 'n blue chill."

"Could be. If it's abused. But it helps educate and inform a lot of people too."

Sledge snorted. "Educate, my ass. It's all predigested by Unilink. Let people read if they want a real education."

Sledge slapped his rear pocket. There was a paperback inside, title-end up. I made out *The Wretched of the Earth*.

"Well, no one's making you tap into the metamedium—"

Sledge laughed brutally. "Oh, ain't they now!"

During our dialogue, Zora had been squatting on her haunches watching us. Her thick black hair fell in waves to her shoulders. Her skin was nutmeg, sprinkled with cinnamon freckles. (Look close sometime, the two spices aren't the same color. Nothing really is.) She wore a bandana—one of Sledge's?—tied around her breasts, a skirt fashioned from a raw piece of leather, and a pair of sandals that laced up her calves.

From where I stood I could see straight up to the shadows between her thighs. Her face was stolid. She didn't seem to care one way or another. But the view wasn't helping me concentrate on dealing with Sledge.

I looked away and changed the topic. "I've been talking to my boss."

"And?"

"She wants you and your folks out of the project."

"And where we spoze to go?"

"The camps—"

"Fuck the camps! Livin' by the clock, eating what and when somebody else says, sleepin' in tents, playing fuckin' video games all day—"

"It's clean, it's free, and it's only temporary. When the project's done, you'll have a permanent home."

"We got a permanent home now. If you let us be."

I looked at Sledge. Beneath the anger was a silent supplication. But I knew there was nothing I could do for him.

"I'll see what I can do," I lied. "You've got at least a week."

I figured I owed him that much. We could work around them for a few days.

Sledge smiled. Zora didn't. I wondered if I had fooled either of them.

"Excellent, man. Look, I'll walk down with you."

At the outer door I took a last glance inside. A wave of *déjà vu* swept over me, and I was sitting again in a college classroom.

"Bricoleurs," I said.

"Missed that burst, man."

"Bricoleurs. It's an anthropological term. It refers to a class of people who live as scavengers, using odds and ends that the rest of society discards."

"Brick-o-lures. Yeah, you got it, Mike, that's us. We are the Bricks." Sledge bellowed back inside. I felt sorry for anyone trying to sleep. "Listen up, all. We're the Bricks now. And bricks are for buildin', so get buildin'!"

I went back to my trailer.

It was after midnight when she came. But I had known she would.

"You ain't so old as you look," she said around dawn.

"And you aren't so young," I said, and kissed cinnamon.

5.

I woke up alone, around noon. The first thing I did after I dressed, even before visiting the commissary roach coach for my vital first coffee of the day, was to stroll over to Doc Hodder's trailer.

Hodder had owned a successful Park Avenue practice at one time. Then he had started peddling skinslip on the side. He had gotten away with it until becoming addicted himself and losing his facade of competence. It's hard to conduct a physical when the movements of your clothes or the feel of the stethoscope in your hand is enough to trigger a thirty-second spasm of involuntary ecstasy.

The judge had given Hodder a choice after his twenty-four-hour detox regimen: Riker's Island or community service. It wasn't a hard choice.

Hodder wore a Solidarity scarf with President Walesa's picture silk-screened on it. They were big that year.

"Hey, Doc, you busy?"

Hodder sipped at a beer that left froth on his mustache. "Not so. Just patched up Bonilla's hand and gave him a tetanus shot. He managed to run a nail through his palm."

"Don't put your needle away. I need an STD booster."

Hodder elevated one eyebrow, but refrained from comment. He dug out the proper ampoule and shot me up.

"Beer?" he said.

I had forgotten it was afternoon. The thought turned my empty stomach. "No thanks. I'll take a coffee, though, if you've got any."

Heating water on a single electric burner, he made a Melita

single cup. When I had it in hand, he couldn't contain his curiosity any longer.

"All our people are clean, you know."

"I know," I said.

"And anyway, I thought you and Holly—"

"Don't bring that up, okay?"

"Well, excuse my big nose, but when our beloved leader comes in looking to have his T-cells goosed, one does feel one's interest being piqued."

I told Hodder what had happened.

He looked down into his beer for something cogent to say. I doubted there were any answers there that weren't in my coffee cup.

"You don't feel that might have been, ah, a tactical error?"

"Tactical? Who was thinking tactics? I'm trying to treat these people as decently as I can, within the limits of my mission here. I'm not a general, I'm a straw boss. If decency includes having some honest human feelings for one of them and responding to those feelings, then where does that leave me?"

"Can't say. Just looks like trouble maybe down the line."

"That, I realize."

Hodder got to his feet. "Well, if you feel the need to have any more of these little chats with ol' Doc Hodder—don't hesitate to go elsewhere."

"Thanks heaps."

I went back to my trailer.

Kerry Drucker was waiting there. He looked like a big goofy puppy. His metagraphix tie of yesterday had been replaced with a black and white one that looked like an enormous bar code. He was the last person I needed to see.

"Can we talk a minute?" he asked.

"Sure," I sighed.

Inside, I spotted a fresh printout lying in the tray of my meta-medium node. I picked it up and scanned it while Drucker talked.

"Those squatters, they're too much, aren't they? I've never seen anything like them. How can they live like that? Don't they know they could have a decent life just by asking? That's what government's for, it's what we're trying to do here, if only they'd get out of the way. Why would a person choose that kind of existence? Are they scared of the government? I don't see why anyone should be. We've only got their best interests at heart. . . ."

I don't know why I told him. It was just something to say in order to shut up his stupid middle-class babble.

"Well, they won't be around much longer. This is their pickup order. As soon as I sign it, the Guard will schedule a bus for next week to take them up to Dutchess County." Fitting action to words, I picked up a pen, signed the order, and ran it through the scanner.

"There, it's done."

"Good. Now maybe we can get back on schedule. That reminds me . . ."

He launched into a discussion of what had originally brought him by.

When I was alone again, I decided to take a little trip.

Hypertext always makes me dizzy. I guess you have to grow up with it to really be in sync with the notion of a completely free-form datastructure. All I know is that I feel old-fashioned whenever I dive into it. But sometimes there's just no avoiding it.

I started out with the entry for "bricoleur" in the online *Britannica*. Jumping from keyword to keyword in the kind of intuitive hunt I've found works best for me, I traversed dozens of linked texts, skittered across a handful of disciplines, piecing together a deeper understanding of the role of these scavenger-survivors across history and the human continuum.

I ended up in Levi-Strauss. Turned out he was the originator of the word. Fascinating guy. A lot of what I read was over my head, but I emerged with the certainty that my flash last night had been on target.

What was even more fascinating was how many patents had been filed over the past decade by bricoleur-types. I watched the figures graph themselves onto the screen. A myriad of mini-improvements—nothing revolutionary, true, but lots of stuff crucial to a smoother functioning of society—had first been developed by this growing subclass of people, operating out of intuition, necessity, and the improved access to information offered by the metamedium. Just the contribution of Perkins's millepore material alone, which could filter all harmful organisms out of drinking water, was incalculable. And Perkins, I discovered, had come out of a group very similar to Sledge's.

Sledge and his people were true bricoleurs, a subculture seemingly essential to the smooth functioning of any society.

And I was sentencing them to cultural extinction.

And also dooming something vital, perhaps, in the mainstream culture along with them. . . ?

I had my orders from Mama Cass. There wasn't any way out. Cultures got flattened everyday all around the world, under the steamroller of consensus reality, for the good of the majority. But mankind went on. Somehow.

I wanted to visit Sledge and his Bricks again, especially to see Zora. But at the same time, feeling like the hypocrite I knew I was, I wanted to stay away.

I postponed the decision by cleaning up my office paperwork.

There was a memo from the folks at Caterpillar, explaining the delay in delivering some heavy equipment. Automation Alley was pressed to the limits of their capacity now. It was hard to remember when they had been the Rust Belt. We could manage without the new machines for a while longer. Not so with the lack of cement. National production of that product was insufficient for all the work being done on the country's infrastructure. We were ready to start pouring, and I had to have my shipments.

I got on the phone and called someone. I won't say who, except to mention that they had been present on every New York construction site since the Dutch had built their wall on Wall Street to keep the Indians out. I wasn't proud of dealing with them, but on the other hand, I had a schedule to meet.

He who sups with the Devil must use a long spoon.

But the Devil's acid broth melts it a little shorter each time.

Finally there came a point where the backlog of nodework was cleared away, and I had no more excuses to stay in.

So I went out.

The warehouse where they had found the toxic waste was down now. So were the three or four other buildings that had been left in that sector. Five crews—Gold, Topaz, Blue, Emerald, and Black—had converged under my orders, and made short work of the remaining demolition. Now, only the brownstone retrofitted with miscellaneous improvements by the Bricks remained standing, a temporary survivor in the war of cultures.

At last, I thought, the whole site was nearly cleared. Already in the northern quadrants crews were driving piles and knocking together the forms used to pour the foundations of the residences, businesses, civic centers, theaters, and stores that would soon swiftly blossom like time-lapse flowers. Society, more than nature, abhors a vacuum. I could feel the incipient tension that the clearing of the ghetto acreage had caused. It quivered like water lipping a too-full glass, or, more exactly, like the formless but energy-dense void of the early universe, awaiting whatever precipitated the Big Bang.

Dust hung over the sweating crew members in the dusk as they clustered in the thick, fading heat around the water coolers, joking, laughing, planning the night's relaxations. A last truck rumbled off, bearing a heap of crushed bricks and timbers.

I was surprised to see that a lot of Sledge's people were mixing with mine. At first I thought that they were just after our water; it was the one thing their home lacked. But then I realized that their sociability was unfeigned. The motley squatters—unwashed, skinny, tough as leather—and my homogenous crewmembers—neat even while sweaty, well-fed, pampered—were getting on famously, like Hong Kong and China.

Not spotting Holly, I asked for her. Behind the Bricks' house was the reply. And that tacit acknowledgement that the brownstone was now someone's property came from one of my own people.

I felt something slipping dangerously out of my hands.

Holly stood next to Sledge, Zora and a couple of others, Goldies and Bricks. A few feet farther off was Runt. Half of his face was laughing. (The dead half, I had learned last night from Zora, was neurological damage, the result of a bad batch of designer PCP analogue.)

Holly spotted me. "Mike, hello! I owe you a beer. You were right about that hose. I was going to send for a mechanic, but Runt patched it up real good."

The repaired compliant trundled toward Sledge's group. I wondered why it was still powered up.

Then I wondered who was gloving it.

It was Runt.

He brought his arm down. The compliant reached for Zora. She squealed, stepped back, then was wrapped with a pneumatic arm that could crush masonry.

Holly blanched. I saw as if through a shimmering haze.

"Runt!" I yelled, although I knew I didn't want to spook him.

He paused. Zora hung six feet up in the air, pushing with both hands against the coiled embrace of the compliant. It seemed she didn't have breath enough to speak.

I tried to be calm. "Runt, slow now. Set her down slowly and uncurl your fingers."

He couldn't figure out yet why we were so worried. "Sure, man, sure, no prob."

He thudded Zora clumsily back to earth, then opened his hand. Zora staggered out.

I was beside her then, Runt too, finally realizing what he had done. "Are you okay?" I asked.

Zora gulped and nodded. "Just—just knocked the wind out of me."

Runt was half-crying. "Hey, Zora, I didn't know. I didn't mean nothing. Honest, you know me, always a dumb joker. Here, look." He stripped off the glove and tossed it to the ground.

"It's not your fault," I said. I looked at Holly. Her tanned face was still drained of blood. Four parallel finger tracks stood out on her neck. "I'll talk to you later, Noonan. Right now though I want to speak privately with Sledge—if it's okay with him."

The leader of the Bricks had stood impassively by during the incident, as if realizing that the responsibility lay within my dominion, not his, and willing to let me handle it.

"Yeah, sure, it's cool. Let's walk."

We moved off. After a few steps, Cassiopeia was the only witness to our conversation.

"Your people seem to be taking well to mine," I said.

"And your folks're cottonin' to mine. But that's how I expected it to go. You see, my people, they don't want much. They just can't stand to live in no institutions. They don't want no handouts or charity. All they ask is to pick through what society don't want, and put it to their own use. I think your people respect that, being self-reliant and all."

"But aren't you worried—" I began.

"Worry! Ain't got no time for worry. Look, Mike, we should both be very happy. Been plenty of times before, when two tribes met, when things didn't go so peacefully as they are now."

He managed to surprise me with the analogy. "Is that how you really see it, as two tribes running into each other?"

"Sure. Don't you? Look, you guys come into the city jungle, clearin' it away like some Brazilians in the Amazon, and you bound to run into some natives. Chances are, some of your folks maybe even go native on you. After all, you guys may be from a bigger, richer society, but you still just a tribe." He gave me a gap-toothed smile. "But I know you ain't gonna be like no exploiters, you gonna treat us with the dignity we deserve, and help us keep our little piece of land."

I shifted the topic slightly. "If we're enacting the meeting of two tribes, what does that make us?"

"We're the chiefs, Mike. Two headmen. Got all of the work and none of the fun, all of the grief and none of the kicks."

I couldn't say anything because I knew he was right.

We started to circle back to the others in silence. Then Sledge spoke.

"When two tribes meet, then you gonna see that old exogamy in action, I figure."

Again he had managed to startle me, the clinical term sounding utterly foreign coming from his lips. I reminded myself not to underestimate this man.

"Yeah," Sledge continued, "I bet you enjoyed your ol' piece of exogamy with Zora last night. She's one hell of a lady. But that's cool, that's cool, exogamy is for bindin' the tribes together. That's why I hope you don't mind me and Holly gettin' it on. It's a fair trade, she can really crank that little thing of hers. Girl go down faster 'n Drano."

Four tracks on her neck. . . .

I swung on him.

He caught my wrist and there was a knife at my throat.

"You a big man, Mike. But not that big."

The knife disappeared. My wrist was freed.

"Let's drop this shit, okay? Won't do for the others to see us rumblin'."

He turned his back on me and walked off.

And once again he was right, and knew I knew it.

6.

Like four slabs of ferrocrete settling on my back, four days passed.

A lot happened.

Nothing happened.

I took delivery on five hundred tailored London plane trees: biofabbed mycorrhizae on the roots to fight disease and help extract nutrients, increase CO_2 uptake, and heighten resistance to pollutants. We were going to landscape as we went, leaving arcades of greenery behind us.

Con Ed sent some people over to help lay the superconducting cable that would carry power throughout the new development. Skeptical at first that my people could manage, the outsiders soon changed their tune. It's amazing what the average eighteen-year-old can do, given half a chance.

My cement began to arrive, the new fast-cure mix. It came in a procession of rumbling, revolving trucks, all driven by guys named Guido. I hoped the bodies in the mix—literal or metaphorical—wouldn't make for weak foundations.

Atop the Bricks' squat, a windmill sprouted, its eggbeater blades clattering noisily night and day in the stiff breezes the open site promoted. Freed from dependence on the limiting fuel cells, the Bricks added more lights, and at night the building blazed like a carnival attraction, topped by its busy pinwheel.

Also on the roof they built a rainwater catchment, of the kind found on many Caribbean islands. To supplement this source of water, the Bricks scavenged a dozen plastic fifty-gallon drums, which they endeavored to keep filled. I looked the other way when Holly sent our water tanker over.

Each night in bed, after our lovemaking, Zora would whisper to me the new improvements they had made that day, always ending on the same note.

"You think we're doing good, Mike? You gonna help us, right?"

I said things she could interpret as she wanted.

I have always loved the wild and the strange. Sometimes I think that's all my altruism, my career of "selfless" helping comes down to: a desire to plunge into alien cultures and environments. I offer the notion not as excuse or indictment, palliation or breast-beating, but simply as an insight, won at some cost.

The whole affair began to remind me of something that had happened in the city about fifteen years ago. A communal group that called itself the Purple Family had taken over an abandoned waste-strewn lot and remade it into a beautiful garden. Then the original absentee owners had come to reclaim it, uprooting all that had been planted. For a few years thereafter, at random intervals, painted purple footprints had appeared all over the city sidewalks, as if a silent, accusing phantom stalked the streets.

I couldn't help speaking to Holly. I managed to keep my voice official, to show neither favoritism nor vindictiveness. Even the upbraiding I gave her for allowing Runt to factor the compliant was strictly professional. She responded at first with hurt incomprehension, then adopted my own cool demeanor. Where we had once had a warm and wordless bond, it was now like two icicles rubbing together.

I found compensation in Zora.

I gathered Holly found hers in Sledge.

But what would happen to all of us in a few days, I could not say.

At the end of the fourth day I got a visit from Mama Cass. Only she didn't really come in person, and it wasn't really her.

At that time in their development, metamedium nodes had no holo output or audiovisual input. It was still a medium of mice and keyboards and monitors, uninhabited by autonomous agents. But there did exist rather simple personal programs that would route a simulation of the owner's face, along with a message, to any node at a preselected time. They were useful as prompts and reminders.

It was around noon that day when Mama Cass's face lit up my screen, interrupting my scheduling work. She had given her image an eyepatch of jeweled copper. Aside from that, it was true to life.

"Mike," said the simulacrum, "I'm sorry I haven't been around lately, but things have been crazy. I'll be in Washington for the week, speaking at the Senate hearings. I saw that you signed the transportation orders on those squatters. Don't let the date slip any further. Catch you later."

Plasma pixels pulsed off.

The ghost's ultimatum left me feeling even further boxed in.

That afternoon, Holly came to my trailer unbidden.

Wiping her sweaty face with a bandana (One of Sledge's? The one Zora had worn that night as a bandeau top? Why should I care?) she looked directly at me with a concentrated distance, as if a chasm only a foot wide but miles deep separated us.

"The Bricks are throwing a nova party tonight. Just decided. They've invited me and my crew. Figured I should check with you first. Are we allowed to go?"

I thought hard. If I ordered my people not to go, they'd probably disobey anyway. As was their prerogative, being adults. I wasn't running a summer camp here. No bed checks or curfews. Besides, what harm could come? In a few days, the Bricks would be gone, willingly or under the coercion of the National Guard, as others had already been taken. Then my problems would be over.

"Sure. Why not?"

"That's what I thought you'd say. Just wanted to check."

Holly turned to go, paused, looked back.

"You'll be there?"

"Wouldn't miss it for the world."

"Thought you'd say that too."

As an excuse for a party, the nova was always reason enough.

Born of violence, the star was something new and shining and perfect. Temporary, certainly, but all life, all human accomplishments are temporary. Who's to say whether it's better to drudge along from day to day, hoarding one's energy, or blow it all off in one spectacular display?

I had almost not come to the party tonight. For a long time I had sat in my trailer, shirtless and in shorts, not thinking, precisely, but just waiting in suspension for something to move me one way or another. At last an inner balance tipped, disturbed by some wind that blew from the soul, and I got up and dressed. At the last minute, I buckled my utility belt around my waist. The shearing fork I had hung there several days ago, when I had helped Leotis and Shayla, slapped against my hip. I guess I wanted some badge of my status as comfort. Or were my motivations even then something darker. . . ?

Leaving the ATV parked, I walked across the empty land between my trailer and the party, wanting to be alone for a little while longer.

Someone in the Gold Crew had brought a boombox that pumped out crank-up hits on DAT, drum-heavy rhythms. There was a makeshift table consisting of planks on two plastic sawhorses, covered with some scavenged curtains as tablecloth. Various cardboard take-out cartons and trays held Chinese food, pizza, fried chicken. Somewhere the Bricks had dug up some styrofoam plates in their original packaging. I hadn't seen styrofoam in years, since the Montreal Protocols got into full gear. To drink there was beer, wine, punch.

I grabbed a bottle of beer and circulated among the dancers and talkers for a while, nodding a hello here and there, but not joining in any conversation.

He stood back in the shadows, watching.

"Mike."

"Sledge."

"Good to see you here, man. Hope it's just the first time outa many."

"Maybe. You plan on standing alone here all night?"

He laughed. "You got my number, buddy. I get too far above it sometimes. Comes with the job. But I don't have to tell you that. No, I'm gonna party down right now. You too, you hear."

"I hear."

We stepped out and walked together, toward a crowd of laughing people.

As we drew closer, I recognized a voice I hadn't expected to hear tonight. Drucker's. Simultaneously fascinated and repelled by the Bricks, he must have heard about the party and jumped at the chance to get close to them. He sounded a little high.

Runt was speaking. "Yeah, after all our work, we really feel we got us a nice home now. Tons better than the streets."

Drucker laughed. "I wouldn't get too used to it. Your transport orders were signed days ago."

In the human silence the music sounded harsh and alien.

Everyone turned to Sledge and me.

"Never did trust you bleedin' hearts all that far," Sledge said.

Reflections snagged on the blade of his knife. I swore I could see the nova caught in its tip, embedded in his junk ring.

"Put it away, brother, it's too late for that now."

"Ain't your brother. And too late depends on what you want." He jabbed upward.

This fight, I caught *his* right wrist with my left hand and squeezed.

You do a lot of lifting on a construction site, even as straw boss.

After a few seconds, he dropped the knife.

"That's cool, Mike, don't need no blade to put you down."

His grip on my throat felt like a compliant's. I knew he would shatter my larynx in a few more seconds.

I fumbled for the fork at my waist, managed to unhook it.

Clamped it against the wrist I still held.

Pulled the trigger.

Sledge staggered back. I dropped what I held. His face wore a look of incredulity.

"So it all just comes down to better tools—" he said, then collapsed.

I stepped away from the crowd flowing in on him. I saw Holly raise a walkie-talkie to her mouth to summon help. She always could keep calm. Like I said, she was the best I had. Then she dropped the box in the dust and rushed in with the others.

I tried to speak, but only croaked. I massaged my throat and looked up.

One-eyed Cassiopeia glared.

Time is a whirlpool that can swallow whole societies, whole cities, whole cultures. . . .

Or whole individuals.

Where is the man now who was so certain of his plans, his convictions, his idealism, so certain that the good of the many balanced the destruction of a few? I look in the mirror, but can't find him.

With Sledge in the hospital, the Bricks lost their center, dispersed, dissolved into the random components they had been

before Sledge forged them into a unit. Most opted for the relocation camps, and eventual settlement in the rebuilt Harlem. Others
disappeared back onto the hungry streets.

The project rolled on under my direction, a tamed juggernaut
now done with its crushing. (I thought of leaving—especially
under the constant silent accusation of Holly's daily gaze—but
realized that to abandon what had already caused so much grief
and bloodshed, without seeing it to fruition, would be the ultimate folly.)

But when the project was finished, when the first of the
quarter-million people who would live there had begun to filter
back, I quit the UCC. Mama Cass couldn't understand. Holly
could, but didn't care.

I went looking for Sledge—and Zora. I didn't know what I
wanted to say to them, but it never mattered. I couldn't find them.
It was as if the culture had swallowed them up. So instead, I went
looking for others like Sledge. Them I found. They existed in
every city, large and small. The forgotten scavengers, living ingeniously on castoffs and detritus, the waste and debris. And when
I found them, these bricoleurs—

I tried to atone.

Here is the Dark Cousin to "Spondulix." Again, a motley lot of underdogs try to better their lives with inspired lateral circumventions of the system. But in Rory Honeyman's world, there is really no presence of evil, a lack which makes all the difference between the broad farce of his tale and the tragedy of Shenda Moore, the dog of love.

As the prefacing quote indicates, I was trying to replicate, channel or borrow some of Phil Dick's broad compassion for suffering, absurd humanity (with a dash of the Hernandez Brothers). I hope I did not dishonor his artistic or spiritual legacy.

My knowledge of Santeria derives exclusively from Migene Gonzalez-Wippler's Santeria: The Religion *(Harmony Books, 1989), for which, my thanks.*

Karuna, Inc.

He learned about pain and death from an ugly dying dog. It had been run over and lay by the side of the road, its chest crushed, bloody foam bubbling from its mouth. When he bent over it the dog gazed at him with glasslike eyes that already saw into the next world.

To understand what the dog was saying he put his hand on its stumpy tail. "Who mandated this death for you?" he asked the dog. "What have you done?"

—Philip K. Dick, *The Divine Invasion*

1.
Memories of the 37th

*M*AYBE HE SHOULD GET HIMSELF A DOG.

A dog—a pet, a constant companion, something to fuss over—might help.

But then again, maybe not. It was so hard to know, to make up his mind.

Considering his unique situation. His special troubles. His extra share of suffering.

Adding any unknown factor to the sad equation of his life

might disguise its solution, remove any answer forever beyond his powers of philosophical computation. (Assuming his life—anyone's life—was solvable at all.)

But how could he know for sure without trying?

Yet did he dare try?

Foolish as the dilemma seemed, it was a real quandary, seemingly his alone.

Others seemed not to have such problems.

For instance. Everyone in Thurman Swan's life had a dog, it seemed. All the people he hung with daily at the Karuna Koffeehouse. (He felt odd calling them "friends," upon such short acquaintance, even though they were starting to feel a little like that.) Shenda, Buddy, Chug'em, SinSin, Verity, Odd Vibe. . . . They were all dog owners, every manjack and womanjill of them. Big dogs or little dogs, mutts or purebreds, quiet or yippy, reserved or exuberant, shaggy or groomed, their dogs came in all varieties. But one thing all the animals had in common, Thurman had noticed: they were inseparable from their masters and mistresses, loyal beyond questioning, and seemed to repay every attention lavished on them in some psychic coin.

Call it love, for lack of a less amorphous word.

Thurman could have used some of that.

The cheap clock radio came on then, dumb alarm-timer, unaware of Thurman's insomnia, activating itself needlessly. The device was the only item on his nightstand. There *had* been a framed picture of Kendra and Kyle, but when the letters and calls stopped coming, he had stored the picture of his ex-wife and child in his lone suitcase on the high closet shelf.

Thurman had already been lying awake for hours, although he hadn't had the energy to get out of bed. He didn't sleep much these days. Not since the war.

The war that had held so many mysteries in its short span, and changed so much—for him, if no one else.

Furnace skies. Sand lacquered with blood. And greasy, roilsome black clouds. . . .

He was in one of the ammo-packed, barrel-stacked bunkers that made up the conquered fortified maze at Kamisiyah, laying the charges that would bring the place down like a bamboo hut in a typhoon. He wore no protective gear, hadn't thought he needed it. His superiors certainly hadn't insisted on it. Dusty sunlight probed through wall-slits like Olympian fingers. Sweat leaked out from beneath his helmet liner. He took a swig from his plastic liter-bottle of water, then returned to work. His deft actions raised spectral echoes in the cavernous concrete room, ovenlike in its heat and feeling.

But exactly what was it baking?

So intent was Thurman on the delicate wiring job that he didn't notice the entrance of visitors.

"Specialist Swan."

Thurman jumped like a cricket.

Major Riggins stood in the doorway. With him was a civilian.

Civilians made everyone antsy, and Thurman was no exception. But there was something extra disturbing about this guy.

As thin as a jail-cell bar and just as rigid, wearing an expensive continental-tailored suit so incongruous in this militarized desert setting, the guy radiated a cold reptilian menace. A stance and aura reminiscent of a fly-cocked iguana was reinforced by shaved head, pasty glabrous skin and bulging eyes.

Major Riggins spoke. "As you can see, Mister Durchfreude, the demolition is calculated to leave absolutely nothing intact."

Durchfreude stepped into the room and began running a gnarly hand lovingly, as if with regret, over the piles of crated munitions. Thurman's gaze followed the ugly manicured hand in fascination, as if fastened by an invisible string. For the first time, he noticed what appeared to be a trademark stamped on many of the crates and drums and pallets.

It was a stencilled bug. A termite?

The civilian returned to the doorway. "Excellent," he dismissively hissed, then turned and walked off.

Major Riggins had the grace to look embarrassed. "You can return to your work, Swan," he said brusquely.

Then his commander left, hurrying after the civilian like a whipped hound.

Thurman went back about his task. But his concentration refused to return.

And a day later, at 1405, March 4, 1991, when Thurman and his fellow members of the 37th Engineer Battalion assembled at a "safe" distance from the bunkers, video cameras in hand, the proper signals were sent, liberating a force that shook the earth for miles around and sending up a filthy toxic plume that eventually covered thousands of surrounding hectares, including, of course, their camp. Thurman, uneasily watching, thought to see the mysterious civilian's face forming and dissolving in the oily black billows.

A commercial issued from the bedside radio. "Drink Zingo! It's cell-u-licious!"

A drink would taste good. Not that Zingo crap, but a very milky cappuccino. More milk than coffee, in fact. With half a plain bagel. No schmear. Thurman's stomach wasn't up to much more.

Now, if he could only get up.

He got up.

In the bathroom, Thurman hawked bloody sputum into the sink—pink oyster on porcelain—put prescription unguent on all his rashes, took two Extra-strength Tylenol for his omnipresent headache, counted his ribs, combed his hair and flushed the strands from the comb down the toilet. In the bedroom he dressed gingerly, in loose sweats and unlaced sneakers, so as to avoid stressing his aching joints. Halfheartedly, he neatened the sweaty bedcovers. No one would see them, after all.

In the entryway of his small apartment, he scooped up pill vials and inhalers, pocketing them. Claiming his aluminum cane with the foam back-bolster clipped to it, he left his two semifurnished rooms behind.

Another busy day of doing nothing awaited. Retiree city. Adult day care. Park bench idyll.

Not the worst life for a sick old man.

Too bad Thurman was only twenty-seven.

2.

Bullfinch's Mythology

"No!"

Shenda Moore burst the shackles of her bad dream with an actual effort of will. There was nothing involuntary or accidental about her escape. No built-in handy mental trapdoor opened automatically, no cluster of ancient guardian neurons on the alert triggered its patented *wake-up!* subroutine. No, it was all Shenda's own doing. The disengagement from the horrifying scenario, the refusal to participate in her subconscious's fear-trip, the determination to leave the grasping fantasies of sleep behind for the larger consensual illusion called reality— It was all attributable to the force of Shenda's character.

Really, everyone who knew her would have said, *so typical of the girl!*

Sometimes Shenda wished she were different. Not so driven, so in-charge, so *capable.* Sure, mostly she was grateful every minute of every day to Titi Yaya for bringing her up so. Shenda *liked* who she was.

But being responsible for *everything* was really so much *work!* An endless roster of sweaty jobs: mopping up messes, straightening crooked lives, building and repairing, shoring up, tearing down, kissing all the boo-boos better. *Mwah!* And now: stop yer sobbin'.

Dancing with the Tarbaby, Shenda called it.

And there was no stopping allowed.

Especially now — with Karuna, Inc., taking off and demanding so much of her time — Shenda awoke most mornings with a hierarchical tree of chores arrayed neatly in her head, a tree where any free time hung like forbidden fruit at the farthest unreachable branch tips.

But even coming online to such a formidable task-array was better than waking like *this.*

Shenda's heart was still pounding like a conga, her shouted denial still bouncing around the bedroom walls. She clicked on a table lamp and swung her slim and muscular caramel legs out from under the sheets, sitting upright in her cotton Hanro nightshirt. She massaged each temple with two fingers for a while, lustrous and wavy black hair waterfalling around her lowered face, while contemplating the nightmare.

It was not the first time she had had the nightmare.

She was on a flat graveled rooftop in broad daylight, level with the upper stories of many surrounding buildings. Tin-walled elevator-shaft shack, a satellite dish, door to a stairwell, whirling vents, a couple of planters and deckchairs. Highly plausible, except that she had never been in such a place.

With her was Bullfinch.

In her hand, Shenda suddenly realized she clutched a tennis ball.

Bullfinch capered around her, leaping up for the Holy Grail of the ragged green ball, begging her to throw it.

So she threw, sidearm, expert and strong. Wildly, without care or forethought.

The ball sailed through the air, Bullfinch in hot pursuit, claws raking the gravel.

Over the parapet the ball sailed.

With a majestic leap, Bullfinch madly, blithely followed, sailing off into deadly space.

In the dream, Shenda screamed her denial.

Now she merely murmured, "No. . . ."

The "meaning" of the dream was plain enough: her duties were getting to her, the weight of her responsibilities to those she loved was making her imagine she might easily fuck up.

Hell, she *knew* she was gonna fuck up sooner or later. It was inevitable. Everyone fucked up continuously. That could almost be a definition of human existence. The 24-7 fuck-up. She didn't need any dream to remind her of that.

All she prayed was that she wouldn't fuck up too bad. Be left with enough of her faculties to pick up the pieces and start again.

Luck came into this somewhere.

And luck was one of the things beyond her control.

Her heart had calmed. Rising determinedly to her bare feet (the purple paint on her toenails was all *chipped*—she'd *have* to make time to see SinSin for a pedicure—not that she had, like, any *man* in her life these days to *appreciate* such details), Shenda went about getting ready for her day.

Her first instinctive action after the nightfright was to check on Bullfinch.

She found the dog snoring in the dining room.

Disdaining his very expensive catalog-ordered puffy cushion bed, Bullfinch had made himself a nest.

Somehow he had reached a corner of Titi Yaya's antique linen cloth (remnant of old high times in Havana) where it hung down from the tabletop. He had dragged the cloth down, bringing two brass candlesticks with it. (God, she must have been dead *to the world!*) Then he had chewed the irreplaceable cloth to the shredded state most suitably evocative of some genetic memory of an African grass lair.

"Oh, Bully! Whatever is Titi going to say!"

Bullfinch swallowed a final snore in a gurgle, then awoke. His wattled, enfolded face peered innocently up at her. Breaking into an ingratiating, tongue-lolling smile, he wagged his stubby tail.

Shenda found her anger instantly dissipating.

Most empathetic people found it impossible to stay mad at bulldogs for long, as they were so mild mannered and goofy looking.

Especially one colored like a canary.

The employee at the animal shelter—a bearded, spectacled fellow with some kind of East European accent and a nametag reading JAN CLUJ—walked Shenda back among the cages so that she could make her choice. Ambling down the wet cement aisle, she found herself wanting to take every one of the abandoned yelping mutts home. But it was not until she saw the bright yellow occupant of one cage that she stopped decisively.

"What's the story with this one?"

"To my eyes, which are admittedly not of the most expert, our friend is the variety of English Bulldog. Was picked up on Kindred Street, near the college. Of tags, none. Meeting his maker in—" Jan Cluj checked the page slipped into a galvanized frame wired to the cage "—five more days."

"But what about that *color?*"

Jan Cluj shrugged, as if the matter were of little interest. "It is unnatural. Most assuredly obtained chemically. I accuse some likely college boys. They are insufficiently studious and given to madcaps."

Crouching, Shenda extended her fingers through the wire separating her and the yellow dog. He snuffled her fingers eagerly and sloppily. She stood.

"There's no roots showing, or normal-colored patches the dye job would've missed."

Exasperatedly: "Dear lady, the dog is as you see him, fit and active by medical ukase, most normal save for his hue. Explanations are superfluous. Will you have him?"

"I will have him."

After signing the relevant forms, Shenda took the happy bounding yellow dog straight to a grooming salon known as Kanine Klips (recommended by Pepsi, who had her poodle, French Fry, done there regularly), where she had the anomalous bulldog dipped and clipped.

Then she waited for his normally colored fur to grow out.

Three years later, she was still waiting.

The dog was some kind of genetic sport. His naturally unnatural coloration was a shade most commonly associated with avian life forms.

Shenda had resisted naming the bulldog until he assumed his true form. Called him "Hey, you!" and "Here, doggie!" for weeks, out of some kind of feeling that to name him wrongly would be to warp his personality. But when the true state of his freakish coat became evident, there was no other possible name for such a specimen.

"Bullfinch," said Shenda with weary patience, "get up off that tablecloth please. It's time for you to go out and do your business."

Bullfinch obeyed. He arose and trotted over to the back door of the house. Shenda opened it and the dog went outside into her small fenced yard.

While the criminally destructive canine was busy outside, Shenda gathered up the precious tatters, surveyed them mournfully, estimating possibilities of repair, then, clucking her tongue, chucked the rags into the trash.

Bullfinch re-entered the house. Promptly, the dog went over to the wastebasket and dragged the ruined fabric out and over to his bed. With great care and exactitude, employing paws and muzzle, he arranged the cloth atop the puffy cushion to his liking. He plopped his rear haunches down on his new dog blanket, and sat regarding his mistress.

Shenda gave up. "I don't have time to play no tug-of-war with you, Bullyboy. My day is fuller than usual. And it starts *now*."

As if to say, *Mine too!*, Bullfinch nodded his weighty corrugated head several times, then lowered his forequarters and was soon asleep.

Shenda showered and groomed. Those toenails *had* to *go!* In a robe, towelling her hair dry, she flipped on the bedroom radio automatically, thinking to catch the news, but then hardly listened. She put her panties on ass-backwards, caught herself, swore, and re-donned them correctly.

Dressed in baggy Gap jeans and a green silk shirt, she ate a chocolate Pop Tart standing up at the sink, washing it down with a tumbler of chocolate milk. Her face was blank, as if her mind were vacationing in a more alluring country than her body.

"—cell-u-licious!" declaimed the radio.

Shenda snapped out of her fugue, looked at the clock, and exclaimed, "Louie Kablooie! Bully, I've got to run! You got plenty of kibbles, and tonight I'll bring you a real treat. Promise!" She scuffled on a pair of open-toed Candies, grabbed up a courier-style satchel and her car keys.

The door slammed behind her. Bullfinch opened one eye, then the other. Seeing nothing that needed his attention, he closed them and returned to sleep.

He could fly. He really could. And that airborne tennis ball was *no problem.*

3.

Frozen Furniture

No dreams, pleasant or otherwise, but rather a mechanical device, awoke Marmaduke Twigg from his Midas-golden slumbers.

Like every other member of the Phineas Gage League, Twigg

was physiologically incapable of dreaming. The relevant circuitry, along with much else, had been chemically and surgically excised from Twigg's altered brain.

As a consequence, he was radically insane. And in the worst possible way.

The mania didn't show, didn't impede his daily functioning. Indeed, Twigg's brand of insanity *increased* his cunning, ingenuity, deftness, manipulative social skills and will to power. Minute to grasping minute, hour to scheming hour, day to conquering day, he appeared to himself and others as a single-minded superman, apparently a paragon of efficient, rational action. Perched on the very uppermost rungs of the social ladder, Twigg seemingly owed all his accomplishments to the secret devastations willingly wrought on his gray matter.

Yet it was as if a dam had been erected in the brains of Twigg and his compatriots, a dam behind which fetid black waters were continually massing.

A dam which must one day give way, taking not only the well-deserving Twigg and his peers to their vivid destruction, but countless others, the more or less innocent and the less or more complicit.

Right now, of course, such a fate seemed vastly improbable.

Twigg thought—rather, *knew*—that he was a new and improved breed of human, superior to anyone not a League member.

He knew that the world was his oyster.

The only thing left to determine was at precisely which angle one should work the knife into the hapless stubborn bivalve, and how best to *twist* the sharp instrument properly.

Crack!

The shell halves fell apart.

And the raw meat was sucked greedily, gleefully, down.

Twigg lay sleeping on his back in the exact center of the mattress of his enormous four-postered canopied bed. His chest-folded arms were clad in ebony silk salted with white dots. Beneath his crossed arms, crimson satin sheets and a crest-embroidered white duvet were drawn up in unwrinkled swaths. (The crest on the coverlet depicted a heraldic shield enclosing crossed iron rods with a superimposed eye, and the Gothic initials PGL.) Resting in the middle of a softer-than-down pillow, Twigg's unlined face seemed the ivory mask of one of the lesser pharaohs.

Suddenly, without visible stimulation, Twigg's pebbly eyes snapped open like rollershades, and he was instantly alert.

Twigg could feel the small unit consisting of pump and segmented reservoirs implanted inside him stop its gentle whirring. The same device (which regulated many hormonal functions previously so crudely performed by now missing gray matter) had sent him efficiently to sleep exactly four hours ago, during which time he had not stirred a limb.

He knew that most of his servants—especially those who had the least personal contact with him, knowing his peculiarities only through rumor—jokingly referred to him as one of the undead. But Twigg cared not.

All the lesser cattle were the true phantoms, without substance, ineffectual. Only he and his kind were truly *alive.*

Twigg's breakfast would soon arrive, carried to him by his loyal factotum, Paternoster. In the meantime, he flew the jetcraft of his mind over the varied terrain of his day.

Meetings, public and private: legislators, aides, ambassadors, presidents, CEOs, media slaves. Acquisitions and sales: companies, divisions, patents, real estate, souls. Phone calls: conferenced and one-on-one. Presentations: from scientists, PR experts, lawyers, brokers, military strategists. Wedged into the interstices: meals and an intensively crafted scientific workout.

All of it absolutely necessary, absolutely vital to keeping all the delicately balanced plates of Isoterm's myriad businesses spinning.

Yet all of it absolutely tedious.

But tonight. Tonight would make up for all the boredom.

For tonight was the monthly meeting of the Phineas Gage League.

Twigg smiled at the thought.

His smile appeared like fire burning a hole in the paper of his face.

Memories of his own entrance into the League trickled over his interior dam. These were not so pleasant. The initiation rituals were stringent. Had to be. No whiners or losers or weaklings allowed. Cull out the sick cattle right at the head of the chute. Still, the shock and the pain—

Twigg reflectively fingered a small puckered scar on his right temple. His smile had disappeared.

To recover his anticipation of this night's pleasures, Twigg reached up to stroke one of his bed's four canopy supports.

At each corner of the enormous imperial bed stood a life-sized naked woman, arms upstretched over her head, thus pulling her breasts high and flat. Each woman supported one corner of the heavy wooden frame that held the brocaded fabric canopy.

These caryatids were each one unique, sculpted with absolute realism, down to the finest hair and wrinkle. They were colored a uniform alabaster. Their surfaces were absolutely marmoreal, as unyielding as ice. Twigg's hand, lasciviously molding the butt of one woman statue, neither dented nor jiggled the realistic curves. Rather, his hand slid over the human rondures as if they were curiously frictionless.

The door to Twigg's bedroom, half a hundred feet away, opened. A man entered, bearing a domed tray. He crossed the carpet with measured elderly steps.

Twigg bounded out of bed lithely.

His black pajamas, it was now revealed, were embroidered with hundreds of identical white termites.

"Ah, Paternoster! Well done! On the table if you please!"

The old and crabbed servant—longish hair the shade of old celluloid—set his burden down.

The table was a large piece of gold-rimmed glass borne aloft on the backs of two kneeling naked men arranged parallel. One of the humaniform trestles was a middle-aged paunchy type; the other young and lean.

Twigg moved to an antique desk of normal construction, where a high-end computer incongruously sat. He powered it up, eager to begin his day of bending and shaping, betrayal and coercion. Simultaneously, with seeming unconcern, he questioned his servant.

"Birthday this week, Paternoster? Am I correct?"

"As always, sir."

"Not thinking of retirement yet, are you?"

A fearful tremor passed over Paternoster's worn features. "No, sir! Of course not! I served your father for his whole life, and his father before him! How could I even *think* of retiring!"

"Very good!" Twigg ceased his typing. As if pondering a different topic, he said, "I *must* find a hassock for this room! Well, I'll get around to it some day."

The servant seemed on the verge of fainting. "Any—anything else, sir?"

"No, Paternoster, you may go."

Twigg's braying laughter escorted Paternoster out.

Whipping the silver cover off the tray, Twigg disclosed his breakfast.

It was a single uncapped bottle of sinisterly effervescent

Zingo, whose label featured the famous lightning-bolt Z.

Twigg grabbed the bottle and downed its bright Cool Mint Listerine-colored contents.

Cell-u-licious!

Setting the empty bottle down, the man picked up a device off the table. It resembled a standard remote-control unit.

Pivoting, Twigg raised the unit and pointed across the vast room.

On the far side of the interior acreage stood a full-sized statue of a Siberian tiger, absolutely lifelike save for its unvarying artificial whiteness. The beast's face was frozen open in a toothy snarl, every ridge of its pallid gullet delineated; one mammoth paw was lifted in midgesture. Separate from the statue, strapped around its neck, was a collar and small box.

Twigg pressed a button.

The tiger's anguished roar filled the room, its striped face a Kabuki mask of rage. Like an orange, white and black express train, it raced at its tormentor. Twigg stood like a statue himself.

Several yards distant from its infuriating quarry, the tiger leaped, its maw a slick red cavern, claws extended.

At the last possible moment Twigg pressed another button.

The stasis-transfigured tiger, now vanilla white, fell with a heavy thud to the deep carpet, nearly at Twigg's bare feet.

"Yes!" said Twigg gleefully. "Like to see even that cool bastard Durchfreude do better."

Naming the Dark Intercessor aloud seemed to cast a shadow on Twigg's pleasure.

The man was a valuable nuisance. Every use of his talents simultaneously decreased his utility and increased the liability he represented.

One day the balance would tip decisively on the side of liability.

And then, Twigg grimly suspected, it would take more than the easy press of a button to put Kraft Durchfreude away.

4.

Espresso Eggs

The wide, welcoming, windowed wood door to the Karuna Koffeehouse had its own unique method of announcing customers.

Mounted inside above the entrance was a Laff Bag: one of those innocuous sacks that contained a device to play tinny mechanical maniacal laughter. Every passage through the door pulled the string that triggered the abridged five-second recording.

Making a pompous entrance into the gaily-painted Karuna was practically impossible.

Not that there weren't folks who still tried.

Fuquan Fletcher for one.

Thurman had just arrived that morning, setting off his own personally impersonal gale of guffaws. This early, he had found his favorite table empty, the one by the moisture-misted south window. Taking a seat, he unclipped the cylindrical foam bolster from his cane and arranged it against the small of his back.

The fragrant atmosphere of the Koffeehouse was filled with the gurgles and chortles of various brewing devices, the chatter of the trio of workers on duty, the savoring sipping sounds of sleepy humans gradually coming up to full mental speed with the aid of friendly plant derivatives. The ceiling-mounted speakers suddenly crackled alive with the sounds of Respighi. A wide-mouthed toaster noisily ejected its crisped bagel passengers.

All was right with the world.

If not with Thurman himself.

Lining up his various prescriptions on the tabletop, Thurman tried not to feel too sorry for himself. An attitude that didn't do any good, he knew from the recent bitter years, though surely easy enough to fall into.

Looking up from his chesslike array of bottles, Thurman saw one of the baristas approaching.

Normal service at the Karuna involved placing one's order while standing at the long, oaken, display-case-dotted counter separating customers from the employees and the exotic tools of their trade, and then maneuvering with the expeditiously filled order through the crush toward an empty or friend-occupied table. The baristas generally ventured out only to clear tables of post-java debris and swab them down. (And even these incursions into the customer area were infrequent, thanks to the unusual self-policing neatness of most Karuna patrons.)

But for Thurman—and anyone else who obviously needed special attention—exceptions were easily made.

Just part of the thoughtful charm that found expression in the Karuna's motto:

The place to come when even home isn't kind enough.

The phrase Thurman always involuntarily associated with the young female barista named Verity Freestone was "pocket-sized."

Pixie-cut black hair topping a seventy-five pound package of cheerful myopia.

Today Verity wore a striped shirt that exposed her pierced-navel belly, brown corduroy pants that would've fit Thurman's twelve-year-old nephew, Raggle, and a pair of Birkenstocks. Verity filled *her* pants, however, in a more interesting—to lonely Thurman—fashion.

Verity pushed her thick glasses up on a mildly sweaty snub nose. "Hi, Thur. The usual?"

"Um, sure. Except maybe just wave the beans over the cappuccino, okay? The old stomach—"

"Thurman, you look *wicked* peaked. Are you okay?"

"As okay as I'll ever get."

Verity eyed the pill vials ranked before Thurman and frowned. "All those unnatural chemicals can't be good for you. Haven't you tried any alternative healing methods? Maybe get the old *chi* flowing. What about vitamins? You take any vitamins?"

Thurman waved the advice away. "Verity, really—I appreciate your concern. But I can't change any part of my medical care right now. Strict doctor's orders. I'm barely holding on as it is."

Verity's expression changed from faintly hectoring to triumphantly assured. "I know just what you need, Thur."

This was more than Thurman himself knew. "And what might that be?"

"Some espresso eggs! They're not on the menu. We—the help, that is—we make them just for ourselves. But I'm gonna fix *you* up some special!"

The treat sounded nauseating to Thurman. "Verity, I don't know if I can take any espresso in my eggs—"

"Oh, they don't have any *coffee* in them. We just call them that because we make them using the espresso machine steamjet."

"Well, if they're mild—"

"Mild don't even come close!"

Before Thurman could object any further, Verity clomped determinedly off.

Thurman plucked the rumpled morning newspaper from the adjacent window ledge and unfolded it. A headline caught his attention:

DISPOSAL LOGS MISSING FROM GULF WAR
CIA BLAMES ACCIDENTAL ERASURES

He made an effort to focus on the smaller print.

Just then the door laughed.

Fuquan Fletcher was the Karuna's coffee-bean roaster. A master at his craft, he was indispensable to the quality of the Karuna's drinks, and thus responsible for much of its success.

That single and singular virtue failed to compensate for the fact that he was an utter prick.

At least in Thurman's eyes. But not, he suspected, in his alone.

Always dapperly dressed and impeccably groomed, the trim mustachioed Black man had no admirers more fervent and appreciative of his immense hypothetical charms than himself. He was a loud walking arrogant billboard for his own athletic, sexual, financial and terpsichorean prowess.

"Ladies!" bellowed Fuquan from the door. "Show me a hot oven, and I'll get right down to some sweaty work!"

Returning to Thurman's table, an unfazed Verity passed by her coworker. "Morning, Fuquan."

The man made as if to embrace her, a move Verity deftly eluded with a twist and a skip, all without spilling a drop of the drink on her tray.

"Freestone! I got you pegged, girl! You're one of them sex elves like I seen in a comic once! Show the world your pointy ears, girl! Let them puppies out to play! Then you and me will go into your fantasy world!"

Thurman was highly embarrassed by this display. For the *nth* time, he pondered putting Fuquan in his place. Once he would have done it automatically. Visceral memories of R&R barroom brawls tweaked his flaccid muscles. But now he had neither the energy nor the ability.

Verity was unfazed by the familiar routine. "Fuquan, you'd better cut the talk and get to work. We're running low on Jamaican."

"One day you're gonna give me some of your good stuff, Miss Peanut."

"Don't count on it. Thurman, here's those eggs I was talking about."

Moving irrepressibly on to other equally futile love conquests and bouts of braggadocio, Fuquan went behind the counter where Thurman could see him donning a neck-to-knee apron.

"Don't you ever get sick of him?"

"Oh, he's harmless. It's the ones who don't say anything you have to watch out for."

Thurman instantly felt that perhaps he was one of those suspiciously quiet ones, and fumbled for some sort of conversational tidbit, as Verity disburdened her tray onto the table.

"Uh, how's your dog doing?"

Verity owned a long-haired dachshund (referred to by Fuquan as, of course, "Hairy Weenie"). "Slinky Dog is just fine. He goes out to stud next week. Slinky makes his girlfriends happy, and I make a little extra cash."

The mention of even canine stud duty saddened and embarrassed the unstudly afflicted Thurman. "Um, great, I guess. . . ."

"Now, try these, Thur, and tell me what you think."

Before him, fluffy white-flecked yellow clouds of whipped and steam-cooked eggs seemed to float an inch off their plate. Thurman had never seen such ethereal scrambled eggs. Plainly, there was a component of antigravity to their recipe.

Thurman forked some up and delivered them to his taste buds.

There was not even any sensation of them resting on his tongue. The sweet creamy taste of the eggs seemed to suffuse directly into his bloodstream. Chewing was definitely superfluous.

"These—these are the best eggs I've ever had!"

Verity smiled and patted his shoulder. "Part of your regular order from now on, Thurman. We'll get a little flesh back on those bones."

Thurman finished his eggs with gusto, as well as his usual plain bagel half and cappuccino (oh, all right: weakly flavored hot sugary milk). Feeling better than he had in months, he settled back to absorb the busy evolving scene around him.

People-watching was Thurman's main recreational activity these days. Cost nothing, and took little strength.

Odd Vibe came in. A quiet and generally unsmiling Norwegian who bore the unfortunately twistable name of Otto Wibe, he was the Karuna's baker.

Thurman could hear Fuquan greet his backroom coworker.

"Odd Vibe, my man! You sleep in those clothes or roll a bum and strip him?"

"Fletcher, you go and sit on a biscotti, by gosh!"

"Oh, sharp one, Oddy! We'll have you playing the dozens yet!"

Around eleven, Tibor "Chug'em" Gruntpat made his daily appearance. Chug'em was a sanitation worker, fiftyish and gnarled, just coming off shift. He had been up since about 3:00 A.M. Without a word, Buddy Cheetah—drummer for a struggling band called the Beagle Boys, who was working the counter with Verity—lined up four double-mochaccinos in front of the gray-haired muscular man, who knocked them back in a total of sixteen seconds. Then Chug'em left to sleep through the day.

Others less and more memorable came and went, the latter category featuring SinSin Bang and Pepsi Scattergood from the Kwik Kuts salon three doors down the block. As usual, the brace of beauticians were impeccably trigged out. The Misses Mode O'Day. And, natch, their hairstyles had changed since last week.

Nelumbo Nucifera, good-looking Italo-American boy who kept all the females happy with his tight T-shirts, came out from behind the counter to clear Thurman's dish and refill his cup.

"Thanks, Nello."

"Hey, want to hear a joke, man? This guy walks into a bar with an alligator on a leash. . . ."

In the buttery sunlight after Nello's departure, Thurman began to grow sleepy.

And then the door's chortles, sounding somehow lighter and more vibrant, announced Shenda Moore.

Her arrival had the same effect on Thurman's nerves as a Scud missile intersecting the Aegis defense system. He came instantly awake, his heart thumping to a salsa beat.

Wasn't she just so achingly damn *beautiful?*

And wow!

Peeking out of her open-toed shoes —

Those Easter-egg nails!

5.

Money Comes

The Tarbaby wanted to *tango* today!

Shenda's hasty departure from her apartment had set the tone for the rest of her morning. From one appointment to another she had raced. Suppliers and building contractors, City Hall and DEM, office supply stores and printshops, the homes of employees out on long-term sick leave. The odometer on her little green Jetta seemed to revolve madly like one of those movie time-machine displays as the decades whipped by. Shenda's Day-Timer was thick as a slice of Sequoia, stuffed with loose business cards that took flight at the slightest provocation, making her feel like an utter *idiot* as she stooped to recover them under the noses of leering sneering straight-edge white guys in *suits!*

(Whenever Shenda heard this putdown tone in her mental monologue, she would automatically pause, disengage the gears on the aggression machinery, and try to radiate a little human warmth, the way Titi Yaya had taught her when she was a little girl. The practice had been hard at first, gotten easier over the years—although the mental trick never ceased to be something she must consciously invoke as a counterweight to natural human impatience. This refusal to hate or impose false separations lay at the heart of Shenda's personal MO, and at the heart of her vision for Karuna, Inc.)

As she dashed about town, attending to all the daily hassles associated with running the expanding set of enterprises loosely linked under the umbrella of Karuna, Inc., Shenda felt a twinge of irreducible guilt.

She had not taken Bullfinch for a walk in days. (That dream—) The dog was uncomplaining, but Shenda knew that he missed the exercise. Hell, so did she!

If walking with Bullfinch pleased them both, then why hadn't they done it in too long?

Was her life becoming the kind of White Queen's Race she had always derided in others?

Was she forgetting what was really important in life?

She hoped not. Natural optimism made her ascribe this un-naturally busy and stressful period to the fact that now, after three hard years, Karuna, Inc., was really taking off.

Maybe soon now she could even hire a helper!

Stopped at the traffic light at the corner of Perimeter and Santa Barbara Streets, Shenda looked idly to her left and saw a big truck emblazoned with some kind of insect logo.

Must be exterminators. . . .

The light went green. Shenda wheeled right on Perimeter toward her final two stops before lunch. (Both stops had been planned to mix pleasure and business, one of Shenda's survival tactics. At Kwik Kuts, she'd get her pedicure and instead of dishing dirt, discuss business. Then, at the Karuna, she'd lunch after tending to their affairs.)

As she expertly threaded the traffic, she thought back to the beginnings of this whole unlikely scheme.

Three years ago, she had been a business major fresh out of the university, temping in a series of dead-end jobs, unsure of the path before her. The *what* and *why* of her life were plain enough, but the *how* was shrouded in mystery. Then Titi Yaya had phoned, a day in advance of her standard weekly call.

"Shen-Shen, dear." Only Titi Yaya called her *that* old child-hood name anymore. "You remember Titi Luce?"

"Of course, of course. I saw her once when I was six. She visiting from Miami?"

"Not anymore, dear. She's dead. Nine days ago. I just got back."

"Oh boy. . . . Sorry to hear it, Titi."

"I know you are, dear. Now, pay attention. I can't get out of the house today. Too much to make ready. So I need you to pick up a few things for the *oro Ilé-Olofi* ceremonies tonight. Seven white candles, a pigeon, eight coconuts, some *cascarilla*, Florida Water. . . ."

Shenda scribbled dutifully, although she was not truthfully looking forward to attending the *oro Ilé-Olofi*. Titi Yaya and the other *santeras* would ask when she was at least going to take the Necklaces, embrace the Warriors—never mind making the saint! —and they would press upon her protective bracelets at the very least—the *idé*—which she would have to refuse, saying that she didn't follow the Religion anymore, had never really done so since reaching adulthood. Unpleasantness would result.

Titi Yaya finished her list. "And be here sharply at nine, dear. Oh, by the way: Luce left you a hundred and fifty thousand dollars. Goodbye till nine."

The connection was severed on Titi Yaya's end but not on Shenda's, as she held the phone stupidly in her hand until the recorded operator's voice came on.

The first thing Shenda did was press the disconnect button on the handset, then dial the temp agency and resign.

The second thing she did was walk (no car then) to the Karuna, where she could sit and have a coffee and think.

In those days, the Karuna looked nothing like its current self. Didn't even have the same name, but was known instead as the Corona Coffeehouse. Drab, dirty, dusty and disagreeable, it was mismanaged by absentee tax-finagling owners and patronized by shady types, the yuppies they preyed on, and a clique of arty poseurs.

Liars and strivers and bores, oh my!

Only a handful of the employees redeemed the joint. Folks glad to have a job and trying their best to overcome bad conditions.

Sitting with a cup of acidic, burnt coffee, thinking alternately of the nameless yellow adopted dog back home in her tiny walk-up and the bequest so cavalierly dropped in her lap by her ever-surprising aunts, Shenda tried to imagine what she might do with the money, how best to put it to work.

There came an unbidden moment then—a moment most incommensurate with the tawdry surroundings, a self-catalyzing timeless nanosecond Shenda would never forget—when the whole world seemed to blossom, to split open like a fruit, revealing the seeds of her whole future.

Shenda was at the bank the next day.

Depositing the bequest and using it as collateral, she took out a loan. With that money, she bought the Corona from owners eager to dump it cheap and write off the loss.

Rechristening the place was easy. Somehow the sound-a-like new name surfaced, recalled from a college philosophy class.

Shenda wasn't quite sure what the *exact* definition of "karuna" was. But it had something to do with warmth and spaciousness, and it sounded suitably exotic. Plus, anyone who went looking for the old "Corona" would likely end up at the new "Karuna."

Firing the incompetent and surly employees had been positively pleasant. Shenda was not one to flinch from necessary triage. The girl could be positively *brutal* when brutal was called for. (She would have made a good nurse or general, and had in fact become a mixture of both.)

Once the Karuna was running on a steady footing (about six months; guess those business courses were worth something after all), Shenda incorporated a holding company that also utilized the Karuna name.

This parent company had but one purpose. Its short prospectus was perhaps unique in the history of capitalism. Shenda was very proud of it. She had written all of it herself.

"Karuna, Inc., is a cooperative overseeing entity whose sole purpose is to facilitate and maximize the functioning of its subsidiaries through any ethical means available, including but not limited to group purchasing agreements; joint bargaining and sales forces; intersubsidiary loans and personnel exchanges; healthcare coordination; shared management, training and education; pooled charitable donations and grants; mutual information sharing; etc., etc.

"A company wishing to become a subsidiary of Karuna, Inc., must first redefine its sole business mission to be the creation of environmentally responsible, non-exploitive, domestic-based, maximally creative jobs to be filled without prejudice or favoritism. The performance of all employees shall be regularly evaluated, partially on accomplishment of defined goals and partially on native abilities and attitudes of employees, with the latter considerations outweighing the former in cases requiring arbitration. While maximum product and service quality are to be always striven for, the primary goal of the subsidiaries shall always be the full employment of all workers meeting the qualifications of good-will and exertion of individual levels of competence. It is to be hoped that the delivery of high-quality goods and services will be a by-product of such treatment.

"Upon demonstration of such a redesign, a company will be admitted as a subsidiary, with all rights and obligations pertaining thereto, upon a positive vote of the Karuna, Inc., board.

"Profit making is naturally encouraged. Each subsidiary shall pay a tenth of its profits to the parent corporation for the fur-therance of the shared mission as outlined above.

"All owners of subsidiaries become members of the board of Karuna, Inc., and at regular meetings—open also to all subsidiary employees and their relatives, as vested shareholders—the board members shall vote to determine any future corporate actions out-side the stated scope of this document, or amendments thereto. A simple majority shall carry all votes. In the case of ties, the vote of the President (Shenda Moore, undersigned) shall be called on. The President may also veto any board decision in the best interests of Karuna, Inc."

Shenda wavered a little over that last bit. It sounded kinda dic-tatorial. (Especially since she really had two votes: one as the owner of the Karuna Koffeehouse, the first subsidiary, and one as president.)

Hell! It was her idea, her money and her effort!

Let anybody who wasn't satisfied stage a coup!

Smith and Hawken. Ben and Jerry's. Tom's of Maine. The Body Shop. Sure, they all tried to live up to *some* of the same prin-ciples Shenda had outlined in the formation of *her* company. But none of these others had as their primary mission the simple crea-tion and sustainment of good jobs for those who needed them. (Perhaps the national figure who came closest to Shenda's concep-tion of how to treat people was Aaron Feuerstein, the owner of the fire-destroyed Malden Mills in Massachusetts, who had main-tained his idled help on a full payroll throughout reconstruction.)

In each of those other companies, the ultimate emphasis was on the *product*, on making and selling it, grabbing market share. Whatever the company rhetoric, when push came to shove, the workers drew the short straw.

"Doing well by doing good" was *their* motto.

"Doing good and maybe doing well" was Shenda's.

It was a real, although subtle, difference.

(And in the end, there didn't even seem to be any *maybe* about it. Loan paid off, house and car bought, the Karuna turning a nice monthly profit. Louie Kablooie! What more could you ask of a business plan?)

Shenda didn't really give a *flying fuck* about product. People were drowning in products, they bought too much too cheaply anyway. It didn't take a genius to turn out quality goods. That part was simple.

What took skill and talent and vision and general resourcefulness — qualities Shenda was a little surprised to find out she had in abundance — was promoting conditions that opened up satisfying, decent-paying vocational niches for everyone. Getting people into a harness that didn't bind and having them all pull together, for the common good.

General Shenda, jetting in her Jetta toward a pedicure and lunch.

Never thought being a general might someday mean having to fight an actual war.

6.

Nailed

Marmaduke Twigg adjusted the bib of his black rubber apron, smoothing the cord where it passed around the collar of his five-thousand-dollar suit. The long, butcher-style garment bore the PGL crest in the middle of the chest.

Unlike the Masons and their aprons, the Phineas Gage League had adopted theirs for strictly practical reasons.

The lovely expensive fabrics favored by the League members reacted so *poorly* to bloodstains!

Confident he was looking his best, Twigg walked forward to the clustered PGL members who had arrived before him.

They stood on a subway platform, lit by a single scanty light. The dusty station was a deserted one, off the maps, reachable only through a certain subbasement's concealed door.

Of course, a League member owned the building that included that subbasement.

Empty for over ninety years, the station possessed a certain Victorian feel to it, wonderfully consistent with the period of the League's founding. Twigg could almost believe that he had traveled back in time, back to that romantic age of the great industrialist Robber Barons: Carnegie, DuPont, Rockefeller, Getty, Rothschild, Hearst, Krupp —

Not that he would have traded places with any of those legendary figures. Sure, they had had a few nice perks. No inflation, no taxes, no government regulations. Truly classy playgrounds like Newport and Saratoga and Baden-Baden. Half the world's resources and population subjugated as colonies under their boots. The respect and ass-kissing admiration of society.

But taken all in all, the present offered *so* much more!

The assembled members—eleven, Twigg quickly counted, making him the last to arrive— hailed him with varying degrees of civility and enthusiasm. Here were important personages— competitors and rivals—who would, upon receiving any news of Twigg's painful demise, lose not a minute in popping their finest champagne, toasting his anticipated afterlife roasting, and pissing the metabolically transformed fluid on his grave. Yet they were constrained by the rules of the League from doing more to his person now, or elsewhen, than uttering a mildly cutting *bon mot*.

Such was the strength of the bond between them.

The League members were a motley assortment of international figures, most of whose faces would be instantly recognizable to the average newspaper reader or television viewer, all leaders of enormous, globe-girdling enterprises, media talking-head sources of quotes and advice.

Twigg catalogued his peers.

Sasha Kapok, of Kalpagni, Ltd.

Ernest Firgower, of Stonecipher Industries.

Isabelle Fistule, of Burnes Sloan Hardin Hades.

Jack Burrows-White, of Crumbee Products.

Nick Potash, of Harrow & Wither.

Edouard Ensor, of Somnifax et Cie.

Alba Cumberbatch, of Asura Refineries.

Osada Sarakin, of Preta-Loka Entertainments.

Abruptio Placentae, of Culex, SA.

Cooper Stopford, of Brasher Investments, Plc.

Klaus Kunzi-Fuchs, of Rudrakonig, GmbH.

Lastly, of course, came the nervous-looking new recruit, Samuel Stanes, of LD–100 Pharmaceuticals, whose initiation would bring the League up to its full strength of thirteen.

After greeting his compatriots, Twigg moved to the absolute edge of the platform and looked down the tunnel for the train. Not seeing it, he made a dismissive noise and stepped back, joining the rest.

Like a group of commuting meat cutters, they waited silently.

At last the train arrived.

Not modern subway cars, nor even antique carriages, but rather primitive open mining cars like riveted iron buckets with seats, pulled by a tough little engine, at the helm of which sat the Dark Intercessor.

Kraft Durchfreude.

Durchfreude was one of the League's rare failures. Something had gone wrong in the procedure that would have made him a full-fledged League member. A portion of his higher individualism and initiative had been unfortunately excised. The team and head surgeon responsible for the screw-up had soon come to wish they had never seen a scalpel. Durchfreude himself had been declared officially dead, and his corporate empire had devolved to a son, who knew nothing of his father's actual fate, nor of the League.

Yet a use and further half-life had been found for Durchfreude. Unwaveringly loyal and obedient, he made an excellent catspaw, a unique tool, disposable if need be, rotating his services among the League's initiates as requested.

And in fact, if no one had a more pressing need for Durchfreude's services, Twigg himself intended to borrow the creature soon for a short and simple private assignment on behalf of Isoterm.

Stepping carefully, the PGL'ers filtered into the various cars, except for the caboose.

That car was filled with bound unconscious bodies.

Men, women, children. Some animals.

Once they were all aboard, Durchfreude rang a little mechanical bell (with what mix of sardonicism and actual childlike glee, Twigg could not discern in the dimness), and the train chugged off, its single kerosene lamp the only illumination.

Not far beyond the station, the tracks began to slope to a nonnegligible degree. Soon, the train's brakes were squealing, the engine's gears in low, as they dropped into the earth's depths, torturing rasping shrieks from the rails.

After a time, the tracks leveled out. A light at the end of the tunnel appeared after they rounded a bend.

The train emerged into a cavernous room hewn from the living rock, and stopped. Naked flames from bracketed torches illuminated the rough clammy walls. Hidden vents created slight air currents that caused the flames to jump and lick like hungry tongues. Thick Persian rugs—stained despite the best cleaning attempts—softened the hard floor.

Durchfreude leaped down and hustled carpeted wooden steps

up to the cars so that the thirteen passengers could dismount.

The room was furnished with various comfortable chairs and couches—as well as shrouded equipment whose shapes implied a more sinister nature. Scattered tables were laden with fine gourmet food and vintage drink, as well as various recreational pills and needles. Full sanitary and ablutionary facilities were half-visible behind a folding screen.

At one end of the room was a kind of dais supporting a lectern. On the wall behind the podium hung a large reproduction of the PGL crest as well as a framed portrait. The painting depicted a mustachioed white man with the looks typical of the mid-1800s. There was, however, a curious deformity to a portion of his skull.

The members dispersed among the furniture, helping themselves to the refreshments, making small talk. After unloading the unconscious cargo, stacking the hogtied bodies like cordwood, Durchfreude had vanished somewhere, down the tunnel or behind the screen.

When the men and women of the League had settled down, business began.

As the oldest member, Ernest Firgower ascended the dais to conduct the meeting. Behind the podium, not much of the short elderly man was visible save for his vigorous shock of silver hair towering over his wrinkled brow (where that same small scar, which Twigg and the others shared, leered obscenely), and his green eyes shining like the tips of poisoned stakes. Twigg fancied that his countryman resembled Bertrand Russell, had that philosopher ever included in his CV the management of, say, a concentration camp.

Firgower coughed, began to speak in a reedy voice. "Fellows of the Rod, let us commence our business. The first matter on the docket is the division of Zairian natural resources—"

Twigg listened with only half his attention. The rest was focused on a blonde woman sprawled atop the pile of warm and gently respiring bodies. Her immaculate features and contorted limbs evoked the air of a Renaissance martyr portrait.

Twigg sucked in her delicious helplessness, tuning Firgower out. Twigg was a man who believed firmly in granting business and pleasure equal status.

At last the humdrum League affairs had all been dealt with. Twigg suppressed a yawn. It was hours before his normal sleep period. Was his onboard pump working as well as it should? He made a mental note to have it checked.

Now Firgower had begun the ritual preface to the initiation of

Samuel Stanes, the last duty before they could all cut loose in that hot red festival that was a simultaneous abandonment and affirmation of their unique privilege.

Twigg perked up in his seat and listened. The old story never failed to enthrall.

"We are gathered together tonight in honor of our symbolic founder, the hapless yet lucky Phineas Gage. While he did not literally lay the first bricks of our organization—that honor belongs to the farsighted entrepreneurial visionaries of our great-grandparents' generation—Gage provided the actual inspiration for our magnificent accomplishments.

"Phineas Gage was a simple untutored manual laborer during the middle of the last century. At the time of his remarkable transformation, he was helping to construct a railroad. The blasting of interfering rock ledges was underway. Gage was assigned to make sure the explosive charges were well in place. Taking his tamping rod, he went to work."

Firgower waved a thin arm backward at the crossed bars of the PGL crest, then almost toppled. He righted himself and continued.

"Gage performed his task a trifle too enthusiastically. At one drill hole in the stone, he created sparks and ignited the powder charge.

"The iron rod was sent rocketing upward, out of the channel as out of the barrel of a gun, through Gage's right eye, blazing a trail of gorgeous destruction across his lobes, and emerging in its entirety out the top of his cranium.

"Let us leap ahead, over the confusion attendant on this accident and the subsequent primitive medical treatment. Gage survived his wonderful injury. But as all his old friends attested, he was utterly changed. From an easygoing, laughing, careless sort, he turned moody and unpredictable and demanding. He seemed to be without the normal constraints of civilization. Regard for his fellow humans, he had none. Completely self-centered, his actions —reprehensible to an ignorant milksop society—led to a life of ostracism and despair.

"We now know, of course, that along with much needless peripheral damage, Gage was the first man to undergo the removal of his brain's ethical nucleus. Or, as some of the more old-fashioned among us refer to it, his conscience.

"Lacking all power, occupying the wrong social stratum, Gage never benefitted from his inadvertent surgery. He could not fully make use of the miraculous ease and fluidity of action which one who is blessed with the destruction of one's conscience experiences. Never to doubt, never to allow pusillanimous sentiments for human cattle to interfere with one's own self-interest, never to waste a moment of one's precious time in introspection. To see clearly the quickest path to one's own ascension. Such is the legacy given to those of us who have undergone the perfected operation."

Firgower stepped out from behind the lectern. "And now, Samuel Stanes, we of the Phineas Gage League invite you to join our ranks. What sayest thou?"

Stanes stood on visibly weak knees. "I—I accept!"

Durchfreude had appeared from nowhere.

"The Dark Intercessor will administer the sacrament," intoned Firgower.

Twigg watched as Durchfreude fastened a stasis box to Stanes's wrist. The leader of Isoterm found his finger straying almost of its own accord to his own temple, and restrained the traitorous digit with an act of will. Someone else flicked a wall-mounted switch, and the hissing of an electric-powered air compressor resounded.

Sweat like an oily evil dew spontaneously broke out on Stanes's brow. He closed his eyes.

Durchfreude brought into view a heavy-duty carpenter's nail gun, its tumescent hose trailing. He placed the muzzle against Stanes's right temporal ridge and squeezed the trigger.

The *pop* of the gun was followed by the crunching sound of the short nail driving through flesh, striking and partially penetrating the skull.

Stanes turned then into a rigid snowy sculpture of himself, as the stasis box was activated by the control in Firgower's veined hand.

Durchfreude caught the unstable toppling figure, hoisted it and loaded it into the train. Mounting the engineer's seat, he drove Stanes off to the awaiting surgery.

No ride home for the others would be needed for hours.

For now the fun commenced. Already, as planned, the victims were waking up.

Twigg moved swiftly to claim the blonde.

But he need not have rushed. There were plenty of subjects to go around.

When Twigg next looked up amidst the screams and howls

and guttural roars—the animals sounding human, the humans animal—he saw Cumberbatch with her mouth incarnadined, a wide red clownlike smear, Ensor holding a fluid-darkened saw, Sarakin pulling tight a noose, Fistule with her arm imbrued, buried inside a dog's split mortal shell.

Not jealous in the least, the superman returned to his own pleasures.

7.

"What's Wrong With You?"

Alert, almost vibrating, Thurman watched the regal and youthfully glamorous Shenda Moore stride swiftly across the Karuna's polished floorboards and pass behind the counter. She set her courier's case down with visible relief.

Verity eagerly started up a conversation with the Karuna's owner, of which Thurman caught only the opening.

"That sleazy new distributor came to the delivery door again, Shenda. This time he had a couple of greaseballs with him. Heavy muscle. Thought I'd be scared or something. Huh! I told them to go fuck themselves—"

Shenda's face darkened into a scowl. Thurman thought her intense and concentrated protective wrath was nearly as attractive as her general wide-focus warmth. She opened her mouth to speak, but her reply (beyond a prefatory "Those bastards—") was lost to Thurman in a sudden swell of noise: kitchen clatter, door laughter, street traffic, patron hooting. By the time things had quieted somewhat, Shenda had disappeared into the rear of the shop.

Thurman slumped down in his seat, cut off from the source of his momentary invigoration. For a moment, he had actually forgot his illness, succeeded in imagining himself whole again.

What he wouldn't give to get a little closer to this intriguing woman! He envisioned the way their conversation would swiftly flow, from easy early friendliness to gradual whispered intimacy. And then, in some quiet, private setting—

At that moment Thurman began to cough. Not a polite, out-in-public cough either, but one of his regularly occurring TB-victim-in-the-isolation-ward, lung-ripping, throat-searing gaspers. Clutching a sheaf of napkins for the expected expectoration, he tried to turn his body toward the window, away from the other customers. His knee jerked involuntarily, bumping the small table and sending his pill vials tumbling to the floor.

In the midst of his agony, Thurman felt waves of searing humiliation.

Nothing could make his embarrassment any worse.

Nothing?

A soft yet strong hand descended on his shoulder, followed by a familiar voice.

"Are you all right? What can we do?"

Oh, Sweet Mary!

It was her!

Thurman struggled to get his body under control. He finished gagging into the napkin wad, then instinctively stuck the filthy mass of tissue (paper) and tissue (cellular) into the pocket of his sweatpants. Trying to compose his mottled features into a semblance of normality, Thurman turned to face a standing Shenda Moore.

A sweet floral scent wafted off her. She clutched half a bite-rimmed sandwich unselfconsciously in one hand. Her exquisitely planed Afro-Caribbean face, framed in lax layered Fibonacci curves of thick hair, was a blend of alarm and curiosity, her taut body poised for whatever action might prove necessary.

Weakly, Thurman found a joke. "I — there was a fly in my coffee."

Shenda laughed. The sound was like temple bells. In a bold tone she completed the old joke: "Well, don't spread the word around, or everyone will want one!"

Then, just when Thurman expected the Karuna's proprietor to turn and walk off, she pulled up a chair and sat down beside him. Now she spoke in more confidential tones, and the watchers attracted by Thurman's discomfort turned back to their own business.

"Do you mind if I finish my lunch here?"

"No, never! I mean, sure, why not? It's your place."

This hardly sounded the note of gracious invitation Thurman intended. But Shenda seemed not to take offense. She waved over Nello.

"Nello, I'll have a Mango-Cherry, please. And — what's your name?"

This information was not immediately retrievable. After a dedicated search, however, involving all his processing power, a few syllables surfaced. "Thurman. Thurman Swan."

"Get Mister Swan whatever he wants."

Thurman had never tried any of the many Tantra-brand juices available at the Karuna. "Um, I'll have the same."

Nello left. Shenda took a bite out of her sandwich, meditatively studied Thurman while she chewed. Their juices arrived. Shenda uncapped hers and drank straight from the bottle, her lovely throat pulsing. Thurman took a tentative sip, cautious as always when introducing new acquaintances to his hermit stomach. Not bad.

Shenda finished her sandwich with deliberation and obvious enjoyment, washing it down with the rest of the sweet juice. She set the empty bottle decisively down. Still, she said nothing. Thurman was dying.

But when she finally spoke, he almost wished she hadn't.

"What's wrong with you?"

Of course. She wouldn't have been human if she hadn't zeroed in on his obvious sickly condition. Still, Hunchback Thurman *had* hoped the pretty gypsy girl could have avoided the touchy subject.

He wearily started to recount his sad and baffling tale with its lack of a clear conclusion or moral.

"Well, you see, I was in the Gulf War—"

Shenda impatiently waved his words away. "I don't care about *that* shit! That's *old* shit, kiddo! I assume you got a doctor for whatever happened to you there. Maybe not the best doctor or the best kind of treatment. That's something you gotta look into some more maybe. But what I want to know is, what's *wrong* with *you?*"

His mouth hanging open, Thurman couldn't answer.

Shenda leaned closer, drilling him with her unwavering gaze. "Look. I see you in here every day of the week, any hour I come in. Now, I certainly don't bitch about anybody taking up space without spending a lot. Hell, that's one of the things this place is *for!* And I'm flattered that you find this joint so attractive. But *no one* should be so desperate or lonely or unimaginative that they've only got one place to go! I mean, like Groucho said, 'I love my cigar, but even I take it out of my mouth sometimes!' "

Thurman struggled to recover himself. "Well sure, I agree, if you were talking about a normal person—"

Shenda banged her hand flat down on the table, raising a gunshot report. "Where's your tail? You got a tail? Show me your tail! Or maybe you're hiding a third eye somewhere?"

Shenda pressed a finger into his brow.

"Ouch!"

"No, I didn't think so. Thurman, you *are* normal. Maybe a struggling kind of normal, but who isn't? No, you've let your spirit get a kink in it, Thurman. You've been dealt a lousy hand, but you're still supposed to play it. Instead, you're down a well of apathy without a bucket to piss in! You need to get out and around, my friend."

The word "friend" was like a life raft. "I—what could I do?"

"How about a job?"

"A job? What kind of job could I possibly handle?"

"There's a job for everyone. Wait right here."

Shenda got up and walked to the counter, where she retrieved her bag. She strode briskly back, dropped down, and removed her appointment book from within the satchel. A single business card shot out under its own volition onto the tabletop. Shenda picked it up and read it.

"Perfect! Go to this address today. This very afternoon, do you hear me? Tell Vance I sent you and said for him to put you to work."

Shenda stood then, extended her hand. "Welcome to the Karuna family, Thurman."

Thurman found himself standing somehow without reliance on his cane. He took Shenda's hand. Her grip was a pleasant pain.

When she was halfway across the room, Thurman impulsively called out, "Shenda Moore!"

She stopped and whirled. "Yes!"

"I like your toenails!"

Shenda eyed Thurman with new interest. Coyly angling one foot like a model, she said, "Me too!"

And then she was out of the Koffeehouse, force of nature dissolving in a burst of laffs.

Thurman sank back down gratefully into his seat, feeling his face flushing. He was *almost* glad she was gone.

Now that he had gotten some small fraction of his crazy wish fulfilled, however unpredictably, he wasn't sure how much of Shenda Moore's intense company he could take!

Someone else was now standing by his table.

Fuquan Fletcher was smiling. But the smile was not pleasant, nor meant to be.

"Big man. Likes the lady's *toenails!* Gonna let the world know it!"

"Fuquan, what's your problem?"

"*You* my problem, man, you try to move in on Shenda Moore. That girl is *mine!* She got her nose open for *me!*"

"Is that so? You sure she feels that way?"

"Sure? I'll show you sure, man!" The irate coffee roaster jabbed a finger into Thurman's chest.

This was the second time Thurman had been poked in the space of a few minutes. Unlike the first educational prodding, this poke made him mad. So—after he did not respond with immediate belligerence, causing Fuquan to laugh coarsely and turn to leave—Thurman felt completely justified in using his cane to hook one of the Black man's ankles and pull his foot out from under him, sending him crashing to the floor.

Fuquan was up and heading with bunched fists for a risen shaky Thurman when Buddy and Nello and Verity intervened, referee baristas holding the opponents apart.

"Hey, c'mon, guys, who started this?"

Neither antagonist said anything. After a tense moment, Fuquan brushed himself off and stalked into the back.

Gathering up his pills and accoutrements, feeling that his life was becoming more interesting by the second, Thurman departed the Karuna.

Outside, he studied the business card.

KUSTOM KARS AND KANVASES
VANCE VON JOLLY, ARTIST IN RESIDENCE
"HOUSE OF THE WINGED HEART"
1616 ROTHFINK BOULEVARD

Thurman checked his wallet. Not a lot of green. But hey—he had a job now!

In the cab, Thurman speculated on what he would find at the end of the ride.

Disembarking, he discovered the wan products of his imagination to be a pale shadow of reality.

He stood facing an old garage: four cinderblock bays flanked by an office space. The entire nondescript structure, however, had been studded with brightly colored glazed ceramic objects in *bas-relief*, executed in a zippy cartoon style. Animals, trees, people, cars, toys, musical notes.

Above the office door was the biggest piece of pottery, big as a sofa: an anatomically correct heart sprouting white-feathered angel wings.

Thurman entered the cluttered office. No one home. He moved into the bays.

The first three were occupied by exotic cars: hotrods in various stages of being gaudily decorated. The last bay was filled with easels and wall-leaning stacks of canvases, also in various stages of completion. The paintings exhibited the same daffy sensibility as the outdoor ceramics. A beat-up workbench held brushes, tubes of color, tins of thinner and crusty rags. A tatty couch with mussed blankets, a metal-topped kitchen table and a small refrigerator seemed to hint at regular overnight human occupancy.

A toilet flushed. Through an opening door—whose frosted glass bore the calligraphic legend INSPIRATION: TEN CENTS—walked a very pale muscular man with a trendy arrangement of dark facial hair offset by a thinning on top. One earlobe, his left, was studded with segments of a severed silver snake, like the colonial DON'T TREAD ON ME. He was concentrating on tucking his paint-splattered green mechanic's shirt into his Swiss Army-surplus wool pants, and so did not immediately notice Thurman. Lacking sleeves, his abbreviated shirt revealed several tattoos, including a winged heart.

"Er, Vance?"

The guy stopped and looked up with neither welcome nor discouragement. "Who're you?"

Thurman, growing more and more doubtful, volunteered his name. Then: "I was sent by Shenda Moore. She said you'd have a regular job for me. . . ?"

"You know kandy-flake? Or striping? I could use some help striping. How about bodywork? Can you do bodywork?"

"Well, I'm good with tools, and I picked up a lot of special skills in the Army."

"Yeah? Like what?"

"Well, basically I was a demolition expert. But I can learn new things quick."

Vance von Jolly had gotten his shirt stuck in the zipper of his pants, and was now struggling mightily to restore his apparel to its proper functioning. Thurman wondered if he should offer to help.

"Jesus! That Shenda! She drives me nuts! All right, I suppose you can start by washing brushes. Any thumb-fingered idiot can wash brushes."

Thurman was hurt. "Wait just a minute now—"

"Oh, did I mention I can't work with anyone who gets pissed off at my dumb mouth?"

"No. Unless that was the warning just now."

Unable to free his shirt from the toothy tangle, Vance ceased struggling and moved to the workbench. Buttoning his waistband, he found an alligator clip and pinched shut the upper open portion of his fly. The clip projected outward like a small groin antenna.

"It was. Okay, let's start by showing you where everything is."

Thurman had one question. "Vance—will I be working with a lot of chemicals? I've had some bad luck with chemicals in the past."

Vance seemed to see Thurman and his condition for the first time. He shook his head ruefully. "Man, someone really fucked you up, didn't they?"

"I guess you could say that."

The painter moved to Thurman's side, hanging an arm over his shoulder. A complex odor of sweat, garlic and solvents wafted off the man.

"Thurman, my pal, I want to let you in on a little secret. The Army made you handle the chemicals of *death!* But here we work with the chemicals of *life!*"

"What's the difference? Chemicals are chemicals, aren't they?"

Vance von Jolly merely tapped a finger against his head and winked.

8.
"Let the Dogs Vote!"

Sun like a fusion-powered pomegranate in a pristine blueberry sky. Whipped cream clouds. Breezes holding kites and balloons aloft and trying to tug high women's skirts and slither up men's pants legs. Acres of open lawn green as celery, with shaded patches the color of new money. Shouts and squeals of running playing wild children. Over-the-top, can't-*stand*-myself canine pack yelping. Bee-buzz adult chatter: gossip, business, philosophy and seduction. Teenage odd-stressed argot in the perpetual search for cool. Pointillistic laughter. Competing music from half a dozen boomboxes, holding the sonic fort until the Beagle Boys finished their cable-laying, equipment-stacking preparations underway 'neath a Sgt. Pepper bandstand. Smell of mesquite burning down to perfect grilling coals, and aromatic dope leaves combusting.

Just another partially organized, partially spontaneous monthly shareholders' meeting of Karuna, Inc.

Shenda thought back to a poetry class.

Rip those boardroom doors from their jambs, rip the executive jambs from the walls, then rip down the corporate walls!

You go, Walt!

Amidst and amongst the several hundred people and several score dogs assembled in Morley Adams Park, Shenda circulated happily, Dame Kind with her flock.

Mama! These festivities always made her high!

Every face smiled to see her, every adult hand juggled drinks or spatulas or books or tapes or purses or babies in order to clasp hers. Children hurled themselves at her as if she were some natural feature of the landscape placed here for their rightful pleasure: a tree, a mountain, a beach. Shenda caught them up, whirled them and set them down. Fur and tongue and tail foamed around her like breakers, then raced away.

A splash of lemon yellow, a flash of jello wattles: Bullfinch scampered to keep up with his fleeter cousins.

This was what Shenda lived for. Not all the petty details of running her brainchild, the squabbling altruistic quasi-corporation known as Karuna, Inc. Certainly not all the hourly, daily, weekly headaches and stress. They all faded like phantoms in the sunshine of this assemblage. Here, under her watchful, beneficent gaze, she could gauge the actual good she had accomplished, count all the people she had helped and observe how that help had spread — was continually spreading — outward in circles of big-heart, wide-mind action.

Shenda really wanted nothing else. (A man, a mate, hell — a date? Well, perhaps. . . .) This gathering was her total and complete yardstick of satisfaction.

This very day would have been perfect, in fact, if not for one matter.

Zingo, that cell-u-licious horsepiss.

The actual owner of Maraplan Importing — this brashly illegitimate distributor new to their city — had visited the Karuna Koffeehouse several times since that day Verity had told his men unequivocally to fuck off. At last managing to snare Shenda, he had delivered one final classic performance of intimidation and blustering. Ignorantly self-assured, crudely sly and warthog-aggressive, he refused to take Shenda's "Blow me!" reply-in-kind for an answer.

"Little lady," said Faro Mealey in their ultimate interview, rasping a simian hand across his chin stubble, "you are not being very smart."

Shenda was a little scared at this confrontation. But stronger emotions were a sense of the scene's absurdity, and utter infuriation at the *nerve* of this guy!

"On the contrary, Mister Mealey. It's you who's acting like a juvenile dumbshit schoolyard thug! You come in here and practically order me to drop my old distributor and replace him with you. Then you tell me that I'll have to take just as many cases of that poisonous antifreeze you call soda as you decide is good for me. Moreover, I'm not the only business you're trying to pull this scam on. You've been to some of *my friends*, as well as dozens of unrelated concerns throughout the city. Does the word 'shakedown' hold any meaning for you, Mister Mealey? Do you know what would happen to you if I went to the cops?"

Mealey unsealed a sporadically gold-capped grin. "Not a fucking thing, babe, I assure you."

Shenda looked the man up and down. Clad like a cheap racetrack tout, Faro Mealey seemed an unlikely type to actually command the clout he now boasted of. Still, Shenda probed for more information.

"Oh, yeah? Who's gonna come bail your ass out? The International Brotherhood of Slimeballs?"

"Very funny. I like broads with a sense of humor. They're always good in bed. No, my business has some important backers. Let's just say that the makers of Zingo take a big interest in insuring their product gets top placement in the marketplace. Now, why doncha think about my proposition for a few days? I should warn you that our terms in the future might not be so generous."

"Mister Mealey, you can take a fucking Zingo enema. Now, get the hell out of here!"

Over the next few days, Shenda had done a little financial-pages, web-searching, library-stack sleuthing, following a not-too-shadowy paper trail.

The company that perpetrated Zingo was owned by another. And that one was owned by yet another. But beyond that level, the path seemed to lead conclusively to something called Isoterm. Who or what motivated *them*, Shenda had been unable yet to learn.

A Nerf football hit Shenda in the side of the head.

"Sorry!" called out little Tara Vadeboncoeur, her face a mix of horrified chagrin and stifled delight.

"*No malo, chica!* That's what I get for daydreaming in a *rowdy* crowd!" Shenda lofted the ball back, and moved on.

She stopped and talked with Joe Ramos of Kan-do Konstruction for a while. His firm planned to bid on part of the new Westside highway job. Shenda gave him a rundown on what she had picked up on his likely competitors through the grapevine. After a gleeful handshake, she left Ramos crunching numbers on a calculator.

Mona Condeluccio staggered by under the weight of two aluminum pans, each as big as an unfolded Monopoly board and deep as a footbath. Shenda quickly relieved her of one, and peeked beneath the foil lid.

"Mmm-mm! Potato salad!"

"And this one's macaroni. I got six more in the truck!"

Mona ran Kozmic Katering. She was providing about half the food for today's bash, partially in lieu of her tithe. The rest was all deliciously homemade. Oh, except for the donuts from Krishna Murphy's Krispy Kreme franchise.

Following Mona toward the picnic tables, Shenda said, "Louie Kablooie, I wish the business part of the day was *over* already!"

After a few spectacular failures, Shenda had mandated that Karuna, Inc., finish discussing all its outstanding business matters prior to falling like wolves and vultures and savages on the food and alcoholic beverages. Otherwise, not a hell of a lot got done. And also, while Shenda didn't mind being heckled, she found that the intellectual quality of the catcalls and witticisms was higher when the audience was sober.

The women deposited their burdens on the groaning buffet. Shenda grabbed the first teenager to fall within her reach. "You, Haley Sweets! What you thinking, standing there like a goofball statue when there's work to be done? Help Mona! Right now!"

Haley Sweets—acne like strawberry fields—gazed at Shenda with besotted puppy love. He gulped, sending a hypertrophied Adam's apple yo-yoing, said without satire, "Yes sir!"—then trotted obediently off.

Shenda laughed silently. *Boy—we got to find you a woman!*

And then she saw Thurman Swan.

Thurman sat on a folding plastic-basketweave lawn chair, his cane hung from the armrest. If his seat had been a gold throne in a Byzantine palace, his enjoyment would obviously not have been increased one iota.

On either side of him stood the gorgeously decorative SinSin Bang and Pepsi Scattergood, owner-beauticians of Kwik Kuts. SinSin was half-Vietnamese, half-Chinese, one of the few good things to come out of the last border war between those two countries. Pepsi was a Nordic-Anglo mix who—Shenda had always privately observed to herself—resembled no one so much as that infamous comix icon, Cherry Poptart.

The two women were fussing inordinately over Thurman. All

they lacked for their role of *houris* were giant palm fronds to fan
him with.

"Can I get you some more juice, Thurman?"

"Would you like another cushion, Thurman?"

"Is that sun too much for you?"

"Have some potato chips, Thurman! They're fresh!"

A burst of jealousy ignited like a Roman candle in Shenda's
chest. What did those two think they were *doing!*

Ever since Shenda had told Pepsi and SinSin that Thurman
had admired her pedicure— Shenda's footwork their handiwork—
they had taken a silly fancy to him.

"You know how rare it is for a *man* to notice something like
that, Shenda?"

"And then to say it *out loud* in a *public place!*"

"Wow!"

Additionally, Thurman's sickly condition had sent their unfulfilled maternal nursing instincts into overdrive.

It was all very innocent and probably good for them all.

But somehow, today, it made Shenda's blood percolate!

Shenda marched over.

When Thurman spotted her, he got guiltily to his feet.

"Un, hi, Shen—"

Shenda cut off the feeble greeting. "You, Swan—come with
me!"

"I'll be right back—

"No, you won't! Hurry up!"

Shenda stalked off, leaving Thurman to stump after her.

When they were some distance away, Shenda stopped under
the semiconcealing foliage of a willow. Fronds whispered at her
passage. Thurman caught up and leaned gratefully against the
trunk, out of breath.

"Do you know what those two are?" demanded Shenda. Without waiting for an answer, she spat, "They're lovers! Lesbians!
Lipstick lesbians!"

Thurman looked puzzled. "So what? I can't be friends with
them? It's not like I want babies or anything."

Shenda's ire deflated. She lowered her head and pinched her
brow. "Oh my god, what am I *saying?* They're my friends too. I
don't care they're lesbians! I never even thought *twice* about it
before! I swear it! That's not *me!*"

Thurman moved next to Shenda. Cane in his right hand, he
took her left in his. He didn't press any advantage that her confu-

sion provided, but simply said, "Don't worry about it, Shenda. You must have a lot on your mind."

Shenda felt immense gratitude for the sympathy. The same tactical pause she employed not to prejudge others, she now used to forgive herself. "I do, I do! In fact—" she consulted her watch "—I've got a meeting to call to order that's already late!"

"Let's go then."

People were already gathering expectantly about the central focus of the bandstand, growing quiet and alert. The crowd parted for Shenda, and she found Thurman somehow still behind her, his face drained from the small exertions.

"Oh, shit, I am so sorry I dragged you around like this!"

"I—I wouldn't have missed it for anything."

"Listen—you can't stand for the whole time, and the only seat is up there with me. Do you mind?"

"Nuh-no," panted Thurman.

They ascended the three stairs, finding themselves amid the band's equipment and instruments. Thurman collapsed onto Buddy Cheetah's drumset stool. Shenda picked up the microphone and tested it. It was on. With a backward glance to make sure Thurman was okay, she shifted into business mode and began.

"This meeting of Karuna, Inc., is now officially underway. Can I have the minutes of the last meeting, please? Ellen Woodrose, are you out there?"

Business was conducted. People ascended the stage as called. Officers read reports. Motions were proposed. Yays and nays were tallied. People were praised or confronted. Plans were debated and modified. Arguments expired in compromise. Agreements were reached. No blood was spilled.

At last Shenda was able to utter one of her favorite sentences. "If there is no more business, then this meeting is adjourned—"

Chef Mona called loudly out from the mass of people. "Shenda, I got a shortage of help and grill space today! Which should I cook first? The veggie burgers or the meat?"

The crowd went into noisy spasms. "The meat, the meat!" "No, the falafel first!"

Then an anonymous voice called out: "Let the dogs vote!"

The whole crowd took up the absurd chant: "Let the dogs vote! Let the dogs vote!"

Children ran off screaming to herd the romping packs up to the tables. Like a madman's cattle drive, the dogs were chivvied toward the food tables.

Shenda knew them all by sight. Spaniels, briards, whippets, shepherds, Scotties, terriers, Great Danes, greyhounds, sheep dogs and many a miscegenetic mongrel. Hounds and lapdogs, hunters and retrievers. Ten thousand years of human-inspired breeding. There was French Fry, Slinky Dog, Muzzletuff, Oftenbark, E. Collie, Dogberry, Wagstaff, Nixon, Tuff Gong, Gromit, G-Spot, Snake, Whiskey, Deedles, Subwoofer—and dozens more.

And of course, sticking out like a bright bouncy beachball, the resplendent Bullfinch.

The kids had succeeded in massing the dogs around Chef Mona. In her hands, she held two patties: one meat, one bean. The crowd fell still as Arctic night.

Strangely, the dogs too had grown calm and composed. They seemed aware of the responsibility that had devolved on them.

Mona bent and offered the patties.

Not a single dog moved forward out of the ring. Instead, they seemed to consult with muted growls and ear prickings among themselves.

Then one animal emerged from the pack as if nominated by the rest, strutting with immense dignity right up to his own personal canine Judgment of Paris.

Bullfinch.

And without a second's hesitation he chose the falafel.

Half the crowd applauded, half booed, before dissolving into a disorganized surge toward the buffet.

On the stage Shenda turned to Thurman, whose face was wreathed in amazement.

"And that's how we do things *por la* Karuna!"

9.

The Illogic of Conquest

In his vast, statue-littered bedroom, before his official busy day began, Marmaduke Twigg sought to fortify himself for his off-the-record meeting with Kraft Durchfreude. The guiding black light of Isoterm lifted his silken pajama top, revealing a small titanium port like a robot's nipple implanted in his side. He attached a transparent feedline leading to an IV sac hanging on a stand. Triggered by the connection, his inner pump began to hum. Blue fluid flowed directly into his veins.

No time to get the Zingo through his slow digestive tract now! Durchfreude would be here any moment.

Twigg dreaded the meeting. All he could picture was Durchfreude holding the nail gun and firing into Stanes's head. The expression on the creature's face! Something not present at previous initiations—a trace of deadly disengagement, of schizoid withdrawal—had crawled beneath the tightly held surface of the Dark Intercessor's face.

Twigg suspected that Durchfreude's unstable brain was finally fractionating. As when a glacier meets the sea, parts were calving off, achieving or struggling for autonomy. The jigsaw pieces of Durchfreude's mind were twitching with a life of their own, hopping out of their former plane of alignment.

Of course, this made the catspaw of the PGL highly unreliable—dangerous in fact—and subject to immediate termination.

Still, Twigg hoped to get just one more assignment out of him. A simple one, to be sure, but necessary.

As the IV bag collapsed with an accompanying mechanical sucking sound from Twigg's thorax, he felt a twinge of regret at Durchfreude's disintegration and imminent demolition. None of this had been the man's own fault, of course. Why, Twigg remembered when Kraft Durchfreude had been the ultra-competent head of Squamous Securities, a legend in the world of cutthroat business dealings. And even after the surgical bungle he had lived a useful life, performing with *eclat* and *brio* the dirtiest tasks the PGL members could dredge up for him. Why, even as far back as six or seven years ago, when Twigg had sent the Dark Intercessor to the Persian Gulf, the monster had still been at the top of his form. Look how ingeniously he had raked Isoterm's nuts from the fire, destroying all evidence of the company's sales to Iraq of CBW *materiel*. Even the highly over-rated CIA had been unable to prevent Durchfreude's access to pertinent records of theirs, which had forever after gone conveniently missing. . . .

But now—now was a different story.

After this job, Twigg would present his suspicions and proofs to the godsons and goddaughters of Phineas Gage. Surely they all must have noticed the falling-off in Durchfreude's performance, the strains in his behavior, and would agree on his lethal disposition, despite any temporary inconveniences.

Twigg suspected that only one real issue, never made explicit, had stayed their hands thus far.

Where would they *ever* find a successor with Durchfreude's exquisite taste in kidnap victims for the monthly rites?

The bedroom door opened as Twigg was unsnapping his feed.

A quivering Paternoster ushered in the bald and skeletal Kraft Durchfreude, then hastily backed out, as if from the vicinity of a cobra.

Dropping his pajama shirt, Twigg manufactured affability out of unease. "Kraft, my good man! Come right in. I hope they fed you well downstairs."

The thing's voice was as uncontoured as a worm. "I ate."

"Wonderful! Never conduct negotiations on an empty stomach, that's my rule. Makes one too eager to have them over! Not that we're performing what one might term negotiations, of course."

"No."

Unnervingly, Durchfreude's popeyed gaze never strayed from Twigg's mouth, as if the Dark Intercessor were contemplating cruel refinements in the form and function of that organ. Twigg stammered, "Yes, well, be that as it may." He tried to project authority. "Here is your assignment. I have recently encountered several nuclei of resistance across the nation, holdouts fighting the introduction of a new Isoterm product. Zingo, a soft drink. I'd like you to visit each of these sites and insure that they are permanently removed as sources of opposition. You should start with one in particular, more organized than most. It's at the head of the list. You'll find the specifics in these papers."

Twigg handed over a file folder. "Is everything clear?"

"Why?"

The simple word stopped Twigg like a wall. He couldn't recall Durchfreude ever uttering that syllable before. Further sign of his slide into mental chaos.

" 'Why?' What do you mean?"

The monster struggled to cloak nebulous thoughts in the proper words. "Why must—why must you go where you aren't wanted? Can't you purchase those who would be purchased, and —and leave the others alone?"

"Kraft, my good fellow, surely you jest! It is my absolute nature to flow into all available niches, to drive out and break all competition, to smash and burn and crush, to grind the faces of the conquered into the dust, until only I alone am left standing, regnant over all I survey, even if that should be a smoking wasteland of my own devising! My categorical imperative is that all my actions must conduce toward the magnification of my supreme presence. Why, had I infinite time and infinite space to fill, it would still not be enough to hold my tremendous vitality! It's not that I particularly want to sell soda pop! Great Satan, no! And there is nothing sinister about Zingo, no addictive properties or brainwashing qualities. In fact, the drink is a not completely unhealthful, if nasty tasting mix of electrolytes, Olestra, Nutrasweet, and some artificial flavors and coloring. Good for keeping the masses fit for the assembly line. And of course, the money is trivial. No, it's simply a matter of not allowing my will, however arbitrary and capricious, to be thwarted."

"I—I see."

Twigg clapped a hand on Durchfreude's shoulder. "Of course you see. You may do no other."

Twigg's shifted line of vision now encompassed the stasis-control device on the tabletop. On a powerful whim, he picked it up, aimed and brought his tiger nemesis instantly to life. At the same time he stepped behind Durchfreude as a screen, so that the tiger would spot that man first.

The enraged wild tormented beast rocketed toward Durchfreude. But the Dark Intercessor never so much as flinched.

Twigg froze the big cat only when its whiskers were nearly touching Durchfreude, who—only upon seeing the threat neutralized—stepped deftly aside to allow it to crash to the carpet.

Durchfreude regarded his employer emotionlessly. Then he turned and left.

Twigg sensed then that he should have let the Siberian finish the job.

But now it was really rather too late.

10.

Karuna Kaput

Thurman really could not think of much he would want to change right now in his life, except of course for the state of his health, the less-than-optimal condition of his tainted organs and flesh and bones. A collection of mismatched parts barely holding together (although seemingly, thankfully, not getting worse).

And yet—even with that grim toe-stepping partner, Miss Function, he was learning to dance, to shuffle gamely around life's ballroom.

After all, as Shenda had said, his problems were *old* shit.

He was really getting his act together at last, after the disastrous end to his Army career. Coming out of his shell, turning over a new leaf, climbing every mountain, and a raft of other natural metaphors.

Why, one day it seemed possible he might even own a dog!

Things looked sweet.

Every morning he arose early after a semidecent night's sleep. (His joints still pained him, his stomach still often rebelled against supper, but somehow his mind was more at ease, and that helped a lot.) Dressed, he measuredly walked the ten blocks to the Karuna Koffeehouse and through the laffing door, where he was treated to Verity-whipped espresso eggs and the latest creation of that baking genius, Odd Vibe: a buttery, cheddary croissant with fractal flaking layers.

"You eat good now, Tor-man, you betcha!"

"Very good, Odd Vibe. Thanks!"

The familiar faces and repeated rituals of the place soothed him. There resounded Chug'em's fourth long slurp, here came Nello with his latest dirty joke, there was Buddy executing intricate rhythms on the countertop with two wooden spoons.

Even the mean scowl and mimed expressions of distaste directed his way each day by Fuquan Fletcher (who had never again verbally or physically accosted Thurman) were an integral part of his daily routine.

The place to come when even home isn't kind enough.

Indeed, indeed.

At a quarter to nine, the taxi from Kall-a-Kab would pull up and beep for him, and he'd ride to his job.

Vance von Jolly had proved to be a decent boss. Any sternness or disdain exhibited by the man was a tartness solely in service to his art, and would just as likely be turned toward himself.

"Thurman, I ask you—have you ever seen such a pitifully derivative waste of canvas? If Big Daddy or the ol' Kootchie-Koo hisself could see this sad excuse for a painting, they'd break all my brushes in half and throw my ass out on the street. Scrape it down, will you, before I barf. I'm gonna go sand down that T-bird."

Having no artistic talent or insight, Thurman simply did as he was told. (When working with potentially noxious chemicals, he wore full protective duds: respirator, gloves, smock. The proximity to pigments and sprays and solvents seemed not to be worsening his ailments anyhow.) His natural obedience and alacrity, modified by his body's limits, seemed to suffice. For the past two weeks he had collected a more than generous paycheck.

And many times a week, he got to see Shenda Moore.

The vibrant, seemingly inexhaustible leader of the Kompassionate Konglomerate (as Thurman had mentally dubbed Karuna, Inc., inspired by its treatment of himself and all others) blew into the garage like an hourglass-shaped twister at unpredictable intervals, bearing directives, advice, questions, checks, official forms, gifts of food and flowers. And she always offered up a personal comment or two, out of that massive Rolodex concealed in her pretty head.

Whenever she wasn't around, Thurman thought he had no illusions about Shenda ever being more to him than a not-too-intimate friend. That moment of connection under the willow tree had been a fluke, never referred to again.

But when her warm and radiant body and blithe spirit actually occupied the same room as Thurman, he was convinced he loved her and always would.

Maybe all he needed was another opening. . . .

Early Saturday evening in Morley Adams Park. Dusk calls of birds, skybowl purpling, lawns releasing their night odors, stone wall still warm against his back, planks of the bench rough under his butt. Hands folded in his lap, Thurman contemplated the foot-gouged trough of dirt at his feet.

What had brought him here? Usually he was abed by now, watching TV or listening to the radio. Hoping to recapture some of that magic willow-shrouded day perhaps. . . .

A tennis ball rolled up to nestle between his V-angled sneakers.

Then a beautifully ugly jonquil dogface appeared, tongue lolling out to drip approximately a pint of slobber on Thurman's Nikes.

"Hey, Thurman, what's up?"

Shenda dropped down beside Thurman. If a transdimensional imp had materialized and hauled a giant cartoon moneybag out of some fold of hyperspace and offered it to him, Thurman could not have been more stunned.

Shenda ignored his blank amazement. "Me and Bully are out for the first time in *days!* I could kick myself sometimes! Get so involved in the *biz,* you know. And what's it all for, if not minutes like this?"

"I agree. Minutes. Just like this."

Shenda said nothing for a time. Thurman recalled the silence she had cultivated prior to blasting his psyche apart, and inwardly flinched. But when she spoke, her words were mild.

"How're SinSin and Pepsi and you getting on these days?"

"Oh, them! Great, fine. They're very nice to me. They even took me to the beach the other day. I don't remember the name of the place, but there was a real big-hair crowd—"

"Uh-huh. Been there once with them myself. You should have seen this one lifeguard. Buff but dim! Well, he just went straight after Pepsi like—"

Shenda's story was long and involved and funny. She rattled on as if she hadn't talked recreationally in too long a time. Thurman had only to nod and interpolate a few monosyllables to keep the narrative flowing. One tale segued into another. Every few minutes one of the humans offhandedly tossed the ball for Bullfinch. When it became too dark for the dog to see anything, he lay beneath the bench and began to snore.

Thurman began to talk a little about himself. Presently he found that their roles had flipped, with Shenda doing most of the listening and nodding.

Around ten-thirty, Shenda jumped up. "Louie Kablooie! I have to make my rounds!"

"Your rounds? At this hour?"

"Before I can sleep, I go around to all our businesses and make sure they're locked up safe. The Koffeehouse is last, at midnight."

Thurman thought this sounded obsessive, but only said, "Even on the weekend?"

"Like maybe thieves don't *work* weekends?"

"Well, I guess I'll say goodbye then—"

"No, don't! Please. You can keep me company."

"Ride shotgun?"

Shenda made pistol fingers and fired a few imaginary shots into the dust. "Dance, pardner!"

The three of them got into the Jetta, Bullfinch sprawled in the back seat, and were soon circulating down lonesome urban trails.

Their small sedate city was winding down by the time they pulled up to the Karuna.

All dark, save for a lone light still on in the kitchen.

"That's probably Fuquan, getting the beans ready for tomorrow so he can sleep in late. He's got a key."

Emboldened by this time spent together, Thurman was about to inquire just what, if anything, Shenda felt for that obnoxious guy.

Then a gunshot sounded, plain as a million dollar vase shattering.

From inside the Karuna.

"No!" yelled Shenda.

The woman and the dog were out of the car before Thurman could even get the unfamiliar door open. Damn, where was the *handle*—!

All hell arrived, with bells on.

An enormous *CRUMP!*, followed by a *WHOOSH!*, and the Karuna burst into flames, sending glass flying like deadly stars into the street.

A stick figure in a business suit emerged from the storeside alley like a demon stepping from an inferno. He walked calmly away from the blazing structure, gun hanging down by his side.

Shenda hesitated, but Bullfinch did not.

The dog raced across the street and catapulted himself at the man.

The living skeleton's reaction was out of all proportion to the unarmed assault. As if facing some supernatural creature, the arsonist-killer dropped his gun, screamed, threw up his arms and tottered backward.

Bullfinch impacted, sending the man over completely to bounce his head off the curb.

By the time Thurman made his lame way over, Shenda was kicking the unconscious man in the side and screaming.

"Bastard! You fucking killer *bastard!*"

Thurman pulled her back. "Shenda, stop!"

Shenda collapsed like a string-and-bead toy whose pushed button releases the tension that sustains it. Thurman kneeled to hold her up. A migraine was flowering behind his eyes.

And then he saw the killer's face.

Furnace skies. Sand lacquered with blood. Greasy, roilsome black clouds. . . .

And to his instant horror, Thurman knew he knew him.

11.

La Iyalocha

Nothing would ever, ever be the same.

And Shenda Moore was the one to blame.

This sad couplet ran and ran in Shenda's brain. Like a mean virus of found poetry self-assembled from fridge-magnet vocabulary. As towers and spurts of crackling fire illuminated her dog and the two men and her own crumpled self on the oil-slicked macadam, Shenda realized with absolute certainty that what she had long awaited and pretended not to fear—like a child whistling in Oya's graveyard—had now found her. The unraveling of all her careful labors. The major fuck-up. The explosion of chaos you're lucky to walk away from. The shitstorm that takes innocent bystanders and chews them up like pumpkin seeds.

Innocents like Fuquan Fletcher.

Poor Fuquan!

And despite all prior pretense of equanimity, the disaster scared her.

Scared the piss out of her—

And made her fighting mad!

Some sick and evil motherfucker was going to pay.

Sirens began to wail like delighted banshees. Shenda leaped to her feet.

"In the car with this pig. Quick!"

Thurman's expression revealed major perplexity. "But the police—"

"The police are whores! They *know* this man and his bosses! They suck at the same hindteat! Believe me!"

Thurman bent and lifted the unconscious killer's arms. Shenda saw the crippled Swan try to hide a wince and grunt.

"Oh, Thurman, I forgot. Can you do it?"

"I can do it—"

Between them they hustled the guy into the back seat of the Jetta. Shenda lashed his arms and legs together with rope from the trunk. Bullfinch leaped in and sat atop the man's chest, proudly on guard. Shenda and Thurman piled in. They tore off in the direction opposite from the hastening firetrucks just a block away.

"Where are we going?"

"To my aunt's house."

Shenda hadn't known the answer to Thurman's question until he asked it. But as soon as she opened her mouth, their destination was obvious.

Only Titi Yaya could help her now.

As she drove, Shenda filled Thurman in on the shakedown moves being directed at the Karuna and other businesses in town.

"This has to be Maraplan's doing. Mealey and his fucking Zingo! He practically told me something like this was coming. And me, the stupid smart bitch, so *muy* competent, thinking I could handle everything myself! Look where it got me. Look where it got Fuquan!"

Shenda could feel tears threatening to spill out. No, not yet. She sought to relieve some of her feelings by smacking the steering wheel with her fists; the car veered; she recovered.

Thurman looked appalled. "Shenda, don't be so hard on yourself. If the authorities *were* in on this, what else could you have done?"

"A lot! I could have hired some security guards, for one thing."

"And then maybe more people would have died. No, these are jokers who don't mind how many bodies they leave in their wake."

Shenda turned to study her passenger's face. "You sound so sure. What do you know?"

Thurman shared what he knew.

"Louie Kablooie," whispered Shenda. *El pulpo* grew more and more tentacles. In a louder voice: "Then the jerks behind Zingo—they're the same ones who fucking poisoned all you Gulf War vets!"

"It sure looks like it."

"I hate them!"

Thurman said nothing for a moment. Presently: "Well, I was full of hate for a long time too. Then you told me it was all old shit."

Shenda was too angry to listen to her own past advice. "Well, it's new shit again. Get pissed."

Their cargo did not awake during their journey cross-town. Within twenty minutes, Shenda was in the neighborhood, parking in front of the brownstone where Titi Yaya lived.

They hustled the killer up the steps like a sack of cornmeal, the pudgy daffodil Bullfinch somberly following, one awkward jump at a time, tags on his collar jingling. Shenda rang her aunt's bell just to alert the woman, but used her own key. They were quickly in the tile-floored foyer without anyone seeing their unconventional arrival.

Thurman was gasping. "Is there an elevator?"

Shenda was winded too. And everything felt unreal. "Not needed. Just down the hall."

They half dragged their captive down the hall. At the end, a door was already opening.

There stood Titi Yaya, elder sister of Shenda's Mom, Consolacion Amado.

La iyalocha.

The small and trim old woman wore a blue-striped white-flannel robe and corduroy slippers. Necklaces and bracelets adorned her form. Long, unbound coal-black hair was at odds with her age-lined, dark honey-colored face. Equally unlikely—yet so comfortingly familiar to Shenda—was a vibrant power, tinged with sexuality, that radiated off her, blazed in her eyes.

"I was not sleeping," said Titi Yaya. "The *cowries* told me there would be trouble tonight, Shen-Shen. And I encountered the twisted branch of Eleggua in my path on the way to the store this morning. I knew that you would need me."

"Oh, Titi! Everything's gone wrong!"

"We'll fix what we can. Although I have to tell you the signs are not good."

They were inside, door shut, as safe as possible, considering.

Shenda looked around. Nothing had changed since the day a scared and tearful five-year-old had come to live here, after the child's father, Tresvant Moore, crack-addled, had killed Consolacion and himself.

All the furniture was old-fashioned and immaculate, much of it in transparent plastic covers. Worn rugs had been vacuumed speckless. Artificial flowers and innocuous prints decorated end tables and papered walls. Smells of cooking, ancient and recent, permeated the air—and below that olfactory layer, the unmistakable whiff of *omiero*, that potent herbal concoction.

So far, so normal, an apartment like that of any other *aleyo*, any other nonbeliever.

But then Shenda's eye traveled to the altars and shrines, earthly homes of the celestial *orisha* gods and afterlife *eggun* spirits. Colorful and cloth-draped, laden with statues, pictures, vases, *sopera* tureens, instruments of sacrifice. Sumptuously bestrewn with offerings of live flowers, toys, cigars, rum and food.

Titi Yaya's apartment was a *casa de santo*, a Santeria temple, site of a thousand, thousand ceremonies, daily, weekly, monthly, yearly observances and propitiations, possessions, beseechings and repayments, spell-castings and curse-cleansings, a refuge for petitioners and meeting place for Titi Yaya's peers, the male *babalawos* and female *iyalochas*.

All of this had been taken for granted by the growing child named Shenda Moore. She had hardly given a thought to the various sanctified weirdness that she had often witnessed. The *tambors*, the *rogación de cabeza*, the *Pinaldos*. It had all been part of the new stability she had experienced upon being taken under the wing of her unmarried aunt.

And yet, somehow, she had never penetrated fully into the Religion—or it had failed to penetrate her. About the time she would have been expected to commit to Santeria, she began hanging with the Black kids at school—her father's seductive heritage —and the Cuban half of her background grew even less interesting to her. Analogue, antique and uncool.

After testing the stubborn strength of her niece's convictions,

Titi Yaya had refrained from coercion. Only an occasional mild reminder from time to time that the door was still open.

Santeria didn't proselytize, didn't do missionary work.

You came to *la iyalocha* because you *needed* the *orishas*.

And now Shenda was here.

But maybe too late.

Titi Yaya stooped to pet Bullfinch and whisper in his ear. The dog's tail propellered. Rising, the *santera* addressed Shenda.

"Get that man in a chair. And untie him."

"But Titi, he's a killer!"

"He can cause no harm here."

With Thurman's help, Shenda did as she was told. Shanghaied into this mess, the man was being more accepting than Shenda had any right to expect.

Thurman whispered. "Your aunt. She's some kind of witch?"

"Not witch. Priestess."

"Oh. Her place is weird. But nice. You know—I had a massive headache when I came in here, but it's gone now."

"That always happens."

Across the room, Titi Yaya, now barefoot, took no notice of them. She made the *foribale*, the prostration before the altar.

The altar of Babalu-Aye.

Louie Kablooie, as five-year-old Shenda had dubbed him.

Saint Lazarus was the plaster Catholic disguise the *orisha* wore: a loincloth-clad, sore-riddled, bearded beggar with crutch, his loyal dog always by his side.

Standing now, shredding coconut husk fibers before the statue, feeding with liquid the saint's sacred stones concealed in the ornate tureen, chanting in Yoruban, Titi Yaya was invoking his help.

She paused, turned to her visitors.

"I need the *derecho*."

Shenda's purse was forgotten in the car. She said to Thurman, "Give me a dollar."

Thuman dug in his pocket and came up with a bill. Shenda passed it to *la iyalocha*, who tucked it into a niche of the statue.

The ceremony was long and complex. The day began to catch up with Shenda. Despite all the terror and turbulent emotions, she found her eyelids drooping. She cast a glance at Thurman Swan. He seemed riveted, as did an alert Bullfinch. The Maraplan-Isoterm hireling remained eyelid-shuttered and unstirring.

Suddenly Titi Yaya spun and was upon them. It was not as if

she had moved, but as if the room had revolved around her.

Behind her face Babalu-Aye dwelled.

The old woman clutched the killer around the waist with both hands. His body jolted as if electrified, his eyes snapping open.

Then she — or rather, the *orisha* within her — lifted him as if weightless, holding him effortlessly aloft.

Babalu-Aye's voice was a guttural growl. "Speak!"

The man began to recite his personal history, starting with his name.

Kraft Durchfreude's story unreeled for hours. Shenda and Thurman sat transfixed at the enormity of the far-stretching, long-living evil his tale contained. Dawnlight filtered through the gauzy curtains before he was done. For the whole time Babalu-Aye held him ceilingward like a doll, a rigid tableau.

When at last the recitation was finished, Babalu-Aye dropped Durchfreude back in the chair. The *orisha* departed his servant, and Titi Yaya returned, her loaned body seemingly unaffected by the superhuman exertion.

Shenda rubbed her grainy eyes. "Titi Yaya, what — what *is* he?"

"An *egungun*, a shell. He is possessed by the dead man he once was."

Thurman spoke. "A zombie?"

"If you will."

"What can we do with him?" asked Thurman.

"I can end his artificial life with the proper spell —" suggested *la iyalocha*.

Shenda had been thinking about the immense horrors wrought by Durchfreude and the Phineas Gage League. Now she spoke.

"No. Wake him up enough to realize what has been done to him. Some of the things he said make it seem he's halfway there already. Then — send him back to his masters."

Titi Yaya reached out to touch Shenda's wrist. "That will set large and uncontrollable forces in action, daughter. You play one *orisha* against another. Are you ready for the consequences?"

Shenda felt emptied of emotions. Pity, remorse, fear, hope, hate — all were just words without referents. Her body was thin as a piece of paper. Only weariness ached inside her.

"All I know is that I don't want to live in a world where such things go on. Let's end them if we can."

"Very well."

Into the kitchen stepped Titi Yaya. Sounds of bottles and tins being opened, bowls and spoons and whisks being employed trickled in to Shenda and Thurman.

She returned with two small vials full of subtly differing cloudy mixtures, one open and one corked. From the open one, she anointed Durchfreude's joints and head, made him swallow the remaining pungent liquid, chanting all the while.

The *egungun*'s eyes showed white, his limbs twitched. Bullfinch barked. Durchfreude got spastically to his feet. When his vision was again functioning, he lurched out of the *casa de santo*.

Shenda knew it was time for them to leave also. "Titi, you know I can never repay you."

"The debt is all mine, daughter. I should have been more forceful with you, made you take the Necklaces, gotten you under the protection of the *orishas*. Now I fear it is too late. The gods do not like being ignored for so long. And they are vengeful when slighted. I will work for you despite this."

Shenda hugged her aunt. "Thank you, Titi! That's all I can ask. Come on, Thurman. I'll drive you home."

Thurman and Bullfinch preceded Shenda. At the outer door, when Thurman was already down the stairs and on the street, Titi Yaya pressed the second vial into Shenda's hand. "This is for your sick boyfriend, dear. It will help him."

Boyfriend?

Shenda regarded Thurman thoughtfully.

Boyfriend.

What *didn't* Titi Yaya know?

12.

A Cavern Measureless to Man

Samuel Stanes wore only a small head bandage a month after his surgery. Even in the dim light of the abandoned subway station, Twigg could detect the powerful knowledge of the limitless freedom conferred by the neuro-alteration alight in the newest member's eyes.

Now the Phineas Gage League was up to full strength. The resulting synergy and competition would doubtlessly inspire them all to new heights of ambition and conquest. At times, Twigg enjoyed the cruel play that flourished amongst them. At other times, he would have preferred to have the entire world to himself, resenting the presence of the others. But such had been the way since the League began.

Not that there could never be changes.

And yet Twigg, even in his speculative heresy, failed to intuit that changes waited literally just around the corner.

Out of the darkness and into the station pulled the little mining train, Kraft Durchfreude at the helm.

The Dark Intercessor looked like a poorly constructed scarecrow from the fields of Dis. He seemed to have spent a longish period of dirty action without bathing or changing his normally immaculate suit, resulting in a shambolic appearance.

Twigg shook his head ruefully. Deplorable and dangerous. Shameful, if such a word could apply. It was like watching a corpse rot. This would have to be the meeting where they dealt with Durchfreude. They could send him on an errand and discuss his fate then.

Climbing aboard with his peers, Twigg noticed two oddities.

The pile of victims in the last car was covered with a tarp.

And instead of the expected whiff of unclean flesh, a strange herbal odor wafted off their driver. Twigg found it instinctively repugnant.

Down the long dark descent the train chugged, finally arriving in the flambeau-lit charnel cave.

The cold flyblown broken meats of their last feast still festooned the tables. The corpses, thankfully, had been removed. But no pleasant repast awaited their delectation. The smells of old rot were gagsome.

Further strangeness: Durchfreude did not servilely hasten to move up the portable steps for their ease of disembarking. He seemed frozen at the controls of the train.

With Twigg taking the initiative, the League members got awkwardly out.

Now Durchfreude did an unprecedented thing. He backed up the train until the last car effectively blocked the narrow tunnel mouth, their only exit from the meeting place.

Twigg began to feel very ill at ease.

Durchfreude stepped down. Jerkily, he moved to the caboose. Awkwardly, he pulled the tarp off.

The victims therein were already unfairly dead, some of them quite messily. With a burgeoning horror, Twigg recognized one of the corpses as a highly placed Isoterm executive. Others he knew as important members of other PGL-led companies, a fact confirmed by gasps and demands made by his compatriots.

"What is the meaning of this?" "Is this some kind of obscene joke?" "I can't believe what I'm seeing!" "Durchfreude, explain yourself!"

Give their senior member full credit for bravery. Creaky old Firgower moved toward the Dark Intercessor, relying on old patterns of dominance.

"We want to know the meaning of your actions right now!" quavered the very illustrious head of Stonecipher Industries.

By way of explanation, Durchfreude reached in among the bodies and retrieved an exceedingly sophisticated automatic weapon.

A rubber apron was not a satisfactory shield. The first blast cut Firgower to gory flinders, giving the others time to scatter.

But in the final sense, there was no place to run.

With stoic lack of affect, Durchfreude calmly potted the screaming members wherever they sought to hide. In their frantic scrambles and inevitable death throes, all the furniture of the chamber was overturned and smashed.

Twigg's mind on the conscious side of the dam was blank. But not for long. A single stray bullet in his side filled his superman's brain with crimson anguish.

He fell to the carpet, facedown, a hand going to his wound.

Metal. He felt metal. His pump had caught the bullet, stopped it penetrating further.

Twigg lay still.

Eventually the screaming and inarticulate gurgling stopped.

But the shooting continued, a single round at a time.

Ever conscientious, Durchfreude was slowly walking around the scene of slaughter, putting a *coup-de-grâce* shot or three into each surgically altered brain.

Twigg opened his eyes.

He was staring into the lifeless blood-freckled face of Isabelle Fistule a few feet away.

Between them lay a familiar machete, often employed for fun, now his last hope for survival.

With infinite slowness he snaked his hand toward it.

Just as he stealthily clasped the handle Durchfreude's shoes appeared in his vision. The man's back was toward Twigg, as he pumped mercy shots into Fistule.

Still supine, Twigg swung up and around with all his strength.

A deep pained grunt.

Hamstrung, the mad assassin collapsed, rifle flying off.

Twigg was atop the creature in a kind of parody of sexual

mounting. The face of the Dark Intercessor remained blank as ever.

Seeking to compose his mind, Twigg felt a greatness invade him from outside. Perhaps it was only his damaged pump flooding him with an uncontrolled mix of hormones and chemicals and soft drink. But whatever the source, amidst the stench and clotting filth, something celestial descended and rode Twigg like a horse.

"Speak," ordered Twigg.

Durchfreude began a mechanical recitation covering the past few days.

When he was finished, Twigg said, "The servant is not to blame for the master's mistakes. Die cleanly now."

Durchfreude's jugular blood sprayed Twigg from waist to head, feeding his power.

Twigg stood up beneath the splattered gaze of Phineas Gage.

Alone. He was all alone, the only one of his kind in all the world.

How wonderful!

13.

Fuquan's Sendoff

In the three days following the burning of the Karuna and the visit to Titi Yaya's, much happened.

Thurman felt dizzied by it all.

First, the police. They had found the dropped gun in the street and conclusively linked it to the bullet obtained from Fuquan's charred corpse. The fact that the only fingerprints on the pistol were those of a long-dead respectable businessman proved only that the weapon had probably been stolen and kept unused for years, then handled by a gloved killer. Much persistent questioning ensued. The firemen had reported a fleeing car, but had been unable to provide positive ID that would link it to Shenda. Still, as with any business-related fire—especially one involving apparent concealment of a death—the suspicions of the authorities turned first on the owner and putatively disgruntled employees and customers.

"Now, Mister Swan," said Sgt. Botcher. A comb-over, a plump ruddy face, and a black vinyl belt distinguished the policeman. This did not cause Thurman to underestimate him however. "Witnesses report that you had a little run-in with the victim some weeks ago."

"It—it was nothing. He got mad when he thought I had eyes for a woman he wanted."

"Ah-ha. I see. A woman. Would you mind divulging her name?"

Thurman knew he couldn't lie, and also how suspicious all this would sound. "It was Miss Moore."

"Miss Moore. The owner. Hmmm. She sure has her hand in a lot of businesses in this city. All properly insured, though, I bet."

Sgt. Botcher made a little tick in his notebook. Then he threw Thurman a wild pitch that appeared to be an attempt to establish a specious bond.

"You're a vet, Mister Swan?"

"Yes. The Gulf War."

"Me too. 'Nam. One long hellacious fuck-up and fuck-over. Yours was penny-ante. Just a few months of the bosses testing some new systems and keeping their hand in."

Thurman tried to imagine his debilitating chronic illness as something penny-ante. Maybe to someone outside Thurman's skin that was how it looked. "I guess. . . ."

"Learned all about guns in the service, naturally."

"Well, sure, the necessary drill. But I don't think I ever fired one in combat. Mainly I was a demolitions man."

Sgt. Botcher's eyes got as wide as camera shutters in a dark room. "That'll be all, Mister Swan. And please—don't leave town without letting us know."

But the police were only a minor upset in Thurman's existence. They were blind and unknowing of the strange new reality that had been revealed by Kraft Durchfreude's hypnotic confession. (And God help the authorities if they were ever unlucky enough to track down that monster!) Tiresome as they were, they grew bored, went away eventually and could be forgotten. A number of other things were more disturbing, less forgettable, and did not seem likely soon to go away.

The shattering of his newly fashioned cozy routine, for one. With the destruction of the Karuna, he had no way to start his day. No familiar faces and rituals, no laughter and jokes, no hearty boost of generosity, goodwill and nourishing food. It left a void at the center of Thurman's day. And whenever he encountered other members of the Karuna family, he saw the same sad feelings at work in them.

"Go home, Thurman," Vance von Jolly told him when he showed up for work the next morning after the dawn departure from Titi Yaya's *casa de santo*. The artist was stretched out on his couch, paint-stained covers pulled over his face. A small rigid tower poked the blanket up at groin level. "Someone's scraped the canvas of my heart with a blowtorch. The palette of my soul is crusted dry. I drag raced with the Devil and lost."

Thurman could take a hint. He left. Back in his lonely apartment, he felt that his life was shutting down again. Old physical and mental aches began to reassert themselves. It would be so easy to slip down that dark bottomless well once more—

Thurman got up and went looking for Shenda.

He found her exiting the Kandomble Brothers Funeral Home.

Shenda looked ragged. Red tired eyes, new downward-dragging lines around her mouth. The mainspring of Karuna, Inc., was plainly unwound. Thurman still found her beautiful.

She hugged Thurman tightly, then released him.

"Fuquan's mother asked me to handle the arrangements. She's old, and doesn't have two nickles. It's all taken care of now. No wake, just the funeral day after tomorrow."

"I'll be there. Shenda—"

She placed two fingers gently on his lips, as if in a blessing. Electricity sparked. "Not now, Thurman, okay? After the funeral. Right now I have to cobble together temporary jobs for Verity and Buddy and the other baristas who are out of work. Then there's a lot of official crap connected with the fire. And I want to find a new home for the Karuna. And the police—"

"Sgt. Botcher. I know. Okay, Shenda. See you back here."

He watched her drive away.

On the morning of the funeral—bright, fragrant, dawn rain-washed, implacably beautiful— Thurman was dressing in his lone suit and leather shoes, disinterred from the closet. It felt strange to be out of sweats and sneakers after so long. Too bad it wasn't a wedding. . . .

The radio was giving the news. There seemed to have been an inordinate number of executive corporate jet crashes over the past twenty-four hours, all inevitably fatal. It was almost as if—

Thurman put *that* notion firmly out of his head.

The Kall-a-Kab dropped him off at the funeral parlor. Thurman thought he'd be among the first. But there was already a crowd numbering in the scores. All the people he knew personally, Shenda prominent, plus dozens of faces he recognized from the happy park meeting. Apparently, every employee of Karuna, Inc., had determined to attend, in a show of solidarity that actually brought tears to Thurman's eyes.

Fuquan's relatives were bunched in a tight, slightly suspicious and leery family knot that quickly unraveled under the warm pressure of greetings, introductions and expressions of condolence. Soon they were interspersed among the Karuna Korps, hugging, crying, smiling.

Inside Kandomble Brothers it was a more somber, closed casket affair, a photo of Fuquan in his off-work finery propped atop the silver-handled box. Foot-shuffling in the general hush, chair-creaking and weeping.

Thurman hitched a ride to the church with the respectful but ultimately irrepressible SinSin and Pepsi in their absolutely fabulous Miata. Now that was a ride and a half! His brain was put to the test to handle the disorienting transitions, from a folding chair in the parlor to a lap perch in the car to a pew in the church.

Thurman hadn't been inside a church in years, and this one wasn't his old denomination. It felt strange but good. Maybe that incredible visit to the *casa de santo* had awakened something dormant in him.

After the preacher spoke his formal eulogy, the lectern was opened to anyone else who had words to offer.

To Thurman's surprise, a steady stream of people trekked up to speak.

Time to toast the roaster.

Fuquan *had* been a prick. The speakers neither dismissed nor highlighted that fact. But he had been *loved.*

People talked about the man's high-energy approach to life, his unique entrances and exits, his unstinting involvement with whatever thrilled or irked him. Memories of brawls and love affairs, ups and downs, flush times and bust times, generosities and ingenious scams were trotted out and lovingly recounted.

Thurman found himself listening with increasing enchantment. There had been a lot more to the feisty guy than he had ever suspected.

As the flow of speakers ebbed, Thurman realized that one important aspect of Fuquan's life hadn't been touched upon.

Without conscious intention, Thurman found himself heading up the aisle to speak.

Facing the sea of attentive faces, Thurman hesitated for a nervous moment, then began.

"I, uh, I only knew Fuquan for a couple of months, and we didn't always get along, so, um, I don't have a lot to say. But I do know one thing. He made a lot of people happy and wide-awake with his coffee-roasting, er, prowess. And that's better than letting them stay grouchy and sleepy. So we all owe him. And who'll take his place?"

Thurman stepped down to loud applause and chants of "Amen, brother!" His face burned and his mind spun. It was only by the graveside, as the large crowd dispersed, that he really returned to earth.

Shenda approached him. She wore a black wool dress molded to her opulent figure and a single string of pearls, black nylons on the strong pylons of her legs. Her high-heels pierced the turf with each step. She laid a hand on his arm.

"Thurman, I don't want to be alone. Come home with me."

Bullfinch was waiting behind the apartment door. He leaped and cavorted about them like a bright sunny jowly gnome, barking in a queerly modulated way.

The humans had little attention to spare for the dog.

Shenda kicked off her shoes and led Thurman into the bedroom.

They were kissing. Then she loosened his tie and began to unbutton his shirt. Thurman felt suddenly awkward. He stopped her hand.

"I used to look better than I do now," he said.

"But I know you only now."

Thurman couldn't argue with that.

Sprawled naked on the bed, face alight, cocoa arms and legs open to him, Shenda made Thurman think of a dryad who shared the hue of the exotic heartwood of her home tree, or of an unburnished copper woman.

Shenda was gentle with his disabilities. At climax, it was as if lightning entered his head and blazed along his spine. Something shifted permanently within him, as when an object was lifted from a balanced tray. A coffeecup, perhaps.

Thurman fell asleep cradled in Shenda's embrace. When he awoke, it was twilight. Shenda still held him. Bullfinch had climbed onto the bed, and was snoring. Thurman shifted to look at Shenda's face. Her eyes were open, and tears trickled down her cheek like the first rivulets of spring.

"What's wrong? Did I—?"

"No, not you. It's only that nothing lasts. But what else is stinking new, right? Like I should be exempt for my good deeds! Forget it."

They talked about many things for the next few hours. At one point Shenda said, "Thurman, the most important thing in my life is the Karuna idea. It has to go on, even if I'm not around. But I never found anyone who could take over. Now I think maybe you could."

"Me? How could I ever do what you do? You—you're like a force of nature! I'm just a washed-up old rag next to you. Besides, you're not going anywhere anytime soon."

"Can't say, Thurman. Never can say."

After some further conversation, Thurman happened to notice a familiar vial atop the dresser.

"Is that the second potion your aunt concocted the other night?"

"Oh, yes, I almost forgot. You're supposed to drink it."

Shenda hopped out of bed. Her hand was reaching for the potion.

The apartment door blew off its hinges with a plaster-shattering crash and two burly men, stocking-masked and armed, burst in.

14.

Tarbaby's Clinch

For the whole day—one whole wasted, unrecapturable day!— after the destruction of the Karuna Koffeehouse and the revelation of the dark forces behind the disaster, Shenda had felt enervated and full of despair. All her efforts, all her hard work of the past few years toward achieving her vision, had seemed a pitiable, naive facade erected against chaos, a tent in a hurricane. She even let the spontaneous blame and guilt that had erupted that fiery night fester and grow.

If I hadn't been so stubborn over my foolish damn principles, if I hadn't stuck my head up above the mass of the herd, trying to change things, then none of this would have happened. Fuquan would still be alive, and the Karuna would still exist. It's all my fault for being so uppity, so arrogant, so greedy to make things better. Why couldn't I have been content with my lot?

But as she got caught up in managing the myriad details of Fuquan's funeral and salvaging her business from the ruins, her natural optimism, tempered and reforged, began to reassert itself.

It wasn't my fault! If some jerk steals my car, do I blame myself for having too nice a car? No! There's right and there's wrong! Titi Yaya taught me that! I didn't light the match under the Karuna, that pathetic egungun *did, following the orders of some bastard named Twigg! Karuna, Inc., is the best and most honest thing I've ever done. I built and he destroyed! That's what it boils down to, making and breaking, sane adult or vicious child.*

This reborn confidence brought something new to light.

Before the disaster, she hadn't thought much about living and dying, just gone naturally from day to day.

After the tragedy, life seemed worthless and she had felt like dying for nothing.

Now, with the change of heart, she felt like living, and, only if need be, dying for *something*.

So when the midnight intruders crashed through her door, Shenda did not meekly surrender.

Her hand closed not on the potion but on a small necklace box atop the dresser and she hurled it at one of the men. At the same instant Bullfinch flew in a snarling rage at the second.

But these were not supernaturally sensitive zombies like Durchfreude, these were hardened mundane professionals.

The first man took the box in the chest without flinching or pausing.

The second shot Bullfinch in midflight. The dog squealed and thumped to the floor.

"No!" screamed Shenda, seeing her nightmare realized.

Thurman was struggling with treacherous limbs to rise from the bed. One of the men was quickly upon him.

"Hey, feeb," said the man, "chill." He used his gunbutt on Thurman's skull.

The other now grappled with Shenda, succeeding in pinning her arms.

Within seconds they had her wrists and ankles secured with duct tape, a strip across her mouth. Then they bundled her nakedness in a sheet and carried her outside.

She was dumped into a car trunk. The car took off.

For a timeless interval her mind raved, visions of lover and dog and her helpless self, spinning in kaleidoscopic disarray.

Then Shenda, with greater effort than ever before, forced her habitual mental pause upon herself.

A curious calm enveloped her now. Always dynamic, always a doer, always proactive, she was now in a situation where she could only lie still, could only react.

Was this the paralysis of the rabbit frozen before the snake? Shenda thought not, hoped not. The calmness felt too big to be simply an instinctive neural shutdown. Instead, it felt more like an opening up, like an activation of an untapped higher function, a heightened receptivity to something she had previously been only dimly aware of.

As the car accelerated toward its unknown destination, a memory came back to Shenda. It was one long sealed away, one she had never had access to before.

She was five years old. Her parents were dead. Titi Yaya had custody of her now. They were on a trip to the ocean. That should be fun.

But they ended up not at a public beach, but at a secluded rock-shored Atlantic cove barren of homes or other people. Titi Yaya had told the little girl to undress then.

"Everything?"

"Everything."

Then *la iyalocha* had given the naked Shenda a white handkerchief knotted around seven bright pennies.

"Step into the sea, child, and offer the coins to Yemaya while you ask for her protection."

Shenda waded out tentatively, the rocks bruising her feet. Waist deep, she tentatively stuck her hand holding the offering under the water.

Something *pulled.*

Shenda didn't think to let go of the coins, and was dragged under.

There was a face below the waters. Kindly and wise and warm. Shenda could have looked at it forever.

But Titi Yaya was already pulling her up, coinless.

"Yemaya accepts your offering, little Shen-Shen. The *orishas* are your friends now forever, as long as you honor them."

The car went over a bump, and Shenda knocked her head.

All this time. All this time she had had help waiting, but had been too proud to heed the numerous offers.

If any flaw of hers deserved punishment, this was it. Trying always to go it alone.

And now she finally was. All alone.

Or was she?

15.

The Lady Is the Tiger

It was very convenient for Marmaduke Twigg that his bedroom was wired, boasting all the electronic conveniences that allowed him to run the Isoterm empire remotely.

For he had found in the days after the massacre underground that, having attained a safe refuge, he could not summon the will to leave his room.

Oh, of course the phobia was quite understandable and certainly only of temporary duration. After all, what survivor of such carnage wouldn't jump at every sharp report or look with suspicion at formerly trusted faces? He just needed a little time to regather his wits and confidence, his sense of the rest of humanity as easily manipulated cattle.

But: dangerous cattle, who could gore.

That had been his mistake. Not to realize that even witless subhumans could inflict pain.

But not as intently and ingeniously as he, Twigg himself, could.

Therein lay his superiority.

Twigg had not delayed in pursuing what would strengthen him.

Immediately upon receiving the requisite medical attention, he had begun to sweep up the crumbling empires of his erstwhile PGL peers. Kalpagni, Ltd.; Stonecipher Industries; Burnes Sloan Hardin Hades; Crumbee Products; Harrow & Wither; Somnifax et Cie; Asura Refineries; Preta-Loka Entertainments; Culex, SA; Brasher Investments, Plc.; Rudrakonig, GmbH; LD–100 Pharmaceuticals. All these firms, unlike more democratic ones, had been particularly susceptible to disintegration upon the lopping off of their heads. Now Isoterm, the insect god of homogeneity, was engulfing them.

With every glorious business absorption, Twigg felt power flow into him.

And yet, something was missing. These conquests were all ethereal affairs of bytes and EFTs, votes and bribes. Too impersonal.

What Twigg needed to fully reinvigorate himself was much more elemental.

Blood. The blood of the cow that had set off the stampede that had nearly trampled him.

And this was the day, now the hour.

A knock came at Twigg's door. He took his feet off his new hassock, pausing to pat the frozen kneeler appreciatively before he stood.

Alas, poor Paternoster. Decades of loyal service undone by one incautious aged stumble while bearing the breakfast tray. Now enjoying his retirement.

Without pension.

"Enter," called out Twigg imperiously.

The unconscious woman carried into the room by the two thugs was not in immaculate condition. Contusions mottled her naked form, and her features were smeared. An arm dangled crookedly. Experts had inflicted a certain high degree of damage on her prior to her delivery here. Twigg had not fully recovered his strength yet, was used to dealing with drugged victims, and had heard that this one was a fiery bitch. Best to have her vitality taken down a notch or three beforehand.

Twigg was not greedy. There was plenty of play left in her still.

The men dumped her on the rug and left. Twigg picked up his favorite knife, a slim Medici stiletto, and kneeled beside her. With expert prickings and a final slap across the face he managed to raise her eyelids.

"Ah, my dear, so pleased to meet you. I'm Marmaduke Twigg, your new best friend. Here is my calling card."

Twigg sliced shallowly across the bridge of her nose. Blood flowed, crimson on brown like lava down a hillside.

"We're going to get along famously, I can tell. What do you think?"

The woman was murmuring something. Twigg had to lean over to listen, since her bruised lips and lacerated tongue had trouble forming words.

"Dog. Your . . . name. A dog."

Twigg straightened. "Oh, dear. How *gauche*. I'm afraid I must register my dismay."

Twigg began to carve.

Delightful hours passed. Despite all his experience at prolonging agony, matters seemed to be reaching a terminal point. So Twigg paused for refreshment.

A deep swallow of Zingo.

Lowering the bottle from his avaricious mouth, Twigg was inspired. He bent over the shattered woman lying curled up on her side.

Her lips were twitching. Twigg thought to hear her mutter, "Lou—Louie . . ."

"He's not here, dear. Would you care for a drink? I know you're famously not partial to this beverage though. Too much like vinegar, I take it? Oh, well, if you insist—"

Twigg emptied the cobalt liquid onto her grimly painted face.

It seemed to revive her a bit. With infinite exertion she rolled fully onto her stomach and began to crawl. Twigg watched indulgently.

She reached the table supported by the two male statues. Using their organic irregularities as handholds, she dragged herself upward until she managed to catch the gilt edge of the glass top.

The active workstation across the room chimed, signalling its need for a share-selling authorization. Twigg moved quickly to attend it, so that he could resume his pleasures.

When he looked again, the woman held the control for the tiger.

"No!"

Too late.

Death roared.

The neuronal dam crumbled.

Twigg dashed insanely for the door.

Impossibly, the woman stood like an iron wall between him and safety.

Something supernaturally strong dwelled now within her.

She clasped Twigg in an iron embrace.

"Come with me," rasped a voice not hers.

And then the tiger was upon them both, claws, jaws and tropical volcano breath.

But tigers are not cruel.

16.

Long May You Run

A key turned in the repaired door to Shenda Moore's apartment. The door swung inward.

First entered Titi Yaya.

Behind her, Thurman, cane thumping.

After him hopped a three-legged Bullfinch with bandaged front stump.

Titi Yaya stopped.

"I know this won't be pleasant. But we need to go through all her papers if we are to salvage what she built. You know that's what she wanted."

"Yes," said Thurman. The word came out of him easier and more evenly than he would have expected, given the surroundings. Apparently, he was, for the moment anyway, all cried out.

He had been dreading returning here, had delayed the necessity till a week after the funeral. (Shenda's savaged corpse had come home to them only through Titi Yaya's string-pulling on both supernatural and earthly powers.) But now, with the future of Karuna, Inc., at stake, they could delay no longer.

"You take the desk here," ordered Titi Yaya. "I will look in the bedroom."

Thurman was not inclined to argue. The bedroom was not a place he cared to revisit. "Feeb—" He sat at the desk chair; Bullfinch dropped down beside him. He began to leaf through papers. Shenda's handwriting was everywhere.

After a time Titi Yaya emerged, bearing various folders, Shenda's big satchel—and a small glass vial.

"What is this doing unopened?" she demanded. "How do you expect to accomplish anything if you stay sick? Here, drink this now!"

Thurman did as he was told. The potion was not exactly pleasant, but not vile either. Musty, loamy, musky, powerful.

"I have to go now, child. Meet me at my apartment when you are finished."

Alone, Thurman sorted through a few more sheets and ledgers. Then an irresistible drowsiness started to creep along his limbs from his feet on up, until it crested over his head and swallowed him entirely. His hand dropped down to graze Bullfinch's back.

He was on a flat city rooftop. Bullfinch was with him, smiling and rollicking, lolloping about on his remaining three legs.

"Throw the ball! Throw the ball! Quick!" said the bulldog.

Thurman realized he held a tennis ball.

"I don't know how! Get Shenda to do it. Where is she?"

"She's everywhere! Just look! She's always here! Now let's play!"

Thurman looked around. The sun, the sky, the commonplace urban fixtures. Was that Shenda? It seemed a poor substitute, a deceitful trade for the living woman.

"Don't you see her? Wake up so we can play! Wake up!"

Bullfinch's last words seemed to echo and reverberate. The rooftop scene wavered and dissolved.

Thurman opened his eyes and saw Shenda.

It was only a picture of her as a child, an old snapshot lying atop the papers on the desk.

But it hadn't been there when he fell asleep.

Thurman stood to go. He reached for his cane, then hesitated. Somehow his legs seemed stronger.

Cane left behind, he moved with increasing confidence toward the door.

Behind him gamely trotted Bullfinch.

Thurman guessed that now he had a dog.

*   *   *

[Compassion or karuna] does not seem to die. Shantideva says that every uncompassionate action is like planting a dead tree, but anything related to compassion is like planting a living tree. It grows and grows endlessly and never dies. Even if it seems to die, it always leaves behind a seed from which another grows. Compassion is organic; it continues on and on and on.

—Chogyam Trungpa,
Cutting Through Spiritual Materialism

*In a collection of stories devoted to various modes of employment —
the classic "working for a living" theme, if you will — the author's
attitude toward the workplace and the marketplace are bound to
emerge fairly strongly — if he's done his job right. Contradictory and
shifting, my take on earning one's bread by the sweat of one's brow
has undergone a number of metamorphoses. But at the core has
remained a distaste for rigid, authoritarian environments, big corporate cube farms and their ilk. Some twenty years ago, when I was
still a COBOL programmer for an insurance company, one of the
goads to leaping blindly into the freelance writer's life was a newly
instituted office clothing policy that required us formerly unre-
strained coders to don a tie. I gave my notice shortly thereafter.*

    *As Thoreau famously advised, "Beware of all enterprises requir-
ing new clothes."*

$SUITs$

I'LL NEVER FORGET THE FIRST TIME I SAW A SUIT. THE sight took five years off my life.

I was hunched over my CAD-CAM station, trying to finish up the specs for a new waste-burning facility (thankfully to be situated in a state far away from mine). The smokestack scrubbers were giving me a hell of a time. I couldn't come up with a configuration that would match both the money allotted and the cleansing capabilities needed. The simulations kept showing we'd either have to spend twice as much as we had in the budget, or end up spewing dioxin over half the Midwest. I could guess which option we'd choose. With EPA pollution credits available comparatively cheap, it would definitely be the latter.

As I agonized over my mouse and keyboard, trying to squeeze out the last possible ounce of utility from the scrubber models available in my price range, I could sense someone hovering behind me, looking over my shoulder. At first, I figured it was just Carl, checking on my progress, and I didn't bother turning around. But as minutes passed and no caustic comment was forthcoming, I gradually realized that it couldn't be Carl. Anne would've laid a hand on my back. Jerry would've been slurping his omnipresent coffee. Marcie would've been popping gum. But behind me was only an eerie silence, and the subliminal sense of someone—or something— watching me.

I swivelled my chair around.

And that's when I saw the SUIT.

The empty cuffs of its perfect wool trousers floated several inches off the carpet. The legs of its pants were bulked out as if they contained living flesh, but I knew instantly and unerringly that they were empty. The suit jacket—one button buttoned, lapels neatly creased—showed the vacant cuffs of a white shirt out its sleeves, and a swath of the same shirt across the nonexistent but shapely chest. The hollow neck of the shirt was ringed with a red tie that hung down neatly.

It was like coming face to face with the Headless Horseman. Only this apparition lacked limbs or torso of any kind.

"Jesus Christ!" I yelled, and scrambled backward in my wheeled chair.

Laughter broke out from the doorway, and I looked.

Carl led a pack consisting of the whole office staff. They had been waiting patiently for my reaction to this bizarre thing, and I had been gratifyingly dramatic.

Now Carl stepped into my office. "What's the matter, Mark? That's no way to greet your new coworker."

I got up and hastily placed the desk between me and the floating clothing. Even with the first shock fading, I found the thing too uncanny. It simply gave me the creeps.

Now that the show I had put on was over, the others were dispersing back to their desks. Soon, I was left alone with Carl and the strange mechanism.

"What the hell is it?" I asked.

"It's a SUIT. Sensor Unit for Interior Telemonitoring. Not only does it keep track of the building's microclimate—dust levels, heat, drafts, things like that—but it also functions as mobile security."

I started to relax just a little, my engineer's fascination with clever gadgetry taking over.

I thought I knew, but I still asked, "How's it float like that?"

"Superconducting wires woven into the fabric. Just like the mag-lev train you hopped to work this morning. It rides the steel frame of the building on magnetic lift. The wires give it its shape, too. Combination of stiffness and interactive fields. And all its sensing circuits, cameras, probes and chips are incorporated right in the material too. Oh, and its power pack as well."

"Well, all right, why can't it look like a normal robot?"

"Why should it? It doesn't need a body because it doesn't have to lift or move anything. But it's got to be roughly humanoid so that it can efficiently monitor the same body space that the average worker occupies. The building management might have decided to let loose another horde of MICE, but the building's crawling with MICE already. So they went with this. And wrapping it in clothing makes it familiar. It's an elegant design. Whimsical, too."

"It's terrifying. It reminds me of a ghost."

Carl laughed. "C'mon, Mark, don't be superstitious! Here, poke it. Go ahead, it doesn't mind."

Suiting his actions to his words, Carl jabbed a finger into the thing. It bobbled backwards on its magnetic fields, then righted itself.

I came up tentatively to the SUIT and tried the same thing.

My finger encountered the sensation of yielding flesh beneath the fabric. Although I knew it was just an electromagnetic simulation of skin and blood, it was almost indistinguishable from poking a living body, save for its lack of warmth.

I shivered, and stepped back. Had I seen the SUIT start to raise its arms, as if against me. . . ?

Shaking my head, I said, "No, I'm sorry, Carl, I really don't like it. . . ."

"You're just jealous because it's wearing—or made of—better clothing than you own."

This was true. The manufacturer had chosen a beautiful designer outfit to modify.

"How many of these things are there?"

"Oh, a dozen or so. There're even female ones."

"No!"

"Sure. Skirt, frilly blouse, jacket, floppy bow tie. Equal employment opportunities for sensing devices too, you know."

Suddenly, the SUIT began to drift away. Its legs, of course, didn't bend in walking movements—and thank God for that! It simply floated silently away like a specter, its empty arms slightly bent at the elbow.

"How did you get it in here?"

"I phoned Sys-Ops and told them to send it to your office, to check a funny smell with its chemosensors. It must've finished just now."

"Someone down in Sys-Ops is guiding these all the time?"

"Not at all. The SUITs run off the server without human intervention most of the time. It's only if something turns up that the heuristics can't deal with that a live operator is called. Doesn't happen that often either. At least not yet."

I paused to consider everything Carl had told me. In the end, I supposed, the SUITs were just one more thing I didn't like about my job.

"Well, please don't ever send one of those things in again when I'm in the middle of concentrating. It's very disturbing."

Once again Carl laughed. "Oh, now that you know what they are, you'll get used to them."

But he was wrong.

The next few months were among the most hectic and enervating of my life. I was burdened and overburdened with work on a dozen projects, each one of them more reprehensible than the last.

Our firm wasn't the biggest contractor in our particular job arena, and it wasn't the smartest. There were competitors out there who could both outspend and outthink us. Practically the only way we could get work was to underbid. And that resulted in cutting some pretty sharp corners.

In the weeks after I first saw the SUIT, I had to make the following compromises:

Switch to a lower grade of concrete for the foundations of a new airline terminal.

Cut back as far as I dared on the number of structural beams in a hotel walkway.

Substitute a thousand two-pane windows for the requested three-pane ones.

Use PVC piping in place of copper.

Find a source of used bricks when new ones had been promised.

Every such morally dubious action I was forced to take left me feeling more and more hollow. I lay awake nights, wondering how I had ended up in such a position. I wanted to quit, but just couldn't convince myself to do it. The paycheck was too regular, my lifestyle too secure. I tried to tell myself that everyone made such compromises, no matter where they worked. That no one was getting hurt with this second-class material even though they had expected to receive first-class goods. That the difference was minimal, undetectable, would never be noticed by the occupants of the shoddy structures.

But somehow, every time I saw one of the SUITs, my whole facade of rationalizations came crumbling down like one of my crappy buildings under a wrecker's ball. They had an emotional effect on me out of all proportion to their reality.

And I swore there must've been more than the dozen that Carl had specified. They seemed to be everywhere. Indistinguishable from one another, they could've been an army whose members were uncountable due to their cookie-cutter identicalness.

Every time I decided to go to the john, it seemed, I'd encounter a SUIT in the corridors. There it would be, hovering mysteriously under a heating vent, perhaps sampling the output; or— far worse—pausing by a window *as if looking out.* (They were only registering drafts, I kept telling myself.)

I found myself instinctively hugging the wall farthest away from the mobile units, as if afraid that they would swing around at my approach and confront me with their faceless gaze, an array of sensors that would read my second-rate soul and report me to some heavenly OSHA.

When I went down to a corner of the lobby for a cigarette, a SUIT would always show up, most likely attracted by my illicit smoke. It would approach unnervingly close, though it never violated my interpersonal sphere of space, having been programmed, I assumed, to respect a person's boundaries. It would hover remonstrantly, like the ghost of smokers past, sending its accusatory telemetry back to the mother CPU in the subbasement. I would always hastily stub out my cigarette and flee, with a feeling of guilt such as I hadn't experienced since childhood.

And they even drifted into the cafeteria, spoiling any enjoyment I might have taken in my lunches. The SUITs had a habit of hanging around the trash cans, perhaps sampling airborne bacteria counts, and it became an exercise in nerves for me simply to deposit my empty paper cup under its headless scrutiny.

Once, one joined the serving line. Moving perfectly along with the flow of diners—none of whom seemed to share my unease, but instead pointed at the SUIT and laughed among themselves—it passed down the line of steam tables, sampling odors through its sleeves, filling its nonexistent belly with data for the Department of Health.

I soon came to fear and despise the female SUITs even more than the male ones. Their feminine clothing seemed a more elaborate mockery of their cybernetic hollowness than did that of the males. (The lack of any woman currently in my life, I realized, had something to do with this feeling.) The designers had even equipped each female SUIT with moderate, subtle curves of hip, waist and bust — a magnetic illusion of fertility — rendering further obscene their bodiless presence — at least in my eyes.

And because their empty skirts ended at knee height, their flying-carpet nature was even more apparent than with the male SUITs. They seemed to swoop down on me with more alacrity than the males, more predatory and harsh.

I'll never forget the time I was standing at the supply cabinet, trying to find an old-fashioned eraser under all the disks and print cartridges. (I still liked to draft a few small plans by hand. It was about the only soothing activity connected with my job.) A female SUIT popped out *from behind the cabinet*, and I felt my heart jump like a rabbit inside my chest.

What it had been doing behind the supply locker, I couldn't guess. (The space between the cabinet and the wall, by the way, was only a few inches. Apparently, the SUITs could alter their shape at will, shrinking to occupy the same dimensions as a regular suit of clothes flat on a hanger.) All I knew was that it seemed at that instant to be hurling itself at me like a giant bat or raptor of some sort, and I scrabbled backward like a frightened mouse.

Luckily, no one was there to witness my humiliation.

After a time, I tried explaining my feelings about the SUITs to Carl. But he only laughed, and shrugged it off.

"You've been working too hard," he said, clapping a falsely hearty palm on my shoulder. And that was when the hallucination happened.

I saw Carl as a SUIT. His head grew translucent, transparent, then disappeared. His hands vanished, as did his feet in their shoes. Then there was nothing but an empty sack of clothing with its arm upraised to my shoulder.

Jerking back, I felt a shout beginning in my throat. But before it emerged, my vision returned to normal, and there was Carl again standing before me.

Now he looked genuinely concerned, if only for the smooth functioning of the workplace. "Mark — are you okay?"

I mumbled something. Carl seemed to come to a quick decision.

"Mark, you're kind of bringing the whole office down lately. Your attitude, you know. I think what I'd like to do is switch you to nights. It would free up your workstation during the days too.

We could pump out some extra specs that way. What do you say?"

What could I say? I could sense that it was either agree, or lose my job.

So I agreed.

The building that housed our firm was fifty stories tall, and held numerous other tenants.

But none of them seemed to work at night.

I was to be alone in the building with the SUITs and the janitor MICE.

The first night, I managed to make it up to our floor without encountering a single SUIT. I turned on every light in the office and locked the outer door.

When I at last dared to look up from my monitor, I saw a flock of shadows clustered outside the frosted glass of the hall door like an army of the undead.

The SUITs.

I slowly got up from my chair. I didn't know what I was doing, or where I was going.

Then I heard the solenoid of the electronic lock click open, under orders from the building's CPU.

I found myself in Carl's office without memory of having run there, leaning against the closed door. With trembling hands, I grabbed a chair and shoved it under the doorknob.

It was several hours before they gave up and left. I could tell by the cessation of the muted rustling of fabric, as they brushed against one another. It was another several hours before I dared to open the door.

Somehow, I made it out of the building unmolested.

When I got home, I took several pills and went straight to bed.

Although I usually wore pajamas, that night I slept naked. Lying on a chair, my garments repelled me. Had I put them on, I was afraid of what the mirror would have shown.

When I woke from the drugged sleep, it was dark again, almost as if day had never been.

I got dressed, and left for work.

Why did I go?

At the time, I recall, I had lots of seemingly sensible reasons. The SUITs were ultimately under human control. They were simply innocent tools or devices, and hadn't meant to hurt me. A feedback loop of some sort had developed, triggered by my unusual presence alone at night. The artificially intelligent software had fixed itself—a task it was perfectly capable of—and would be fine. I had to show up, or be fired. I had to show up, or admit that spooks and hallucinations had broken me.

Good logic. But none of these were the real reason, I now realize.

I wanted to see what the SUITs had to show me.

When I let myself into the building—there were no human security guards anymore, with the SUITs in place—they were waiting for me.

Just two, a male and a female.

But it was enough.

Flanking me, the SUITs conducted me to the elevator.

When its door opened, without my summoning it, they boarded with me.

Their shoulders brushed mine in the narrow confines of the elevator, substantial yet meaningless.

The door whooshed open on my floor.

The whole level was full of SUITs.

Scores and scores of them.

They were engaged in a perfect simulation of a normal day.

SUITs stood around the water cooler in attitudes of relaxed conversation. SUITs sat at desks in postures of typing and writing. SUITs moved to and fro on errands. SUITs opened and closed file drawers with invisible magnetic appendages. SUITs stood eagerly by the fax machine. SUITs bent paperclips in meditation or boredom. SUITs stapled papers. SUITs held clipboards and pens.

Fascinated, I stepped away from my escorts, who left me to join their fellows in their solemn stolen enactment. In a daze, I moved through the office.

In the conference room, a dozen SUITs sat around the long wooden table in earnest confab. One passed the metal water pitcher to another.

In the men's john, SUITs stood at the urinals with their metal zippers down.

And in Carl's office, two SUITs were screwing.

A female SUIT lay on its back on the desk, with a male SUIT pumping its vacant crotch against the empty skirt.

Thus did they reproduce.

I picked up a phone and dialed Sys-Ops. A recording came on.

"The Faber Building is currently under heuristic monitoring. No human personnel are available. If you wish to page a human operator, please call this number. . . ."

I dropped the handset, and the recording began to recycle tinnily.

Then I left the building.

The driver of the cab I hailed was a SUIT. Made of jeans, flannel shirt and leather jacket, not cut from the same elegant material as those in the Faber Building, he was a SUIT nonetheless.

I let him drive me to the airport, magnetic hands on the wheel, magnetic foot on the accelerator, and I tossed the fare in his magnetic lap.

The enormous concourse was filled with SUITs. SUITs behind the counters, SUITs dispensing coffee, SUITs manning the X-ray machine, SUITs wheeling suitcases!

A SUIT sold me a ticket on my credit card.

A ticket to far, far, far away.

A small island in the tropics, where there are no SUITs.

Because there is no one there but me.

And I go naked all day.

When Bruce Sterling contacted me for permission to reprint my story, "Stone Lives," in his soon-to-be-historic Mirrorshades anthology, I was elated. This was the first reprint request I had ever received, and for what counted, depending on your definition, as either my first, second or third professional sale. Truly, I felt I had finally arrived on the real SF scene. Hugo and Nebula Awards lay glittering just around the corner of my career path. (Now, fifteen years later, I can laugh at my naiveté without too much ironic bitterness creeping into my guffaws.) So when Bruce wrote a short time later that he was hoping I'd let him switch his anthology choice from "Stone Lives" to "Skintwister," I brashly refused. Let Bruce live with the hasty decision he had made, I thought. I'll save "Skintwister" for best-of-the-year volumes and Hollywood options.

Needless to say, the story has never again seen the light of day until now. The resounding silence that greeted its original appearance was the first step of many on my long road of hubris-snuffing education in the ways of publishing.

My mate, Deborah Newton, helped me de-sappify the original ending of this tale, where all the protagonists exchanged hugs and kisses. She's justifiably proud of her editorial touch, and I think she still expects her Hugo Award "Real Soon Now."

Skintwister

*K*EATS WAS WRONG.

Beauty is not forever; and alone it is not even enough. Anything permanent is suspect. All is vanity and mutability, flash and eternal change. Fashion is truth, and truth fashion. That is all ye know, and all ye need to know. Society changes daily, hourly, and so must the individual, even if it's to no purpose. As a visionary artist of the last century once sang when filled with ennui, "I wanna change my clothes, my hair —

" — my face."

And the high priests of transformation, those perceived as the almighty trendsetters and arbiters, are in reality its most debased servants, unable to locate their true selves amid the welter of arbitrary change they foster.

Ask the man who knows.

Yours truly, Dr. Strode.

The girl lay in bed like an anxious Madonna. I had forgotten her name. Here at the Strode Clinic, the patients came and went so quickly, and in such numbers, that I often lost track of their individuality. But Maggie Crownover, my head nurse, briefed me before we entered the girl's private room.

"Hana Morrell is next, Doctor," Maggie had said, all brisk efficiency. "She's fourteen, a technician at the Long Island cold-fusion station. Her credit's solid. No organic defects. Strictly a makeover."

"No organic defects" was an understatement. The girl was a perfect beauty.

Propped up on pillows, surrounded by bedside monitors, she nearly stole my breath away. Blonde hair like incandescent light filaments framed a heart-shaped face with skin the color of powdered pearls. Her eyes were an arresting gray, her nose had an insouciant tilt, her lips were a feature Rubens might have bestowed on his favorite model.

She smiled, and I thought, *My God, how the hell am I going to improve on this face?*

I extended my hand and we shook, slim hand strong in mine. "Hello, Dr. Strode."

"Ms. Morrell, good morning. I understand you're here for a facial biosculpt." I tried to keep any disapprobation out of my voice. Her credit was all I should be concerned with.

She nodded timidly, as if only in my presence had she realized what she was planning to do.

I spoke quickly and confidently, to get her over this last hump. She had signed the consent form already, and I wasn't about to lose the easy fee she represented by allowing her to vacillate now.

"Let's have a look at your new face, then, shall we."

Maggie took her cue and stepped to the holocaster. A bust formed of light and color suddenly filled the air above the girl's bed, translucent in the bright sunshine that flooded the private room and its luxurious furnishings.

Subtle disappointment welled up in my throat. Like a fool, I had thought that perhaps this girl would be different. Her beauty had misled me into thinking her desires would be commensurate. But she was like all the rest, following the latest trends as helplessly as a surfer caught in a tsunami.

The holo was a woman of vaguely Eurasian/Polynesian features: skin olive-bronze; epicanthic folds around the eyes; strong chin; thin lips; nose rather small; glossy hair jet-black. It had been assembled from stock graphics in real time on the clinic's computer-aided-design system, under the direction of the patient. Ever since the amalgamation of Hong Kong into the Hawaiian-Japanese prosperity sphere last year, this face, or something almost identical, had been chosen by sixty percent of my female patients.

"Fine. . . . It will look wonderful on you," I lied. Sick at heart with contemplating the natural beauty I was about to destroy forever, I moved toward her to get the whole thing over with.

"Wait," she said nervously, before I could lay my hands on her face. "Could you just brief me once more on exactly what's going to happen?"

Now I was starting to get annoyed. "I assume you've read the literature the clinic provides, Ms. Morrell. It's all spelled out there."

She smiled wanly, and I buckled.

"Okay. A quick refresher. I am going to peek you and initiate changes in your cells that will, more or less, return selected cells temporarily to an embryonic state."

Her look of puzzlement made me sigh.

"Ms. Morrell, have you ever considered how you ended up with the face you now possess?"

A negative shake.

"During embryogenesis, your cells differentiated and accumulated in definite patterns. These patterns resulted from the play of energy as it was dissipated into the embryonic environment against various constraints. You might think of a mountain stream pulled along by gravity and being configured by the shape of the streambed and channel and rocks in the flow. Although all individuals share the same cell-adhesion mechanisms, your unique genes dictated the temporal and spatial constraints of your development, and hence your unique morphology. Following me so far?"

"Yes, I think so."

"Very well. What I am about to do is influence your cells directly through Banneker psychokinesis. I am going to reawaken their potential for development—which, as an adult, you have lost. By peeking selected sites, activating cell-loosening enzymes such as trypsin, and planting my own constraints in place of your predetermined genetic ones, I will rebuild your face in the shape you desire."

Naturally bright, she had followed my more elaborate explanation with real understanding, and seemed to be losing her anxiety. "Exactly what's going to happen to my old face?"

I tossed her a bone. "Good question, Hana. Under normal conditions, your epidermis is constantly sloughing off, as new cells are produced subcutaneously and rise to the surface to take the place of the old ones. On the average, a new cell takes a month to migrate to the surface. An extinct disease like psoriasis represents what happens when epidermal replacement occurs more frequently, say in a week. What I am going to provoke in your body is something like that. For roughly a week, you are going to look very ugly indeed, as your old features slough away and the new ones manifest themselves underneath. This is an uncomfortable but entirely safe process, and you will be monitored throughout. Also, I will be making daily adjustments based on how I read the changes. The treatment could even be conducted on an out-patient basis, if the temporary disfigurement weren't so drastic."

But then, I thought, *I wouldn't clean up on daily room charges.*

"Are you gonna have to alter my bones?" she asked.

I considered the holo. "It appears not, although I could, by regulating your osteoblasts and osteoclasts. The face you've chosen goes well with your current skeletal structure."

She opened her rosy lips for another question, but I cut her off, fed up with her vain hesitation. My bedside manner definitely had its rough edges today.

"Ms. Morrell. Either you want this treatment or you don't. My training consists of eight years at Johns Hopkins and four more at the Banneker Institute itself. I have been running this clinic for ten years and have performed more biosculptures than you have fused atoms. Now, can we proceed? I have other patients to see."

She nodded yes meekly, and I felt the perverse thrill of having another human entirely obedient to my will. I tried to suppress it, but couldn't completely succeed.

Disgusted with myself, I placed my hands on her soon-to-be-lost face.

Then I dove beneath her flesh.

How do you convey extrasensory modes of being in terms of the five senses? I haven't found a way after all these years. It may be impossible. Better minds than mine have tried. Synesthesia comes close, offering the feeling of skewed perspectives, of the mundane transformed, but in the end, it, too, fails to capture the reality.

Still, how else can I tell it?

My surroundings vanished. The first thing I tasted was Hana's health and youth, refreshing as the heat of the sun. I could have reveled in it for hours, and had to pull myself away. Her vitality was so different from what the hurt and sick people, the broken ones, had given me in school. That was a taste I couldn't stomach, the reason why I used my talents as I did. Next I went beyond surfaces, to bathe in the noisy cellular automatons I proposed to change. They hummed a blue light like ginger, happy and content in their stubborn ways. I felt the configurations of muscles and bones, swam along the maxillae and up the zygomatic arch to the temporal bone and down to the nasal bone, even unto the cartilage at the tip. When I was certain I knew her face in its entirety, I began to initiate the changes.

A writer I like once proclaimed, "There is no art without resistance of the medium." I was an artist by any standards, and my medium was one of the most recalcitrant. The plastic stuff I worked with had its instructions on how to behave, and resented my intrusions. Membranes squeezed out lugubrious sparks against my mental tweaking. Pseudopods of angry noise attempted to push me back. Still, I persisted, knowing the battle would be mine. I ordered growth here, diminishment there. Melanin, marshal your forces and march! Lymph system, retreat! Sebaceous glands, surrender!

At last I was satisfied. I swam out of her skin, back to the external world.

The return of sunlight caused me to blink painfully. I stepped back awkwardly, fatigue heavy in my limbs. Maggie steadied me, anticipating my confusion.

"Wow," Hana said. "What did you do? I feel like ants were crawling under my face."

"Get used to it," I said. "It only becomes more intense."

I turned to go. At the door, I stopped, guilty, and said, "Ms. Morrell—I'm sorry if I was rather brusque."

But she didn't even hear me, both hands on her alien face, as she felt the changes massing beneath her forsaken flesh.

Scarves of smoke ghosted the trapped air in the club. Twisting ceilingward, they encountered shafts of colored light that tinged them gaudily, lending them a brief vitality much like life.

Almost everyone in the noisy, crowded room was smoking— both tobacco and California sinsemilla. When a Banneker graduate could peek away your lung cancer for more money than a prole made in a year, then smoking—once almost extinct—became yet another exclusive status symbol of the rich.

And we—Jeanine and I—were indeed among the rich tonight.

After a tiring day at the clinic, I had felt I deserved the best night out I could manage. That meant one place: *Radix Malorum*, atop the Harlem Pylon. Just the view south from its sweeping windows was worth the inflated prices. Manhattan looked as if some angry god had ripped down the night sky, shaken the stars into geometric patterns, and laid the priceless carpet at our feet.

Jeanine was telling me about her day. I half-listened, sipping my overpriced drink at intervals, letting the alcohol have its way inside me without interference.

"I swear," she said, "These kids I teach are getting smarter every day. Pretty soon they're going to have to lower the franchise again. Can you imagine it at twelve? When we were growing up, I remember everyone said fifteen was too low. What's in that latest release of mnemotropins anyway? Sometimes I can barely keep ahead of my students."

I muttered something about reversing evolution, reverting to the self-sufficiency of most other mammals soon after birth. Truth to tell, I was busy wondering if tonight was going to be the night I dared satisfy my curiosity about Jeanine.

We had met over a year ago, at a party given by one of my clients. From across the room, her radical beauty had overwhelmed me. Her thick black hair fell in waves to her shoulders. Her long face, with its high cheeks and prominent nose, achieved a composite beauty greater than the sum of its parts. Deep luminous eyes were fringed with the thickest lashes I had ever seen.

My first thought had been: *What genius built that face? I don't recognize the style at all.* Then I muttered aloud, "You cynical bastard. Why can't she be real?"

I had come on to her shamelessly, with all the intensity I could muster. Despite my gaucheries, she had seen something attractive in me. That night, upstairs in our host's bedroom, atop a bed piled with coats, we became lovers. She excited me so much that I forgot to dive beneath her skin and search for traces of alterations.

Since then, I had deliberately forborne. She meant too much to me now for me to know another sculptor had swarmed beneath her flesh. But not to know was killing me, too.

I shook my head. Jeanine asked, " 's matter?"

"Nothing," I said. "Just thinking about this crazy world we live in. Why can't things be simpler, like, say, about fifty years ago, when those loopy Kirlian auras and biofeedback were as close as anyone got to the notion of reading and altering bodies like books?"

She took my hand across the real linen cloth. "I've never heard you talk this way before, Jack. You must have had an awful day. Why don't we just head home now?"

That sounded good to me, so we summoned the waiter—a

human, of course, not a mek, at these prices—and he arranged the crediting of the restaurant's account, not neglecting his gratuity.

Shuffling between packed tables, we made for the door.

Halfway there, a tug on the hem of my quilted dinner jacket stopped me.

I looked down. A man's choleric, beefy face stared aggressively up at me. He was obviously drunk and belligerent. I thought I knew him, but couldn't remember where from.

He slurred his speech. "If it's not the illushtrious Dr. Strode, demigod and paragon. Sit down with us and have a drink, Doc. Just to show there's no hard feelings about throwing us out of your stinking clinic."

I regarded his companions, one of whom was a thin, dandified man, and it all came back to me.

"Listen," I said, "my policy is not to handle illnesses, especially something as critical as failure of the immune system. I couldn't do anything for your friend."

"Tell the truth, you high and mighty bastard. You *could*, but you *wouldn't!* And every other honest peeker has more cases than they can handle. So now Mitch is on monoclonal antibodies, which are only, like, eighty percent guaranteed. While you waste your talents skintwisting."

"I am a biosculptor, not a 'skintwister,'" I said. Jeanine was pulling at my arm. The restaurant had grown quiet as all heads swiveled.

"I say you're a lousy skintwister," the man said, and started to rise.

I grabbed his shoulder while he was still coming up. His life aura stunk of fear and bad living. It took me less than a second to give him a shot of angina that folded him up in a gasping heap. Let him try to prove I had anything to do with it. He had the physique where such an attack could be purely natural.

"Let's go," I said to Jeanine.

She stared at me as if I were Satan himself—or at least Faust. And she wouldn't let me touch her at all that night.

I studied my hands with unnatural calmness. I knew something bad was about to happen.

I felt weird inner tremblings and quiverings. Something prevented me from diving into my own flesh and finding out what was wrong. Instead, like anyone else, I was forced to watch it all from the outside, my own body a mystery.

Immense pain shot up each finger from my wrists. The dorsal surfaces of my hands suddenly blackened, puffed, and split, like pork in an oven, revealing bloody red meat and white phalanges beneath the blistering epidermis. The ruined skin began to fall away in rotten strips, until it hung like a diseased orchid from my carpal bones.

I shot up in bed, my pulse pounding, sweat drenching the sheets. Jeanine wasn't beside me, having left me soon after the scene in the club.

It took me longer than it should to restore my bodily equilibrium, but at last I got my blood pressure down to 110 over 80. I turned on the light then, lit a cigarette, and thought about what had just happened.

One of the first things they made us read at the Banneker Institute—right along with *On the Origin of Forms*—was an old essay by a doctor of the past century named Lewis Thomas, called "On Warts." It was his graceful speculations on how warts could be cured "by something that can only be called thinking." The instructor cited this as one of the seminal pieces in our field. But he directed our attention to one of Thomas's offhand comments that all of us had missed:

"I was glad to think that my unconscious mind would have to take the responsibility for this, for if I had been one of the subjects I would never have been able to do it myself."

"Unlike Thomas," the instructor continued, "you special people are quite capable of taking charge of what were once perceived as autonomic functions managed by the unconscious. I can tell you from my own experience that the urge to meddle constantly in your own body will prove to be an almost irresistible one. I have one word of advice for you: don't.

"Your unconscious, properly trained, is completely capable of monitoring and policing your body with more efficiency than your rational self. We will see to it that you receive such training. After it, you will function at the peak of health for more years than we have yet put a number to. All provided, of course, that you give up any incessant tinkering that is sure to do more harm than good. It is a prime paradox of our profession that while we exercise complete control over the bodies of others, we must practice a certain powerlessness over our own, lest we be caught up in a destructive feedback loop of incremental changes.

"One of the little side benefits of a trained unconscious, I think you will be surprised to learn, is the suppression of nightmares . . ."

I hadn't had a nightmare in over a decade. Dreams, yes, but nothing like this bloody vision that had shattered the night for me. I couldn't afford to. Nightmares were the mark of an unconscious at war with itself, at least in people such as myself. They were bound to result in malfunctioning of my careful homeostasis.

Lying back, I ran through a dozen mind-cleansing techniques before falling asleep again.

I had no more bad dreams that night.

But in the morning my hands were sore and stiff.

Most days I was reasonably proud of my office. The diplomas and AMA citations hanging on the real wood-paneled walls; the thick burgundy carpet; the mahogany sideboard holding antique *objets d'art* and a jagged crystal from the Russian settlement on Mars (I had to perform four nose jobs and two breasts lifts for that alone); the holo of the Banneker Institute, a building evoking instant recognition and respect. The whole effect was one of serenity, calmness, and prestige, intended to put prospective patients at ease.

This morning, after the horrors of last night, it seemed a tawdry stage set. I wanted to kick the cardboard walls down and flee. But of course I couldn't. I had my practice, my reputation, and my self-respect to consider.

Or at least two out of those three.

Dealing with the woman sitting on the other side of my desk was not making the day any more agreeable.

It wasn't arrogance or hauteur on her part that was getting under my skin; I had encountered those often enough to have quick and effective ripostes at my fingertips. Instead she exhibited a kind of scatterbrained ditziness that was giving me a headache. Every question I asked seemed to elicit a senseless torrent of references to people and events I couldn't possibly know or care about. All I needed was a straight answer to what she wanted done with her body. Instead I got her social diary for the past six months.

Her lack of wits appeared an even greater shame when I considered her looks.

If the Winged Victory had survived the centuries with its face intact, I'm sure it would have looked something like this woman. A classic, aquiline profile complemented her long, slender neck. Her eyes were penetrating but essentially empty, like a cat's. Her platinum hair was feathered close to her magnificent occipital structure. She wore fur and silk like a queen.

I let her wind up her latest reply without really paying attention. My life seemed suddenly full of women lately. Jeanine; the girl, Hana, whom I had found myself thinking of all morning; and now this personage—Amy Sanjour, she had named herself. I supposed I had always favored the company of women over men. Was it because I found them easier to dominate? Jeanine's frigid treatment last night and Hana's ineluctable haunting of my thoughts seemed to portend a table-turning in the works.

"Ms. Sanjour," I said when she ran out of breath, "I believe your problem is a general lassitude." I had fastened on this recurrent leitmotiv in her rambling discourse.

"Why, yes," she gushed. "How perceptive of you, Dr. Strode. That's my trouble exactly. I just can't seem to keep up with all the things that I have to do. Parties, charity affairs, travel—it's all too wearing lately."

"I prescribe a general toning," I said, calculating how much she was good for. "I'll work over your muscles, maybe boost your ATP production—Can you arrange to check in tomorrow for about a week?"

Her face was so transparent that I could almost watch her running over her appointment book in her head. When her forehead wrinkles disappeared, she said, "Absolutely, Doctor. My health comes before anything else. I simply *have* to get back on my feet."

"Fine." I stood to escort her to the door. She rose like a flower unfolding in stop-motion photography. Her expensive scent filled my nostrils. What a sorry mismatch of beauty and brains.

At the door, she offered her hand.

I didn't know any better, so I took it.

The room seemed to invert itself and reform faster than light. I caught my breath and shook my head, plainly dazed.

"Are you all right, Doctor?" she asked, solicitous as a nurse.

"Uh, yeah, I guess. I had a bad night. Probably not quite recovered yet. It's nothing, really."

She smiled dazzlingly. "Well, don't work too hard. I'll be needing you tomorrow."

"I'll take care," I said.

Then she left.

On the way to Hana Morrell's room, I initiated a quick internal diagnostic on myself. Everything seemed fine. Yet if nothing else, the memory of my shredding hands still remained, an unexplained abnormality.

Maggie was waiting by Hana's bedside. As I came up, she finished explaining how to use a terminal mounted on a swivel arm that projected over Hana's bed. IV tubes threaded the girl's arm. Her face—

No matter how many times I saw it, I was always taken aback by the overnight transformation. People—most of them quite good-looking but unsatisfied—came to me, I laid my hands on them, and they turned temporarily into something resembling plague victims.

Already a scaly scurf overlaid Hana's lumpy features. No more was she the beauty who had occupied the bed yesterday. Clumps of her hair bestrewed her pillow, the old falling out to make way for the new.

"Hana, how are we feeling?"

"Okay. Weird, but basically okay."

"In that case, I'm going to go forward with your treatment. Ms. Crownover's explained the idiosyncrasies of our network hookup, I see. You'll be communicating your wishes and needs through that now. I'm going to paralyze your vocal chords for the remainder of your stay here. It's simply to remove the temptation to talk. No sense straining your facial muscles while they're reforming. As for eating—they've already got you on your gourmet menu."

She eyed her IV and laughed. "Right."

"Okay, then. I'm going in."

My hands cradled her abused flesh.

The diving was rough today. I felt swept away by the turbid currents of her transitional self. I had to exert all my powers to manage a simple reading of the progress of the changes. Making the minor adjustments necessary was almost more than I could accomplish. Her larynx fought me like a malignant snake. I got out of her susurrant, scarlet-spicy interior awkwardly, in a hurry.

I mumbled something about seeing her tomorrow, and hurried off.

Later in the day, when Maggie asked me if anything was wrong, I told her roughly just to tend to her end of the business.

She was too professional to cry in front of me.

But I learned of it after.

Naked, Amy Sanjour differed from Victory in one respect: no wings.

This was one body I was glad I didn't have to amend. Contemplating her elegant contours as she dressed unselfconsciously in one of the clinic's white robes, I found familiar thoughts running through my mind.

Why was it that every advance in man's powers seemed to lessen his regard for the accomplishments of nature? As soon as the first cathedral was finished, the forest began to seem puny. The airplane made an eagle's accomplishments paltry. Each city canyon decreased the grandeur of the Grand Canyon or the Valles Marineris by a perceptible amount. The ability to mold the body made what left the womb unsatisfactory. You would think just the reverse would be true. After struggling so hard to achieve his small skills, man should appreciate the effortless workings of nature even more. But such was not the case.

And who was I to alter affairs?

"I was going to suggest some cosmetic attention to your epidermis, in conjunction with toning," I said as she sat down on her bed. "But I can see it won't be necessary, Ms. Sanjour."

"Please, call me Amy. If I'm going to spend a week here, it would be tiresome for you to be always 'Mizzing' me."

"That seems like no problem—Amy. Have you made the tour of our facilities yet?"

"Yes. The pool is splendid, and so's the gym. I really feel at home here. I think this week will turn out to be just what I've been needing."

"I hope so. Maybe you'll recommend the clinic to your friends. Now, shall we begin?"

She reclined wordlessly, her legs primly crossed at the ankles, yet somehow managing to convey a sense of wanton invitation.

With restraint, I managed to touch her quite neutrally on the shoulders. An affair with one of my patients would have the Review Board down on me in seconds.

I hesitated for a moment before leaving the external world behind. I still remembered the unexplained vertigo that had followed my last contact with this woman. Was there a cause-and-effect relationship I was missing, or had it been strictly coincidence?

Time to find out, I figured.

I dipped tentatively beneath her surface.

Almost instantly I popped back out.

"What quack did this to you?" I demanded.

"Did what?" she asked, seemingly genuinely puzzled.

"Your muscles are pouring out fatigue poisons. You may as well be running a daily marathon. No wonder your energy's down."

"I was seeing a psychokineticist for a time. I prefer not to name names, though. He's a friend of the family. I can't believe he's responsible."

"It's the only explanation. He should have his license revoked."
Only then did I remember clutching the heart of the man in the
restaurant. I swallowed my hypocrisy, tasting bitter gall. That had
been different, hadn't it? I was provoked, and drunk. Surely miti-
gating circumstances.

"Can't you just restore things, without knowing how they got
that way? I won't go back to him—I promise."

"It's unethical—but without your cooperation, I don't see what
else I can do."

"That's that, then. Let's go on."

I went into her secret self of raucous tissues and proud bones
once more, and began the repairs. So demanding were they that
I had to exercise greater concentration than I had called upon in
years. Time passed in a quantumless blur.

Exiting, I anticipated the vertigo I had experienced at our first
contact.

It wasn't there. But instead I felt an odd inner disturbance, as
if, while rewiring Amy, some unseen individual had been busy
inside *me*.

"That felt wonderful, Doctor," she said with a smile.

Have you ever felt something slipping away from you and been
unable to stop it? Perhaps a lover became unexplainably cold,
without a reason you could discern. (If you knew what was wrong,
you *would* change, wouldn't you?) If you're an artist, perhaps you
felt your powers waning in inexplicable ways, as if fleeing misuse.
(Could it be the drinking, the carousing, the hack work?) Or
maybe it was nothing as easy to finger as these examples. Maybe
it was just a diffuse sense of losing your grip on life; of becoming
something you swore you'd never be.

I think you'll know what I mean now if I tell you this was how
I felt during that period that coincided with Amy's stay at the
clinic. My mind felt like a dusty bottle of forgotten wine in a cellar
no one would ever visit again. I made the rounds of my patients
with such an absentminded, distracted air that I'm surprised none
of them got up and left, rather than entrust themselves to such
sloppy care.

Cautiously, I plumbed my own depths at intervals, trying to
ascertain the source of my troubles. A malfunctioning unconscious? There had been no more bad dreams. Something wrong
in an objective physiological sense? If so, it was nothing I could
pinpoint with my talents, a loss of focus more subtle than anything I could name.

I fought not to let it interfere with my work, with mixed results. Amy's progress seemed to be fine, her body gradually regaining normal functioning. I was proud of catching and reversing deliberate damage, and I found myself visiting her twice as often as necessary, performing the laying on of hands more than she actually needed to continue mending. I told myself it was innocent and motivated solely by the pleasure I took in wallowing in her healthy aura. She was a pleasantly cooperative patient, and I had experienced no more untoward side effects after diving her vibrant flesh.

Other cases were not going so well. Hana's, for instance. Hers was the only full facial biosculpt I happened to have that week. I don't think I could have handled another. As it was, I barely handled hers. I began to treat her in a perfunctory manner. Are the melanocytes doing their job to get her complexion the right shade? Good, let's get out. A little malformation in the mandibular area? Tweak it fast and forget about it. Why was I acting so unprofessionally toward Hana? I asked myself at lucid intervals: Did I resent her willful and vain decision to replace her natural beauty with a product of the fashion marketplace? I had had no such compunctions about similar cases, and could hardly afford them anyway, being one of those responsible for encouraging such trade.

After a few days I deliberately ignored the dilemma. I went on like a talented zombie, reaming out the atherosclerotic arteries of the self-indulgent, dissolving adipose tissue, killing hair follicles in inconvenient places.

The outside world seemed to be conspiring to remind me of what I was, and had forsaken. There was a disaster in one of the orbital factories; hundreds injured, including the resident physician. Medical volunteers were needed. I didn't respond. Workers dismantling an archaic fission reactor received inadvertent rad overdoses. Repairing the cell damage required the talents of many peekers. I turned the sound lower for the rest of the newscast.

One morning I was sitting alone in my office, dreaming that my talent worked on inorganic matter instead of living substances alone. What would I do then? Turn lead to gold? Make a fortune at the roulette wheel? Anything had to be better than what I was doing now.

The door opened without warning, and Maggie hurried in, concern written plain on her face.

"Doctor, I think you'd better come at once. It's Ms. Morrell. Something's happened overnight."

Together we rushed to her room.

Hana's racking sobs greeted us at the door. Lacking a mirror, she was running her frantic hands over the ruins of her face.

All my work had been undone somehow. Instead of the porcelain-figurine features that yesterday had been almost finished, loose folds of corrugated skin hung in obscene draperies and convolutions. It looked as if someone had melted a plastic doll with a torch.

"Oh, my Christ," I swore, my stomach turning inside out.

"I get readings indicative of a massive disturbance of the lymph system," Maggie said. "Almost like elephantiasis."

Through her wails, out of her swollen lips, Hana cried, "Doctor, do something!"

But I couldn't bring myself to touch her.

The man removed his hands from my face.

"Someone's been walking all through you like you were a public park," he said.

That was the last thing I had expected to hear when I had called in one of my colleagues. Madness, some strange virus, poisoning—a hundred implausible explanations had thronged my brain. Everything but the truth.

"Just what the hell do you mean?"

He regarded me with a minimum of cold sympathy. "Exactly what I said. One of us has been peeking you like a patient, and there was no way you could see it for yourself. Once he got in the first time, he set up dozens of blocks on your own talents, forbidding corrective measures or even recognition of trouble. After that he had free run of all your systems. And what a massive tangle he caused! It was very elegant work—some of the best I've ever seen. The goal seems to have been not to totally disable your skills, but rather to misdirect and ball them up. I'm surprised you didn't kill someone, you were so screwed up."

I couldn't believe it. But I had to. What else could it be?

"So I caused the girl's disfigurement?"

"Damn right. Toward the end of her treatment, every move you made had an unpredictable result, almost as if you willed your hand to scratch your nose and found yourself raising your foot."

"Did you calm her down and start repairs?"

"Yes. And I think I managed to convince her to keep quiet about the whole thing. I had to promise you'd refund your fee and compensate her for any missed time at work."

"Good. And me?"

"I restored everything I could spot. And with the blocks on your inner perceptions removed, you should be able to handle any residual cleanup."

"I owe you," I said, getting up to accompany him out.

"Just find out who did this to you, and stop him. We can't tolerate a rogue."

I thought I could find out who, all right.

But what could possibly be the answer to why?

That night, clutching Jeanine tightly as she slept, I craved some certainty in my life. I penetrated her essential self, reading the record of her cells, searching for the imprint of past manipulation on gross morphological scales.

All of my best efforts revealed no such tampering. She was as life alone had made her. But could I have any certainty in the result? Were my talents truly restored? How would I ever be certain of anything again?

The night seemed like an endless cave without egress or a safe corner, Jeanine's body a cold stone corpse, petrified by millennia of slow mineral drips.

As the registered physician of Amy Sanjour, I had a limited access to her datafiles. I couldn't get to her financial records or voting history, but certain innocuous biographical data that might have a bearing on her treatment were mine to command.

I brought up her employment history. The current entry read UNEMPLOYED. That much I had known. She had counted on me looking no further, and I had unwittingly obliged. I scrolled forward now to the next entry, backward in time.

PSYCHOKINETICIST, GRADUATED BANNEKER INSTITUTE 2045. SPECIALTY: NEUROPATHOLOGY. ABANDONED PRACTICE 2053 FOR PERSONAL REASONS . . .

That bitch. But why?

I went hastily through the rest of her files, looking desperately for some motivation. At last I came to one entry whose significance hovered at the edge of my understanding like a moth batting at a screen:

SISTER, ELIZABETH SANJOUR, BORN 2029, DIED 2053. CAUSE OF DEATH: INTERNAL HEMORRHAGING INCURRED IN SKIING ACCIDENT.

Skiing. The single word triggered memories I had tried so desperately to forget. . . .

✻   ✻   ✻

Med school was so easy. I had always been a quick study, sharp and bright, and the chemistry and anatomy, dissection and lab work were a snap. When I tested positive on the Banneker exam, I was carrying a straight 4.0. Entrance to the institute was guaranteed.

Even in the first few months there, I had no trouble. I remember how they started us on bacterial colonies and little quivering cubes of vatflesh, where our amateur psychic probes could cause no irreparable damage. Those initial forays into the mysteries of living tissue, combined with the new mastery over my own body, were heady experiences. I felt like God himself. When we were ready, they brought in the sick ones. I was eager to show what I could do, to cure and heal like a beneficent deity.

I can't explain why I had such an adverse reaction to the tainted auras of anyone suffering severe traumas or illnesses. It was the last thing I had been expecting. All I know is that when I dove the flesh of the cancerous, the mutilated, the dying, I lost all my nerve. Forgetting all I had learned, I floundered amidst their gaudy, excessive pain, as inept as a norm. I came out of their bloody shells shaking, tachycardia thundering in my chest, the requisite work barely done. I tried to hide it, but my instructors eventually found out. No therapy worked to cure me. I graduated only with the tacit understanding that I would enter biosculpture.

That was why, when I came down the expert slope at Innsbruck and found the beautiful woman wrapped moaning around the pine tree, blood leaking from her mouth and staining the snow an unholy color, I just kept going, making for the lodge, where I notified the staff doctor, a norm. But by the time he and the rescue team coptered in, she was dead.

I had thought no one at the lodge knew who I was.

But I had been wrong.

She rested peacefully in bed. When I entered, she sat up and brightened, donning her mask of brainlessness. She opened her mouth to utter some silly remark. But something on my own face must have told her the game was up. Her beautiful features underwent such a transformation that she looked like a new, more savage person.

With malicious spite, she asked, "How are you feeling, Dr. Strode?"

"Listen, Amy—"

"Don't soil my name, you murderer!" she spat.

A burst of anger shot through me. What the fuck did she know about me and my life? Did she think I liked living with the knowledge of what I was? She had almost ruined what little beauty I had painfully ransomed from the hard and transient world, and all for selfish revenge for something I couldn't have altered.

As if reading my thoughts, she said, "You could have tried to save her, you crud. But instead you just zipped by."

I lost control then, and my hands went for her throat. I put no pressure on it, though.

Not on the outside.

If she knew my body from a week of sabotage, I knew hers from a week of loving treatment. Entrance was as easy as slipping into an old shoe. I knew that she was diving my flesh at the same time, eager for the kill. But my unconscious defenses were restored now, and I left my safety to them.

Now she was going to learn just how good her own were.

I swam her noisy arteries, heading for her heart. She stopped me in the atrium, where a squad of bright lights chased me off with lemon fire. I shot to her gallbladder, and squeezed burning bile into her duodenum. Before she could find me, I was up in her lungs, collapsing alveoli. She caught up with me there, and I barely escaped. I raced toward her brain, hoping to overload her synapses. A blockade was in place, a thorny mesh of blue hatred, and I had to be content with loosening her teeth in their sockets. I managed to snap a ligament in her shoulder on the way south. Lord knew what she was doing to me.

For an indefinite time the battle raged, each thrust of mine being met with a swift reaction from her. Every inch of bloody ground I gained was recaptured by her prowess. I knew, simply from the fact that I wasn't dead yet, that my own defenses must have been holding up as well.

At last, in wordless concert, admitting the stalemate, we disengaged.

I returned to a body in deep pain. The room swirled as I hauled myself unsteadily off her recumbent form. My limbs were puffy with edemas, and I was pretty sure one knee was broken. I wasn't up to rationally cataloging the rest of the damage. My unconscious had its immediate work cut out. Already it was snapping painblocks into place.

Amy looked no better. Her face was webbed with burst capillaries, and one hand hung awkwardly from a shattered wrist I didn't even remember attacking.

As we eyed each other suspiciously, something like remorse

stole over us as we realized the full extent of our transgressions. Two physicians, bound by a sentimental, implacable oath half as old as civilization, trying to kill each other. Whatever had driven us evaporated—or at least subsided.

"I could make a lot of trouble for you with the authorities," I finally said.

"And me for you."

"So where does that leave us?"

She was silent for some time. Grudgingly, she said, "You're pretty good."

"You, too," I admitted.

"What the hell do you get out of this work?" she asked, waving her good arm to encompass the clinic.

I shrugged. "A living."

She nodded, calculations plain behind her gorgeous eyes.

I couldn't think of anything else to say, so I kept my mouth shut.

Just when the silence seemed to stretch to the breaking point, she spoke.

"I don't forgive you, Strode, but—"

"Yes?"

"Maybe I can help."

No editor among the U.S. sf/fantasy magazines leaped at the sequel to "Skintwister," but the story happily found a home with the perspicacious and welcoming Chris Reed in the United Kingdom. It occurs to me to mention now that both "Skintwister" and "Fleshflowers" owe their existence to Norman Spinrad's kick-ass "Carcinoma Angels," another early instance of my imprinting on superior work, from 1967.

I suppose the ending of this tale begs a continuation of Doctor Strode's career, but it seems unlikely that I'll ever write one. If a genre author is at all prolific, his or her career is littered with abortive series, orphaned by lack of interest from the marketplace, changing authorial aspirations, or a combination of the two. I myself have at least three such truncated story cycles, and will probably accumulate more.

It's all just part of the strange trade of fiction writing.

Fleshflowers

*H*ERE IN EXILE, I HAVE LEARNED HOW MUCH IT IS possible to miss the Earth.

Oh, don't mistake my meaning. It's not as some repository of metaphysical meaning that I miss it. Birthplace of humanity, ancestral globe, big blue marble on a black cloth sprayed with diamond chips. What a load of bullshit. No, I miss only the luxurious life I had there, civilization and all its tinsel trappings. The money, the prestige, the women, the food and wine, sleek imported Brazilian cars and elegant Harlem apartments in the clouds.

I can hardly believe now that I used to pity myself then. Sure, I had had a few rough breaks. Failures of will and nerve that rankled, disappointed expectations, evaporated dreams. But my work had its rewards—when it was going good, and I could lose myself in it—and the material comforts more than compensated for the spiritual pangs. Compared to the lives of most people, mine was an easy lark.

Or so it appears now, from the vantage of another world. A world empty of everything I once coveted, a world where the glittering ranks of society consist of a few dozen men and women, preoccupied with science and survival.

When I can't stand their fatuous faces anymore—and the face

of one in particular—I find I have to get outside the domes, and let the elements abrade some of the emotional callous from my soul.

I must start initiating the changes a couple of hours before I want to step out. It's a demanding process, and I can't do it that often—maybe once a month. (Of course, I could just suit up, but then I'd feel encapsulated, as if I were carrying the colony with me. And besides, it's more dramatic this way. I know it creeps the others out, to see me do it. They watch me through the transparent walls until I disappear from sight, disbelief plain on their silly faces. It reinforces my failing sense of superiority.)

Anyway, about three hours worth of self-tampering—much against my old instructor's advice—allows me, rather like certain seals, to supersaturate my bloodstream with enough oxygen to last for half an hour's expedition. A slight structural change in my hemoglobin suffices. I toughen my epidermis with a layer of expendable cells that will later messily slough off, stoke the metabolic fires, thicken my corneas, don a pair of insulated boots as my only concession to heat loss, and cycle through the lock.

Not breathing, I step lightly among the red grit and windfluted parched pebbles, kicking one now and then. Their motions are strange in the low gravity, they seem to take forever to fall. A frigid dry scentless breeze strokes my altered flesh like a straight razor dipped in liquid hydrogen. Too much of this caress would be lethal even to me. In the leeward sides of the larger boulders, fine-grained brick-hued dust is piled high.

Fifteen miles away to either side of me rear the canyon walls: immense, pocked, riven, mile-long slopes whose steepness is obscured by great slumps of eroded rock clinging precariously to their faces. Crumbled talus litters the valley floor at their feet; side cuts open out onto dead-end tributary valleys.

When I am far enough from the base for solitude, around a slight bend, having used up half my stored oxygen, I stop.

I look up.

At dusk, like a man immured in a well on Earth, I am able to view the stars while the weak sun is still up. They stand out faintly in the slit of darkened Martian sky, occulted perhaps by a high lonely transient cloud, blurred slightly by my horned corneas. I try to find the blue-green star I have convinced myself is Earth.

For a few precious minutes, I dream of returning.

What I don't know yet is how reality will exceed my dreams.

As I turn to go back, I feel like the only person in the universe.

No one can reach me here. Even if others were to arrive in suits, they would still be isolated from me. I am at once utterly exposed and totally shielded.

Then I involuntarily recall what I have been trying to forget. There is one who could stand here unsuited beside me, as an equal. A woman at this moment also exiled to Mars. One bound to me by something different from, but no weaker than, love.

And stronger than hate.

I was standing rapt among the cacti when the news first came.

One of the big linked geodesic domes that comprised the only human settlement on Mars was filled with giant saguaros, multi-armed, towering almost twenty-five feet high—as tall as specimens a century old, although they were only five years removed from biofabbed seeds. Their fantastic growth had been forced by the will of the Banneker psychokineticist who had preceded me.

Now the cacti were my charges, along with the humans. My fellow exile and I were responsible for the health and continued functioning of both.

I preferred tending to the cacti.

Now, fingertips in contact with the solid spined-barrel trunk of one specimen, I had lost myself in their being.

I dived down, among the busy cell factories of the cactus I touched, thrilled by a sense of repleteness that came from water riches stored safely away. Further and further into the trunk my perception raced, assaulted by a distorted mix of sensory input it had taken me years to learn to untangle. Those tarragon-scented, fuzzy violet tangles were chloroplasts, these bloated electric spar-kles were vacuoles. I reveled in a vegetative serenity somehow dif-ferent from the same mechanisms when present in humans. . . .

Deeper now, below the soil, down into the unnaturally thick and elongated filamentary roots, probing, searching with blind tropisms for the water locked as ice beneath the Martian surface. Thirst-seek, thirst-seek, thirst-seek—

Someone was shaking my shoulder. As if from a great distance, I sensed it. Pulling my psychic feelers back in, I returned to my own body.

Joelle Fourier, the colony's aerologist, removed her hand from my shoulder. My face must have expressed some of my annoy-ance, for she stepped back warily.

"Doctor Strode, I wouldn't have disturbed you if it wasn't important. The expedition is returning, and there's trouble."

English was the lingua franca of the colony. Fourier's was pleasantly accented. She wore a white quilted coverall with an embroidered ESA patch showing an antique Ariane rocket above the breast. She was a veteran in her abstruse field, already an ancient eighteen. After three years' association with her, I knew nothing about her save this bare minimum of appearance, name and age, and didn't care to.

"What kind of trouble?" I asked.

"Why, medical, of course. The messages have been vague, but that much is clear."

I turned away. "Let Sanjour handle it. It's her watch."

"I cannot make Doctor Sanjour answer. She is locked in her quarters."

"Shit. She's probably cell-burning. Okay, let's go roust her before she smokes her entire cortex."

The cacti occupied circles of raw Martian soil separated by sintered rock paths topped with a ceramic glaze that was microgrooved for traction when wet by occasional spills made when tapping the saguaros. I followed Fourier toward the dome exit. I fantasized that the cacti all bent toward me, reluctant to let me go, wanting to clutch me in their friendly deadly arms.

The two domes containing the living quarters were subdivided into truncated pie-pieces that opened onto central plant-filled atriums scattered with chairs and cushions.

At Sanjour's door other colonists had gathered, sensing something was up. Their garments exhibited all the different patches of the many nations and organizations that made up the Comity. Their faces looked pale in the weak Martian sunlight that filtered down through the transparent dome top. The mostly young men and women shuffled nervously from foot to foot and whispered among themselves as I approached with Fourier. Make way for the pariah who holds your lives in his hands, folks. . . .

They cleared a path to the door for me. I tapped the OPEN button on the security keypad. The red LOCKED light lit up, there was a beep, and the door stayed shut.

"Who's got the override code?"

A boy I recognized as one of the astronomers stepped up.

"Holtzmann left the codes with me," he said. "But I don't know about breaching Doctor Sanjour's privacy—"

I saw as through a crimson curtain. "Listen, kid, we've got an incoming POGO full of sick citizens, and one of the two available medicos is locked in her room most assuredly burning her fucking neurons up for kicks. I suggest that the situation amounts to enough of an emergency to violate *anyone's* privacy. But if you want to call it differently—"

I shrugged and made as if to walk away.

"No, no, you're right, of course. I just didn't realize— Look, I'll open it right up."

He frantically keyed in the code. The door retreated into the wall.

I stepped inside.

The sight of a naked body I knew almost more intimately than my own, both surface and interior, greeted me. Amy was sprawled slack-limbed across her bed. Her eyes were closed, and a rivulet of saliva drooled upon her chin. She might have been just a sloppy sleeper. But she wasn't. She was lost in a self-induced, self-sustaining bonfire of near-orgasmic pleasure, a pyre fed by the destruction of her own brain cells, which, continued too long, would result in her death.

Suddenly I felt overwhelmed by pity and loathing for the two of us. What a couple of pathetic feeble cripples! How had we come to this sorry state, myself lost continually in the no-thoughts of plants, Amy hooked on cell-burning? How—?

The first time I saw Amy Sanjour naked was as a patient, back on Earth. She had waltzed into my biosculpt clinic, the perfect image of a flighty hypochondriac with the money to indulge herself in a general somatic toning under my capable—and, I admit now, eager—hands. I was utterly taken in by her.

What I didn't learn until much later—when she had successfully jiggered and booby-trapped all my PK talents, nearly resulting in my causing the permanent disfigurement of one of my other patients—was that she was as much a peeker as I. No lowly skintwister, she had had a flourishing practice in neuropathology, treating Alzheimer's, Parkinson's, and the like.

This practice she had abandoned upon the death of her sister —a death I arguably could have prevented.

She had come after me for revenge.

When I confronted her with what I had learned, a fight ensued. More than a fight. A psychic battle fought on the alternating terrains of our two bodies, a war waged in veins and cells, organs and bones.

We had stopped short of killing each other—not out of compassion, but inability. Our skills were too evenly matched to allow either one to gain a permanent advantage.

So there we stood in Amy's private room at the clinic, out of our mental clinch, bleeding, contused, puffy-faced, with snapped bones. Already our capable bodies were automatically healing themselves. That left only the intractable problem of our relationship to solve.

I could sense that Amy shared some of the embarrassed remorse and uneasiness I felt. In the space of a few long minutes, we had probed each other so deeply, come to share such a perverse kind of physical intimacy, that there was almost nothing left to say.

But in the end, Amy did discover something that could be said. "I don't forgive you—but maybe I can help."

I accepted that statement without quite knowing what it meant.

I soon found out.

That very night, when we were basically recovered from our physical wounds, we became lovers, completing our intimacy on the same bed where we had nearly killed each other. Our fucking —I can use only that term to describe the animality of the impulsive act—was a transposed extension of that earlier encounter.

At that time, I was already involved with another woman, a teacher named Jeanine. I had considered her the sexiest, most beautiful woman I had ever seen.

After that night, she came to mean nothing to me.

There was nothing to compare to sex with a fellow peeker. Throughout medical school, I had avoided the experience, out of a certain nervous reluctance to allow PK access to my body, and out of a sense of my peers as competitors, not friends. Beyond school—well, peekers were not that common, and I simply didn't have many social contacts with others of my kind. And I had never guessed that the sensations of having a partner freely roaming inside me, while making more conventional love, would be so intense.

Imagine ghostly feelers opening the taps of lust, stoking biological fires—

And of course, it didn't hurt that Amy was outwardly beautiful, a tall, powerful woman, taut as a cable on the Bering Strait Bridge.

After that night, things moved too quickly to stop, impelled by strong emotions, bereft of logic.

I stopped seeing Jeanine. It was a messy parting. Amy became a partner in my clinic. She moved into my apartment. For a few months, she was satisfied performing facial and bodily makeovers with me, milking the vain rich of their unearned dollars. Then she got greedy, and revealed an unbelievable scheme. I listened warily. I remember thinking that the trauma of her sister's death and her aborted, transfigured schemes of revenge on me had completely erased any altruism or professional scruples she had once possessed.

And since I had never had any, and was hopelessly fixated on Amy, I went along with what she proposed.

We waited for the perfect mark to approach us on his own, to allay suspicions later. He turned up in the form of a billionaire with several patents on room-temperature superconductors. With the build of a flabby flyweight, he was in the market for a new physique. Over the course of a few months, we gave it to him. Along with a time-delayed embolism. But before that fatal attack, triggered weeks after he left the clinic, we had already insured our share of his fortune. From his bed he had summoned his lawyer and richly endowed a foundation in our names, for the entirely plausible reason of being impressed with our mission to bring beauty to the world. Eyes open, lips moving, he had been unconscious the whole time. Amy, one hand unobtrusively on his shoulder, had manipulated his vocal cords like a puppetmaster. He was to have no memory of the event when he awoke.

On the day of the billionaire's death, when he still hadn't learned of his involuntary donation nor attempted to rescind it, we were congratulating ourselves at home when the cops arrived. Suspicious relatives had requested a peeker autopsy, the only way our tampering could ever have been detected.

The trial went fast. We couldn't mount much of a defense. The prosecutor demanded that both of us get two consecutive terms of ninety-nine years each—which we probably could have served, given our superior homeostatic functioning.

It was at this point that the AMA stepped in. They couldn't stand the thought of two ex-peekers sitting out all that time in jail. Every five years a "do you remember?" story in the media, continual bad publicity for the whole profession. . . . So they arranged in behind-the-scenes negotiations a "more clement" sentence, one that would get us off the stage of public opinion, and make it appear as if we were intent on absolving ourselves.

The Russians established the first Mars colony as a unilateral enterprise in 1999, taking advantage of Earth's close orbital approach to that world. This was in the days before the Comity, the de facto alliance that—first delicately, tentatively, then more and more strongly—had grown out of *glasnost,* and the sloughing off of Eastern Europe from the USSR. In those heady early Comity days of fading militarism and joint ventures, all attention had been turned toward remaking the Earth into a better world. The Mars colony had somehow been neglected, struggling along for fifty years as an archaic remnant of Russian aloofness.

Then, in a freakish but ultimately predictable cataclysm, the colony had been wiped out. A small vagrant asteroid had impacted nearly atop it.

Suddenly the world was unanimous in the need and desire to rebuild the base. What everyone had ignored became the only topic of conversation. Society could afford to turn its attention outward now, after half a century of peace and progress.

The Comity colony had been established for two years when our sentencing became an issue. Support for the base was still as strong as ever.

The colony's resident doctor had just died in a climbing accident on the slopes of the Tharsis Ridge. (Even a peeker can't recover from a crushed skull.)

We were nominated his successors. Transportees, exiles, penitent prisoners in the service of humanity.

They shot us up with anti-gee drugs and shot us off on the next supply mission. We had peeker-planted blocks on our powers that wouldn't dissolve until after a fixed number of metabolic reactions, equal to the length of the trip.

But once on Mars, there was no way they could really make us serve.

I was down on my knees by the bed, the crowd clustered at the door behind me forgotten. My hands hovered above Amy's bare midriff, shaking a bit, hesitant. Her abdominal muscle tone was shot to shit. My nails were longish and dirty. Christ. . . . Where was Amy's former superb tonus, where were the manicured hands of the self-important Doctor Strode, which had stroked and reshaped the bodies of wealthy socialites?

Ready to dive beneath Amy's skin, I was halted by an unusual compunction. Did I have any right to drag her back from her destructive pleasures? What else was left to us, the untouchables of the colony? We'd never fit in, the only coerced laborers among all these committed, idealistic volunteers.

Well, hell—when you came down to it, what did rights count for? The only thing that mattered now was that I didn't want to spend the rest of my life alone among these fresh-faced zealots.

I slapped palms to flesh and went under, for a stroll down blood lane, through the gardens of organs and bone.

The stupid bitch had set up roadblocks for me, just like the last time. But she had been in a hurry to get burning, and had been sloppy. Plus her talents were suffering because of her addiction. She lacked some of the deftness now that had almost killed me during our first fight, so long ago.

I got past the buzzing lime-colored clots and the angry fibrillary nets, shot through the blood-brain barrier, and was in her hypothalamus before she could arouse herself to stop me.

She had that organ locked in total production of jazzed-up neurotransmitters and endorphins. These opiate-like substances were flooding the receptors in her brain and spine to produce a heavenly buzz, poppy-sweet. Trouble was, both the originating and receiving cells were burning themselves out, all metabolic resources allocated to the output and uptake of the pleasure-juices. She was killing off these and adjacent cells at an alarming rate.

I intervened in her cortical jury-rigging and got the cells back to normal. Then I initiated some hasty regenerative processes. Brain cells, of course, resisted regeneration more than any other part of the body, and I was hard pressed to force them to obey. Someday Amy would overextend the natural resiliency of her cells, and suffer permanent brain damage. That day, I sensed, was not far off.

Then I pulled out.

I could have woken her up from inside.

But I wanted the pleasure of doing it the old-fashioned way.

Back in my own shell, I slapped her four or five times across the face with stinging force.

Suddenly she shot up in bed and grabbed my wrist. I braced for her to enter me with her talent, but she applied only physical pressure, strong enough at that. I had to give her credit for a quick recovery. But then again, she had had the best peeker on the planet inside her.

"Stop it," she hissed, her olive eyes large.

"Tell me you don't love it."

"You fucking bastard."

I broke her grip and stood up. "Time enough for sweet nothings later, dearest. We've got an audience, in case you've been too busy melting your skull to notice." The watching young faces reddened and turned away. These kids were so easy to shock. "Put some clothes on—unless you consider yourself dressed—and meet me by the lock. We've got incoming trouble of some sort."

I left her getting shakily out of bed.

The crowd dispersed uneasily, remembering their duties. I was left with Fourier, who seemed to have been delegated my keeper. Her youthful innocence appeared untouched by the recent pitiful performance, and she seemed genuinely sorry for both Amy and me. Without meaning to be, I felt myself affected, softened, by her attitude. Then I realized that this was what someone—undoubtedly Holtzmann—had wanted to happen. Ah, he was a sly boy, that one. I updated my mental note never to underestimate him.

We walked through several domes, toward the garage with its lock.

"Any more news?" I asked.

"No. There was just that one radio contact, then nothing."

"What's the ETA?"

"Half an hour from now."

"Nothing we can do but wait, I guess."

She lifted her shoulders slightly, as if to calmly say, *One cannot act without information.* Jesus, these kids might be easily embarrassed by emotional scenes, but they were cool as clams in a crisis. I tried to remember if I had ever been that young and self-assured. But I couldn't make any contact with that past self—the lines were down, the distance insuperable—so I gave up.

Halfway through the wait, Amy joined us at the lock.

She emerged from between the parked crawlers, striding strongly, dressed in green. Her skin shone from a sonic cleansing. Disregarding regs, she had washed her short platinum hair with a week's personal allotment of cactus water, which always seemed to leave it thick and shining. Her features were alert, signs of her formidable intelligence written plain across them. I felt a sharp pang. She looked so right, so familiar, so lost—

"What's up?" she demanded.

I told her what I knew. She nodded sagely, all business. We went back to waiting.

Fourier saw the POGO appear first, and directed our attention to it. For a second it stood atop the northern rim like a Masai warrior on one leg, or a sleeping stork. Then it bounced up and over, and began to descend the long slope in puffs of dust.

The Comity base was situated in the middle of the bottom of the Valles Marineris, that wide, continent-long rift on the Martian equator. The decision to plant the colony there was psychological, a reaction to the destruction of the first base. The valley seemed somehow to offer more shelter than the barren plains—although another determined asteroid would have no trouble fitting into the thirty-seven-mile-wide cleft. Also, the decision reflected long-range plans. The eventual goal was to roof over the entire valley, section by section, and establish a shirt-sleeve environment. Lots of living space for the bucks, and a damn sight cheaper than terra-forming the whole world.

Other colonists had come to the garage to help, although no one knew precisely what would be required. The POGO bounced closer and closer, eventually stopping about fifty feet away from the dome. It was too big to enter through the crawler lock. Its passengers would have to disembark and walk. If they still could.

A hatch opened in the stilted pod. A ladder of plastic chains unfurled.

I didn't know what to expect. Victims of decompression or explosion or rock fall, limbs torn or puffy or mangled, carried out by limping survivors—

The last thing I expected was to see five agile figures drop down the ladder, jumping off while still ten feet above the red soil, and begin trotting for the dome.

They entered the lock and were lost from our sight.

The speaker above the inner door came alive while the lock was cycling.

"Clear everyone out except the medical personnel," said Holtzmann's officious voice, a trace of nervousness underneath. "Have cots set up in the chipfab clean room. We're going to use it as an isolation chamber. We'll reach it by Alleys Eight and Twelve. After we've passed, have the whole route disinfected. We've just sterilized our suits, and won't be cracking them, but we can't take any chances."

I punched the intercom button. "Holtzmann, are you crazy? You're talking like you're infected. You know as well as I do that except for whatever imported terrestrial organisms might have escaped and survived, Mars is dead."

There was silence for a long ten seconds. Then Holtzmann said, "Not anymore, Doctor Strode. Not anymore."

Weddig Holtzmann was thirteen years old. He had sharp Teutonic features and a blond brushcut. An East German, he was the product of their super-accelerated neurotropic education. I had never agreed with those who claimed the miracle catalysts allowed everything an adult needed in terms of sheer knowledge to be force-fed to someone by the time he was only thirteen. I was relieved when Congress—despite the pressure from the Gerontocrats, who wanted plenty of young workers to support them—killed the bill to lower the U.S.'s franchise to that age.

Fifteen was just right; those extra two years made a big difference. I know that I myself wouldn't have been ready for college at thirteen. As it was, by the time I emerged from Johns Hopkins and the Banneker Institute, at age twenty, I was hardly mature enough to handle my powers. As can be adduced by the way I've fucked my life up.

Now, at thirty-one, I felt practically ancient next to Holtzmann and his peers. I knew Amy shared these feelings, for we had spoken of it, in our more rational moments, as one of the causes of our sense of alienation.

Holtzmann, whether as a by-product of his hothouse growth or due to congenital tendencies, was a perfect little martinet. No doubt one of the reasons he had been chosen as leader. I always called him "Weegee," because it pissed him off.

Standing now in the makeshift isolation chamber with Holtzmann, Amy and the other expedition members, I considered foregoing the jibe today.

There were no conventional hand weapons on the base. They would have done little good against the one real threat of asteroids, and nations at peace had seen no need to arm their representatives against one another. But Holtzmann had remembered the flare pistol aboard the POGO, and he now had its ugly wide snout pointed squarely at my gut. Its self-propelled, oxy-fed load would punch a hole in me that no amount of peeker skills would be able to rebuild.

"You're going to find out what's wrong with us," said Holtzmann sternly, an almost imperceptible quaver under his words, "and fix it. And this time there'll be no tricks."

I had to smile then at the memory. He was referring to the last time everyone had come to us for a bone toning. In the lower gravity of Mars, minor osteoporosis was a problem, and we had regular sessions where we dealt with it, as well as searched out incipient skin cancers due to Mars's high UV. This time, out of boredom and disgust with our roles as captive shamans, Amy and I had added a little fillip to the treatment.

The morning after, all the colonists had woken up bald, their hair bestrewing their pillows. The uproar was wonderful. Things had taken months to get back to normal.

And the best part was, they couldn't even really discipline us, needing us as they did.

I carefully considered Holtzmann's emotional state, the muzzle aimed at me, and my integrity, then said, "Whatever you want —Weegee."

Holtzmann's finger tightened visibly on the trigger, I made ready to fling myself aside—when Amy stepped between us.

"Listen, so far we're totally in the dark. What's wrong with the five of you? You look okay. What happened?"

Holtzmann passed the back of his free hand across his sweaty brow and made a visible effort to calm down. "You're right, Doctor Sanjour. I've been remiss. I should have explained everything over the radio, and made the arrangements for the antiseptic precautions ahead of time. But we were all too preoccupied in running what tests we could. You know that Kenner doubles as our biologist." Holtzmann indicated a dark-haired seventeen-year-old sitting on a cot, hands folded morosely in his lap. "Well, he's been unable to learn anything about what's gotten into us."

Seeing our puzzlement, Holtzmann backtracked.

"You know we were making the first real survey of the ruins of the original base, at Pavonis Mons, to see if there could possibly be anything salvageable, or any surviving personal effects for the relatives of the colonists. Also, we wanted pieces of the asteroid that wiped out the base, since we seldom get a chance to study such objects uncontaminated by terrestrial organisms.

"Well, the first part of our mission was fruitless. The base was entirely destroyed by the shock waves of the strike, which must have been measurable in megatons. The inhabitants, I'm sure, died almost instantly, as painlessly as possible. There were no artifacts left.

"However, we did succeed in finding portions of the asteroid itself. They're in the POGO now."

Holtzmann paused. "Oh, Christ, did I say not to let anyone near the POGO?" He walked to the wall and issued the order over the base's PA. My stomach muscles—which I hadn't even known were tight—relaxed.

Still slumped by the curving wall, Holtzmann turned back to us, raising the gun almost absent-mindedly.

"We kept most of the samples in isolation, so as not to contaminate them. But one piece—one small piece—we handled with our bare hands, all of us marvelling, I think, at the distant origins of this innocuous rock, and how it was fated to wipe out so many lives. And now, God knows, it appears ready to do more destruction."

Amy said slowly, "You believe that you've been infected by an organism from the asteroid fragment?"

"It's not that implausible, Amy," I interrupted. "We know that interstellar clouds seem to contain free-floating amino acids. And those famous Antarctic meteorites on Earth appeared to have prebiotic molecules on them. There was even a theory—the guy's name was Doyle, Hoyle, something similar—that the late-twentieth-century epidemics were caused by extraterrestrial microbial agents."

Holtzmann jerked erect, gun quivering. "There's no need to debate so coolly, people. We're compromised. Our bodies are hosts now to something unknown. There is no doubt, no doubt whatsoever."

"Well," I said, almost tauntingly, not quite willing to believe yet, "what are the symptoms, Weegee?"

Holtzmann's hand shot to the chest seam of the coverall he had worn beneath his discarded pressure suit. He ripped the fabric away from himself. Velcro peeled apart with an insulting noise.

There are colors, shades and hues, which human flesh does not normally wear—at least not on the surface. The yellow-brown of rotten bananas. The mottled purple of bruised plums. The green-tinged gray of wet sharkskin. Yet these were the colors visible in the intricate shiny folds and convolutions of the growths bursting from Holtzmann's chest and abdomen.

I was next to the man before I knew I had moved. Amy too. We didn't touch him at first, but only stared.

Each growth was only about as big as an infant's fist, and there were only seven of them, irregularly spaced. It was their startling incongruity that had made them at first appear to dominate his body, from across the room. They emerged subtly from his skin, the alien colors, textures, and shapes grading away into normal skin.

Their shapes—consider brain coral, roses, ranunculus, anything complexly enfolded and recomplicated, gleaming slickly, throwing back highlights from the room's illuminants. They differed slightly, one from the other, like individual faces.

Holtzmann seemed a garden of exotic blooms, his body cultivated soil.

"There are more on the parts of me still covered," he said,

"although their numbers have stopped increasing. Luckily, we are still able to sit and walk, although lying on them is—uncomfortable."

Amy and I both raised our hands in unconscious synchronization, and made ready to enter him.

"No," warned Holtzmann, gesturing with the gun. "Treat the others first. I'll go last."

It was impossible to tell if he spoke from sense of duty, or fear. But it didn't matter, since we had to obey in either case.

The others had opened their coveralls down to their waists, after their commander's example, as if to offer mute testimony to their common affliction. One of the two women had symmetrical fleshflowers on both breasts, where her nipples had been. A man sprouted one from his armpit. I felt my own skin crawl.

Amy moved to delve into one of the women. I went to Kenner, sitting on the cot.

In and down, down, down, past his ephemeral agonized epidermis, into the arteries and cells and meat.

I had expected to spot signs of the infectious agent everywhere. I was disappointed. It had to be something like a virus, I was assuming, but the man's bright blood was clean of any such deadly packets. There weren't even any raised levels of antigens, no pockets of invaders hiding inside macrophages or T-cells. Kenner's psychic aura was one of utter health, tallying with his lack of debilitating symptoms.

Alien tropisms, alien life cycles, meant alien patterns of conquest, I thought to myself.

I had been avoiding the obvious locales of the invaders, the fleshflowers themselves. Now, stymied elsewhere, I moved my perceptions cautiously toward them.

There were outriders to the colonized territory: sentry organisms, far from the main concentrations, whose like I had never before encountered. I tried to pin them down for examination, but they squirmed out of my mental pincers. Trapped in some Heisenbergian quandary, I could not both hold them and pick them apart.

I have used my PK talents on everything from mosquitos to man, microbes to elephants. The Mars colony's cacti presented no resistance to my skills. But all life on Earth stems from a common ancestor, has a shared biochemistry. These things were the product of some completely alien course of evolution, with different mechanisms of life.

While I was planning my next move, the organisms counter-punched.

I never got anywhere near the main flowering bodies. Somehow, in an inconceivable manner, I was repelled, my advance thwarted. I got a fleeting impression of masses of single-celled viroids, alien genetic material coiled snakelike in their nuclei, massing, breeding, preparing to fission—

Kicked violently out of Kenner, I opened my eyes. Amy was reeling back from her patient, obviously dealt a similar defeat.

"Are you done?" Holtzmann demanded. "Did it work? Are they dead?"

I rubbed the stubble on my chin. I caught Amy's green eyes. I spoke.

"Uh, I think we've got them on the run. . . ."

That night Amy and I slept together for the first time in months. And I mean simply slept together, for our sexual encounters had always continued, even during our worst periods. We fell exhausted into her bed after a hasty meal and pointless discussion of what we had experienced.

Holtzmann had been reluctant to let us leave the clean room, after our exposure to their bodies. I convinced him of the truth, which was that we had not been infected. He had been forced to believe us, and let us go. There was nothing any of us could do right then but get some rest.

As I held Amy's sleep-slackened body from behind, my mind drifting aimlessly for the few minutes I took to fall asleep, I thought of all we had been, all we had become—

Then I dreamed.

Peekers don't generally dream.

As a side effect of our training, we lose most of our dreamlife. A fully integrated subconscious both attends to superior autonomic functioning, and dispenses with the necessity of sorting through experience and filing it away as dreams.

The last time I had dreamed, it had been a nightmare, a vision of my hands rotting, indicative of my confusion at the time.

Tonight's started pleasantly enough, but turned nightmarish too.

Amy and I stood on Earth again, atop a high hill, covered with grass and tall multicolored flowers on waving stalks. There was a breeze, and sun on our faces. We held hands like children. We were happy again.

Then the flowers began to attack.

They whipped around our ankles and calves, growing upward to strangle us. We pulled and twisted, Amy screaming, myself howling, to no avail.

Suddenly, a pair of scissors appeared in Amy's hands. She tried clipping the flowers, but they writhed away.

"Hold them, Jack, hold them!"

I grabbed a stalk, immobilizing it; Amy snipped off the bud; the thing withered and died.

In a few moments we had destroyed them all.

We fell down to the soil. Our clothes were gone. We made love.

I awoke in the middle of the night with an erection which, for a change, I hadn't willed into being. Which I soon convinced similarly awakened Amy, using more gentleness than I had employed in a while, to help me with.

But even better, I had an idea that might help us. An idea that needed no explaining, for I had been under Amy's skin during the whole dream and she had impossibly shared it all.

The five infected colonists were miserable that morning, having hardly slept for fear and physical discomfort. Their eyes were pouched in shadows, their postures poor. They looked wilted— except for the glossy vitality of their fleshflowers.

Holtzmann glowered at us as we entered.

"Have you worked on the problem? Do you think you can rid us of this contagion?"

He was so anxious he forgot to threaten us with the flare gun.

"Yes, we've got an approach we think might work. But first, I want you to consider something. What if we had killed off all the organisms yesterday?"

"I don't understand—"

"Weegee, you surprise me. This is a long-awaited event, man's first contact with an alien life form. Microscopic, I'll admit, but still nonterrestrial life! Don't you think the scientific community on Earth might be mildly interested in such a thing?"

Holtzmann nodded. "Of course, we'll send them samples of the asteroid."

I had to convince him that what I was about to propose was the only solution. "How do you know they'll be able to culture it again? What if your bodies hold the only viable members of the life form? Do you want to take a chance on exterminating them forever?"

Holtzmann paled. "You're not suggesting that we just let it continue to breed in us, as if we were lab animals . . ."

Amy broke in. "No, we'll take the bug. We should be able to keep it alive in ourselves, while holding the manifestations down."

"On conditions," I added. "Return passage to Earth, of course. And a complete pardon. Or else we'll let you and the others just bloom until you can't move. And believe us, they're ready for a replicatory burst. We both saw it yesterday."

Holtzmann fingered the gun on the cot beside him, hesitating.

"C'mon, Weegee, face it, it's a great deal. You can kill us, but you can't force us to cure you. But if we get what we want, you all walk out healthy. And you'll have a legitimate reason to replace us with a peeker who's here because he believes in what you're doing."

Holtzmann sat rigid for a minute before speaking. "If you succeed—"

"Oh, we will," I answered with more confidence than I felt. "I take it we have a deal."

He was too mad to speak, and could only shake his head.

"I assume you still want to be last," I told him, just to twist the knife a little. In front of the others, he couldn't deny it.

Amy and I moved to one of the women. We both placed our hands on her shoulders.

Then we were inside her, working as a team, merging our skills.

This time we shot straight to the stems of the fleshflowers.

For a moment, sharing this patient with Amy, I felt exposed, as I did standing unsuited on the Martian surface. Amy could commit any treachery now, attack me through the channel of our mutual patient. Would our truce hold? Was it real?

It dawned on me that she must be having the same doubts.

Then I didn't have time to worry anymore.

The first sentries awaited.

Just as in my—our—dream, I pinned the first organism down immobile, and Amy lysed its cell wall.

Novel organelles, unlike anything on Earth, spilled out, trailing rainbow sparks, dying without their cytoplasmic support. I could leave them for the body's macrophages. I dove into the free-floating nucleus and unspooled its genetic material. The bases were strange, stranger, and they were coiled right-handed, the opposite of all earthly DNA. No wonder it had thrown us. Amy and I studied it for a timeless interval. This look was all we had needed.

Now we could kill. Alone, or together.

We shot through all the nodes of unhealthy, warped flesh, slaughtering invaders by the thousands. We left their carcasses behind us, peeking regenerative changes in the humans that would soon erase all traces of the fleshflowers.

When we were done with the first woman, we moved on to one of the men.

Despite being able to kill the virus separately now, we tackled him and the others together.

It just felt good.

Finally, we had only Holtzmann left.

In the heat of the crisis yesterday, if Holtzmann hadn't stopped us when we instinctively moved to probe him jointly, he probably would have been cured by now. But he did, and we had tackled the viroids separately, and we had failed. And had enough time to conceive our little blackmail scheme.

He seemed to realize this now, and the knowledge rankled. But he was at our mercy.

Amy and I laid our curative hands right atop four of his blossoms. It was the first time we had touched them. They felt cold and hard, like certain fungi.

"Let's do it," I said.

It took no time at all to exterminate Holtzmann's unwanted guests. All except for a few in the colonies beneath our hands.

At the proper moment we split our flesh, opened up bloodless wounds in our palms, and also in Holtzmann's fleshflowers. We drove the remaining alien viroids up into our stigmata, and closed the exit.

It was just like slaughtering Indians, and corralling the surviving few on a reservation. What man had always excelled at.

We came back to ourselves.

Holtzmann spoke.

"It's over," he said with relief.

"For you," said Amy.

"But for us," I said, "it seems to have just begun."

This is the most autobiographical story I have ever written. Many of my relatives were employed in New England textile mills, before those mills closed their doors in the wake of, first, the industry's flight toward cheaper conditions in the southern United States, and, more recently, foreign competition. I myself spent a fair number of summers earning college tuition in such a clangorous, dusty, dangerous setting. But as I try to convey in this story, the old milltown communities — mostly vanished already by the time I encountered their sparse remnants — had their own allure, a kind of tight-knit (pun intentional) camaraderie of the working man, many of whom gratefully fled the uncertainty of rural existences for indoor work and the security of a steady paycheck.

The Industrial Revolution — and hence in a sense science fiction itself — was led by the textile industry and its quest to automate ancient processes. But that era has come and gone. Our world will never see such all-encompassing mills again.

But will the future? Perhaps, perhaps.

In its first draft, this story ended with the fourth section. I owe editor Kim Mohan thanks for urging me to write the necessary coda.

The Mill

BRICK DUST MOTTLED THE STILL VALLEY AIR AROUND the noisy scrambling boys, rising and quickly falling like their cries and shouts in thin ragged clouds that puffed from beneath their hands and feet as they clambered clumsily upon the vast irregular pile of broken and discarded bricks. Its dry powdery sun-baked scent—as familiar as the odor of homemade waterwheat bread—filled their nostrils, even as the settling pale orange-red powder layered their dull black clothing, penetrating its very weave and filtering through to veneer their skins with an ineluctable talcum, so that mothers, washing these boys later, would exclaim, "I swear by the Factor's immortal soul, this brick dust is leaking out from inside you. Why, I wouldn't be surprised to discover you're nothing but a human brick yourself!"

But the kettle-filled tub and the scrubbing with smoke-colored sea sponges and the gentle feminine upbraiding would come later, and was not to be worried about now. Now only the mad, ecstatic spirit of competition held sway, raging in their veins like the Swolebourne at flood. On and around the huge tumulus of bricks the boys swarmed, in a single-minded and almost desperate game to reach the top. Hands relinquished their holds to reach for the shirttails of those who surged ahead, to yank them back with savage glee. The boys seemed oblivious to the impact of the corners and edges of the broken blocks on their knees and shins and forearms, intent only on achieving the instant and insurmountable but fleeting glory of standing upon the pinnacle of the heap.

The boys ranged in age from five to just under twelve. No distinction in treatment was made between younger and older, all ages giving and taking equally in the mutual ferocity of the jagged ascent.

Dislodged bricks tumbled down the pile with a resonant clatter, and it seemed as if the pile would soon be leveled before any individual could reach the top. In the next instant, though, one boy emerged above the rest, eluding the outstretched hands that sought to capture him and deny him the top. Bent almost parallel to the slope of the heap he clawed like an animal with hands and boot-shod feet working alike to reach the apex of the mound. Sweat turned the dust upon his face into a crimson paste.

All the boys seemed to realize at once that victory for this upstart was now foregone, all their own chances lost in the sudden burst put on by the boy now nearing the top. Instead of reacting badly, they gave in to their natural inclination to cheer an honest victor, and exhortations and encouragements replaced their wordless exclamations of struggle. "Go it, Cairncross!" "Yay, Charley!" "They can't stop you now, Charles!"

With the cheers of his peers ringing in his ears, the boy reached the top.

His heart was pounding, and he could hardly see. His white sweat-soaked shirt clung to him like the mantle of a cape-wolf. He feared he might faint, but knew also somehow that he would not. It was not destined for his body, the instrument of his victory, after all, to spoil this moment. Getting his feet precariously under himself, he stood erect atop the crumbling mass, panting, bruised, sweaty, triumphant, and surveyed those below him, who had come to a complete cessation of movement, as if they had finally assumed the earthen nature of the brick they had so long played upon.

For the first time in all the years he had been competing in this brutal, vital, irreplaceable game, he had won. He had won. And there could be only one reason why. Tomorrow he turned twelve. When you turned twelve you entered the Mill to work. You played on the bricks no more. This had been his last chance ever to stand here, in unique and poignant relation to his fellows. And he had been granted the privilege. Through some unseen intervention of God or Factor, unwonted energy and determination had flooded his limbs, urging him on to the top, where now he stood with shaky knees. He had won.

For the next twenty years this moment would be the highlight, the indescribable epiphanic summation and measure of Charley Cairncross's life. Neither his first kiss from his betrothed nor commendation from his superiors; neither the birth of his children nor the praise of the Factor himself would equal this heartbreaking moment.

Moved by a premonition of what this moment meant, under the impulse of forces he could neither identify nor control, Charley, risking a tumble and cracked skull, began to jig and prance, whooping and yelling in a giddy crazy dance atop the bricks, unimpeded by his heavy leather shoes, like a fur-faced South Polar savage gloating over the skulls of his vanquished enemies. The boys below Charley watched in fascination, as the skinny lad flailed his arms and legs about. No one had ever done this before, and they were utterly baffled, but at the same time respectful.

There was no telling how long Charley might have continued his victory dance, had not noontime intervened. From some distance away came the loud tolling of a big bell, echoed up and down the Valley by remoter cousins. Its brazen strokes pealed out, shattering both Charley's visionary state and the hypnotic trance of his audience. Immediately boys began to descend the heap of rubble, brushing futilely at their clothes.

Charley, recovering from his ecstasy, looked up at the cloudless summer heavens. Several kites and cliff kestrels glided lazily in the depths of the aquamarine heavens. The enormous blue-white sun was directly overhead. Noontime indeed, and lunch still had to be delivered, despite the unique and magnificent events of the day. Not even for transcendence—*especially* not for transcendence—could the routine of Mill and Valley come to a halt.

Lowering his center of gravity so as not to topple, Charley crabbed backwards down the pile. By the time he reached the ground, all the other boys had already vanished among the houses not far off. Charley hastened after them.

The brick dump lay on the outskirts of Charley's village, just beyond the outermost houses. In neat, garden-broken ranks the brick bungalows marched alongside the Mill with geometric precision. They clustered familiarly together, despite the abundance of open space in the Valley, as if making a united front against the mystery of the world around them.

By tradition, the master masons of Charley's village for centuries had dumped their waste here, on the last bit of level cleared ground before the land became wooded and began to slope up, forming the eastern side of the Valley. All the subsequent decades of weathering and decomposition had permeated the original soil with the sterile runoff from the pile, rendering it mostly fruitless. Among the trailing tendrils of discarded brick grew only the hardiest weeds. Sourpeas, their gaudy spring flowers only a memory now, their poisonous yellow pods harvested occasionally as an emetic; dangletrap, its jaws snapping softly on the odd insect; maidenhair, its black tendrils lying wispily atop red shards. . . . A foot-beaten path, trod by generations of boys, led back to the houses.

Halfway across the waste, the path was intersected at a right angle by a twin-rutted dirt road with a thin grassy median. The road, like the Swolebourne, like the Mill itself, ran north and south, leading in the latter direction down the length of the Valley to where the Swolebourne emerged from its human-made brick shell. Here, new construction was always going on.

Once among the shadows of the somber brick dwellings—each two stories tall and divided by an interior wall so as to house two separate families, whose compact and well-tended garden plots flanked each proud owner's door, serving in lieu of useless grassy lawn—Charley speeded up his pace. He knew his mother would be waiting for him. More importantly, so would his father.

On the paths threading the village, Charley passed many boys bent on errands identical to his. They had already been home, however, and now raced by carrying tight-lidded tin pails that they swung by their handles, and stone bottles stoppered with ceramic plugs and wire caps, and suspended from twine knotted around the bottlenecks. The stone bottles were slick with condensation, their contents cool from all-morning immersion in the family wells.

Soon Charley reached the doorstep of his house, indistinguishable from all the rest and yet so deeply and immutably known by him as his. A woman with plaited honey-colored hair stood impatiently in the doorway, tapping a foot beneath her long baize skirts and holding his father's lunchpail and beer crock. The left corner of her lips twitched the big dark beauty spot above it in a familiar gesture of annoyance.

His mother cut off Charley's attempted explanation of his

lateness and disheveled condition. "No excuses, boy. Just get your Da's meal to him before it gets cold." Without even stopping, Charley grabbed the pail and bottle and took off.

Down the narrow cindered lanes — which had just lately dried completely after the final spring rains — Charley raced, his tough leather-soled high-topped shoes crunching the grit as if it were rock candy. Eventually he caught up with the other boys, who had not been so far ahead of him after all, and who — by an unconscious and daily urge to gregariousness, as if they were determined to offset now the future semi-isolation they would endure when tending their machines in the Mill — had funneled together from their various starting points and subsequently moved in a jubilant pack through the last shadowy stretch of serried houses. Occasionally a pail would bang up clumsily against one of its mates, eliciting dull clunks and anxious belligerent warnings to "watch out for my Da's dup, you clodder!" Some boys carried two or more pails, for both brothers and father.

Sighting Charley, many of the boys whooped out fresh congratulations for his recent performance on the brick heap. Several of them mimicked his celebratory dance, infusing it with an absurdity he had surely not felt. Had he really looked so foolish? Or was it the perceptions of his friends that was distorting the reality of what he had experienced? Not for the first time, Charley felt distanced from the other boys. He wondered whether anything as intense as what he had just experienced could ever be truly communicated or understood. . . .

At last the boys burst out from the maternal embrace of the houses, leaving behind shadow for diamond-hard translucent sunlight that fell sharply on a wide swath of wildflower-spotted, untamed emerald field that stretched away to the Mill. The cindered path continued across this intermediate zone between home and work, heading toward the immense brick structure that was the Mill.

The Mill was ungraspable from this vantage in its entirety, looking merely like a high endless madder-dark windowless wall capped by a mansard roof whose expanse of thick slates looked like the spine of some unknown beast. It stretched to right and left as far as one could see, dividing the Valley like a ruler laid across a bear-anthill. Its majestic presence was so much a given, so taken for granted, that the boys truly did not even really see it. Their attention was focused on meeting their fathers.

The boys moved on through the fragrant waist-high unscythed

grass, spreading apart a bit, some stopping to investigate a flower or insect, then having to run to rejoin the rest. In a minute or so they had crossed this interzone and entered upon the territory of the Mill proper. Here, as at the brick heap, the ground was bare of anything but the most tenacious and hardy of weeds, due to the accumulation of generations' worth of waste oil. The smell from the organic detritus—Charley had once heard that the oil came from a special kind of plant that did not grow hereabouts—was dense but not overpoweringly unpleasant, especially to those who had lived with its smell engrained in the creases of their fathers' rough hands ever since those selfsame hands had first reached to absent-mindedly stroke the new babe in its cradle. The air here smelled rather like slightly rancid fried food.

Charley and the others hurried across this oily waste toward an opening in the Mill's flank. A wide double-doored portal of thick planks, this entrance was marked by the rising of a clocktower up from the roofline above its location, and also by a heterogenous collection of backless benches scattered around just beyond the entrance. Above the benches, the gilded hands of the clock hung at ten past the hour, scything inexorably toward the inevitable return to work. Under their stern progress, the benches were already filling up with sweaty, hungry, brawny, tired-looking men, and many of their older sons, looking like shrunken or as yet uninflated replicas of their sires.

When the lunch-carriers saw their relatives waiting they picked up their feet even more fleetly and began to cry out like a flock of particularly limited birds. "Da! Da! Da! Da!" The men and workerboys perked up, hearing these youthful voices and knowing their meals had arrived. More and more laborers—those who worked farther inside the depths of the Mill and so had farther to walk for lunch—continued to pour out of the doors.

Straggling alongside Charley in the rear was poor Jemmy Candletree. The boy had six or seven pails to lug. His mother, a widower, supported herself and Jemmy by supplying meals to childless and unmarried men.

Charley silently took one of Jemmy's pails; the lad smiled gratefully.

On the far side of the Mill, Charley knew, this same scene was being mirrored. It gave him a curious sense of twinness to think about it.

Now the lead boys had begun to circulate among the men, handing out the lunchpails and stone jugs they had ferried from hearth to hand. The men assumed a certain dignity with the arrival of these tin vessels and crocks. Each set his shoulders back somewhat more stiffly beneath his coarse jacket (donned in the morning upon departure, doffed once inside the Mill to allow shirt-sleeved freedom, and re-donned at lunch), as if to say, "My wife and oldest homeson have both done their part once again. Let all see and note this." Then they fell to disassembling their tripartite pails. A twist unlocked the first section from the second. Removal of the top lid, which was balanced carefully on the knee throughout the meal, always revealed inside this first container an enormous slab of dense waterwheat bread smeared with orange butter, nearly a quarter of a loaf. The container below this held the main course: a hot, fragrant stew of rocklamb and capers, say, or two groatgoat chops, or some kind of meatloaf redolent of greennut shavings. The final sealed container held dessert. Berry cobbler, stuntapple pie, spicebark cookies.

The sounds of restrained but hearty eating filled the summer air. The men were as yet too intent on sating their Mill-born hunger to engage in conversation.

Charley shuffled from foot to foot, awaiting the arrival of his father, who worked in roving, some distance away. He examined the lone pail he now carried while he waited. His father's initials —RC—were awkwardly engraved on cover and bottom. The alphabetic furrows in the tin held ineradicable dirt from a thousand handlings, which, scrub as she would with boar-bristle brush, his mother could never totally remove.

Suddenly, without warning, Charley experienced a revelation. Tomorrow, he would not be carrying this pail. That task would fall to his little brother, Alan, whose small hands would have to manage two lunches. He—Charley—would have his own lunchpail. Already it must have been bought at the Company Store, and even this minute was probably sitting on a shelf in the kitchen. Tonight he would have to scratch his initials on it. CC. Tomorrow he would be sitting here with his father, probably famished and more tired than he had ever been before. No more eating at home with his mother and Alan and Floy. . . .

CC. See, see. See, see what would come.

It was all too strange for Charley to really fathom. How could he travel from his temporary yet eternal enshrinement atop the brick heap to the interior depths of the Mill in less than a day? It seemed impossible. . . .

Charley lifted his gaze once more to the door. His father was coming through.

For one brief moment, as the man became visible just within the tenebrous interior of the Mill and yet had not fully emerged, he was dusted with light. All over his bare skin and clothing danced tiny motes and atomies of radiance. He looked dipped in some marvelous powder that did not reflect light, but created it, engendered it of its own miraculous being and nature. Charley's father wore, for the briefest second, a chatoyant suit of fireflies. It was, of course, only a coating of the airborne fibrous lux particles that were everywhere within the Mill. And as soon as the man came completely into the sun-drenched outside air his suit of lights disappeared, leaving him clothed like the others, in drab utilitarian fustian weave.

Charley ran to his father and handed over his pail and beer crock. The man nodded wordlessly, tousled Charley's brown hair, and moved to an empty spot on a bench. He dropped wearily down, as if his bones were lead. The inner containers soon ranged along his leg as on a serving board, Roger Cairncross dug out a spoon from his pocket, polished it on his sleeve (thereby probably depositing as many particles on it as he removed) and began to eat, shoveling stew beneath his droopy mustache like a man filling a ditch.

Normally Charley would have rejoined his peers in their roughhousing as they waited for the empty pails, which they had to bring home. But today, he wasn't quite sure who his peers were. So he hung quietly by his father's elbow while the man and his comrades ate, not venturing to speak.

His father seemed not to mind. At least he did not gruffly order Charley to move off. Perhaps he too recognized the in-between nature of the day and of Charley's state of mind. At last, with a final swipe of his bread through the remnant gravy, the elder Cairncross was done. He packed up the assemblage of containers neatly and handed them back to Charley. He brought a pipe out from within his jacket, filled it with smokeweed and began to puff. His fellows were doing likewise, down almost to the youngest. Charley coughed as the acrid smoke reached his nostrils. He vowed then and there never to acquire so inexplicably vile a habit.

The lofty clock-hands stood at half-past the hour. The first man to speak addressed not his fellows so much as the air in front of him.

"I hear that the new mill is nigh finished."

It was a kind of unmistakable intonation that differentiated "mill" from "Mill." The latter word, of course, referred to the whole vast multiunit complex that stretched from the northern end of the Valley more than three-quarters of the way to the south, a distance of nearly five miles. Big-em "Mill" meant more than the building and its contents and products, too. It stood for some numinous ideal, a community that included everyone in the Valley, something larger than any individual, and deserving of the ultimate loyalty. Something that stretched ultimately to the stars.

With a more familiar and less respectful tone, "mill" meant literally the individual production units that made up the Mill. Each small-em "mill" was a collection of men and machines capable of taking the raw lux fibers and producing finished cloth. These mills commanded a more earthly loyalty, a certain fierce pride in the ability of one's mill to outproduce all the others in quantity and quality, and to field a ball team that would win the annual championship. Each mill was approximately twenty years older than the contiguous one immediately to the south of it.

Charley's mill was not the oldest, nor the youngest, being situated somewhat toward the middle of the whole complex. The youngest mill was still under construction. The oldest was a desolate mass of charred timbers overgrown with bramblevines and fronded at their bases with waterplants through which the Swolebourne rushed at the start of its channeled and tamed subterranean passage beneath the Mill. This progenitor mill had caught fire and burned down in a time beyond Charley's conceptions, when there had been only three mills. Now there were fifteen. "Many mills make the Mill" was a saying often trotted out when one wished to indicate that there was strength in numbers, or diversity beneath a common facade.

"Aye, that's what I hear also," said another man. "And we all knows what that means. A new flood of clodders in from the farms, looking for an easy life. Probably some hellacious towners who've gotten one too many gal in trouble and been drummed out. A trapper or three who's getting too old to walk his lines anymore. Well, they'll soon learn. They all settle down to Mill life after a while. I reckon we was all clodders back somewhen."

The men all nodded agreeably at the old wisdom. They knew that after a decade or two the workers at the new mill would be indistinguishable, save for perhaps a slight accent, from those who had lived in the Valley all their lives.

"They'll not be any challenge in the games at first," said a man with a missing arm. "Especially not to the Blue Devils." Everyone smiled at the mention of their own team, as they pictured the frenetic sweaty pleasure of summer twilight games, kicking and passing the scarred lucky leather ball until the moon and stars themselves were inveigled out to watch. It seemed then that the remainder of the talk would center on the upcoming season's games. But Charley's father—who had been frowning and staring down into the oily dirt since the first mention of the new mill—diverted the talk with a blustery outburst.

"And why do we even need a new mill, I ask you?"

All the men turned their eyes on Cairncross. Charley felt nervous, worried and defiant for his father's sake, all three emotions jumbled up together.

"Ain't life hard enough," Cairncross continued, "trying to produce the best goods we can, so's that the Factor will give us a rich weight of gold that will guarantee a fair share for every worker, enough to tide us through the year between his Lord High Muckamuck's visits?"

Cairncross stopped for breath, glaring intently at the others, who appeared not a little frightened at this mild derogation of the Factor. "Now we've got a new set of competitors, more mouths to divide the Factor's beneficence among. Unless the Factor ups the yardage he's willing to purchase, we'll all owe the Company Store our very breaths by the time the new mill is geared up to full production."

An older man spoke up. "The Factor must know what he's doing, Roger." (Here the elder Cairncross mumbled something that only Charley seemed to hear: "He's only human.") "He told us nigh twenty years ago to start building the new mill. He must understand his market, wherever he sells the luxcloth, out there among the stars. Could be he's expecting a big surge of new customers, and needs the new production. You're too young, but I remember when the last mill started up, almost forty years ago. People were saying the same thing back then. And look, we still earn a good living."

Cairncross spat. "Aye, a good living, if you call it fair that the sweat of a man and his sons goes for naught but to survive until he dies—and dies too young most times at that—with not an hour or an ounce of energy left for anything but a game of ball. Think what the Factor could do for us and our world if he wished—"

Now the men laughed. Charley winced for his father's sake.

"Sure," said one, "he could make us all deathless like hisself and we'd all fly through the air all day and live on moonbeams and calculate how many angels fly 'tween here and the stars. Away with your stuff, Roger! It's enough for any man to make the cloth and raise his bairns and tussle on the game fields. That's life for our kind, not some airy-fairy dream."

It seemed that Cairncross wanted to say more, but, feeling the massed attitudes of his fellows ranked against him, he only stood, pivoted and stalked off back into the mill. The subsequent banter about ballplaying was muted and desultory, under the pall raised by Cairncross's wild talk, and the men soon shuffled back into the mill, a few unprecedented minutes before the tolling of the bell that signalled the end of their break.

The boys stood amid the benches for a time after the men had gone, idly picking at the weather-splintered bleached wood of the seats or kicking greasy clods of soil. Their mood seemed touched by the dispute that had arisen among the men. A few boys looked curiously but not accusingly at Charley, as if he somehow could explain or account for his father's untenable position.

Charley could do no such thing. He was too confused by his father's arguments to explicate them. He had never seen his father act precisely like this before, or spout such unconventional ideas—although there had been times, of course, when his father was quietly sullen or explosively touchy; whose father wasn't?—and he wondered if his own near-future entry into the Mill had anything to do with his father's novel mood. Charley returned the boys' glances boldly (some of his exaltation at conquering the brick heap still lingered like a nimbus around and inside him) and soon they looked away. A few seconds later, their natural exuberance had returned and they raced off back across the flowery strip, toward home and an afternoon's boisterous roistering.

Charley did not follow. He still felt too confused to abide by his regular schedule of mindless afternoon gameplaying. He had to go off somewhere by himself, to think about things. Swinging his father's empty pail and jug by their handles of tin and twine, keeping to the strip of waste-sown ground, Charley headed north, the serpentine bulk of the Mill on his left, the massed and brooding houses on his right. When he passed the northernmost house belonging to his own village, with the southernmost houses of the neighboring village still some distance off, he turned east, away from the Mill, across the trackless meadows. The hay-scented, sun-hot layer of air above the chest-high grass was filled with darting midges, the way he imagined the lux-thick air in the Mill to be filled with lux. Charley batted them aside when they swarmed annoyingly about his face.

The land began to slope up: houses fell away, behind, below, to south and north. Slender sapodilla saplings, advance scouts for the forest ahead and uphill, made their appearance in random clumps. Jacarandas and loblollies began to appear. As tree-cast, hard-edged shade blots started to overlap, the grass grew shorter and sparser. The final flowers to remain were the delicate yet hardy lacewings. Eventually, under the full-grown trees, the composition of the floor changed to leafduff and gnarly roots, evergreen needles and pink-spotted mushrooms. Small rills purled downhill at intervals, chuckling in simple-minded complacency, bringing their singly insignificant but jointly meaningful contributions to the Swolebourne.

"It takes many mills to make the Mill. . . ."

Charley labored up the eastern slope of the Valley, not looking back. The air was cooler under the tall trees, insects less prevalent. Only the isolated thumb-thick bark beetle winged like a noisy sling-shot stone from tree to tree.

In the arboreal somnolence, so reminiscent of Layday services, with the buzzing of the beetles standing in for the droning of Pastor Purbeck, Charley tried to sift through the events of the morning, from his triumph on the brick pile to the confusing conversation among the men. There seemed to be no pattern to the events, no scheme into which he could fit both his joy and his bafflement. So he gave up and tried just to enjoy the hike. At last he came out upon the ridge that marked the border of the Valley, the terminator between familiar and foreign.

Here, high up, there were bald patches among the trees, places where the rocky vertebrae of the hill poked through its skin of topsoil. Walking south along the ridge, Charley came out of the trees into such a spot. Sun-baked stone made the air waver with heat ripples. It felt good after the relative coolness under the trees, like snuggling under the blankets warmed by heated bricks on a midwinter's night.

Setting his father's lunchpail down on the grass, Charley climbed upon a big knobby irregular boulder, got his feet beneath him (no one contested this perch with him), and looked around, away from his home. The crowns of the nearest trees were far enough downslope to afford a spectacular vista.

Beyond the Valley, unknown lands stretched green and far to the east, ending in a misty horizon. Sun shouted off a meandering river. Charley suspected it was the Swolebourne on its post-Valley trek, but was not sure. There was no immediate sign of man to be seen, but Charley knew that somewhere a day or so away there were towns and villages and cities and farms, where shoes and meat and the harvested lux came from, in tall-wheeled, barrel-loaded wagons drawn by drowsy wainwalkers, their horns spanning wider than a man's reach. Those places were too unreal to hold Charley's interest. He was Valley born. Back toward the rift that held his world he turned.

He could see the entire length of the Valley from this vantage. It was an impressive spectacle. In the north, the Swolebourne tumbled in high frothy falls from over the lip that closed that end of the Valley. There was a legend that claimed that a whole tribe of aborigines had hurled themselves from this precipice to their mass suicide, rather than submit to the presence of the first human colonists. The mournful chortling which at times could be discerned under the falls' roar was said to be their ghostly lament, and did indeed resemble the noises which the fur-faced natives made, according to those trappers who had actually penetrated to the current-day haunts of the abos.

From its creamy violent pool the river rushed down its man-modified channel, its energy for some small distance untapped by the machinery of the Mill.

Soon enough the water ran among the blackened beams and crumbled fragments of walls that could barely be discerned at this distance and which betokened the original mill that had long ago gone to its destruction as the result of some careless use of fire, a danger each child was warned against daily. The brawling river vanished next beneath the first still-functioning mill, through masonry arches. A gentle susurrus from river and Mill machinery filled the Valley.

Funny, thought Charley, how you only noticed some things when they were remote. . . . Charley's eyes followed in one quick swoop the variegated length of the Mill, each of its sections distinguishable by the subtle and unique coloration of its bricks: generational shades of rose, tawny, pumpkin, autumnal leaf. He let his eyes bounce back from the southern end, where the Swolebourne emerged, a pitiful tamed remnant of its upstream proud valorous self, and where the minute figures of hired out-Valley laborers could be seen finishing the upper courses of the new mill.

Starting with the oldest section, Charley recited aloud all the familiar and comforting names of the Mill.

"Silent Sea Warriors, Swift Sparrows, Deeproot Willows, Wild

Wainwalkers, South Polar Savages, Red Stalkers, Factor's Favorites, Longarmed Bruisers, Blue Devils, Lux Jackets, Eighteyed Scorpions, Landfish, Ringtails, Greencats, Blackwater Geysers."

This litany of mill names was vastly reassuring, a bastion of every child's daily talk and boasting, source of endless speculation and comparison, during winter idleness and summer game-fever.

Suddenly Charley wondered what the new, sixteenth mill would call their team. How strange it would be to have a new name associated with the other time-hallowed ones. Would such a thing ever happen again in his lifetime, or was this the last mill that would ever be built? It was all up to the Factor, of course, and his motives were beyond fathoming.

Charley's attention turned to the houses that paralleled the Mill on both its eastern and western sides. A village consisted of the families on both sides of the individual mills. Each section had its mirror-image dwelling places bunched together opposite each other, with the Mill itself intervening. There was a single corridor that ran straight through the width of each mill permitting access over the river and between halves of a village. This corridor had no doors into the mill proper; that privilege of entry was denied both women and underage children.

Gaps—playing fields fringed by wildness—separated each mill's housing from the rest on the same side, contributing to the team feeling and individual minor differences that marked each small subcommunity.

Charley tried to imagine what life would be like in another community. He felt an uncommon sorrow for girls who had to move out of the villages of their birth if they married a man from another section. Would such a thing happen to his sister Floy? He hoped not, for he would miss her.

Thoughts of Floy made him want to see her, and so he clambered down off his rock, retrieved the lunchpail, and began his descent to the Valley floor. He guessed he felt better for his walk. He chose to disregard his father's bitter talk about the Mill. The Mill was the only life Charley desired. He wanted to enter more deeply and completely into its ritual-filled activities and complexly articulated duties, not to examine or criticize them. He would not let tomorrow— the day that marked his first steps into such a life—be spoiled.

Back down in the Valley, Charley rushed home. He burst into his house, swinging his father's lunchpail just like he had seen the men swing their lanterns as they walked in front of the wagons at

night that carried people back from far-off games down one end
of the Valley or another. He found his mother, Alan, and Floy all
in the same room. Alan was playing with a set of wooden blocks
while Floy, sitting in a chair, was having her hair braided by her
mother. Floy was inordinately proud of having the same honey-
colored tresses as her mother, and wore her traditional plaits
proudly. Such elaborate, time-consuming hairstyles were a mark
of status in the village, showing that mothers could afford to spare
time from housekeeping and cooking and washing, and there were
few women who would deny their rare daughters such attention.

"Where have you been?" asked Charley's mother first thing.
Her voice, while somewhat stern, was also shot through with a
kind of maternal concern the likes of which Charley had never
quite heard before. Was this change, too, connected with his upcoming transformation?

"Oh, for a walk," Charley said. "I didn't feel like being with the
other boys today."

Charley's mother said nothing, but continued to weave her
fingers among Floy's rich hair. Charley grabbed a waterwheat
biscuit, sat and munched and watched until the task was done.

"All right, Florence," said her mother. "You may go out now
if you wish. But be back in before the bell tolls three, since I need
you to baste the roast."

Floy stood, her head with its coiled grandeur held high, and
Charley grabbed her hand. Alan got to his feet and tried to follow
them, but before Charley could deny him, their mother caught up
the younger boy, saying, "And you come with me, mister, for
there're peas to be shelled."

Charley and Floy left the house, heedless of Alan's shrill pro-
tests.

Outside they meandered down the narrow, close-graveled
streets. Odors of cooking drifted from each open window, along
with household noises: the clatter of pewterware, the clink of
glasses.

Holding his sister's hand as he always did on their walks, Charley
felt an unlooked-for estrangement in place of the comfort he had
expected. Floy looked somehow older and different to him today,
inexplicably more mature than her fifteen years. Her starched
white ruffled shirtfront seemed more like his mother's bosom than
the flat expanse of linen he remembered from yesterday. Could so
much have changed in a single day, or was it just his senses playing
tricks? The changes left Charley feeling tongue-tied. Finally, he
ventured an observation on the matter closest to his heart.

"Tomorrow I enter the Mill, Floy."

"I know," said Floy rather blandly. She seemed distant from Charley today, more intent on casting her gaze about as if for witnesses to her coiffed glory.

Charley was discomfited. "Well, will you miss me?"

Floy favored her brother with a look of impatience. "I'll still be seeing you each night, won't I? You'll hardly be getting married yet, I think."

Charley felt frustrated. "No, of course I shan't. You know I don't mean any such thing. But I will be gone all day with Da, and we won't be able to talk and play for hours as we used to, nor take our lessons together. Will you still think of me, when I'm in the Mill? What will you do all day with yourself? That baby Alan can't take my place, can he?"

"No," said Floy in a somewhat absent-minded manner, as her attention was distracted by the sight of showoff Hal Blackburn chinning himself on the branch of a pear tree. Blackburn was inordinately large for his age, and his biceps bulged as he pumped himself up and down. Charley found his leering expression distasteful.

"I don't know quite what I'll do," continued Floy. She released her brother's hand and primped at her hair. Blackburn switched to a one-handed grip and began to hoot and scratch at himself like a purple vervet. Floy turned away from him in a huff. "I suppose I'll find something, though."

This was not the protestation of undying grief that Charley had been longing for and, in truth, half expecting to hear from Floy (he had even, he admitted, pictured tears), but he supposed it would have to do, and he sought to find some solace in it.

They promenaded among the houses in silence for the rest of their final afternoon together, each preoccupied with his or her own thoughts. When it was time for Floy to help with supper, Charley went and sat on their stoop, awaiting his father. The man returned at last after six. He had been gone since seven that morning. He looked utterly vanquished, and barely noticed Charley as he brushed past him.

After supper, his father sat on the wainwalkerhide chair (still owed for at the Company Store) that was reserved for him alone and silently smoked his pipe. The children played quietly, and their mother darned clothing. Buttery light from the oil lamps flowed over forms and faces, furniture and floor.

After a time, their father spoke. "That blasted Otterness was on my back all day. Claimed I wrongfully mixed two incompatible

luminances on my machine. Ever since he made Master Luminary he's been unbearable. At forty he's the youngest ever, and if
you imagine he'll once let you forget it, then you'd believe the Lux
Jackets could take the championship."

Charley's mother said nothing, realizing that attentive silent
agreement was all that her husband wanted at the moment. The
man smoked in silence for a full two minutes before speaking
again.

"I tried telling them today what I believed, Eliza, and they did
naught but laugh."

Charley's mother put down her work. "You know no one likes
to hear bad things said about the Factor, Rog. I don't know why
you even bother."

Charley's father slapped the arm of his chair. "Damn it, it's not
even as if I'm proposing anything other than that the Factor leave
us alone. If he won't share the knowledge of his starways with us,
at least he should take his superior self away, and let us try to find
our own path again. As it stands now, he's like a dam across the
stream of our progress. There's been naught new done since the
Factor came all those centuries ago. Things were different then,
and could be once more. We were picking ourselves up from the
Dark Times, learning what we could do again. Then came the
Factor, and knocked the spirit right out of us. Since then we've
stagnated. It's not healthy, I say. No more than if the Swolebourne
were motionless and covered with pond scum."

Shaking her head, Charley's mother said only, "I don't know,
Rog. I can't say. Life seems good."

Charley's father puffed furiously on his pipe, but said no more.

As Charley lay in bed that night he puzzled over his father's
words, but could make no sense of them before he fell deeply
asleep. That night he had no dreams, not of his triumph atop the
brick heap, nor of the day to come.

And in the morning he got up and had a breakfast of porridge
with his father and he saw *his* lunchpail sitting beside his father's
on the shelf and he realized he had forgotten to cut his initials into
it and would have to do so later and he set out into the dewy
morning beside his Da down a familiar path that looked utterly
strange and soon he was across the oily waste and among the clot
of men and boys, some mingling and joking and some silent, and
intricate odors were wafting out of the open Mill doors at him and
the line of men was moving forward and beyond the doors his
light-adjusted eyes could not penetrate the darkness and as each

man or boy entered—save Charley alone—his clothing sparked with lux and before Charley knew it he had stepped over the threshold inside.

2.

The pale gray leaves of the dusty-miller tree diffused a scent like minty talcum. The branches of the dusty were long and slender, withes useful in basketry, and arced and drooped to form a secret bower around the bole. From some distance off, fatwood torches spiked into the turf on the sidelines of the playing field cast their wavering illumination over the ghostly foliage, sending shadows skittering over the tapestry of leaves without penetrating the deeper darkness of the arboreal shelter. The shouts of the spectators clustered around the sides of the game field rose and fell in linkage with the action of the players, the one an enthusiastic reciprocal of the other. Panting and grunting accompanied the fervent play, intermixed with the solid thump of shoe leather making contact with a scarred leather ball. The game was in its final quarter, and the Blue Devils were battling to maintain their one-point lead over the Landfish.

Inside the canopy of leaves Florence Cairncross leaned in a swoon against the rough trunk of the dusty. The familiar odor of its leaves filled her head with a piquant strangeness. Everything was so much altered. . . . The excited voices of her friends and neighbors and family sounded like the inhuman cries of birds or animals. The light of the torches seemed to issue from watery depths, as if drowned beneath the Swolebourne. An exclamation from one of the players reached through the tangle of leaves. "Pass it, pass it!" Was that her brother, Charley, calling? Perhaps . . . It was so hard to tell; his voice had changed over the last year, maturing into a novel male roughness. And under present circumstances. . . .

Florence felt a tugging at the laces of her camisole. Her starched outer shirtfront already gaped apart, one bone button missing, lost amidst the dead leaves of past seasons which bestrewed the ground at her feet. The fingers at her laces suddenly found the simple knot that secured the top of her undergarment, found its trailing end, pulled and undid it. Those same fingers poked through the crisscrossed laces halfway down her midriff and tugged. The lace-ends slid through the double-stitched eyelets as easily as water through a sieve.

She could see nothing in the tenebrous enclosure, but closed her eyes anyway.

Those fingers. . . . How was it possible for a grown man to have such skin, unscarred by machinery, untainted by the stink of lux and oil? Despite his maturity, they were still so smooth and uncallused, almost as smooth as a girl's. That had been one of the first things she had noticed about Samuel. . . .

The game that Layday had been scheduled for noon, to allow time for morning services. A night game during the workweek would have involved too much travel for the Blue Devils, who had promised to give their fledgling opponents the advantage of their home field. Although the actinic sun was high, the game had not yet begun, for heavy rains the previous day had washed away the chalk lines of the playing field, and the men were still busy demarcating the borders of their eventual struggle. Under a spreading horsetail tree there was the usual broad trestle table set up with food and drink. Big stone jugs of pear-apple cider, both hard and soft; pies and loaves; cheeses and hams. People crowded around the refreshments, chattering. A bit more than half the faces were familiar. The new village was still underpopulated, all its houses and outbuildings still raw-looking, and the visitors, although representing only a portion of Florence's community, actually outnumbered their hosts. This was the first engagement between the Devils and the Tarcats, as the newest mill had denominated their team, the first time the two villages—one long-established, the other barely settled—had had a chance to mingle.

Beyond the village the Valley mouth opened out onto misty blue-green horizons, the hills on either side sloping away into the flat plains like tendons disappearing into the torso of the earth. It was the closest Florence had ever been to the Valley's embouchure, and its nearness made her giddy.

Talking with her best friend, Mabel Tench, one of the few village girls her own age, Florence reached for the handle of a cider jug at the same time the stranger did. His soft palm fell atop hers, engulfing it in a strong yet velvet grip. Florence felt the blood rush to her cheeks.

She turned her face to the stranger, who had yet to release her hand. His eyes were as blue as gillyflowers, his smooth jaw as strong as the rocks from which the Swolebourne tumbled. He was dressed in a ball-playing outfit: a jersey striped with his team's colors—green and gold—and leather shorts. His legs were well muscled and very hairy. Florence felt her flush deepen.

"Please excuse me, Miss," said the man, his words accented strangely. "Mere thirst is no excuse for inconveniencing such a beauty as yourself. Allow me to fill your mug for you."

Finally he released her captive hand. Hooking the big jug's handle with his forefinger, he somehow swung it neatly up into the crook of his arm without spilling a drop. Relieving Florence of her mug, he poured a golden stream of tart juice into it, then handed it back. At that moment one of the man's teammates called him. "Snooker, the game's about to start!"

The man set the jug down, made a little mock bow, then trotted off to join his team on the field.

Florence winced a little at the name. Could such an elegant fellow really answer to "Snooker?" She felt a twinge of proprietary anger, then caught herself. What connection existed between them that could give her the right to even worry about such things? Quite obviously, nothing. Nor would there ever be. Most likely. . . .

Through innocent questioning Florence discovered that the stranger was named Samuel Spurwink. Along with several other villagers he had relocated from distant, cosmopolitan Tarrytown. She found one of his townsmen standing on the sidelines, a short older man with a brown beard thick as thatch.

"That fellow who just scored a moment ago. He plays quite well."

"Snooker Spurwink? Aye, I suppose so. If you fancy a style where you dart about like a drunken hummingbird, stopping to ogle every petticoat on the marge. Oh, he's a sly one, that Spurwink. More used to indoor sports, if you take my meaning. Bending an elbow, letting fly a dart."

Florence felt irked at the man's denigration of Spurwink. "If he's such an idle tosspot, then what made him come to the Valley? Although our work is noble and much esteemed, as bringing honor from the Factor to our humble world, we don't have an easy life here, turning raw lux to fine cloth. I can't see a figure such as you paint voluntarily abandoning all the pleasures of town for our strictured Mill life."

"Well, you see, young Sammy had quite a surfeit of working in his Da's butcher shop. Blood-covered aprons clashed with his finery, it seems. And then there was talk about Sammy and the Mayor's wife— Say, young lady, just how old *are* you?"

Florence huffed. "Old enough to know not to listen to idle gossip." She moved off, leaving the man chuckling to himself.

During the game Florence found herself cheering the Tarcats—and especially Spurwink. Her parents and fellow villagers smiled indulgently at her. "Such a good girl, to make these new-comers feel welcome to the Valley, even with her own brother out there playing his heart out."

The Tarcats lost to the Blue Devils, ten to one.

But Spurwink that day won something invisible.

His lips were on her neck now, and she swivelled her head to expose more of that graceful expanse to his nuzzling. Her labori-ously fashioned plaits, pinned atop her head with blue-bone clips, rubbed against the tree and came loose, falling to frame her face. Then his hand was inside her undone camisole, molding itself to her breast, cupping the fruit of her flesh as he had cupped her hand only a short month ago. He smelled of spicy cologne. Florence had never known a man to wear scent before. His sig-nature smell mingled with the perfume of the dusty-miller leaves in a heady blend.

His kisses stopped at the base of her throat. "Oh, Sam, lower—" He complied, while the crowd roared a million miles away.

The second time they met had been at a night game between the Devils and the Red Stalkers, the latter a team upstream of the Devils. Spurwink had materialized at her side as she stood apart from and on the outer edge of the spectators. From behind he had covered her eyes and whispered, "Hello, Miss Pretty Puss. Can you guess who this is?"

She was both surprised and unsurprised to have him there. On one level she had had no thoughts of him, her thoughts drifting among the minutiae of her daily life. On another, deeper level, she had somehow known he would come. In that first moment her surprise and consternation weighed slightly heavier in the balance of her emotions, and she hesitated before speaking.

"Come now, don't you have a pleasant word for a man who's labored like a dog all day, then walked an hour to be by your side?"

"I—I'm flattered."

Spurwink uncovered her eyes and twirled her around to face him. No one was looking, collective attention massed on the game. "Then show it," he said, and kissed her on the lips.

Florence pushed Spurwink back, both hands on his hard chest. When he was at arm's length, however, she did not remove her palms from his shirt.

"You play rather fast and familiar, sir."

"Have you never heard that fortune favors the bold?"

"In some endeavors, perhaps, but not all."

"It remains my universal motto nonetheless."

"An intriguing steadfastness. Would you care to explain more?"

"By all means. But let's meander to quieter pastures."

"If you wish."

They walked away from the crowd and the torchlight, the trodden night-damp grass exuding its living breath. Spurwink attempted to press his hip to Florence's, but she skipped away. He sighed melodramatically. She ignored him. He began to talk.

Spurwink's exotic speech, his foreign tones, his barely concealed insinuations, all combined to fill Florence's head with dreamy visions, colored in all the brilliant shades of the rainbow missing from the drab black and brick-red environment of the Mill. His words seemed to pass directly from his lips into her imagination, with barely a stop to be interpreted by her conscious mind. Her familiar surroundings disappeared, to be replaced by peacock images of sprightly dances, airy pavilions, candle-lit canopied bedchambers. . . .

Florence had come to a stop by a stand of jojoba shrubs. Spurwink advanced, backing her up into their prickly embrace. He clasped her face in his hands and kissed her again. Florence did not resist.

"Floy! Floy! Game's over! Time to head home!"

It was her foolish little brother Charley calling, shattering the spell she had been in. Florence pushed Spurwink back, rearranging her skirts where the shrubs had rucked them up.

"Factor's ballocks! This damn Mill schedule makes sleepy larks of us all, willy-nilly! If we were back in Tarrytown, we'd watch the sun come up and glint off the wine bottles we'd emptied. But here, you have to be abed by nine just to rest up for the next day's drudgery." Spurwink's tone became tinged with self-pity. "And I've got an hour's walk ahead of me yet."

Hastening toward her parents, Florence called back, "Next week we play the Landfish. They're only three mills up from you."

Spurwink fell back into his gallantry. "If it were three hundred damn mills, I'd still come for you."

The desire in the man's voice made her stumble on nothing. She reached her parents still flustered, but they were too elated with the Blue Devils' victory over the Stalkers to take much notice. Charley, however, recognized enough amiss to ask her if she was feeling well.

Florence felt an immense condescending superiority toward her brother. She tousled his sweaty hair and said, "I'm fine, Charley. It's nothing you'd understand anyway."

Charley regarded her quizzically. For one brief moment his eyes widened, and she was convinced he knew. Then he turned away wordlessly and mounted into the bed of the wagon for the journey home. Ridiculous, she thought, to imagine such a thing. . . .

And the third time she and Spurwink had met—that time was now.

Spurwink's left hand still plumped her right breast. The soft fabric of her camisole felt stiff as burlap on that nipple, so sensitive was it. His mouth ringed the summit of her other breast. His right hand was on her belly, stroking it in circles that grew wider and wider, like the ripples cast from a stone thrown into one of the Mill's many holding ponds. She felt as if her belly were filled with hot coals, like a bedwarmer on a winter's night. Eventually Spurwink's lower hand strayed deliberately beneath the waistband of her skirts. More cunning and experienced this time in the fashions of the Valley, it quickly found the ribbon that upheld her petticoats.

Florence started, and laid a hand atop Spurwink's cloth-covered one.

"Do you really want to stop now, Pretty Puss?" he whispered, relinquishing her breast, yet with his breath still hot upon it. "Tell the truth now."

"I—I don't know."

"Well, you must realize I don't. Not with a Factor's Paradise so near for both of us."

"Then—do what you will. . . ."

He tugged the knot apart. Then, with both hands beneath her clothes, he pushed her single undergarment down, his smooth hands sliding over her rump and hips. The cloth fell from beneath her skirts to lie with the generations of dry dead dusty leaves, a presage of the autumn to come, so seemingly impossible at summer's height.

Without being told, she stepped out of her knickers.

Florence lost a moment then. The next thing she knew she lay on her back on the ground, her skirts pooled around her, Spurwink's muscled weight atop her, his mass centered below her waist. It took a moment for a strange sensation to register. Spurwink had removed his wool trousers and was now bare also.

"I think you'll like this, my poppet."

Florence faltered. "I want— I want—" What did she want? In the end she could not say, and lamely concluded, "I want to."

"And you will, you will. . . ."

When it was over Spurwink fell asleep for a minute or two on the duffy turf. Florence lay awake staring up into the branches of the dusty-miller tree. Judging by the roar of the crowd, the ball game was reaching some kind of climax. She put both hands between her legs and closed her wet thighs on them. What had she done? She could not feel sad about it, but neither did she feel ecstatic. The moment's brief rapture had vanished, elusive as morning mist on the Swolebourne, whose waters seemed to flow now from her center. . . .

Spurwink awoke with a startled grunt. "Oh my aching bones. What time is it? By the stars, girl, you were good! I'd fancy another ride if it weren't so late. But duty calls, and I must hie homeward." Climbing to his feet, Spurwink fumbled with his trousers in the darkness.

Florence remained on the ground. A coldness crept into her flesh. "When shall we meet again, Samuel?"

Spurwink replied airily. "Oh, at one game or another, I'm sure."

"That hardly seems such an enduring pledge as you were uttering earlier."

"I'm afraid it will have to do, my lass. If there's one thing I cannot abide, it's to be trussed up like one of the rocklambs in my father's abattoir. You must take me as you find me."

Florence used the tree trunk to climb somewhat painfully to her feet. Without stopping to alter one iota of her disheveled appearance she marched out of the bower and toward the game field.

"Wait, wait," Spurwink called nervously, attempting to maintain a discreet tone. "Make yourself presentable first, girl."

Florence gave no reply, but strode steadily on.

Spurwink lost all self-assurance. "Stop, you little idiot! What do you think you're doing?"

Widening the gap between them, Florence paid no heed to Spurwink's orders. He darted a few steps after her, thought better of it, then ran off in the opposite direction.

Florence marched toward the Blue Devil and Landfish villagers, who had as yet taken no notice of her. Half of her mind was all icy cold precision and a determination not to feel anything.

That was the half that showed on her face. The other part was a mix of bewilderment, pain and confusion. That was the part that huddled and mewled deep inside like a lost unweaned tarkitten.

Above her head the stars Spurwink had invoked to praise her shone with a frigid radiance. Were there truly men out there, humans who bought the luxcloth? Men like Spurwink? It seemed all too possible. Were they watching her now? Their powers were unknowable. The ten bright stars that formed the constellation Factor's Ship seemed to glare with a particular accusation.

Once she stumbled. This time, however, the cause was not excitement, but only a rodent hole hidden in the grass.

The game had ended when Florence came up to the crowd. The players were leaving the field, victors triumphant, losers consoling each other and boasting of success in the eventual rematch. The spectators had broken up into congratulatory clusters around their various relatives. Florence crossed the perimeter of torchlight and stumbled blindly into their midst, her skirts aslant across her hips, her breasts shamelessly exposed.

There was a moment of stunned silence. Then everyone was hovering about her, the men loudly blustering with outrage and moral indignation, the women all practical earnest solicitude, various children watching wide-eyed. Everyone was trying to get her to speak. Florence opened her mouth, but nothing came out. Somehow all she could focus on was the face of a little girl hanging onto her mother's skirts. Had she ever been that young herself?

Someone tossed a blanket around her shoulders, covering her nakedness. Then her parents were there. Her mother held Alan, the youngest, on her hip. She rushed up to Florence and tried to hug her. But she forgot to put Alan down, and ended up awkwardly embracing both her children. Charley was somehow beside her next. To Florence, he looked inexplicably taller than earlier in the night, as if his exertions on the field had stretched and matured him. He clutched her hand and stroked her hair. "There, Floy, there," was all he said, but somehow it was enough to start her tears flowing.

Roger Cairncross was shouting into the night, at no one and everyone. "Who knows anything about this! Speak up! Speak up, damn you!"

When he received no reply he turned to his daughter and gripped her by the shoulders. "Who did this, girl! Do you know? Are you protecting him?"

Her father's mustache was laced with spittle. His face was red as clover. Florence dropped her eyes from his. When she did this, he began to shake her back and forth with a violence that rattled her bones.

"Trollop! Tart! Is this how you were brought up? Is this what I work for from sunup to sundown? I'll have his name out of you if I have to beat it out!"

Charley was pulling his father away. The older man shrugged him violently off. Then other villagers, his coworkers, were on him, separating him from Florence.

"Can't you see she's in shock, man? She needs to get home and be cared for, not abused. Your daughter's a fine lass, she'll come round. Just give her some time."

Cairncross began to calm down. "And what of the bastard who touched her?"

"He can't leave the Valley without giving himself away. There's no out for him. Don't you see?"

Cairncross nodded in agreement. "All right then, let's get home."

In the homeward-bound wagon Florence sat shivering in a corner, wrapped in the borrowed blanket, her head in her mother's lap. Every few minutes the musty-smelling wainwalker pulling the vehicle would emit a plaintive bellow, as if to complain about being kept up so late. She recalled all the festive rides back to their familiar village, how she had sung and laughed with her friends. Would there ever be such days again? She began softly to sob. Why couldn't she speak? A slow anger began to smolder in her. Why should she have to speak? Couldn't they leave her alone until she had sorted everything out for herself? What right did they have to pester her with questions? The more she thought of this, the angrier she got. By the time they reached their village, Florence had ceased her sobbing. She now wore an expression of stony indifference.

The wagon stopped outside the Cairncross home. Their neighbor—a middle-aged bachelor who supported a widowed father who had grown too frail to work in the Mill—emerged from his half of the house to stare and cluck his tongue with a mixture of sympathy and reproof. Averting her face, Florence let herself be helped inside.

Once in the parlor, Florence spoke for the first time since she had left Spurwink. "I want to wash up, please."

"Well, by the Factor's grace, you've found your tongue," said her father somewhat sarcastically. "Maybe now we'll learn the cause of you bringing so much shame upon our family."

Florence said nothing, but merely went to her room. Her mother soon brought a white basin and a pitcher full of water heated on the wood stove, some towels and a washcloth. When she was alone, Florence used the chamber pot, then scrubbed herself free of Spurwink's detestable scent. She dressed in gown, robe, and slippers trimmed in bluefox fur around the ankles. She knew now that she would never say anything about what had happened that night, come what may.

Back in the parlor, Florence sat on the couch, the center of her family's baffled looks. Gently at first, then, as she refused to answer any of his questions, more and more roughly, her father tried to elicit what had happened from her. Florence maintained her silence throughout all her father's cajoling and threats, his attempts at logic and reason, his appeals to honor, duty and affection. Her mother's pleas also she ignored. As the night wore on, Roger Cairncross grew more and more irrational. Several times he gestured as if to strike her. At last he did, bringing his open palm across her face.

Florence took the blow without uttering a sound. A wild look of despair and self-disgust flashed across her father's face. He jumped to his feet and fled the house.

Charley had sat through this cross-examination silently, offering neither consolation nor accusation. Now he arose also and left.

Soon her father returned. With him was Pastor Purbeck.

Pastor Purbeck had lost an arm to the Mill's machinery at age twelve, some fifty years ago. That same year had seen the demise of Pastor Topseed's youthful catechumen, a boy named Hayflick who had fallen prey to a pack of dire wolves forced down from their mountain fastness by an unusually hard winter. Young Purbeck, barely recovered from his wound and the equally traumatic surgery, had been immediately compelled by his family—a disreputable group led by a drunkard father and a termagant mother— to take his devotional vows. Shortly thereafter his family left the Valley. Upon the death of Pastor Topseed some ten years later, Purbeck had become the Valley's youngest cleric.

Purbeck lived now in the one-room rectory attached to the Blue Devil chapel, a building on the far side of the Mill from the Cairncross home. He was tall and thin, and bore a good-sized wen at the hinge of his jaw. His eyes fairly radiated his devotion to the religion symbolized in the icon of the Factor hung on a chain around his neck. These features, combined with his empty right sleeve, formed a presence capable of frightening even grown men. More than one poor child, hurrying through the cresset-lit windowless tunnel through the Mill's body, rushing from one square of light to another, had had the wits startled out of him by being abruptly grabbed on the shoulder by the single hand of Pastor Purbeck and questioned on elements of his catechism.

In the homey atmosphere of the Cairncross parlor Pastor Purbeck lost none of his imposing sternness. Florence shivered upon seeing him, recalling no specific incident but only the general air the Pastor had always carried, an air of suspecting everyone of guilt and sin. Tonight, she feared, she merited his suspicions.

Purbeck took off his wide-brimmed cleric's hat. Then he sat on a footstool directly opposite Florence. He rested the hat on one bony knee. He flicked some luxdust from it with a contemplative slowness. He lifted the silver figure of the Factor on its chain to his lips and kissed it. Then he raised his gaze to Florence. She braced for a flood of accusations and threats of damnation.

Purbeck's voice was soft and flat. "Ah, young Florence, it seems only yesterday to me that you were being consecrated into the faith. Such a pretty little girl you were. But even then rather willful. I remember when you joined the choir. 'Why must I sing with all these others?' you asked. 'I prefer to sing alone.' I found it amusing at the time, and so I let you have a solo part that Layday. Do you remember the song, Florence? I do. It was 'Our Hearts Shine Like Lux in the Factor's Sight.' A lovely piece. Written over a hundred years ago by Holsapple. And your voice was equally lovely, dear. So sweet and piercing, such a contrast to all those massed tenors and basses. You were guaranteed a solo every Layday afterwards. Such beauty, I thought, could only serve to glorify the Factor."

The Pastor paused a moment, turning his hard eyes ceilingward before fixing Florence with them again. "But now I reproach myself for my vanity, as well as for yours. For what good is beauty without the soul behind it? It is like putting stucco on the Mill. Underneath would still be the brick. And when the heats of summer and the chills of winter—the trials of life, if you will—had flaked all the plaster off, the brick would once more be exposed. Yet my analogy is imperfect. In the case of the Mill, we would not be ashamed to see the noble, homely brick, the true substance of our days. But in your case, my dear, we are all of us ashamed to see what lies beneath your lovely exterior."

Now the Pastor's voice began to modulate into those tones it assumed just prior to the inevitable moment when he would bring his single fist down on the pulpit. "Your beautiful exterior, my dear, is cracking. You have let it be mishandled and mauled, and now your soul is starting to show through. And what a sorry sight it is! Its lineaments are those of greed, selfishness, impetuosity, and stubbornness. You have revealed yourself to lack a sense of gratitude to your parents, of duty to your village, of devotion to the Factor. You have revealed yourself to be a thoughtless, reckless, immature little girl. And to compound your errors, you refuse now even to make amends for your sin by disclosing the name of your partner."

Leaning forward, Purbeck took hold of one of Florence's hands. She tried not to flinch, but failed to repress a slight movement. The Pastor did not comment on this, but instead launched onto a different tack.

"Do you think, my dear, that your partner will turn himself in and save you performing what you wrongly regard as a betrayal? If so, you must disabuse yourself of such a notion immediately. Although it pains me to say it, there are few men in this Valley who would move a little finger to save a woman's virtue. But that is the sad fact of a male's composition. That is why a man is bound by natural law to support his family—if he is lucky enough to have one—by the sweat of his brow all his days. That is why the Factor made a disproportionate number of men. They are expendable and imperfect.

"But a woman, dear Florence, a woman is different. They are so few and so rare, that their natures cannot help but be more refined and heavenly. It is woman who perpetuates our race on this sad world. When a girlchild is born—so rarely, only one to every two boys—we rejoice. All her youth she is cosseted and petted, perhaps made too much of. But we cannot help it, for we see in her a visible sign of the Factor's grace, proof that although he has made life hard, he has not made it impossible. It is woman who must act as the conscience of our race, the moral light. So you see, all the burden of resolving this affair must devolve to you."

Florence's mother was crying; her father was tugging thoughtfully at one end of his mustache and nodding, as if to acknowledge his own male unworthiness. Pastor Purbeck gave her hand an extra squeeze and eyed her hopefully. Florence looked at all of them in disbelief. Then she yanked her hand away and shot to her feet.

"I won't have it! I won't be part of it, do you hear! Special! Holy! Duty and honor! That's all I've heard all my life! Why, I'd rather work in the Mill thirty hours a day than spend one minute as the kind of creature you paint. But you won't have a woman in there. 'Too dangerous, too coarse,' you say. 'Stay home and have babies, lots and lots of babies!' For what? So that they can live out their tiny constricted lives in this narrow Valley, bowing and scraping before the Factor? Why should I raise more little slaves for him? Ask my father's opinion of the Factor, if you want to hear something that makes sense. No, I'll go to my grave unwed, I swear it!"

Pastor Purbeck dropped to his knees, crushing his hat in the process. "This is close to blasphemy, girl. Much worse than mere fornication. I am going to pray for your soul now. Let those who would, join me."

Florence's mother got down on the floor, then Roger Cairncross too, more reluctantly. They were bowing their heads when Charley came in.

"Get up," he said. "Get up, all of you. There's no need of that. I've known all along who the man was, and now that I've had time to think, I've decided to tell."

Florence yelled, "Don't listen to him, he's lying! There's no way he could know."

Charley regarded his sister somberly. "It was his scent, Floy. I smelled it on the playing field when I tackled him, and on you tonight. It's that new clodder, Spurwink, Da. From the Tarcats."

Roger Cairncross leapt up. "The Devils and I will fetch him. Keep our girl here."

Florence threw herself on Charley, knocking him down. She rained blows on his head and shoulders, shrieking, "I hate you, I hate you, I hate you! You awful, hateful prig! You and your stinking Mill can burn!"

Charley made no motion to protect himself. Eventually Florence's rage subsided, and she crawled back to the couch. Charley raised himself off the floor. Tears washed tracks through the blood from his nose.

Spurwink was not much more bloody than Charley when they marched him into the house. One eye was swelling, and he favored one leg. Florence had feared worse. His demeanor was subdued, but still somewhat insouciant.

"Since they tell me we are to be wed soon, I might as well salve my pride and ask if you'll have me. Well, poppet, what shall it be?

Pretend you have a choice and answer me now. Will you be my wife?"

Florence was exhausted. She had no reserves left. "I am yours," she said wearily. Spurwink grinned, thinking it was him she had addressed.

But Pastor Purbeck knew it was himself. Or rather, the Valley, the Mill, the Factor.

3.

The bulky man chafed his hands in an abstracted way. For several minutes he merely sat, rubbing those large hands together, squeezing first one then the other. At the end of this period he abruptly ceased all motion, his hands freezing into position. His conscious mind had caught his limbs again at their independent life. An expression of distaste flickered across his features. He jerked his hands and they flew apart as if they were similar poles of a lodestone. He placed them carefully down on the desk in front of him, palms flat on the felt blotter.

What made his hands betray him? Was it anxiety? Most likely. He had so much on his mind. His mill, the Factor's upcoming visit, Alan's strange behavior of late. . . . Yet why look for such deep-seated motivations? Perhaps it was only the chill. An unconscious seeking of warmth? His breath did not fog, but felt as if it should. And well it might, were the potbellied stove in the corner, sitting four-pawed on its raised hearth of green-enamelled tiles, to slacken its output any further. Yes, that was probably it. Just a basic animal instinct, nothing complicated about it. . . .

The man leaned back in his chair and regarded his traitorous hands. They were big-knuckled and hairy. The wiry hair disappeared at his wrists beneath the cuffs of his jacket. The hair was still black on his hands, but the short-cut stubble carpeting the enigmatic lumpy contours of his skull was mostly gray. His eyes were dark, his nose showed signs of having been broken more than once, as did so many ballplayers' noses — although those days were long behind him — and his jaw was blunt and perpetually outthrust.

Old. He was getting too old for this job. How many more years could he cling to this position? Just as long as he earned a good share of the Factor's largess for his mill. But how long would that be? Long enough to train his protégé and insure his accession, he hoped. Factor grant him that much, he prayed.

The room, the man suddenly realized, felt chillier than just a minute ago. Looking up from the plain scratched woodgrained surface of his desk beyond the blotter—upon which were scattered pasteboard rectangles punched with holes and scribbled with figures, through which were threaded hanks of shining luminous threads of various subtle hues and intensities—he spotted the stovetender asleep, something he had not registered with his earlier glance.

The boy wore a red coat with brass buttons that he put on each morning from his wooden locker among the others just inside the Mill doors. This was the badge of the stoveboys, those who formed, along with the stockboys, the lowest rank of Mill workers. The boy sat on a short three-legged stool beside the sooty coal stove that was rapidly cooling. His chin hung on his chest, his eyes were closed, and his breath buzzed in and out as if he were acting the part of a diligent bellows.

The man regarded the boy with a mix of good-humored solicitous pity and mild aggravation. He knew how hard it was for these youths—coming into the Mill at age twelve, having known mostly freedom and few responsibilities—to be burdened with one of the most important tasks in the Mill, that of guarding and ministering to and always watching the contained fires that heated the Mill during the winter, and which must never be allowed to escape. Also, it was no easy physical task, constantly hauling scuttles of coal up the long flights of stairs.

On the other hand, these boys were now workers. They were getting paid, drawing a share of credit from the commonly held gold which derived from the Factor's purchase of their cloth each year. These boys had to learn proper work habits early on, if they were ever to be relied upon to intelligently manage the various machines that all contributed toward producing the luxcloth.

And the luxcloth—that unbelievably splendid and gorgeously unique product of this humble uncharted world drifting forgotten and unknown and nameless amid the welter of Factor-visited suns—

The luxcloth was everything.

The luxcloth was his life.

Preparing to rise and shake the boy awake and at the same time administer a severe upbraiding, the man paused. Something about the boy struck him as familiar. Naturally there was a surface identicalness in the incident to many others. He had overseen the initial development of more than half a hundred such boys in his career as Master Luminary, and it was only natural that many of them would more than once be caught napping. But there was something about this lad that tugged more acutely at the strings of his memory. Something about his face. . . .

Of course.

The boy resembled Charley.

The man's thoughts fled back down a tunnel whose ribbed walls were years.

Charley had entered the Mill in the summer. That meant that he had gone directly to the stockroom, that cavernous brick and timber hall—its high rafters plainly visible, unlike the other dusky chambers of the Mill—where the luxcloth was stored, a cathedral of radiance so intense that the stockboys must wear smoked-glass goggles as they worked.

The Master Luminary had not particularly noticed the new boy then, having the whole production of his mill to keep in mind. In the winter, a quarter of the boys had been shifted immediately to stovetender duties. (The other three quarters would be rotated out of the stockroom in turn, in order to save their eyesight, as the long cold months went on.) Charley had been one of the first transfers, and he had ended up in the man's office, sitting right where the current boy now sat dozing. The man's hair had been less gray then, and the little stool had had fewer initials carved into it. But aside from that, the situation had been identical.

Something about Charley had attracted the man's close attention. A ceaseless curiosity and darting focus that played about the boy's placidly intelligent features seemed to resonate with something inside the man himself. He made a mental note—along with all the other memoranda regarding the seemingly endless details of his mill—to keep an eye on this boy for future use.

And when Charley's stint as stovetender was supposed to end, along with the old year, the man retained him by fiat in the office, denying three other faceless boys their turns, and perhaps causing some slight incremental damage to their vision as they continued to labor in the stockroom the whole winter.

This small harm he tried to forget, striving to convince himself that the good inherent in his actions outweighed the bad. His life was a patchwork quilt of such ethical trade-offs and judgements. And the quilt frequently scratched his conscience.

Busy years attached themselves like ambulatory Pagan Sea coral to the edifice of the man's life. Always, among his overt duties, he took a covert interest in the progress of young Cairncross. After Charley was promoted from stovetender, the man watched him move from the gillboxes to the spinning frames, from the winders to the converters, always exhibiting a deft proficiency and keen understanding of each step in the intricate process of fabricating luxcloth. The man noted with quiet pleasure the quality of the work that the young man—for by now he was no longer a boy—turned out. After a while, the man felt he knew Charley's secret soul and essence, how it was bound up into the luxcloth's very weave, as was his own.

The only thing the man could never figure out was how such a progeny could spring from the loins of a soured old agitator like the elder Cairncross. That man was a bad egg. And to have also engendered another son such as Alan, so different from both Charley and the old man— The mechanics of destiny were hidden from mortal sight. Perhaps the Factor could explain it.

But one might as well hope for the secret of the Factor's immortality.

The cranky misanthropy of the elder Cairncross, however, was not what the seated man wanted to ponder, and he put it off as ultimately inexplicable. He wanted to consider Charley some more, to recall more of their twenty years of association. Such daydreaming was certainly allowable from time to time, as long as one did not overindulge.

Finally, after nearly a decade of observation, the day came when the Master Luminary approached Charley on an errand he, the Master, had never before performed. Charley was a foreman by this time, supervising a score of workers, among whom was his own father, who had never gone further than machinetender, a post whose duties were changing gears and oiling bearings.

Out on the twilit floor, where the only illumination came from the dancing threads running through the machines like liquid moonlight and from the refulgent yarn on cones and bobbins piled high in hand trucks, and where the noise of the leather belts and the pulleys and the gears—all powered off the Swolebourne —was enough to shatter concentration, the Master found Charley supervising the changing of the worn rollers on an idled machine.

"Cairncross," the man said. "Leave this now and come with me."

"Yes, Master Otterness," Charley replied.

They walked across the width of the mill and up a flight of stairs to the third and topmost floor, all the while silent. In the anteroom to Otterness's own office, the Master Luminary indicated with a wave a tall spidery clerk's workbench and accompanying high rail-backed chair.

"You will sit here," said Otterness. "Begin studying the sample cards that chart the standard luminances. Start with the Whaleford set. They're the classic gauges from which all others derive. I doubt if you will get much beyond those today."

"Yes, sir."

Otterness turned to enter his own office, heard Charley cough, and swivelled back.

Charley's face wore a look of hurt disappointment. "Sir, may I ask why I've been relieved of my former duties? I hope I have not disappointed you with inferior production."

"To the contrary. Your work has been exemplary. The best I've ever seen. That is why I am now nominating you as Apprentice Luminary for this mill. I believe you have the talent for such a post, and understand the grave responsibilities involved. On the rightness of our luminance choices and the resulting attractiveness of the cloth, the whole material well-being of the Blue Devil village rests. I trust you will repay my faith in you, and let neither me nor the mill nor the village down."

Charley bowed his head for a moment. When he lifted it, light from the oil lamp glinted in his tears. "I will, sir. I will. I mean, I won't. Let you down, that is."

Otterness suppressed a smile. "Very well."

Now he came back to himself in his office. The stoveboy still slept. Otterness considered the scullion's dreaming features. He knew he would never have occasion to choose another apprentice. He would die in his job, or be dismissed by a committee of his peers from the other mills if his performance became senilely awful, whereupon in both instances Charley would become Master, with the consequent right to select his own apprentice. But the fact that Otterness was not always on the outlook for talent anymore did not mean that he could risk alienating the skilled. Who was to say what role this snoozing boy would possibly play in the future? The mill—and the Mill—needed all the competent hands it could get. His unnecessarily brusque reprimand here could have unforeseen consequences years down the line. No, better to handle the lapse—after all, it was only the boy's first—in a subtler manner.

Otterness deliberately pushed back his chair with a loud scraping noise, his face averted from the stoveboy. He had the satisfaction of hearing the regular breathing suddenly stop in a panicked reaction, then the noise of the boy's booted feet as he stood up and the clunk of the stove door opening and the chunky rattle as he began scooping coal into the stove.

Getting to his own feet, Otterness turned to the boy—who was drowsily rubbing his eyes with one hand while dishing out coal with the other—and said (pausing a moment while he recalled the boy's name), "Pickering, have that stove good and hot by the time I get back, if you please."

Now furiously tossing coal with a two-handed motion, little Pickering said, "Yes, sir! Of course, sir! Before you return, sir!"

Otterness stepped outside his office. The anteroom was empty. He knew Charley was out somewhere on the mill floor, among the turbulent, clattering, endlessly breaking-down machines, watching and directing the myriad workers who strove to reify the newest type of shining cloth which he and Charley envisioned and sometimes, it seemed, actually dreamed into possibility, after much contemplation and discussion of possible blendings. Having something vital he must discuss with Charley—the original object of the intense pondering that had allowed him to let Pickering fall into a doze and his own hands to escape—Otterness set out to find his assistant.

Leaving the relatively quiet anteroom—whose thick panelled walls, bearing sconced oil lamps, served to mute the continuous roar of the machinery—was like plunging into a surf of shadow and sound and odor. Pausing while his eyes adjusted to the silvery gloom, Otterness drank in the glorious chaos from which his beloved luxcloth emerged.

The Mill had no lighting except in its offices. All its other operations were conducted in the ethereal glow of its product. The luxfibers, in their various unfinished forms such as raw combed tops or spun threads, had to be protected from sunlight or artificial radiance, and so all activities in the Mill took place in a diffuse illumination that amounted to the light one might encounter when both moons were full. This illumination had to suffice. There was no alternative without ruining the product. The reason lay in the very nature of the lux.

Lux was a common plant, native and unique to this world, easy to cultivate and harvest. In the daytime it was an inconspicuous crop: tall waving fronds of a silvery green with tough fibers visible just inside its translucent stalks. But at night—at night it could be seen to glow. With the sun's competition gone, the lux visibly re-radiated stored sunlight. At least this was the most commonly accepted theory. No one—save perhaps the Factor, and he was unapproachable on such matters—could quite agree on the reason for the lux's remarkable properties. A rival to the sunlight theory was that the lux absorbed certain glowing minerals from the soil, which, becoming part and parcel of its very being, allowed it to continue shining even after being chopped down and processed in a dozen different ways, shattered and pulled and twisted and recombined.

Whatever the true explanation, one fact was certain: continued exposure to any light above a certain threshold after the lux was harvested would drastically affect its desirable qualities in an unpredictable fashion. Thus the lux led a most secretive afterdeath existence, like some noble god fated to an underworld imprisonment. Hurriedly reaped and crammed into cunningly crafted barrels in the fields under starlight, it was loaded onto wagons which were then covered by canvas tarpaulins as further insurance. These wagons were kept indoors by day and traveled only at night. Still a faint luminance came from them, revealing that all the best precautions could not insure a light-tight seal.

Upon arrival at the Mill, the lux plunged into the massive building's lightless depths, never to emerge until it had undergone a final wet chemical finishing that fixed the radiance once and for all. The luxcloth, then, could be exposed to daylight without ruining its miraculous qualities.

The fact that there were different kinds of lux was the simple pivot that made Otterness and his peers the most important men in the Mill, and which allowed competition between mills to exist. Had there been only one kind of lux, all would have been simple. Only a single variety of cloth could have been produced, and the Factor would have bought equally from all sixteen mills. But every region where lux was produced experienced different conditions: soil, sunlight, clouds, precipitation, all contributing toward the individual qualities of a region's lux. Some shone with an opal whiteness. Another kind might exhibit a diamond purity. A third was nearly blue, a fourth celery green, a fifth amethyst, another the faintest of yellows.

Within hundreds of miles of the Mill, there were as many different types of lux produced. From all quarters they funneled into the unduplicated manufactory that was the Mill. The dishwater-colored harvest from Teaford; the ale-colored harvest from Claypool; the silver harvest from Goldenfish; the lilac harvest from Albion Cay; the ginger harvest from Clinkscales; the pewter harvest from Yellow Hedges; the pinkish harvest from Fireflats; the champagne harvest from Shining Rock—each with its gradations of luminance also. The number of blends were astronomical.

There were well over a hundred known luminances. Whaleford, Emberstone, Sleet, Silent Sea Wine . . . The catalogue went on and on. A Master Luminary had to be able to instantly recognize each kind without error, so as to spot inadvertent mixes and stop them before they got too far into production. Moreover, the Master Luminary had to know all the standard blendings, and also those poor choices which resulted in muddy or eye-shattering fabric. On top of all this, the Master Luminary had to be a creative experimenter, developing his hunches about what new blends would turn out to be marketable, thus securing one's mill an inordinate share of the Factor's patronage. (And even after four centuries of trial and error, all the blends were not known.)

Additionally, the Masters engaged in bidding wars for each region's crops. They had to be skillful traders as well as perceptive visionaries.

In short, the fortunes of a mill and its village, the day-to-day standard of living of its families, rose and fell with the Master Luminary's skillful or clumsy decisions.

Otterness was a fine and expert Master. He knew Charley had the potential to be even better. It felt good to think of the mill being left after his death to such a successor.

But first, Otterness reminded himself, we must get past this latest obstacle.

Moving off in search of Charley, Otterness savored the noisy clatter of the belt-driven machines that marched in ranks down the unbroken length of this mill section, and inhaled the ripe smell of the vegetable oil used to lubricate them. He could sense in his bloodstream the harnessed and dedicated power of the Swolebourne far down beneath the Mill, where its constricted currents turned the great wheels that transmitted their power via an intricate system of gears and shafts throughout the building.

Otterness took the time then to issue a brief prayer for heavy snows, so that during spring and summer the Swolebourne would rush even more mightily and much work could be accomplished in a last burst before the Factor arrived in the autumn.

Down in weaving Otterness found Charley watching the warpers thread a loom with a warp of Sleet Nine, which had a tendency to break easily. Here was virtual silence. The looms were the only unpowered machines in the Mill, the process being too delicate and complicated to automate, and much skill being required in the casting of the shuttle and the beating of the woof. No one had ever been able to devise mechanical substitutes for the human weaver's hand and eye, and Otterness was confident no one ever would. At times, he regarded the looms as a bottle-neck in the production process, but always quickly reminded himself that the old ways that had persisted for centuries were undoubtedly the best. If the looms ever could be automated, the quality of the work would probably plunge, and where would the mill and its workers, not to mention Otterness's reputation, be then?

"Charley," called Otterness, above the staccato clicking of the myriad flying shuttles, "I need to see you."

Charley gave a final pointer to the warpers and came up to Otterness. "Yes, sir. What's on your mind?"

"I prefer not to discuss it here, son. Let's walk out on the floor."

Charley nodded assent, and they left the weaveroom. Boys trundled noisy wooden-wheeled hand trucks past them, moving yarn from one part of the mill to another. Otterness thought in passing about all the myriad skills needed to keep the Mill going: carpenters, masons, engineers, machinists, beltwrights, oilers, stoveboys . . . Sometimes it amazed him that such a complicated extravagant delicate assemblage of people and machines could function for even a single day.

"Charley," announced Otterness after they had walked a few yards, "I've decided. We're going to devote a full fourth of our pro-duction after the Factor leaves this fall to the new Idlenorth and Palefire blend."

Charley stopped in midstep and turned to face Otterness. "But sir—the Idlenorth is a new breed. We're not even assured yet of steady supply. What if the growers have a bad year? And the Palefire—my God, that's one of the trickiest yarns to spin. I know the sample of the blend we ran off was breathtaking. But a quarter of our output— Sir, I just don't—"

Otterness held up a palm toward Charley to stop the torrent of speech. "I have considered all these issues and others you might not even stumble upon for months. I do not say this to boast, but merely to reassure you that I do not plunge into this without ade-quate forethought. But it is our only recourse. I do not blame you for not immediately coming to the same conclusion. You are miss-ing part of the equation, one vital fact that forces our hand."

Otterness resumed walking down the aisle dusted with lint

that ran between the twisting machines. Workers looked up with momentary interest, then quickly turned back to their demanding tasks. For a moment, shining motes of lux hovered around Otterness's head in a chance-formed halo and Charley regarded him with more than a little awe evident on his face. Quickly catching up to the Master Luminary, Charley waited for him to explain.

Instead, Otterness asked a question. "How long have you been working in the Mill, Charley?"

"Why, nearly twenty years, sir."

Otterness nodded sagely. "You confirm my own memories, which I sometimes doubt. In that case, then, you were probably too young to really notice the lean years we passed through right about then, when the Tarcats started production."

The naming of the sixteenth mill seemed to trigger some sudden flood of remembrance in Charley, for his face grew distant. "I remember—I remember that period well. And now that you mention it, I do recall some talk about how the new mill would affect us all. But I don't really remember tough times, no. Always enough food on the table, new clothes when needed. . . ."

"I take that as a compliment to the way I handled the challenge," said Otterness. "The Tarcats were diligent and inventive. Their workers had a hungry desire to establish themselves, which we complacent older mills sometimes lose. Three years after the Tarcats started up, they earned ten percent of the Factor's gold. All other mills earned correspondingly less—some much less, some not so much. And when the dust settled, some of those mills—you can probably name them if you think about it—never recovered their former status. Of course, the Factor compensated somewhat, by buying overall a slightly greater quantity of cloth than before, but not enough to make up for the new mill's total production. It was as if—I don't know. As if he were encouraging competition for competition's sake. Perhaps his buyers grow jaded, and this is the Factor's method of shaking us up and producing newer, more exotic goods."

Charley remained silent, and it seemed he was trying to digest all this uncommon and startling information—or rather, this new perspective on old events. Otterness lowered his voice, and Charley had to strain to hear his next words.

"What I am about to tell you must not be bruited about. The common folk will discover it soon enough anyway. This fall, the Factor is going to bid us start construction on another new mill. He warned us Luminaries last year."

Charley drew in his breath sharply. Otterness grabbed his arm. "I'm not going to be caught flatfooted this time, anymore than the last. I know the new mill won't come online for many years. Still, it's none too early to experiment with new blends. If we can grab the Factor's attention now, we'll be more likely to hold it during the rough years. Do you see, Charley? Do you see what we must do?"

Charley regarded the blunt-faced man with a direct and serious gaze that locked their visages — young and old — into a composite like those illusory drawings of vases that suddenly transform beneath one's attention into two profiles. "I do, Master Otterness. Roland, I do."

A wash of affection swept through Otterness at Charley's use of his first name. How different it sounded out of his mouth than off Alan's lips of late. . . .

"Now, secrecy is paramount regarding this decision, Charley. You and I are the only ones who know of this. Were the other mills to discover our plans, we would lose all advantage. I do not want this to turn into another debacle like the Sandcrab mess. How the other Luminaries ever discovered our schemes for that mix, I still cannot say."

"Nor no more I," interjected Charley hurriedly.

"I'm not blaming you, son, for the leak. Too many wagging tongues knew about that game strategy. The tattler could have been any of a dozen, in whose numbers you're definitely not included. But I'm just speaking aloud my own fears."

Charley nodded in understanding.

Otterness clapped a hand on Charley's shoulder then, saying, "But enough of such dire talk, son. We'll be discussing this issue oft enough in the years to come. Let's speak of more pleasant things. How are your wife and son lately?"

Libby Straw, from the Swift Sparrow village, a member of one of the Valley's oldest families, had become Charley's bride five years ago, and had come to live in the Blue Devil village.

"Fine, sir," replied Charley, though he still seemed ruminative. "Both healthy and fit, the one still beautiful and the other still a red-faced squaller."

"And your mother and sister?"

"Also hale. Floy I saw just last week, when she came over from the Tarcats for the quilting bee."

"She is happy there, then?"

"Yes, although even after all these years she still misses Blue Devil ways at times."

"It was a shame, the way she was plunged headlong into that match. Your father was never the same after it. But I'm glad to hear she's matured into it."

"Oh, she has. She even deigns to speak to me now."

The men shared a chuckle then at the folly of women. They walked on unspeaking . . . After a time, Otterness broke the silence, rather timorously for one usually so confident.

"And your brother, Alan—does he ever speak confidentially to you about his feelings toward me?"

Charley looked gloomy. "Alan keeps his own counsel, I'm afraid. Mother continues to coddle him, and his lack of a job has not improved his character. No, sir, I cannot report anything on Alan's inner thoughts."

Otterness tried to put some unfelt joviality into his voice. "So be it. I'll have to muddle along on my own with the young rascal."

The men reached the rear lamplit staircase and began to climb. Charley spoke.

"Sir, might there not be another way to improve production, in order to meet the new competition? I am thinking of certain modifications in the machinery, and perhaps even in our method of power. I have heard Tarrytown rumors about steam—"

Otterness recoiled visibly. To hear such talk from his protégé was perhaps the most disturbing thing that could have happened at this crucial juncture in the Mill's existence. He wondered suddenly if young Cairncross could have inherited any of his father's wild-eyed cynicism. Best to probe gently around the roots of this heresy and then yank it up for good.

"What you are advocating, Charley," Otterness said slowly, "is the first step on a very slippery slope. If we begin to tamper with our time-honored methods of production—which the Factor has endorsed implicitly by his continued visits—then we risk all. Consider the upheaval in Mill hierarchies and procedures which new devices would bring, not to mention the radical alterations in village life. Do you wish to precipitate such things?"

Charley said nothing for a minute, then said—with what Otterness took for sincere conviction—"No, sir. No, I do not. Please forget I ever proposed such a foolish step."

"It's not your father who's filling your head with such ideas, is it? I know he's been especially bitter since the probation incident."

Charley leapt to his father's defense. "No, sir, he's not been preaching those things anymore. And as for the probation—he admits that losing two month's work was only fair for what he did. I don't know what came over him, sir, actually to light his pipe in the Mill. God, I like my smokeweed as much as the next man, but to think of what could happen in this oil-soaked warren if a single spark should land in the wrong place— He's promised me personally never to do such a thing again, sir. He was only tired and unthinking, is what it was."

Otterness softened his tone. "I understand, Charley. We all make mistakes. I have nothing personal against your father, you understand. It's only that occasionally . . . Well, you know what I mean."

"It's all right, sir. No offense taken. You've got the welfare of the whole Mill at heart, I know."

Otterness felt relieved. "That's just it, Charley. We're all only partially cognizant of the real nature of things, you know. And I feel that my perception of reality is just a little more valid and complete than your father's. It's the big view, Charley, that you and I share. That is why the workers trust us to guide the affairs of the mill. And that's also why we can't seek after new ways, Charley. Because we don't know enough. Don't you think that the Factor—with his vastly superior knowledge—couldn't lift us up out of our traditions if he chose? But since he doesn't so choose, then we must have the best life we're fit for. It all comes down to trust in the end. Either we trust the Factor's decisions, and the workers trust ours, or everything collapses."

"I see," said Charley.

Otterness thought of a last image to persuade Charley, one that he frequently resorted to when doubtful himself. "We're all just bricks, Charley. Just bricks in the Mill. And we can have no greater idea of the whole grand plan than a brick has of the immensity it forms a part of."

Charley seemed struck by some personal resonance in Otterness's trope. "Just bricks," he muttered. "Just bricks."

When they reached the office again, Pickering had it cozily hot. Dismissing the stoveboy to insure absolute secrecy, the Master Luminary and his Apprentice set about outlining the transition to the new blend. The hours passed in intense absorption for the two men. The final bell tolled, sending all the regular workers home, and still the pair toiled on. At last, closer to midnight than to sunset, they broke up their labor for the evening.

Outside the Mill they walked together across the crunchy snowfield, silent in their individual thoughts. Among the quiet snow-shrouded houses they parted, Charley to join his family, Otterness to greet an empty home.

Looking up for the first time only when he stood on the stoop of his house, Otterness was startled to see a light on inside his rooms. With his heart pounding, he opened the unlocked door and stepped inside.

Alan Cairncross was a slim young man with blond hair and thin lips. At age twenty-five, he still had hardly any cause to shave daily. Unadept at ballgames, he excelled at the annual spring morris dances. Even walking through the village, he carried himself with unusual grace. Slouched now in Otterness's favorite chair, he retained this allure.

Otterness's mouth was dry. Memories rose to plague him. The first time he had seen Alan, at a dinner at Charley's house, some six years ago. Summer nights spent lying together outdoors on the meadowed Valley slopes. Winter nights like this one by a roaring fire. Old. He was getting too old. Old men had too many memories.

"Alan, it's so good to see you again. Will you have a drink? I could easily mull some ale. . . ."

Alan straightened up. "No, thank you, Roland. I'm not here to stay the night. I just wanted to talk a bit. How is everything with you? How's work?"

Seating himself across from Alan, Otterness found himself beginning to babble like an adolescent. Alan listened attentively. Then, for some reason, he reached out to grab Otterness's hand. The Master responded by squeezing the other's upper thigh.

"Roland, stop, I cannot continue with this deception."

Otterness's heart crumbled inside him, like a brick powdered by a sledgehammer. In a blinding instant he knew what Alan was about to say. But he had to hear it from the young man himself. "What—what do you mean?"

"For the last two years I've been a spy, a serpent in your bosom. The Scorpions have paid me handsomely to learn of your plans in advance. Actually, it was not them alone. Others too. That's why I've been so cool to you lately. I've hated myself every moment we've been together. I can't stand it any longer. I've come to say goodbye."

Otterness surprised his hands together again, rubbing, squeezing. Alan's neck was so thin. . . .

He forced them apart. Maybe if he had blurted out the latest scheme. But he had not. Thank the Factor for small favors, however ironic.

"Why?" he managed to ask.

Alan shrugged. "I could say it was the money. That was what I thought at first myself. But I realize now that it was because you loved the Mill more than you loved me."

Otterness tried to deny the charge. But he could not.

"And you could never reconcile yourself to that status, if it had to be?"

"How can my answer matter, after what I've done?"

"Just tell me."

"I—I don't know. I could try to understand."

Otterness put both hands on Alan's thighs. How much better they felt there, than around his throat.

"Then just try. That's all I ask."

Alan's eyes widened in astonishment. "That's all?"

Otterness smiled. "And why not? That's all life asks."

4.

Seen from three miles high, the autumnal Valley was an abstract composition illustrating the beauty of pure geometry and color. By far the greater part of the Valley was a mass of brilliant fiery foliage: from both ridgetops, down almost to the outhouses that were the most distal structures from the Mill, spread a carpet of orange and red and yellow treecrowns threaded with green, like a bed of inextinguishable coals salted with minerals.

Trees bracketed the Mill and the dwellings of the workers. The Mill's slate roof stretched straight down the Valley's length, a fat gray line that swallowed a skinnier silver-blue and rippling turbulent one at the north and disgorged it at the south. The clustered houses—each village separated from the others on its side by sere brown fields—punctuated the exclamation mark that was the Mill like bisected umlauts somehow gone astray from their vowels, the punctual Mill and its outliers as a whole signifying the exclamatory pronunciation of some obscure but vital word.

Beyond the Valley other settlements could be dimly apprehended. Of course, under further magnification they could be resolved to any required depth.

The Factor, regarding the aerial view on the screens of his titanic spherical ship now hovering directly above the Mill, thought—insofar as he was capable of appreciation—that it was a rather esthetically pleasing vista.

He was glad that he had gotten a chance to come here at last. As with all places in this miraculous universe, it was a sight worth seeing in and of itself. But it took on special meaning when one considered the remarkable product that was produced here and only here, in this archaic and time-lost Valley. From what he had heard, he had quite a reception in store when he set foot below to redeem the goods that had been stockpiled all year against his coming. He couldn't know for sure, of course, until he jacked in, never having been here before.

It was time now, he supposed, for that particular precontact necessity. Yet for a moment the Factor hesitated. He was unwontedly sentimental today, outside all his parameters. He supposed it stemmed from the fact that he was visiting this world for the first time in his long and limitless life span. His yearly round of planetary visits normally took him only to worlds he had been to at least once before. His coming here was a newness to be savored, arising from the rare disappearance elsewhere of the Factorial ship previously assigned here. The next time he visited this world, it would be as one returning to the familiar. There would be no exciting thrill of the heretofore unseen to add a touch of spice to his unvarying and solitary life. And although the Factor had been designed to tolerate a degree of boredom and regularity which would have driven a human insane, he still found newness a thing not unwelcome in small doses.

So for a few minutes the Factor merely reclined in his chair and studied the view offered on his remote panels. When he had drunk his fill of these visual stimuli, he reached with both hands up and behind his padded headrest, grasping a node-studded wire cage which he swung up on its arm until it rested securely atop his skull.

Then he jacked in.

When he arose a second later, he knew the whole history of this world. Not dating from its initial settlement by humans, of course. Those records were long ago vanished, destroyed or mislaid when the Concordance disintegrated in a galaxywide psychic calamity, or evolutionary leap. No, the history that the Factor had so effortlessly internalized began after the Inwardness, when the Factors had been created, almost as an afterthought, to partially resume a role that most of mankind had abandoned. Interstellar travel no longer appealed to those human societies capable of it. Integrating themselves into the Bohmian implicate order that underlay external reality, they had moved on to other, less visible concerns. Still, those who had turned Inward had not wholly severed themselves from their primitive cousins elsewhere, the mental Neanderthals who had failed to make the transition, and continued to maintain an obscure and manipulative concern with information and products from other worlds.

Not that those who had turned Inward could really use material goods as they once used to.

The Factors now obediently and disinterestedly served to link, in an almost gratuitous fashion, the scattered and devolved human communities around the galaxy that had not turned Inward.

The Factors had discovered—or rediscovered—this world over four centuries ago. They had fastened on one product as being of interest to their human motivators. They had encouraged the production of the luxcloth in the manner that seemed best to their semiautonomous intellects, stimulating competition and diversity every generation or so by ordering a new mill complex to be constructed. Elaborate rituals had evolved around the visit of a Factor—which ceremonies were not discouraged, contributing as they did toward respect and compliance.

And now the cycle had come round again. It was time for this Factor to initiate the familiar exchange which he had never actually participated in before. And also time to order the new mill built. That was imperative. The old Factor's resolve to order new construction was plain in the inherited memories the new Factor had received. He had no worries that the populace would balk at the commands, no doubts that this might not be the best course for them and their world.

Such concerns were simply not an issue that mattered to the Factor or those who directed him, and hence were not included in his complex programming.

The Factor moved off his couch. He was tall and supple-jointed, clad in a slick almost rubbery black suit that merged imperceptibly into boots. His features were nondescript almost to the point of invisibility; his head was hairless; his limbs, although not heavily muscled, seemed powerful. His irises were silver.

Beside a metallic cabinet tall as himself, the Factor stopped. He picked out a sequence on a keypad blazoned with icons. In a slot at waist level materialized a bar of worthless atomically pure gold. The Factor crooked his right arm, picked up the ingot with his other hand, and placed it on his horizontal forearm up near his elbow. Another brick appeared; it went next to the first. This continued until the Factor held, apparently effortlessly, about a score of stacked ingots that must have weighed well over two hundred pounds.

Without haste the Factor exited the main cabin of his ship. Passage through corridors and portals brought him to a huge bay filled with auxiliary craft. There the Factor entered a landing pod. He piled the gold neatly on a floating pallet waiting inside the spherical pod. He sat in the command chair, activated the pod's screens and drive. Several panels showed various views of the Valley, while one disclosed the big ship itself, as if seen from a small device already on the ground. In this last screen the Factor witnessed his pod's departure. Like a cell budding, the daughter craft separated from the floating sphere and rapidly dropped, down toward its tradition-bound meeting.

Within less than a minute, under swift acceleration and deceleration whose forces the Factor did not appear to feel, the pod came to a rest on the earth. The Factor got to his feet. He caused the outer door to open.

The natives awaited him. It was impressive in a primitive way, as a school of bright fish might be.

The pod had arrived roughly halfway along the length of the Mill, settling in the middle of a vast playing field in a compacted bowl-shaped hollow worn by the accumulated landings of four hundred years. Here it would stay during the seven Days of Festival—a celebration that began soberly but soon escalated to what amounted to a bacchanalia utterly unlike anything indulged in during the rest of the year. A curious custom, thought the Factor, and one he would welcome the chance to observe.

Stepping to the port, the Factor made his ritual initial appearance. The field had been decorated with bright pennons and streamers, all strung from a multitude of wooden poles. Numerous booths had been erected by outsiders to the Valley, who arrived each year to share in the new prosperity. Here were sold such items as food and drink and clothing, jewelry and geegaws, and other novel diversions distinct from the familiar goods in the Company Store. This was the only time hoarded coins circulated in the Valley, as the elaborate credit and barter system utilized by the Valley dwellers could not extend to outsiders, who demanded payment in solid currency.

Beyond the booths were sixteen billowing tents, striped with the colors of the individual mills, their flaps closed against competitors and the curious. Inside these awaited samples of the year's luxcloth, trucked from the various storerooms, ready for the Factor's inspection.

A ramp extruded itself from the Factor's feet to the ground. At the foot of the ramp waited sixteen men, mostly old, wearing their freshly cleaned and pressed black suits and white shirts and heavy shoes, all so drab compared to the shining stuff they produced. Beyond them clotted a tremendous crowd, all respectfully hushed.

The Factor raised a gloved hand. The hush intensified in an indescribable fashion, as if silence could be doubled and redoubled like noise, until it reached a magnitude almost painful.

"I am here to judge and to winnow," said the Factor, shattering the loud silence with the words instilled in him, "to separate dross and chaff from the pure and valuable. Whatever satisfies me I will buy, and the fame of your work will travel with me among the stars."

"We are ready," the Master Luminaries chorused simply.

A nearly visible wave of relaxation coursed through the crowd of workers, as the greeting was completed according to form. Murmurs of speculation and excitement sounded like a minor duplication of the Mill's normal purring, which was absent during the Festival.

The Factor descended the ramp, the Master Luminaries parting to allow him into their middle. As a group, the men and the Factor moved off.

Now the Factor experienced the familiar yet always disorienting doubling of perceptions and memories that never failed to accompany jacking in. He possessed all the memories of all his brother Factors who had ever visited this world, yet not totally integrated into his private consciousness. Thus all he saw appeared at first mysterious and strange, then a second later, totally explicable and mundane.

Striving to completely internalize his artificially acquired past, the Factor still found time to appreciate the spectacle before him. He had landed during late afternoon. Invisible tethers hauled down the big white sun, like some impossible dirigible, to below the western ridge. How good its autumnal heat felt, after the time spent within the ship, how clear and penetrating the blue-white light. And the smells of harvest time, the slight dampness and chill in the moving air. . . . They tingled on his chemoreceptors.

Did these backward, unsophisticated folk realize the wonder of their world, of any world? Did they know how lucky they were just to inhabit such a bountiful globe, out of all the charred and dead and frozen ones the Factor had seen? For a brief moment the Factor almost envied them their uncomplicated primitive existence. They were so unlike the aloofly superior humans who had ventured Inward. The Factor felt a paternal care for these primitives envelop him. He was glad to be able to provide such a focus for their simple lives.

It did not matter to the Factor then that he had been engineered to feel just such an emotion. After all, considered rationally, every creature, whether organic or not, was engineered to feel certain things.

And this charming divertissement, the Days of Festival! What a lot of work and preparation had gone into this Mill Valley Mardi Gras! As a proportion of the Gross Planetary Product, expenditures for this affair were quite significant. The Factor directed his gaze all about, careful to record everything, since he knew that when he returned to his human motivators his memories would be minutely and exquisitely probed and analyzed and correlated by those cryptic beings, for whatever they could extract and utilize in their enigmatic schemes.

One of the Master Luminaries, the Factor suddenly realized, was addressing him. The Factor turned to face the man, as the group continued their traditional promenade among the booths, for the purpose of allowing everyone to circumspectly gape at the Factor and ascertain his awesome unchanging immortal reality for themselves.

"Factor," said the man, who had short grizzled hair and a thick jaw, "we realize it is late in the day, but perhaps we can still make a tour of the mill of your choice, so that you can see that we continue to abide by the old ways of production."

The Factor, after a fractional hesitation while he matched facial image to memory, replied, "Indeed, I think we can fit the tour in, Master Otterness. As I recall, I visited the mill of the Red Stalkers last year. This year. . . ."

The Factor considered his choice. It would be well, he thought, to pay an honor to this very man, who had a record of being one of the Factor's staunchest partisans. "This year, let it be your mill, the Blue Devils."

Watching the man swell with pride, the Factor congratulated himself on the political wisdom of his choice. It was good to sow envy and contention, for it raised the levels of creativity.

Hearing the Factor's decree, the Luminaries now directed their course toward the distant Mill. They soon reached the edges of the crowd. Ready to strike off down the path to the Mill, they were halted by Otterness's sudden darting escape back into the crowd, from which he dragged forth a young man to join them.

"Factor," said Otterness, "you remember my assistant, I hope."

"Certainly. Charley, how are you?"

The young man tugged at a short-billed cap he wore and inclined his head respectfully. "Very well, Factor. Very well. I— we're all glad of your return."

Nodding beneficently, with an air of much wisdom, the Factor said, "We are all part of a master plan, Apprentice Cairncross, and I merely fulfill my part."

The Luminaries expressed their appreciation of this sentiment with various wordless sounds.

After their mutual cooing was over, Otterness spoke the next words of the ritual. Chosen as host by the Factor, he could request the presence of one other member of his mill on the tour of inspection.

"Factor, I wish to nominate as the extra member of our party my protégé, Charley Cairncross. After all, someday he will stand in my place, and might as well become accustomed to his future duties."

The other Luminaries harrumphed and coughed, jealous of the extra attention focused on the Blue Devil mill. But such unexpected shifts and seeming favoritism were necessary to keep this little hive of humanity humming. (The Factor even recalled, in his secondhand way, how one of the mills—not by far the strongest today—had been given reason to once name itself Factor's Favorites.)

"Of course, Master Otterness. I fully approve your choice."

Not daring to contravene or protest, the other Luminaries settled down to a ruffled acquiescence, and the group, enlarged by one, left behind the noisy, exuberant crowd and entered the shadow of the Mill.

The tour of the strangely silent mill took several hours. In the elfinlit twilight the little party moved from section to section, among the resting hulking machines: carding, gilling, doubling, twisting, roving, spinning. . . . They ended up in the weaveroom, inspecting the unfinished lengths of lambent cloth. The Luminaries were all eyes, eager to see any secret blends Otterness might have carelessly left in the open. But the resident Luminary wore such a look of self-satisfaction that they knew any such things would have been hidden well in advance, in anticipation of just such a visit. After all, had they not taken just such precautions themselves?

At last the tour of inspection was over. The Factor signified his approval of all he had seen, and the group rejoined the crowd outside. Now it was early evening. Odors of cooking drifted among the huge bonfires that had been lit. The material for these pyres, the Factor knew, was partially composed of discarded household items contributed by each family, in a ceremony of renewal that intrigued him. How easy if burning the old were all that was required to create the new. . . .

The Factor was now brought to a long table draped with a piece of luxcloth that added its glow to the light from lamps and fires. He was seated at its middle, with eight Luminaries on either side. They all fell to eating. The Factor pretended to enjoy his food. Meanwhile he watched the crowd. There were no tables for the common workers, only scattered benches, and they took advantage of the constant movement of the crowd to circulate past the Factor's table, watching him eat as if it were the most marvelous thing in the world.

A familiar figure caught the Factor's eye some distance away, and he magnified his vision. It was Charley Cairncross, with a group of people that the Factor surmised must be his relatives: a young wife with a toddler, an elderly couple that had to be his parents, a thin graceful youth and another young woman, whose resemblance to Charley made them his two siblings. Everyone in the little cluster seemed tense, the focus being the father. Charley, standing, bent over the seated patriarch in a cajoling fashion. The older man wore a sour face and stubbornly stared into the middle distance, apparently refusing to listen to his son. The Factor boosted his hearing and ran through several filter sequences, finally managing to extract a bit of their conversation from the general hubbub.

"Da, try to be more cheerful. Alan, Floy, tell him he's acting like a senseless old bull. There's nothing to account for such an attitude. It's Festival, after all, and we're here to celebrate."

"What have we got to celebrate?" the father demanded. "What but another year of servitude?"

"Da, don't . . . ," said the brother, Alan.

"Don't talk to me, you little catamite. You're as bad as your sister."

The Factor's attention was distracted from this interesting display by the rising of the Master Luminary at his right, a skinny middle-aged man he identified as the overseer of the Landfish. The Master Luminary coughed several times until he had the attention of those closest to him. They fell quiet, and from them the silence spread among the workers, who began to draw in closely to the table. Soon the entire gathered populace, save for those at the very farthest extremes, was hushed and expectant beneath the watching stars.

The Master Luminary spoke loudly. "The Factor will now address us." Then he sat down.

On cue, the Factor arose. He made the requisite internal adjustments, and when he began to speak his voice boomed out without distortion, carrying almost over the entire crowd. Of duty and reward and the happy unchanging durable nature of their lives the Factor spoke at length, varying his speech only slightly from previous years. The crowd seemed to appreciate it, in a sleepy fashion. But the Factor's closing words caused them to grow alert.

"And now I call upon you—you lucky ones, who labor for worthy ends in the Mill, and share in the bounty of the system—to extend your generosity. I call upon you to arrange construction of a new addition to the glory of the Mill, so that more outsiders may share your humble, shining way of life, and cause the wonder of the luxcloth to spread even farther throughout the stars."

The Factor ceased speaking. There was silence for a strained moment from the assembled listeners. Then someone vented a loud if dutiful huzzah, and soon the night air was split with calls and cries and whistles and yells. The bonfires blazed higher, and the crowd began to move again.

Sitting, the Factor received the congratulations of the Master Luminaries, all of whom pledged their best to hasten the construction of the new mill.

Curiosity subroutines moved the Factor to look for the Cairncross family once more, when the hullabaloo had died down a bit. But the affecting tableau they had formed was nowhere to be seen, broken up and dispersed like flotsam in a stream.

The night wore on. The Factor catalogued many more experiences in his unwearying way. Everything and anything might be of interest to his masters.

The first man to spot the fire break through the roof of the Mill ended the celebration. His sickened curdled shouts of "Fire! Fire in the Mill!" brought the Master Luminaries and the Factor to their feet.

All eyes now turned to the Mill, there to confirm the alarm.

From the roof of the immense structure licked as yet tiny tongues of flame, evilly alive against the dead hide of the stolid creature that was the nonsentient but ensouled Mill. Even as the dumbstruck people watched, the flames seemed to grow in strength and power.

Otterness broke the trance. "Get men down into the cellars!" he shouted, referring, the Factor knew, to where the hidden river could be reached. "We must form the bucket brigades!"

Otterness moved then as if to lead the rush to his threatened beloved mill, but the Factor restrained him. "There is no need to endanger your people. My ship is quite capable of ending this blaze. I will issue the commands from my pod."

Shouts of "Praise the Factor!" quickly mounted. Otterness looked uneasy, however, but restrained himself. The Factor traversed the short distance to his pod and gave orders for the mother ship to drop and begin spraying.

He returned to the table of Luminaries. All the Masters looked nervous. The Factor noticed Otterness was missing. He asked where the man had gone.

"To the Mill," replied the Landfish Master. "He and his Apprentice insisted on going in. We tried to stop them, Factor, but they would not listen. Honestly, they wouldn't."

The Factor considered. The substance his craft would soon begin spraying was a chemical flame retardant which might asphyxiate the men. He could not be responsible for their deaths. That was an integral part of his programming. His policy of benign neglect of their whole society was not consistent with this individual and particular loss of life.

"I will rescue them. Please insure that no one else tries such an irrational thing."

Then the Factor was off.

Moving faster than any human could have, he covered the distance to the Mill in a blur.

At the entrance doors he looked up. Like a falling moon his ship had descended. Even now it was beginning to discharge the retardant. Without choice the Factor went in.

Here on the first floor the only signs of the fire were smoke and hot dead air. With crystal-clear memory the Factor summoned up the location of the stairs. In seconds he had gained the second floor; seconds later, the third.

A smoky crackling inferno greeted him at the head of the stairs. The incredible popping noise of destructing bricks resounded sharply at intervals. Heat assaulted his senses, and he could barely see. He switched to infrared. The loci of flames leapt out of the confusion. Stepping out onto the floor the Factor set out to find the men, who he was fairly certain would have rushed uselessly here, to the center of the disaster.

All the ceiling timbers above the Factor were ablaze. He heard the rain of chemicals descending, but knew that this third floor at least would definitely be lost, no matter what.

"Otterness!" bellowed the Factor. "Cairncross! Where are you? There is no need!"

The Factor's supersensitive hearing seemed to distinguish faint calls from deep within the Mill. He pushed on, ignoring the flames that frequently lapped at him. Twice he had to lift a fallen flaming timber from his path.

Emerging from one such barrier into a relatively clear eddy, the Factor realized he had come upon the men.

Oddly, there seemed to be three. The Factor switched back to normal vision to resolve the discrepancy.

Yes, three men struggled in a mass. One was the elder Cairncross. He held a can of oil in his hands with which he fed the flames. Trying to restrain him were Charley and Otterness. But the wild man's strength seemed indomitable, and he continued to sprinkle his oil like a satanic priest asperging his congregation of devils.

The Factor rushed forward and effortlessly scooped up Charley and Otterness like two weightless sacks, tossing them over his shoulders.

Charley's father, now released, raked them all with a final frantic glare and, letting forth a tremulous soul-bursting scream comprised of years of pent-up inexpungable frustration and bitterness, hurled himself headlong into the nearest flames.

"Da!" screamed Charley, and tried to break free. But the Factor held him tight. Gripping the men with steely strength, the Factor turned and made for the stairs. He moved so fast and unerringly through the least damaging flames that by the time he emerged out into the open air Charley and Otterness had suffered only minor smoke inhalation and burns.

Depositing his burdens upon their own shaky feet, the Factor turned toward the Mill. His ship was dropping mechanical remote units into the building through the gaps in the roof to battle the remaining spot fires. Everything seemed under control.

Sensing a vast crowd behind him, the Factor turned to confront it. Surprisingly he saw that their shocked attention was concentrated on him rather than the subsiding conflagration. Raising a hand to command them, he realized why.

The Factor's suit had burned away in many spots. So had much of his artificial flesh. The hidden titanium armatures that articulated him shone through. Touching his face he found it gone.

"It is all right," the Factor said. The people backed away unconsciously when he spoke out of his charred indestructible self. "It is all right," the Factor uselessly repeated. "The fire is under control. Everything will be as it was."

But even as he said it, he knew it wasn't true.

5.

At the mouth of the Valley, the caravan came to a halt. The lead steam-carriage, an elegant Whaleford six-passenger landau, shuddered to a stop, bringing the ones behind it—a mixed lot of cargo carriers, with tents lashed to their roofs—to an obedient standstill. Geartrains disengaged, the cars thrummed with the silent power of their coal-fired Tarcat boilers.

The lead vehicle, as were all the others, was emblazoned with the gilt crest of Factor's Head University: a blank-eyed mechanical face replete with fanciful rivets, surmounted by a depiction of the constellation known as Factor's Ship. Completing the heraldry was a banner bearing the motto: "Growth From Ashes." The hood of the landau bore a silver ornament in the shape of a wainwalker, those stolid beasts gone these many years from the streets of Tarrytown City where the University was located.

The doors of the landau swung open now, revealing plush-padded inner panels, and its passengers emerged into the bright summer sunlight. Overhead, a soaring cliff kestrel banked and let out a scream.

The driver of the Whaleford was a middle-aged man dressed still in the professorial garb he affected when in the classroom: a lightweight vested suit of flaxen dreamworm cloth, imported from the tropics, and a pair of ankle-high leather boots. In this conservative outfit he resembled any of his fellow pedants. Only in his choice of neckwear did he exhibit any oddity or individuality of taste. For the man wore an antique tie made of the old-fashioned stuff known as lux. In the light of the sun it cast its own radiance. An expert in antiquities had confirmed family legends regarding the tie: it was a blend of Palefire and Idlenorth fibers, one of the last fabrics ever created by the defunct Mill.

Now the passengers of the lead car—four men and two women—were joined by others from the cargo vehicles. These latter folk were plainly laborers. Together, the crowd faced north. Shading their eyes, they raised their faces to the sky.

Someone whistled; a woman gasped; one of the laborers said, "I'll be a fur-faced abo—"

The driver of the landau spoke. "It's impressive, all right. Especially up this close. I've had the Factor's Head explain it to me a dozen times now, and I still don't understand the exact nature of what keeps it up there. I don't think we'll be ready to grasp it for another generation or two. But remember—strange as it seems to us, it's only science."

What captivated the visitors to the Valley was the sight of the Factor's mother ship. Suspended like a lost silver moon above the ruins of the Mill halfway up the Valley, it hung as motionless as a mountain. The only evidence of any sort of imperfection was several open hatches. Thus it had remained for decades, tenantless and unvisited, by either planet-dweller or one of its mates from the stars.

The leader of the expedition spoke again. "Well, we'd best continue. We need to set up camp before nightfall, and we've still got a few miles to go to reach the site. And if the old road ahead is anything like what we've traversed so far, it'll be slow going. This is hardly the Grand Concourse. No pavement here."

"Nor no ladies of low virtue either," added one of the laborers, provoking much laughter which served to relieve the slight tension they had all been feeling.

The crowd broke up. One of the other drivers opened wide the door of his vehicle's boiler, exposing the open flame to add more fuel. At that moment, someone shouted.

"Professor Cairncross! Look!"

From out of the undergrowth paralleling the track emerged a squat mechanism. Big as a footstool, it moved stiffly on three spidery legs, advancing on the carrier with the open firebox.

The intruder was suddenly the focus of a dozen rifles and pistols carried as protection against dire wolves and other wildlife. Professor Cairncross stopped the men before they could fire.

"No, don't—I think I know what it is. . . ."

The automaton homed in unerringly on the open flames. Once upon them, it swivelled a nozzle at the heat source. A sound of dry pumping ensued. After a few moments of this fruitless activity, the little mechanism lowered its nozzle in defeat, collapsed its legs underneath itself, and sank to the ground.

"Let's go," said Professor Cairncross. "And remember,

whatever curious things we may see, they'll all be as harmless as what you've just witnessed."

In the car and once more in motion, the passengers of the landau were silent for a time. Then one of the women spoke.

"Are you really so certain, Charles, that we won't encounter any dangers?"

"Basically, Jennifer, I am. The oral history and the written accounts all tally. The Factor's ship never disgorged anything except him, his lighter and the clockwork firefighters. It's true that after the Valley emptied other constructs may have landed, but it seems highly unlikely. It was all under the Factor's control, and once he suffered his fate, he was unable to contact his ship via the lighter. He's told me so often enough. And though one must always take the Head's talk with a grain of salt—the damage it suffered manifests itself in strange ways—I'm inclined to believe him in this case."

"Well, you certainly sounded confident enough. I'm sure the workers were heartened."

Professor Cairncross appeared embarrassed. "Just part of my job, after all. We wouldn't have much success in our dig if we were always looking over our shoulders for some alien menace. No, I expect that the most we'll meet will be a few friendly ghosts."

The road was indeed nearly impassable in spots. The expedition had to stop often to fell with axes the larger trees which had grown on the median strip; the centuries-compacted dirt ruts had proved more impenetrable to seedlings. Through the dense foliage running alongside the old track, they could catch occasional glimpses of the Mill and its many associated dwellings, the residences all broken-roofed and shatter-windowed. They encountered no more ancient firefighters, but the going was still slow. It took till dusk to reach the site selected by Professor Cairncross and his fellow archaeologists.

The Field of the Festival was nearly all overgrown with copses of sapodilla and jacaranda. However, a grassy clearing about the size of a ballfield remained, not far from the road. Here they chose to pitch their tents, leaving the vehicles lined up in the track.

While the tents were being raised, Professor Cairncross took Jennifer and the rest of his University colleagues on a beeline across the tree-dotted field. What directed him, he found hard to say. Surely hours of studying old maps had a lot to do with his certainty, as did hours of listening to his grandfather and namesake ramble on in his half-cogent, half-dotty way about life in the Mill

Valley. But there was more guiding him than these things; it was an instinct almost genetic, a rising of ancestral feelings and memories.

Within minutes they had come upon the Factor's little ship, trees growing right up to its walls. Grass—having sprouted in wind-deposited soil on the very ramp—licked at the door, into which leaves had blown. The scat of some animal wafted pungently from inside the vessel.

Professor Cairncross's excitement was nearly palpable, and transmitted itself to the others. Sweaty, dressed for city streets rather than cross-country trekking, their faces showing the rising welts from branches, his comrades did not protest when he said, "Let's press on, toward the Mill. I want to find the Factor's skeleton."

They burst from the marge of the woods, and stopped. The oily waste strip had resisted organic encroachments much more easily, and only the toughest weeds grew there. They had an unobstructed view in the gold and purple twilight of the sad, silent, sag-roofed Mill, parts of it crumbled by flooding of the Swolebourne, its middle portion still exhibiting the effects of the fire that had unmasked the Factor and precipitated his demise and the abandonment of the Mill.

Professor Cairncross scanned the waste fruitlessly. Then Jennifer said, "There, that glint—"

The metal armature of the Factor was wreathed in maidenhair, as if the earth strove to clothe it.

Professor Cairncross shivered. "I can feel it as if it were yesterday. I'd sit on my gran'da's knee, and he'd tell me how the Factor was decapitated with a dozen blows from a huge wrench, wielded by his old boss, Otterness. Once I thought I'd found the very wrench, an old rusty thing in my father's shop. But it turned out to be much too new. I think I'd date my desire to do archaeology to that moment."

Jennifer said, "And look where it's led you. To something much more exciting than an old wrench!"

Back at the camp, a fire was already going. All throughout supper, they half expected more clockwork visitors, starting at every sound from the surrounding woods. But in this they were disappointed.

As he fell asleep in Jennifer's arms that night—their betrothal had been announced last month, and it had not taken them long to get a jump on the actual marriage—Professor Cairncross thought wistfully how wonderful it was that this expedition, the first such, could include women. The Head's revelation a generation ago of the dietary deficiency that had limited female births for so long, and how to correct it, was having far-reaching changes already. . . .

In the morning, Professor Cairncross arose before the others, with first light. He felt the need to be alone with his thoughts and emotions.

Wandering away from the camp without any intentions, he soon found himself among the brick houses of a Village. In one such, his ancestors had passed their whole lives. It was nearly inconceivable. . . .

Outside the Village, he came upon an old midden of waste bricks, nearly concealed by vegetation. Time and the elements had softened what must have once been a formidable pile. Moved by some urge he could not explain, excitement mounting in his breast, Professor Cairncross climbed awkwardly to the top. It took only a few adult steps.

Yet when he stood atop the brick pile, sourceless tears tickling his cheeks, he felt master of all he surveyed, and king of the world.

Am I being fair in allowing this sour little parable to close out a collection of stories revolving around the theme of work? It's certainly a bitter ending for a volume that strives to offer balanced portraits of a variety of vocations and workplaces, and attitudes toward same.

On the other hand, who hasn't felt—while sitting through a useless meeting or while performing a pointless task—just like the Kafkaesque protagonist of this tale?

As Arthur C. Clarke has blithely remarked with a godlike perspective, "Work is a temporary aberration in the history of our species."

I say we get our licks in against the institution while it's still around!

The Boredom Factory

*S*OMEONE HAD TOLD P. HE MUST FIND A JOB.

He could not now remember whence the admonitory voice had issued. He had heard it so often that the repetitious and separate sources had merged into one amorphous imperative. His wife, his parents, his teachers, the state, the television, his own children—someone had definitely informed him of his responsibilities. Frequently. And in no uncertain terms.

P. had to find a job. It was his duty, his right, his privilege and his only hope of fulfillment. He would never be at ease until he was performing a useful role in society. That would only come when he had a job.

For some time P. continued to put off this vital task. He would read the classified advertisements every morning over his breakfast cereal. Sipping the last of the sweet candy-tinted milk from his lifted bowl, he would afterwards announce that nothing suitable had presented itself. He was saving his skills for something grand, something commensurate with his talents and ambitions. P. also refused to deal with state employment agencies or independent placement services, claiming they did not offer sensitive service, but were only intent on jamming any square peg into any round hole.

So the days passed. P. was unable to truly enjoy his freedom from work, as the pressure to perform some vital function continued to mount.

One morning there was a different kind of ad in the newspaper. P. studied it curiously.

THE BOREDOM FACTORY
HAS OPENED A SUBSIDIARY
IN YOUR TOWN!
WE ARE NOW HIRING
BY THE THOUSANDS!
NO SKILLS NECESSARY,
EXPERIENCE A MINUS.
LIGHT WORK, HEAVY WORK,
DELICATE WORK, CRUDE WORK,
WHITE COLLAR, BLUE COLLAR,
WOMEN, MEN AND CHILDREN!
ALL MAKESHIFTS
MINIMAL WAGE GUARANTEED
PHOTO-OPPORTUNITY FOR ADVANCEMENT

"This sounds like the thing for me," P. announced to his family and the alert television. "I think I will go apply this morning."

His family greeted this news with delight and acclamation. P. set off for the address given.

Out on the edge of town he found an enormous new sprawling multistory windowless structure. P. walked across the huge deserted parking lot up to the door marked PERSONNEL. He knocked politely and walked in.

P. had expected to find crowds of people waiting to apply. Instead, the office was empty, save for himself. As P. puzzled over this, a man in a nice suit walked through the inner door.

"Hello," said P. "Are you hiring today?"

"Yes," said the man. "Just one person, though."

"I thought your ad said there was employment for thousands?"

"There will be. Tomorrow we are hiring two people."

"I see."

"The day after, we will be hiring four."

"I see."

"And after that, eight."

P. contemplated this pattern. "Will the day after that be sixteen?"

"Yes."

"At that rate, you will soon employ the whole world."

"This is true. However, today we need only one person. That is why the ad appeared only in your copy of the newspaper."

"What if I choose not to take the job?"

"The Boredom Factory will not be able to begin operations."

"This is a large responsibility."

"Take your time in making a decision."

P. thought about it. Everyone kept telling him he must take a job. Here was a job offering itself to him alone. Could any decision be clearer?

"I will take the job."

"Very good. Follow me."

The man led P. out of the personnel office and onto the factory floor. Vast echoing spaces ranked with obscure machinery stretched on for miles. P. and the man ascended many levels and finally ended up in a moderate-sized room. The room featured a conveyor belt. One end of the conveyor entered through a hole in the wall shielded with a leather flap. The other end terminated in midair above a set of mechanical jaws. There was a chair midway along the conveyor's length. Next to the chair was a box filled with enigmatic parts.

"You will sit here," the main in the suit explained. "At intervals an object will come down the conveyor. You will stick a part in the appropriate socket. That is your job."

"How will I recognize the appropriate socket?"

"There is only a single socket."

"There seems to be a number of different parts in here. Will any one do?"

"Yes."

"I believe I understand the job."

"Good. If you need assistance, press the button on the chair arm."

P. sat down. The man left. The conveyor belt started up with a petulant jerk and began to slowly travel its endless loop. P. waited tensely for the unknown object to emerge. A half-hour passed without a sign of anything. P.'s tension abated, becoming transformed into sleepiness.

Suddenly a cubical gunmetal case pushed aside the hanging flap and approached P. on the slow conveyor. P. grabbed a random part from the box. When the case drew abreast of him, he quickly spotted the socket on top and had plenty of time to insert the part.

The assemblage traveled on down the belt. It reached the end and fell off into the mechanical jaws, which promptly closed and crushed it with a grinding noise.

P. grew angry. He had been regarding the assemblage with pride in his workmanship. It had hurt to see it destroyed. Perhaps this was a malfunction. Perhaps his initiative was being tested. P. pressed the button on his chair arm.

The man in the suit entered. "Yes?"

P. explained what had happened.

"Very good. But it is not necessary to inform me of each satisfactorily completed unit."

"So then—all is proceeding as you wish?"

"Yes. You are doing a good job. Keep it up."

The man left. P. waited for the next unit to come down the conveyor. When it did, about an hour later, P. inserted a part and watched as the implacable jaws crushed the resulting construction.

After the third such event, P. felt no anger, but only a growing apathy and boredom.

The lunch hour was signalled by the stoppage of the conveyor and the arrival of the man in the suit. By this time P. had completed four assemblages, only to watch them all be destroyed.

"Allow me to show you the lunchroom, P."

P. wondered how the man knew his name. He supposed if they had managed to deliver the unique newspaper to his house, then learning his name would present no problem.

The lunchroom was enormous. One wall was completely filled with little automat doors.

"Please enjoy your lunch, P. Compliments of the Factory."

P. went to one window. It was labeled CHEESE SANDWICH AND MILK. P. did not care for cheese sandwiches. He investigated another window. It too held a cheese sandwich and milk. So did a third. Eventually P. became convinced that the thousands of doors all held cheese sandwiches and milk. He reluctantly took one. Tomorrow he would make sure to bring his lunch from home.

P. sat down at one of the thousands of empty seats and ate his lunch. When he was done the man returned for him.

During the afternoon P. completed six assemblages. Then it was time to go home.

"See you tomorrow, P.," said the man in the suit.

That night P. explained about his job to his wife and children.

"I am sure the units are not destroyed," said his wife. "Those jaws do not crush, but merely reform the device into its next stage."

The hopeful speculation gave P. the strength to return to The Boredom Factory the next day.

This day, carrying his lunch, he entered by the door marked EMPLOYEES. The man in the suit was waiting for him.

"Congratulations, P., you have been promoted to supervisor." The man shook P.'s hand warmly.

"Whom will I be supervising?"

"Today's two new hires. I have already set them up at their stations. Come with me."

The man brought P. to what was perhaps the same room P. had labored in yesterday. If so, an alteration had been made.

Today, instead of ending in midair, the conveyor belt made a U-turn and exited parallel to its entrance. Two chairs were positioned opposite each other on different sides of the conveyor. The one P. had occupied — if indeed it was the same — still commanded a full box of parts. Beside the new chair was an empty box of equal size. There was also a third chair behind a small desk whose surface bore a single sheet of paper and a pencil.

There were two men waiting nervously in the room. The man in the suit introduced them to P., and explained that P. would be their boss. He bade the men take up their stations, and then guided P. to his new desk.

"You will draw a line down the middle of this paper, P. The right column will be headed 'Assembly,' the left 'Disassembly.' Make a hash mark in the appropriate column for each operation you witness. At the end of the day, total the columns and make sure that the two sums are equal. If there is no discrepancy, sign your name. If there is a non-equivalence, notify me, and we will adjust it the next day. As before, you may summon me with this button."

"I understand."

"Good."

P. sat at his desk. The men sat at their workstations. The conveyor jerked to life. Forty minutes later the first cube emerged. The man with the box of parts inserted a part. P. made a stroke in the "Assembly" column. The cube traveled around the bend in the conveyor. The second man removed the part and dropped it into his empty box. P. recorded the action. The cube disappeared through the wall, naked as it had arrived. The two men looked to

P. for approval. P. was slightly embarrassed. He waved his pencil to indicate his approval, and found himself repeating the words of the man in the suit.

"Very good. But it is not necessary to inform me of each satisfactorily completed unit."

Chastened, the men returned their gazes to the conveyor.

The day proceeded in a completely uneventful fashion, all going to plan. The workers inserted and removed parts, P. recorded all. A miasmic fog of boredom gradually began to permeate the very air the three men breathed.

At lunch time, the workers ate cheese sandwiches together, while P. sat apart, trying to enjoy his lunch from home. The food seemed tasteless, however.

At the end of the day P. totalled his columns, verified their identicalness, and signed his name. The man in the suit took the sheet from him.

"Excellent work, P. I foresee a great future for you here."

When P.'s wife heard of his promotion, she was overjoyed. P. did not have the heart to tell her how boring the work actually was.

The next day P. found he had six workers to supervise. The cubes emerged now with three sockets, which were filled by half the crew and emptied by the others. P. anticipated that the additional strokes he would be required to make would add some interest to the job. However, in what seemed to be a compensatory change, fewer cubes emerged.

When eight workers were added the next day, making a total of fourteen, the cubes emerged with seven holes. That day they did only three units.

P. knew this could not go on forever. At least he hoped so. Sure enough, the next day brought a big change.

There were now thirty workers. Twenty-eight of them occupied seats along the conveyor. The two who had started immediately after P. had received promotions. One would record the Assemblies, one the Disassemblies. P. would merely check their work, making no strokes himself.

With so many people now performing these useless tasks, the sensation of boredom within the room was akin to being muffled in yards of fiberglass insulation.

Soon it was time for paychecks to be issued. Even this stimulus failed to raise the pall of boredom by more than a fraction.

Further days brought more sophisticated divisions of labor to the line. Eventually, though, all possible refinements in the process had been made. When this happened, the man in the suit approached P.

"This room is functioning fine without you. We need your help now to open up a new division."

"Whatever you wish," said P. He knew enough now not to grow excited at the prospect.

The man brought P. to a gigantic room filled with smelting and casting equipment. "Tomorrow we hire hundreds of people. The machinery is almost entirely automated, so there should be no problem in operating it. You will supervise as before, making sure that the net output of the room remains at zero."

"As you say," replied P.

The next day the big room was alive with greased machinery and sweaty people. Blast furnaces roared, iron flowed in orange molten streams into troughs and molds. The finished ingots were recirculated as raw material for the furnaces.

P. supervised as he had been instructed, although truthfully even his services were unnecessary. At day's end, the man in the suit spoke to him again.

"Our rate of hiring is now growing exponentially. We will be opening a new division each day, and expanding into other shifts. Your former underlings are being promoted daily, but you still outpace them. Your performance has been very satisfactory. We will continue to use you to open new divisions."

"Thank you," said P. without emotion.

Thus commenced many days of new activity. Each division whose start-up P. oversaw was different, insofar as the actual activities that took place inside varied. Stacking and unstacking; painting and stripping; polishing and abrading; sorting and scattering; cleaning and dirtying; packing and unpacking; threading and reaming; cutting and welding; raising and lowering; digging and filling; filtering and mixing; weaving and unraveling; drilling and plugging; inscribing and obliterating; layering and shredding. . . . However, the foregone nature of the net results was so identical that he could not summon up any interest in the various industrial procedures themselves.

Meanwhile, as more and more workers exerted themselves to perform the useless tasks, the blanket of apathy, boredom and monotony increased in weight and duration, and began to spread.

By the end of a month, when The Boredom Factory was running at a fever pitch — hundreds of divisions employing thousands of people in millions of perpetually nullified actions, whose workers ate thousands of cheese sandwiches for lunch — the morass of boredom could be psychically and viscerally apprehended miles away from the Factory itself.

This then, P. realized, was its true output.

Soon, P. knew, the boredom would invade his home, as it already had crept into the domiciles closest to The Boredom Factory. At such a time, there would no longer be any difference between home and the Factory.

And, ultimately, this was why he continued to go to work.

Strange Trades Drabble

ONCE A GROUP OF FICTION MAGAZINE ENTHUSIASTS gathered online.

Their conversation flourished until the advent of virtual reality.

Then they all began to quarrel over avatars.

"I'll be Tarzan!"

"No, me!"

"Take off that deerstalker, you second-rate Sherlock!"

"Make me!"

All civilized discourse ended when five people simultaneously appeared as John Carter.

Once the fighting had temporarily ceased, the wise list-moderator stepped in. "Ladies and gentlemen, we must resolve this sensibly. I suggest we each adopt the persona of a famous editor, assigned by lot. There'll be no fighting then."

He was right. Now faced with being editors, everyone left!

Three thousand copies of this book have been printed by the Maple-Vail Book Manufacturing Group, Binghamton, NY, for Golden Gryphon Press, Urbana, IL. The typeset is Elante, printed on 55# Sebago. The binding cloth is Roxite B. Typesetting by The Composing Room, Inc., Kimberly, WI.

12-01